The Courtesan and the Sadhu

A Novel about Māya, Dharma, and God

Satya Avatar

Dharma Vision LLC

The Courtesan and the Sadhu
A Novel about Māya, Dharma, and God

ISBN: 978-0-9818237-0-6

The Courtesan and the Sadhu: A Novel about Māya, Dharma, and God/ by Satya Avatar
Library of Congress Control Number: 2008934274

This is a work of fiction. All of the characters, names, incidents, organizations, and dialogue are either the products of the author's imagination or are used fictitiously.

Cover illustration and book layout by Nick Inglish

Printed in the United States of America

To My Mother

Table of Contents

Preface

My family has followed *Sanātana Dharma* since the beginning of time. While we have tried to teach our children the tenets of Dharma as best as we could, there is not always a straightforward way to explain all the tenets of the faith given our busy day-to-day life. Growing up in modern times, this can sometimes lead to fundamental questions about Faith in a teenager's mind. That is exactly what happened in the case of my own son. More than four years ago, my son came to me and asked me how we related to God in Sanātana Dharma. Followers of Sanātana Dharma know that the answer to that question is not simple and requires some thoughtful analysis. It promptly sent me on a sojourn in which I started taking notes from Sanātana Dharma Scriptures. As I progressed in formulating an answer to my son's question, it occurred to me that the best way to explain the basic tenets of Sanātana Dharma to my teenage son was to write a novel set in ancient India and explain the tenets through the spiritual journey of the characters in the story. This is how the idea of *The Courtesan and the Sadhu* was born. My hope is that, this way, the reader will learn not only about the tenets of Sanātana Dharma but also about the history and culture of the Indian sub-continent. The goal is to explain Sanātana Dharma in an interesting way so that the reader will grasp the true meaning of God's Dharma in the end.

As I progressed with my writing, I realized that there are multiple answers to my son's question even within the Sanātana Dharma traditions. My intent, however, was to provide an answer that was universally acceptable within the Sanātana Dharma umbrella. With that in mind, I have based most of the interpretations of the tenets of Dharma in the novel on the teachings of The Bhagavad Gita, which my mother introduced to me when I was a teenager. In a sense, I am continuing with the family tradition.

A project like this would not have been possible without the support and help of my family and friends. In particular, I am grateful to my son, Rohith, who read the novel and gave me continuous feedback to make it better. More importantly, he raised the fundamental question that started this whole project. I am also thankful to my editor Shiva Prasad Nagaraj who did a diligent job editing the manuscript. In addition, I am thankful to my focus group that included Vjayashree Basapur, Anantha Ramu, Cathy Reisler, and Divyashree Ishwar for the valuable suggestions and input that I received.

I would also like to give my thanks to my daughter Seema and my wife Meena for their support and encouragement throughout this project. Without their moral support, I could not have made this book a reality.

Finally, my special thanks go to Professor Ruben Habito of Southern Methodist University, Dallas, Texas, and Professor Robert Wigton of Eckerd College, St. Petersburg, Florida, for their reviews and for their valuable suggestions and feedback. I am truly indebted to them.

Plano, Texas   Satya Avatar

Prologue

Vishnu Gupta was having his monthly meeting with the top officials from his agency. He took these meetings very seriously and had them conducted in utmost secrecy. They were always in a chamber hidden deep inside the building that housed his agency. His agency was the most powerful government office in the *Mauryan* Empire and had the ultimate responsibility to gather, analyze, and act upon intelligence from every corner. Its mission was to protect the Empire from any internal insurgency as well as from any unforeseen belligerency from outside. The agency had met this goal with all the five principles that are so vividly described in ancient *Pancha Tantra*[1] stories. Vishnu Gupta had achieved this by employing thousands of agents from all occupations from all over the Empire. There were farmers, carpenters, traders, priests, prostitutes, and even *Sadhus* who worked as his field agents.

Everyone knew that the Mauryan Empire was the largest Empire ever built since the days of Alexander the Great. The Mauryan Empire covered the entire Indian subcontinent and extended beyond into the Bactrian lands. Vishnu Gupta's agency was the machinery that ensured that the Empire was intact, that the enemies were in check, and that there were no internal subversions or rebellions. Gupta, which was how he preferred others to call him, believed in eliminating problems before they even surfaced. It certainly cost a lot less to the treasury to eliminate

---

1 Pancha Tantra means five principles or strategies. Five strategies addressed in the ancient tales: loss of a friend, gaining a friend, creating dissention among friends, separation, and union.

the enemies by subversion or assassination than waging a full-scale war at a later stage. Furthermore, peace guaranteed prosperity and a happy citizenry. Moreover, it ensured that dharma flourished.

When it came to intelligence analysis, Gupta had set a very high standard. He believed that how the state acted upon the intelligence collected was even more important than gathering the intelligence itself. As such, he continuously evaluated other departments in the Empire on how effective they were in utilizing the intelligence gathered.

Gupta and his field officers sat around a large table in the secret chamber without any windows. The room was almost dark except for the burning lamps on the four walls of the chamber. Gupta spent the first hour of the meeting assessing the overall health of the Empire; his main goal was to identify potential trouble spots. He would then hold a detailed review on regions that had even marginally troubling intelligence reports. He was a man on a mission who would drill his officers for every minute detail. He had an enormous memory, and his intuitive powers were legendary. He saw trouble before anyone even imagined it in their wildest dreams. He was always several steps ahead of his enemies. His reputation as someone who would ruthlessly suppress opposition to the state was known all over the Empire. Perhaps, because of his reputation, enemies of the Empire seldom tried any misadventure at all.

He would listen carefully, ask tough questions, analyze the data in real time, and have run a myriad of scenarios in his head before the meeting was over. He would make decisions on the spot on what was necessary to eliminate potential trouble spots, and he would then let the mercenary unit or the security forces handle execution of the decisions. He had some of the most powerful and ruthless mercenary units at his disposal. He had assembled the best soldiers from all over the Empire to build that unit. The soldiers were highly skilled and willing to undertake any mission. They had utmost loyalty to Kautilya and the emperor.

Gupta was a protégé of Kautilya, who was the most powerful man in the entire Empire next to the emperor himself. The emperor himself had enormous respect for the Brahmin from Taxila and let him oversee all agencies of the Empire. After all, Kautilya had discovered the young Chandra Gupta and anointed him to be the emperor. He was the prime minister to the emperor and was the most respected person in the entire

Empire. He was also the most feared. Kautilya and Gupta knew very well how an entire Empire could collapse if they were not vigilant about potential enemies. They also knew how difficult it was to regain and rebuild an Empire once it was lost to the enemies. They had first hand experience of that. An Empire needs to be vigilant about threats from both outside and within. While an external threat is easier to monitor, it was the threat within that could often blindside even the most powerful Empires. For that reason, Gupta, who was in charge of intelligence, had the least tolerance level towards treason. In the Mauryan law, treason in any form was a crime punishable by death sentence. This was a rule endorsed by Kautilya himself who nevertheless abhorred killings. As a trained priest, he believed that the Lord was in everyone's heart, and therefore, no one had the right to kill. However, he also believed that being easy on people who committed treason would only weaken the Empire and would even eventually lead to its destruction. Where would dharma be if the state became weak? He was convinced that a strong and stable Empire was essential to maintain dharma, and death penalty for anyone who committed treason was a just punishment, albeit in a secular sense. Moreover, Kautilya avoided mixing his religious beliefs with secular laws.

Today's report from the central region would test Gupta on his interpretation of treason. He sat at the head of the table with officials from all the regions gathered around. He glanced at the official from the central region.

"So Kumara Verma, tell me, what have you gathered from your field agents?" Gupta questioned.

"Well, Sir," Kumara Verma stated, "everything seems to be normal. Nevertheless, I have this report about a Sadhu, which is a little troubling."

"What is it about this Sadhu that troubles you, Kumara Verma?"

"Well, he does seem to be harmless. He was once a resident at the ashram[2] run by the great seer Bharadwaja. Before he joined the ashram, he was a bikku.[3] He is so charismatic, people from all over my region long to hear him. He is not an enemy spy. We have concluded that. It is the sermons he gives that trouble me."

---

2   A religious school usually located in a secluded area.

3   A Buddhist ascetic.

That intrigued Gupta. He slowly got up and started pacing around the table. Gupta was a burly man with a friendly face, and as he paced slowly, his steps seemed to cause reverberations in the room. He was intent on knowing what it was about the Sadhu that troubled his official. Kumara Verma continued, "Oh! His sermons are the usual religious stuff. It is usually about God, Soul, and *Moksha* (reaching God's abode). He continues to attack ancient Manu; he encourages his audience to reject *Varnas.* "[4]

That caused Gupta to stop his pacing. His face got red and was no longer friendly. How could this Sadhu preach against the Varna system? It was a God-revealed system that was in the Vedas.[5] Gupta looked at his official from the central region and quizzed him.

"Does he say why one should reject the Varna system?"

"He has his arguments. He quotes the *Bhagavad-Gita,* argues that the Lord is in all of us, and says there is no need to have divisions among men and women."

That seemed completely logical to Gupta, and he closed his eyes for a moment of prayer. Every one in the room closed their eyes for a moment. Invoking the Lord's teachings had that effect on them.

Yes, the Sadhu is right in a theological sense, Gupta reasoned. However, Gupta's duty was not to protect theological purity. His duty to Kautilya and the emperor was to protect dharma, and the Arya[6] way of life. In his mind, Varnas were an integral part of the Arya way of life and were *non-negotiable.* Gupta, torn between his duty to the emperor and his own conscience, struggled to find a proper action. In the end, his loyalty to the Arya way of life won over. He had to stop that Sadhu from inciting people to rebel against the Varna system. The Sadhu's seemingly innocent actions could lead to anarchy and provide an opening for the enemies of the state. This could eventually lead to the collapse of the Empire. An unjust and immoral regime could seize power, which could lead to the collapse of dharma itself, the very thing that the Sadhu professed to support. He tried to remain calm as he searched for an appropriate response to silence the Sadhu. However, it was difficult for

---

4 Varna System (Caste System) which divides the society into four castes.

5 Vedas are the fundamental *Scriptures* for followers of *Sanatana (Eternal) Dharma.*

6 Arya refers to those who were within the Varna System.

him to do so. Every time dharma seemed to be under attack, real or imagined, Gupta was like a man fighting mysterious demons. His face turned red and he started to sweat profusely. His assistants knew what was going on, as it was not the first time they had witnessed such a reaction. Indeed, the reaction this time was somewhat subdued compared to some of his previous outbursts. There was an absolute silence as no one said anything, and they all waited for Gupta to speak. He finally regained his composure and responded.

"Tell me, Kumara Verma, how large are his audiences?"

"Well, that is the troubling part. His sermons started out as small gatherings. However, these days, he is drawing thousands of people from several towns and villages. His fame seems to be spreading fast. A few rich merchants have now built him an ashram; he calls it *Dharma-Ashram*. People come in droves to listen to him in his ashram every day," elaborated Kumara Verma.

Gupta was not a happy man now. He did not like anything about this wandering Sadhu. Nevertheless, he kept his exterior cool and kept methodically pacing in the room. He finally came back to his seat, slowly sat down in the chair, and looked around the table as if he were searching for the right answer. One of the older officials, troubled by the tone of the ongoing discussion, spoke politely.

"May I interject a different perspective into this? Perhaps, we are reading too much into all this. We have always had multiple interpretations of the Holy Scriptures. There are theologians who even describe the material world as unreal and question everything we do in our daily lives. For them, running the state itself is a meaningless exercise. We do not look at them as troublemakers. Why should we be so hard on this Sadhu? He seems to be harmless."

"He is right. If we really think that the Sadhu is a threat to our way of life, let us monitor him for a few more weeks. We can take a more definitive decision if we find anything troublesome. We can do that in the next meeting," agreed another official.

Gupta silently nodded his head. He appeared to agree.

"He is right. Do not worry about this Sadhu, Kumara Verma. Let us give him a couple of months, and he will lose his charm. You know, Sadhus come, and Sadhus go."

They all laughed, and Kumara Verma felt like the burden of a large weight had melted away from his shoulders. No one else had any pressing intelligence report, and with the meeting settled, the officials left the chamber in an orderly fashion.

Soon a guard closed the door behind the departing officials with Gupta sitting alone in the room. That was something he did after the meeting every month. He would sit there absorbing all he had heard from the top officials, contemplating his next actions. If he ran into a situation when he did not have a definitive answer, he would consult his boss Kautilya. However, on internal security matters, Gupta had complete autonomy and made his own decisions. He kept thinking about the Sadhu, his sermons, and what he had to do about him. He was not in agreement with the way they had closed the matter. He was not going to risk a rebellion. There was peace and prosperity in the entire Empire and people were content. The Mauryan Empire was now the land of dharma, and the Arya way of life was flourishing. A rebellion against the Empire was very unlikely. However, his job was to focus his energy and resources on events that had minute probabilities. One thing he had learned in his life was that seemingly remote possibilities could explode with minor shifts in western winds. There could be a famine, and people could get anxious and insecure, which could cause instability in the Empire. Any such natural disaster coupled with the Sadhu's religious fervor could be a dangerous recipe. He continued to ponder and wondered if everyone in the Empire was happy. There are always people who are unhappy, and they could easily exploit the Sadhu's teachings to incite trouble. Although he was convinced about the appropriate action to take, he had not made up his mind for the time being.

What should he do? Should he assign a couple of mercenaries to kidnap him, kill him in a remote jungle, and make it look like a robbery? No one would believe that robbers would attack a helpless Sadhu, and that could only cause more problems later. Should he use some agents to poison the Sadhu? Would that be moral? What could happen if he did nothing? Could the enemies within use the Sadhu's teachings to incite the citizens to rebel against the Empire? Would the Sadhu start his own religion and cause more future problems to the Empire? Was this something that required him to consult with Kautilya?

Finally, he had come to a decision. He decided not to bother Kautilya on this. He was ready to bear all the responsibility of what he was going to put forth in motion. He asked one of the guards to come inside. The guard opened the door and quickly came towards him waiting for the order.

"Send someone to the main dance hall and get me their massage expert to come and give me a massage in an hour."

The guard acknowledged the command and quickly retreated to get the message to the dance hall, which was a block away from Gupta's office. Of course, Gupta was tired and needed a good massage. However, that was also a code to summon one of his top agents, Chitralekha. She was a dancer in the dance hall who was of mixed heritage; her father was an Arya, and her mother was a Yavana.[7] She was extremely beautiful – some even considered her the most beautiful woman in the city of Pataliputra - and was an excellent dancer. What mattered to Gupta, however, was that he considered her as one of his top agents. Of course, she was committed to dharma, and he only brought her in for important missions.

Within a few minutes, there was a coded knock at one of the doors at the back of the room. That particular door led to a hallway attached to the meeting chamber. At the end of the hallway was a hidden chamber that led to a tunnel that connected Gupta's office and Chitralekha's chamber in the dance hall. This allowed them to confer, whenever required, without giving away her identity, her real identity as a royal spy.

As she walked into his chamber, Gupta was very pleased to see her. He was very fond of her and treated her like his own daughter. His admiration for her skills as an agent of the Empire was endless. Indeed, she had helped his agency solve many difficult cases by gathering intelligence that they thought was impossible to come by.

"Come in and sit down my child," Gupta welcomed her.

Chitralekha knew that Gupta had a special assignment for her. He would not summon her that way unless there was an urgent matter to address. As she sat down in a chair, she politely enquired.

"Is everything all right, Gupta? What can I do to serve the emperor?"

---

7   Yavana is the ancient Sanskrit word for Greeks.

"Well, my dear Chitralekha. There is a wandering Sadhu in the central province that seems to be planting dangerous ideas into the minds of ordinary citizens. He is a disaster waiting to happen. We need to remove him before it is too late."

Clearly, Gupta despite his best efforts to stay calm appeared agitated as he spoke to Chitralekha. She had rarely seen him so disturbed before and wondered what it was that the Sadhu had done to upset Gupta so much. She had seen Gupta age in his job. She had witnessed Gupta transform from an amicable innkeeper to a powerful head of the intelligence agency. As his powers had grown, he had become more rigid, often making unilateral decisions. Recently, Chitralekha had been concerned about his health. She had noticed that he had gained appreciable weight and was somewhat edgy whenever she saw him. Perhaps, the enormous burden of continuously gathering and analyzing information from the intelligence network of the Empire was finally taking a toll on him. She knew that Gupta worked endlessly every day and was completely dedicated to his work and Kautilya. She often wondered what drove him so hard. It was certainly his dedication to dharma. However, was his concept of dharma the right one? Was he making decisions based on his own twisted interpretation of dharma? Although she was no expert on all the intricacies of dharma, she knew the answer to that question. She, however, did not say anything, and just gave a blank stare at him. Sensing that she was looking for some explanation, Gupta continued.

"He is traveling from village to village preaching against the Varna system, which is the basis of the Arya way of life. It is the basis of our dharma. His popularity is growing fast, and soon enemies could use him to incite people to rebel against the Empire. As I have always said, get rid of the problems before they become too big. We need to eliminate him before it is too late."

Chitralekha knew where his logic was going. She was searching for a way to reason with him. Gupta got up from his seat and started pacing again. He then stopped and instructed her in a matter of fact way.

"I want you to take a couple of flute players with you to one of his sermons. At the right time, have one of the flute players shoot a poisonous arrow at him. You know the routine."

He was referring to highly skilled flute players who carried small poisonous arrows hidden inside the flute and could shoot the arrows as they played the flute. Gupta and his agents often employed them to eliminate dangerous enemies.

Chitralekha thought about the mission. It seemed too ruthless to kill a wandering Sadhu just because he had some crazy ideas. She even thought that Gupta was extrapolating the consequences a bit too much. She felt very uncomfortable with the mission. However, she had never refused a mission assigned to her by Gupta. She was never disloyal to him as he was her mentor; he had protected and helped her when she was at the lowest point in her life. He had only shown pure fatherly affection to her. Out of loyalty, she agreed to carry out the mission anyway. Moreover, she was very loyal to both Gupta and Kautilya. She smiled and assured Gupta.

"I will do it, Gupta. You do not have to worry about this Sadhu anymore."

Gupta was pleased and spoke to her with a big smile, "I knew I can always count on you Chitralekha. I will get you more details tomorrow. Now you go back to your chamber and get ready for your mission."

Chitralekha left his office through the same door she had entered Gupta's office. As she walked into the tunnel leading to the dance hall, she had the strange premonition that this latest mission was going to be her last mission.

A few minutes after she had left, Gupta heard a knock on his door. As he instructed the guard to come inside, the trusted guard brought a massage expert to give him that relaxing massage he badly needed. Gupta then slowly walked towards his quarters with the massage therapist.

Part I
Kautilya

Chapter 1
Taxila

It was a pleasant autumn morning, and Kautilya got up before the sunrise. He was always up before dawn, a habit he had developed as one who practiced the Vedic dharma in its true spirit. He finished his early morning meditation and yoga, and he took a relaxing bath as he planned the morning classes; he was planning to review the first book of *Rig Veda.*[8] He was in perfect health and could not remember the last time he had fallen sick. He knew very well that it was all due to his healthy routine – the yoga exercises, the meditation, and the strict vegetarian diet. He strictly adhered to *ekadasi*, a Vedic tradition of eating only raw vegetables and fruits on the eleventh day of the lunar cycle. Keeping with his daily routine, he walked into the backyard garden and sat on a boulder that was right at the edge of the flowerbeds. He had been sitting on the same boulder every morning several hundred times over the years. He sat there motionless, gazing at the heavens, wondering what was in store for the Land of Five Rivers that everyone called *Aryavarta* – the land of Aryas. He sat on the boulder immersed in the mild breeze generated by the early morning wind. The wind made an almost inaudible whisper as if someone were trying hard to tell him something. He tried hard to listen to the whispering wind as he had often done in the early morning hours before the classes. Quiet moments like these helped him find answers for many important questions.

---

8 Rig Veda is the oldest of the four Vedas.

However, many times, he just wanted to sit on the boulder and soak the sweetness of the morning silence until the dawn slowly broke. He found silence to be the sweetest thing, especially when he was into deep thoughts. Silence helped him get in touch with the spiritual dimension of the universe. Indeed, Kautilya was very spiritual and was convinced that there is a divine energy that permeates this material world, and all one has to do is to seek that energy for answers. For him, the whispering wind was the link to the divine energy, and the boulder was the place where the whispering wind would carry him for a communion with the divine energy. Was it really the whispering wind? Was he seeking the answers from within? Moreover, it is in the scriptures: *Tat Tvam Asi* (Thou are That)!

Whether it was listening to the whispering wind or seeking answers from within, moments like these were precious for him, and he wondered why so many in this world were ignorant of the easy path to get in touch with the spiritual energy that blanketed the material world. Many times when his students asked him about the inner meaning of life, his reflex answer was, "Listen to the whispering wind. You will find the answers."

The breeze was soft and soothing as he listened hard for the answers. It was a full moon day, and the moon was still visible in the far end of the sky. Millions of stars were visible as there were very few clouds in the sky. He gazed at the stars and wondered what was in store for Taxila, his school, and the Arya lands in general. Recent events had made him uneasy, and there was a sense of sadness in his heart. As he sat there gazing at the stars, something moved in a nearby tree, and distracted his thoughts. As he focused on the tree, he realized that it was a bird; a closer look revealed that it was an owl, and its sharp, green eyes were staring at Kautilya with great intent. Feeling uncomfortable, Kautilya quickly turned away from the bird, and looked in the other direction. Owls were a bad omen, and he did not want to make eye contact with the bird. Suddenly, the owl swooped down like an arrow and caught an unsuspecting hare that was hiding in the bushes behind the boulder, and carried him away to a far off tree. It happened so fast that Kautilya was startled a little and was sad that the little hare had met sudden death. He reasoned that it was all a part of the karmic cycle, and that it was inevitable. It was the owl's karma to hunt for the hare, and the hare's karma was to be the next meal for the owl. He sighed, slowly got up, and walked back into the school.

He had a busy day ahead of him, and he wanted to make sure that his students did not miss any of the classes despite the extra work that he had accepted that day. He took the sacred texts out of his bag, which everyone referred to as the Vedic Bag. The scriptures written on palm leaves were so ancient that no one knew how old they were. Kautilya had gotten them from his father, who had inherited it from his father, and so on. Kautilya did not know to whom he would pass those sacred books. He had never been married. For him, his students were like his sons, and all he wanted to do was to impart the true knowledge of the Vedas to those boys. Kautilya was a scholar in all the four Vedas. He had mastered and debated all the *Upanishads.*[9] Kautilya took particular interest in the rules of dharma. He had studied and mastered Manu's Dharma Shastra - *Manu Smriti*[10] in its entirety. There was nothing more important to him than keeping the Vedic tradition alive and making sure that the secrets of the sacred Vedas were passed from generation to generation. Moreover, according to ancient texts, a Brahmin who taught the Vedas was superior to Brahmins who did religious services in temples. For Kautilya, there was nothing more important than teaching the Vedas to younger generations; with that in mind, he had opened his school a long time ago.

Kautilya's Vedic school was located just outside of Taxila, a bustling city that connected the plains of the Indus and Ganges with the Panchashir valley. The trade route between India and Greece went through Taxila, and the people of Taxila often traveled to far off cities to conduct business. Culture and religion flourished, and the people of Taxila considered themselves sophisticated in art, music, science, and literature. Nevertheless, their culture and tradition were deeply rooted in the Vedic tradition and they were proud to be upholding the Vedic mores and values, the foundation of the Arya society. Kautilya's school was a medium sized building with a good-sized prayer hall, which was where he taught his students. It had a separate hall for performing the Vedic

---

9 Sacred Vedic texts that are considered part of the Vedas in a larger context.

10 *Manu-Smriti* specifies the laws or codes for the followers of Dharma.

rites and several rooms for the students who all lived with him during their studies. There was also a large kitchen with an added area for dining. Kautilya had a resident cook who took care of all the culinary needs, and there were several servants during the day that took care of other mundane jobs. There was a gardener to tend the garden and assistants to the cook to cut vegetables and bring groceries from the market place. In addition, a housekeeper did the common chores for the school and was always busy cleaning the house. The school owned several acres of fertile land gifted by the king of the Land of Five Rivers. The farmers who lived in a nearby village had leased the land. The farmers and the school shared the proceeds from the sale of the crops that was the main source of income for the maintenance of the school. Of course, there were also the generous donations from rich merchants in Taxila and the contributions from the parents of students who studied there. Kautilya never had to worry about funds for the school even during the years when the rains failed. Indeed, there was always a surplus every year, and he often used it to support families in nearby villages that needed material help. Of course, he was always open to provide spiritual counseling for anyone who came to his school. He also had a guard who stayed in the school and made sure that the children were safe from outside intruders. He was not only a very trustworthy guard; he was also an excellent horse rider and took care of horses in the stable that was just outside the school at the far end of the garden. There was also a horse drawn carriage in the stable. Kautilya and his students did not have to worry much about intruders since everyone in Taxila and beyond respected Kautilya and his scholarship. People often called him the pious one. Kautilya or his students rarely had to venture out of the school, thanks to all the help they got from the servants. Kautilya seldom went into the city of Taxila unless an Arya family wanted Kautilya to perform special Vedic rites. Today was such a day, and that was the reason he felt a bit hurried.As Kautilya got back to the school, he heard noise coming out of the rooms that housed his students; the boys were talking to one another trying to wake up completely. He shouted to one of his older students, "Vasudeva, make sure that all of you are clean and ready in the next thirty minutes."

"Yes, Sir, we will be ready on time. We always are," replied Vasudeva. Sensing that the student sounded somewhat unappreciated, Kautilya reminded:

"Remember we have to go to Vijaya Verma's house and perform the *homa.* "[11]

He often took his students to assist him in such ceremonies. He always looked forward to such occasions; they gave him a venue to preach to the public about the sacred Vedas. It was also an opportunity for his students to showcase what they had learned at his school. This year he was a little anxious about the whole thing. This was the first time he was going to give a public chanting since the Yavanas had occupied Taxila and the Land of Five Rivers.[12] He thought about the Yavanas and Alexander the Great. While everyone considered Alexander a great warrior, Kautilya was the least bit impressed. Everything he had heard about Alexander convinced him that he was nothing but a tyrant who had very few moral values. Everyone knew that Alexander had murdered his own father and his infant half-brother. For Kautilya, Alexander was a barbarian who had no sense of dharma.

He often longed for the days before the Yavanas; how wonderful things were before the Yavanas came swarming into the Indus valley. Commerce was good, and trade with foreign lands prospered. There was peace and prosperity everywhere and dharma flourished. Just two years ago, Kautilya had thirty-two students; students from all the four Varnas - there were fifteen Brahmin boys, ten Kshatriya boys, five Vyshya boys, and two Shudra boys.[13] Although ancient Manu specified that only the first three Varnas were entitled to learn the Vedas, Kautilya nevertheless taught it to anyone who wanted to learn the scriptures. Kautilya believed that the Vedas were beyond any synthetic divisions. People were happy and content, and they were eager to learn the sacred Vedas. In the opinion of most of the people of Taxila, Kautilya, who was famous for his spiritual knowledge and depth, was the best person to teach the Vedas to the youngsters. Indeed, his reputation as the best teacher to train the

11 A Vedic fire-ritual.

12 Modern day Punjab.

13 Brahmins are priestly class, Kshatriyas are warrior class, Vyshyas are merchant class, and Shudras are labor class.

youngsters in Vedic skills and knowledge had reached remote corners of the Land of Five Rivers. Naturally, every prominent Arya family in Taxila wanted their sons to attend Kautilya's Vedic school. People were happy; the Arya classes were in complete control of the land: Brahmins took care of the spiritual aspects, the Kshatriyas ruled the land and protected the land from outside invaders, while the Vyshyas took care of trade and commerce. Shudras were farmers whose hard work fed all the people. The four Varnas were like the four parts of a body that would be incomplete with any one of them missing. This was indeed mentioned in the Rig Veda. However, suddenly, all that changed without any warning. A young Yavana by the name Alexander with a large army had invaded the Arya land. Alexander and his army had come face to face with King Porus, who ruled the Indus plains. On the banks of the Indus River, Alexander and his army collided in a major battle with King Porus. King Porus was a brave and fair king. He was truthful to *Dharma Shastras*,[14] and was a king who did his best to rule his land accordingly. Naturally, his subjects were happy and loved him. At the same time, because of his military prowess, his enemies feared him. Kautilya himself was very proud of him. The battle was fierce, and long. Porus and his army fought bravely, but in the end, Alexander with a larger force, was able to maneuver to a victory, and surrounded Porus. However, Alexander was impressed with Porus, and left the eastern part of the Land of Five Rivers to Porus. Alexander, however, gave the western part including Taxila to his generals. The local military leader who was now in charge of Taxila was a Yavana by the name Stallios. Kautilya was not very happy about all this, and he often wished that the Yavanas would go away, or an Arya prince would drive them away. However, the Arya land, fragmented with many small kingdoms, was in no position to drive the Yavanas away, and he knew what he hoped for was just that – a dream.Most of the Aryas considered Yavanas unclean as they were outside of the Varnas. For Kautilya, what bothered him most was their lack of Vedic knowledge and tradition. They seemed to be educated, and philosophical, but they just could not grasp the depth and the secrets of the Vedas. Moreover, since the start of Yavana rule in Taxila, Aryas were more into material comforts. They were more interested in women and wine. Finer things

---

14 Laws of Dharma.

in the material world like gold, silver, ivory, and silk became more fashionable. Trade and commerce expanded further, and these developments made most of the people happy; the Yavanas running around in the city were just a minor inconvenience to them. For Kautilya, it was the spiritual decay since the Yavanas came that bothered him the most. They were a bad influence on the Arya communities, and this troubled him endlessly. Kautilya considered the number of students in his school as a good indictor of spiritual health of the people of Taxila, and the Arya lands. Since the Yavanas had ruled, the number of students had gone down continuously, and now he had just ten students in his school, all Brahmin boys. This hurt him the most.

Kautilya's worst fear was that the Yavanas would contaminate the Arya society to such an extent that they would drift away from the laws of dharma and the entire Arya society would become corrupt and materialistic. Just the thought of such a possibility made him feel sick, and he shuddered in disgust. How could he prevent such a possibility? He had to do all he could to stop that. He, as a Brahmin, was saddened that he had to think about cleansing the lands and protecting dharma. Under the Vedic tradition, it was the duty of the Kshatriyas to protect dharma. He sensed that the Vedic tradition was at stake here, and it seemed like a crisis of the greatest proportions to him. The more he thought about it, the more he got agitated. It was as though some demons had possessed him; not that Kautilya believed in demons. What was really happening was that the seed of *Māya*[15] was slowly entering into his head. It was ironic that Kautilya, the scholar and preacher who taught his students about the traps set by Māya, was soon going to drown in the ocean of Māya. Māya is so subtle and so invisible; it would engulf Kautilya before he even realized the impact of his next moves. His next moves would alter the history of the Indian subcontinent forever, and one could even argue that it was all part of a Divine plan.

All the boys were now cleansed and ready for the classes. They came to the prayer hall and sat around Kautilya. Kautilya would randomly pick one of the students and ask him to recite a certain hymn from the Vedas. He would then ask his senior students to give a commentary on the student's performance. An ordained teacher teaches the Vedas in only one way - to

---

15 God's material energy that permeates the entire world.

his pupils, who have committed to dharma, which is the right way. The pronunciations had to be perfect; the spacing between words had to be just right. The pitch and tone had to adhere to the ancient metric. This took years of learning and practice. The Vedas, which were handed down from generation to generation existed since the beginning of time. God Himself revealed the Vedas to the people of Aryavarta, and it was the supreme duty of Brahmins to protect and keep the Vedic tradition intact. Kautilya, as a Brahmin, took this responsibility very seriously.

For today, he had chosen the Rig Veda. He wanted the students to practice *Mandala* (chapter) one. He asked one of the students to chant the thirty-second verse in the first Mandala. This was a hymn dedicated to Indra, god of thunder. The student began earnestly:

"... Let me now praise Indra, and his heroic deeds.
This was the first deed god Indra, the thunderbolt wielder performed,
He slew the dragon and then opened the channels for the holy waters,
... With his great and deadly weapon, the thunderbolt, Indra killed
Vritra the mighty dragon...
Indra who wields the thunderbolt in his hands is the king of all that moves
And moves not ... "

The chanting continued, the student meticulously continued, and Kautilya was pleased. He now wanted all the class to chant the hymn praising Indra. When it was over, a student stood up, and said:

"Excuse me, Sir. I have this nagging question. Is Indra God?"

Kautilya smiled. He looked at one of his older students, Mukunda, and said, "Mukunda, do you want to answer that question?" Mukunda was delighted that the esteemed teacher called out his name. He replied, "The answer is a definite no. Indra is just one of the glories of God. He represents the glory of God that destroys evil".

"Then, why do we keep praising Indra? Why cannot we just praise God?" The young boy quizzed.

Mukunda tried to clarify further, "Rig Veda is the beginning. We need to learn about all of God's glories before we delve into our relation-ship with the Creator Himself. It will become clearer as we learn the Upanishads. You need to delve deeper into the Vedas to learn about the true nature of God. Vedas will lead you to God."

The young student was satisfied with that answer, and Kautilya himself was pleased. The students started their breakfast after the classes were over. Kautilya did not eat anything as he was fasting that day. Just as the students were finishing the breakfast, a large carriage drawn by horses appeared at the front of the school. The carriage, which belonged to Vijaya Verma, was there to pick up Kautilya and his students. Kautilya and the students took their books and essentials for the Vedic ceremony and boarded the carriage. They were on their way to Vijaya Verma's home.

There was a festive atmosphere in Vijaya Verma's house. His was a large house that was almost like a mansion. The decorations were impressive, and the guests, all well dressed and wealthy, were appreciating the elegance and beauty. There was also a large garden in the backyard, and the homa was to be in the garden. Vijaya Verma had requested Kautilya to perform a homa for the god Varuna.[16] Varuna is the god who protects *Rita* (the sacred law). He watches men for their deeds, rewards those who are truthful to Rita, and punishes those who broke the sacred laws. He is the god who rewards the good, and for that reason, all Aryas worshipped him for worldly good.

Several guests had gathered for the homa. Most of the prominent Arya families from Taxila were present there. Women wore beautiful dresses and expensive jewelry. Kautilya and his students sat at the center of the assembly and started arranging material for the homa. He took out the books from his bag, instructed his students to take their proper places, and asked Vasudeva to start the homa fire. Now that the fire was blazing in full glory, he asked Vijaya Verma and his wife to sit in their designated places. As Kautilya settled in his seat and glanced around the gathering, he noticed that there was a Yavana in the audience. It was none other than Stallios, the Yavana general in charge of Taxila. Kautilya was a little perturbed to see his presence, but he did not let it bother him too much. The homa started in earnest. The students and Kautilya started the hymns praising Varuna.

---

16 Varuna is the Vedic god of sky.

*"O Varuna, free us from the sins committed by our fathers, and those
we have committed with our own bodies...
The deeds were done not by our own will, but by wine, anger, dice...
Let this praise bring us your blessings...
Keep danger away from me, O Varuna, Emperor of sacred order...
...I cannot bear to live away from you even for a blink of the eye..."*[17]

The hymns continued in full swing with Kautilya's students keeping
the Vedic fire in its full glory. The audience was very pleased with the
chanting and admired the skills shown by Kautilya's young students.
After the homa was over, there was a grand feast for the guests. Vijaya
Verma and his wife were pleased with the way the homa went and came
to Kautilya to offer a token gift for his services as it was customary for the
host family to honor priests at the end of a religious ceremony. They gave
Kautilya several gold coins that made him wonder what he would do with
all the gold coins he had collected over the years for his services. Little did
he realize that the very thought about gold coins was Māya lurking.

When Kautilya and his students were ready to get back to school,
Stallios walked up to Kautilya and praised the way he had performed
the homa. Kautilya was a little surprised to see that the Yavana had
developed interest in the Vedic tradition.

"I liked the way you and your students performed the homa. I am thinking of doing one myself. I would like you to be the priest in my ceremony
as well," said the general. Kautilya was somewhat taken aback. He did
not know what to say. Should he say no for he was outside the Arya fold,
or should he accept his request and bring him to the Arya fold? Was that
right? While the Vedas were clear that only a trained priest should perform
the homa, nothing in the scriptures prevented any one, even outsiders,
from sponsoring a homa. He, therefore, took an enlightened approach, and
decided that he would perform the homa in the general's place.

"I will be pleased to perform the homa. Which god do you have in
mind? Indra, Varuna, Agni,[18] or any other Vedic god?" said Kautilya.

Stallios looked at Kautilya as if he was not pleased with his way
of thinking.

---

17 Rig-Veda 2.28 and 7.86.

18 Agni is the Vedic god of fire.

"Surely, Brahmin, you are smart enough to know what is in my mind."

"Sorry for my confusion, General. Do you want me to choose an appropriate god for your homa?" inquired Kautilya.

"Why perform a homa on some Vedic god? Maybe you should perform a homa praising my deeds? Embellish the Veda, and put my name in place of one of your gods," said the general with a wicked laugh.

His laughter hit Kautilya like a monstrous wave, and his insensitivity towards the sacredness of the Vedic hymns made Kautilya extremely angry. What Stallios was asking was blasphemy. *Embellish the Vedas? Replace a sacred Vedic god with this mortal?* Kautilya's mind was getting dizzy. *Alter the holy hymns? I would never do such a thing in my life. I would rather die!*

He could sense his veins swell from the blood rushing towards his nostrils and ears. His face was turning red and Kautilya was trying to do his best to control his anger. He closed his eyes and took a deep breath to calm his senses. After all, a Vedic scholar should never lose control of his senses. Finally, Kautilya managed to suppress his anger, and without losing his graciousness, he replied, "I will think about it, and I will get back to you in a couple of weeks. General, you realize that it is not easy to change the Vedas just like that; a lot of work is necessary."

The general was pleased and parted from Kautilya saying, "I will be ready for you in two weeks".

At that time, Vijaya Verma's carriage was ready to take him and the young students back to the school.

The students recognized that their teacher was very upset; they had never seen him so upset during their stay at the school. Yes, Kautilya was almost sick the day he found out that King Porus had lost to Alexander the Great, but, even then, he was not this upset. The young students kept quiet the whole time during their journey back to the school. They quietly went to their quarters as soon as they could. Kautilya walked into the prayer hall and sat there for a while shaking with anger. He finally decided to meditate to calm himself down.

Later on, Kautilya kept pacing in the prayer hall. There was no way he could fall asleep that night. He then walked to the garden and sat on his favorite boulder. He remembered what had happened that morning; the owl he had seen was signaling trouble. While it was not clear what trouble was in store that morning, there was no doubt about the danger he was in right at that moment. If he did the unthinkable and accepted to perform a homa praising Stallios and his deeds, he would be committing a sin against the sacred Vedas. On the other hand, if he refused to please Stallios, his life itself could be in danger. There was only one answer to his predicament; freeing the Arya lands from the Yavanas. With all his thoughts engulfed in driving the Yavanas out of the Arya lands, Kautilya kept searching for a plan.

Over the years, Kautilya had evolved; he had grown spiritually, realizing that everything in this material world was driven by Māya. After all, Māya was the root cause of seemingly absurd behavior among humans. Not even learned scholars including priests like him were immune from the effects of Māya. He remembered a brief exchange he once had with a student in one of his classes. The student wanted to know everything about Māya – an impossible goal. Only God as the *controller* of Māya knows *everything* about Māya.

"What is Māya, Sir?" the student had enquired.

Kautilya thought about it for a while; he wanted to give an answer that was as accurate as humanly possible. He struggled to find one that was simple to explain, and easy for a beginner to grasp the true meaning of Māya.

"Māya is that energy that drives the material world," he started his explanation. "It is that energy which makes us desire things; good things and bad things. It is that which drives love and compassion, and is also the force behind hate and lust."

His goal was to give a somewhat basic explanation but at the same time lead the student in a direction to pursue a deeper understanding of Māya.

"So Māya can be both good and bad?"

The student looked confused. Kautilya explained, "It is not Māya that is good or bad, it is what you do under the influence of Māya that is good or bad."

"In that case, how do we escape from Māya?"

"There is no escape from it, my child. Only the Lord is free from its influence, for He is the one who controls it."

"Then, you are not free from the effects of Māya, Sir?" The young student was quite disturbed that his esteemed teacher was not free from the effects of Māya.

Kautilya thought about that conversation and thought how apt that statement was. Indeed, the young student was right. He could see himself entering the vertigo of Māya; he could feel it, but at the same time, he felt infinitely helpless to overcome its effects.

Kautilya's ultimate spiritual goal was to attain *Moksha* –to be free of the cycle of birth and rebirth and reach God's abode. He knew very well that any attachment to the material world would prevent him from achieving that goal. He did his best to overcome Māya – he had overcome the Māya of food, the Māya of desire to be near a woman, and so on. However, there was one thing that he had struggled to overcome all his life. It was his short temper. While he had an immense amount of patience in achieving his goals, trivial things would cause him to lose his temper. He could never analyze that paradox. Maybe because of this, he always avoided getting involved in anything other than things that concerned the school and the students, lest the emotional cycles that were part of worldly affairs engulf him. No one can really stay away from Māya even if one is deluded into thinking so; Kautilya was the last one to be deluded that way. However, he now realized that he was slowly drifting into the very things – the political affairs of the material world - he had avoided all his life. It was Māya in full swing; he now knew that he was drowning under the influence of Māya. Sadly, nothing was going to save him from this. Absolutely, nothing could save him. Again, it was perhaps Providence. One may even say it was God's will, destiny, or karma. He had to go through that torturous path.

Kautilya was destined to be a Vedic scholar. He had excelled in all Scriptural studies; he had mastered the four Vedas, and the one hundred and eight Upanishads. He had excelled in other matters of scholarship as well; he was an excellent student of mathematics, logic, military strategy, and grammar. Indeed, military strategy was one of his favorite subjects. When he was a child, once his teacher had asked him a tricky question, "How many sides there are in a circle?"

"Too many sides, Sir!" was his prompt answer.

This was astounding given that the answer was coming from a child. His observation powers were unmatched. He could observe very few events and make accurate conclusions based on his superior logic. He could have been a counselor to a king, a military strategist, or a diplomat in a king's court. However, he wanted nothing of that sort; all he wanted to be was a simple teacher teaching the sacred Vedas.

Under the influence of Māya, right at that moment, his outlook was undergoing a transformation; the more he thought about his current predicament, the more he was thinking about a military solution. He was sad that the Aryas had let the Yavanas occupy their lands; he was upset that the Kshatriyas had failed in their duty, which was to defend and protect the Arya lands. Nevertheless, what was the use in blaming others? He himself had to do something about the danger the Vedic tradition was in; he was beginning to suspect that what happened to him in Vijaya Verma's house was a part of the bigger Divine plan. He was not going to resist it anymore. Kautilya sat on the boulder looking for a sign that it was the Divine calling. He closed his eyes, prayed, and begged God to give him some sort of signal. He sat in that position with his eyes closed for what seemed like several hours. He now felt the breeze strengthening and opened his eyes. Everything was dark, he could not see the moonlight, and he realized that dark clouds had moved in from the southwest. He could hear the thunder all over and he soon realized that a major storm was brewing in the sky. There were blinding lightning streaks, and there was a sudden storm with blistering winds and torrential rains. Within minutes, he was completely soaked. Surprisingly, all this pleased Kautilya immensely. He was convinced that the storm was the signal from Providence he was desperately looking for.

The storms gave him the extra push, and he concluded that he had to leave Taxila. However, where would he go? Kautilya thought about Pataliputra, the capital of the Magadha kingdom, which was more than a thousand miles to the east of Taxila. Its ruler was a brave king by the name Dharma Pal, and Kautilya had heard many good things about him; his subjects were fond of him, and he followed the true spirit of dharma.

"Perhaps, I could join his court and render him my Vedic services and convince him to drive these wretched Yavanas out of our lands," reasoned Kautilya. He could even become his military strategist. From the accounts, he had gathered about the Alexander-Porus battle, he knew exactly what mistakes King Porus had made. He also knew the weaknesses in the Yavana military strategy. He was confident that given a sizable army, he could devise a military scheme to oust the wretched Yavanas.

Kautilya slowly walked into the school not a bit bothered about the storm. Neither the deafening thunder nor the blistering wind bothered him. All he was thinking was about his impending journey to Pataliputra. He decided to pack his necessities for his long journey: his books, his clothes, and other needed priestly material. In addition to the palm-leaf books that contained the sacred Vedas, he had many empty palm-leaf books containing slots in the pages to hide gold or silver coins. Over the years, Kautilya had collected several gold coins that he hid in these books; he now had a collection of such "wallet" books. He added the coins he had collected from the morning services into one of the wallet books and wondered what he was going to do with all that money.

"I have enough money to raise an army," he mused.

He went to the guard's room and woke him up. The guard sat up thinking something was gravely wrong.

"Is anything the matter, Sir? Is everything all right?" he enquired with a worried look on his face. He was a light sleeper, and he too was woken by the fury of the thunderstorm. His name was Bhima Sen, and he had been serving the school from the very first day Kautilya had built it. Never had Kautilya woken him up in the middle of the night, not even on a stormy night like this one, and he knew instantly that something was gravely wrong.

"The children are safe, and there is nothing to worry. However, I need to discuss something important with you," replied Kautilya.

Bhima Sen was confused and had no inkling about what was going on in Kautilya's mind. As he sat there trying to make sense of what was happening, he saw myriads of emotions go through Kautilya's mind. Staring at Kautilya's face was like seeing into a kaleidoscope of emotions. He saw anger, frustration, sadness, and even a flash of helplessness. Most of all it was determination on his face. What was causing all this?

Seeing the puzzled look on his face, Kautilya continued, "Yavanas are asking me to do the unthinkable. They want me to alter the Vedas to praise their deeds. Taxila is not a safe place for me any more. I have decided to go east where I am safe from them."

Hearing this made Bhima Sen overcome with emotions, and all he could do was weep. However, he did not try to stop Kautilya; he knew that it would be a waste of time. His main concern was Kautilya's safety. He wanted to obey his orders and signaled with his hand that he would do whatever Kautilya wanted him to do. Kautilya gave him further instructions.

"Take me to the trade route that runs from Pancha Shir to Varanasi and drop me near a guest house or an inn outside Yavana control. I will take care of myself from then on."

He then took some gold coins from his "wallet" books, and placed them in Bhima Sen's right hand.

"Bhima Sen, you have been a dear friend to me all these years at the school. I now have to take leave of you to achieve some urgent goals, and I do not know when I will see you again. It is very hard for me to leave you and my beloved students. However, one must listen to the Divine calling, and I must move on. I know deep inside that I will be back some day. Meanwhile, take good care of the students and the school."

Kautilya's eyes were moist from the raw emotions he was trying so hard to suppress.

Bhima Sen did not want to see an emotional Kautilya; he was still trying to control his tears. He took the bags and went outside to get the horse ready. Riding a horse was safer than taking the carriage. Moreover, with a horse, they could take remote routes and avoid Yavana soldiers. Kautilya thought about the boys; should he walk away from them as Gautama had done almost three hundred years ago. Would that be too cruel?

Kautilya was not going to be cruel to his students as Gautama had been to his wife and child. At least he was going to bid goodbye to his beloved Vasudeva and Mukunda. The other students were too young to handle the situation. Kautilya woke up Vasudeva and Mukunda and quietly took them to the prayer hall to explain to them his decision to leave Taxila.

"Vasudeva and Mukunda, listen very carefully to me. I need to explain an important decision I have made," Kautilya began his most difficult task he had faced as a teacher. He knew very well that all his students were going to be devastated from his decision to move way. It was not an easy decision for him either. He had invested almost all his adult life in building and nurturing the school. He was emotionally distraught just thinking about moving out of Taxila. He knew he was abandoning his duty. However, he had concluded that the call of duty to protect dharma was the highest duty, and the only way to bring back the control of the Land of Five Rivers back to the dharma fold was for him to move away. The Vedic scriptures are very clear about it. There are levels of duty, and the ultimate duty is the protection of dharma itself.

The two boys were not clear about what was going on, but they knew something important was at stake, because Kautilya had never woken them in the middle of the night.

"I have decided to move out of Taxila. It is too dangerous for me to stay here," Kautilya was carefully weighing his words as he spoke to the boys.

"Why, Sir? We will do anything to protect you. We are willing to die for you," said Mukunda, still a little naïve in worldly affairs.

Kautilya felt emotional by his sentiment, but he tried to keep his focus. "You need to understand this; if I stay I will be forced to do things that are considered the gravest of sins in Dharma Shastras,"

Vasudeva, the elder one, had a slight idea what was going on from his keen observations. He looked into Kautilya's eyes as he spoke,

"Are you talking about something like blasphemy?"

"Yes. That is what the Yavana general is asking me to do. He wants me to alter the Vedas. If I refuse his wish, he is sure to kill me."

"Oh, I hate the Yavanas," Mukunda cried."Do not worry, Mukunda. Remember, hate is destructive. Everything is going to be all right. I am going in the direction of Varanasi. I will bring help to get rid of the Yavanas. Indeed, I will not return to the school until the Yavanas have left the Arya lands. If anyone asks about me, tell them that I went on a pilgrimage to Varanasi," replied Kautilya.

"But Sir, the Yavanas are too powerful. How is anyone going to do that? Even King Porus could not stop them."

The two boys burst into tears to protest Kautilya's decision. Deep inside their hearts, they knew that their teacher had made up his mind, and it was a futile argument to make him change his decision. Once they realized that they might never see their beloved teacher again, the two of them were overcome with fear and despair, and started sobbing uncontrollably. Kautilya tried to calm their fears, "You two are the oldest now, and you both have mastered the Vedas. I want you to continue to run the school. I have left some of the books for you. Bhima Sen will help you run the school. I have given him some money for emergencies. Have faith. Things will change. Some day, Taxila will be free of the Yavanas, and I will return then. Until then, be truthful to the Dharma Shastras."

He then hugged them and went outside to mount the horse. Soon Kautilya and Bhima Sen rode into the darkness in the pouring rain.

They rode through the dense forests to avoid contact with anyone. Bhima Sen knew all the secret routes that went out of Taxila. After riding for several hours, they were safely outside the land under the control of Yavanas. When they finally reached an inn that was on the trade route, Kautilya decided to rest.

"Let us stop here, Bhima Sen. I will rest in this inn. You go back to the school and take good care of the children."

He stopped and took Kautilya's belongings inside where the innkeeper was more than eager to help them.

Kautilya hugged Bhima Sen and bid an emotional goodbye to his loyal guard. He stood outside the inn for several minutes as the old guard rode into the darkness back towards Taxila.

Meanwhile, unknown to Kautilya, events had unfolded in Pataliputra that would have a profound impact on his plans.

Chapter 2
Journey to Pataliputra

K autilya stayed in the inn for three days, hoping to join a trade caravan traveling east. For some strange reason, there were no traders going east for several days. There were many travelers and traders going west, but the traffic going east was non-existent. This frustrated Kautilya, for he was getting uneasy at the thought of some Yavana soldier coming after him from Taxila. A lot had changed in Pataliputra in the last few months. What he did not know was that Dharma Pal was no longer the king of Magadha. A Palace coup ended with the murder of Dharma Pal. The leaders of the coup Dhana Nanda and his two sons had assumed the rule of the Magadha kingdom. The saddest part for the citizens of the Magadha kingdom was that the Nandas had no regard for dharma. Consequently, the citizens of the kingdom missed Dharma Pal whom they loved dearly. Ever since the Nandas had taken over the Magadha kingdom, there were riots by citizens, which led to brutal purges by the royal forces. Every one was a suspect in the eyes of the Nandas. What if some Vyshyas and Kshatriyas got together and raised an army to overthrow their rule? The Nandas hated the Vyshyas, for they controlled most of the commerce, and therefore the economy. They were the intermediaries that controlled the flow of goods and materials. No monetary transaction happened in the kingdom without the Vyshyas being involved. It was no wonder that the Vyshyas took the brunt of the Nanda wrath. All this meant that no trader wanted to go to Pataliputra with an unstable political situation.

There were some traders, however, who went as far as the Holy City of Varanasi and then traveled southeast to reach the kingdoms in the south. The next morning Kautilya went to the clerk with the intention of finding out the reason for the absence of caravans to Pataliputra. He knew that something was terribly wrong. The Magadha kingdom was the richest in Aryavarta, and no trader wanted to miss opportunities in selling goods there. The innkeeper was a young man and smiled at Kautilya when he saw him. He knew at once that Kautilya was a priest, and with all the due respect for the priest, he asked, "May I help you, Sir? Is everything all right with your stay?"

"I am all right young man. There is one thing that is puzzling me. Do you know why there are no trade caravans going east?"

The innkeeper got a little nervous when Kautilya asked that question. He did not want to say anything aloud. He always worried about Nanda informants lurking around. He gestured Kautilya to come closer and whispered into his ears, "Something terrible has happened. There has been a coup in the Magadha kingdom. The Nandas have killed Dharma Pal and taken over the rule of the land."

This came as a terrible set back to Kautilya. His whole plan was to recruit Dharma Pal in his efforts to drive the Yavanas out of Aryavarta. Now, with Dharma Pal gone, he had to rethink the whole plan. Besides, he did not know anything about the Nandas. *Who were they? Were they good for dharma?*

"What do you know about the Nandas?" Kautilya whispered back. He had to rethink his plans. However, he also knew that there was no going back to Taxila either.

"Not very much is known about them, Sir. There are reports of continuing battles between pro-Dharma Pal forces and the Nanda soldiers. We all hope peace comes soon."

Kautilya thanked the clerk and walked back into his room. He mused about traveling on his own. He could buy a horse. Indeed, he had enough gold coins with him to buy several horses. He could then ride alone to Pataliputra, the capital of Magadha. He decided to drop that idea, as he did not want to travel alone on such a long journey. He had often heard stories of lawless thugs attacking helpless travelers.

20

That evening, just after his dinner, Kautilya came to the front of the inn to get some fresh air. Being a person who spent the majority of the days communing with nature, he had found the inn to be suffocating. Nevertheless, he did not want to venture too far outside until he was sure he was safe from Stallios and his soldiers. He stood outside enjoying the fresh breeze and debating in his own head about his next moves. Just as he was contemplating his plans, a group of traders came into the inn, and one of them walked to the clerk. Kautilya tried to listen to the conversation.

"We are looking for three rooms for the night. Do you think that you can accommodate us?" enquired one of the travelers.

"Very well, Sir, I can certainly arrange that," replied the innkeeper.

"That is excellent. We have come all the way from Gandhara. We are on our way to the Holy City of Varanasi," added the traveler.

"No problem, Sir. I will have some servants help you with your belongings," replied the clerk. He then remembered about Kautilya and wanted to know if the merchants could take on an additional traveler with them.

"By the way, Sir, would you have room for one more traveler? The Brahmin priest over there is looking for a ride to Varanasi," the clerk added pointing to Kautilya.

Kautilya who heard the whole conversation was pleased that he had at last found some company to travel east. However, when he surveyed the group, he was a little disappointed. The group was a mixed crowd with both Yavana and Arya traders. After the bad experience he had with Stallios a few days ago, he was hesitant to travel with any group that involved the Yavanas. Could they be spies in disguise? Just then, the eldest of the Yavanas, who was older than Kautilya, came to him and greeted him with utmost respect.

"We are pleased to see you, good Brahmin. Are you interested in traveling with us to Varanasi?" asked the old Yavana.

Kautilya was somewhat taken aback. He did not expect the old Yavana to be civilized to know the traditions of the land like how one should interact with the priests. The old Yavana had such a pleasant presence and demeanor that Kautilya with his sharp intelligence quickly realized that he was not one of those Yavanas who had come to the land of the Aryas with Alexander the Great. He must have been one of those Yavanas who had been in touch with the Vedic civilization for several years, perhaps decades. Kautilya quickly overcame his reservation and replied, "That would be very helpful. I shall pay you for your offer."

The old Yavana laughed, "That won't be necessary. I see that you are a very learned scholar well versed in the Vedas. It will be our pleasure to give you a ride. Perhaps, as a favor, you can enlighten us about the Upanishads."

Kautilya was surprised that a Yavana wanted to learn about the Upanishads. He was always a willing teacher whenever there was an eager student. Finding no trace of deceit in his demeanor, he gladly accepted the offer. "That sounds like an excellent plan. When is your party leaving for the journey?"

"It won't be long. All we need is a good night sleep, and off we go on the trade route. By the way, my name is Demetrius. What is your name learned Brahmin?" The old man asked; he was very polite and refined, which pleased Kautilya.

"I am Kautilya. I am on my way to Pataliputra. May I know your final destination?"

"Well, we are going to Varanasi first, and from there we travel south a few hundred miles to a place called Swarnapuri which is famous for silk clothes with golden embroidery. We buy silk from there and travel west to Bactria and Greece. We have some wine from Bactria we plan to sell in Varanasi." Demetrius gave Kautilya his entire itinerary. Kautilya was happy that he had found company to Varanasi at least. He would stop for some rest in Varanasi and could travel with another group to Pataliputra. As he was contemplating his plans beyond Varanasi, Demetrius continued, "Well let us all get together early in the morning. After a quick breakfast, we will be ready to continue with our journey."

Next morning, Kautilya was up early and finished his meditation and yoga. He had a light breakfast with his newfound travelers and was soon on his way to Varanasi.

It was early fall, and the weather was perfect. The rains were gone, the temperature had moderated, the sky was blue; they could not have picked a better day to travel.

Demetrius was the talkative one, and he started the conversation. "You are probably wondering how we all got together, right?" he said.

"I will tell you our story. We all come from a town called Mahanagar, near Gandhara. Our city has a big name, but it is really a small fort-city. There are maybe one thousand of us. Most of the town people are Aryas, but there are some Yavanas like me. There are also people from places like Bactria, Panchashir, and Persia. We are all traders, and we love traveling along the trade route. We are on the road most of the time going east as far as Pataliputra and traveling west as far as the Yavana islands."

Kautilya found that very interesting. "That is really fascinating. What about your faith and tradition?" he asked.

"We all follow the Vedic tradition when it comes to our religion. However, we have adopted elements of other traditions in our music, clothing, food, and dance. We do not like wars and invasions. We do not like Alexander's men. They are just beasts. All they want to do is pillage and destroy. They are not like the people I grew up with."

Demetrius was very vocal about his displeasure towards the Yavana soldiers who had recently settled in the Arya lands.

"How long have you lived near Gandhara?" inquired Kautilya.

"Oh, maybe thirty years. I liked the town so much that when my wife died, I brought my daughter and settled down in Mahanagar. Indeed, my daughter is very well versed in the Vedic traditions. She has married an Arya man and they have a beautiful daughter. Her name is Chitralekha".

"I must be boring you with my life story. Let us talk about you now," added Demetrius.

"I am not bored. It is all very fascinating. Anyway, I am just a priest traveling to Pataliputra. I hope to find a job as a priest in the palace," replied Kautilya. He was still cautious and did not want to reveal more details about his current situation.

That worried Demetrius a bit, and he could not hide it from Kautilya. Kautilya was surprised to see that and wondered what worried Demetrius about his plan.

"Is something bothering you? You seem to be distracted."

"Well, you are right. When you mentioned Pataliputra and a job in the palace, I remembered some of the things I had heard from my fellow travelers. These new rulers, the Nandas, seem to have one bad reputation. Be careful, Kautilya."

Kautilya thought about that. It was the second time someone had said not so kind things about the Nandas. After all, his plan hinged on getting the support of rulers of Magadha to drive the Yavanas out of the Arya lands. He was getting worried that his plan could run into a dead end if the Nandas were not motivated.

"Thank you for that information, Demetrius. I will heed your advice," replied Kautilya. That pleased the old man who then turned his attention to the Upanishads.

"Anyway, since you are a priest, I have a question about the Upanishads. In almost all Upanishads, there is so much discourse on *Brahman*. Who is Brahman? Can you enlighten me on that?"

Demetrius was now more serious. He really wanted to learn about the wisdom of Upanishads. Kautilya thought about his question. Although his question sounded very basic and simple, he knew that it required a thoughtful answer. Indeed, many of his advanced students had struggled to find the right answer to the same question that the old Yavana had brought up.

"We all know that the material world we dwell in is just an illusion," Kautilya started. "It is an illusion in the sense that it is not permanent. However, a careful examination of the world around us reveals that there is a lot more than is obvious to the naked eyes. It is not just the matter around us. There are invisible forces involved. Matter taken together with these forces constitutes the material world. One may even say that a divine force binds us to this material world. In addition, a force binds all living creatures to one another and to nature as a whole. What is that force? How are we bound to one another in this material world? These questions have challenged our intelligence since the beginning of time."

Kautilya began to lay the foundations for his discourse. "Of course, the next question is: Is there a Supreme Being who controls this force? Is this a force, or is this a form of energy?"

24

Demetrius was all ears at this point. He found Kautilya's discourse fascinating. He and his fellow traders were becoming mesmerized. Kautilya continued, "You may start looking inwards and ask similar questions. Who am I? Am I merely this body full of blood, flesh, and bones? The body ultimately perishes. Does it mean I cease to exist? Am I not real? Am I just a discrete speck in the continuum of time?"

"The Upanishads provide the answers to these?" asked the old Yavana.

"The answer is affirmative, my friend. If you read the Upanishads, you will begin to find answers to all these questions. You need to start from the basics. Upanishads means the knowledge that destroys ignorance. It is that knowledge that liberates one from *Samsara*, the cycle of birth and death," replied Kautilya.

"Is that knowledge Brahman?"

"Well that is an eternal question that men have asked for ages. I will try to explain. But to really understand the true meaning of Brahman, we need to realize the knowledge that permeates this material world."

Now Demetrius was getting anxious. He wanted to know more. "Tell me about that knowledge," he asked in almost a pleading way.

Kautilya was now getting deeper into the meaning of Brahman.

"The obvious components of the material world are the elements: earth, wind, fire, water, and so on. We think that the world is just that, a complex interconnection of the manifested elements and forces. It is seemingly perpetual, and yet we know almost everything that is alive and moving is temporary. Have you thought about how this visible world really holds together? Who makes it look like this material world is forever? Isn't the material world an illusion?" Kautilya continued with his discourse.

Demetrius was fascinated. He had never thought about those questions; he certainly had no answers to them. He knew Kautilya could answer them all. He listened carefully as Kautilya continued with his monologue.

"My friend, the energy that holds this material world together is Brahman. It is not just any ordinary energy; it is the source for all that is spiritual. It is not something you can feel through your sense organs. The spiritual energy is everywhere. You can only reach that energy through *Adyātma Yoga*."

25

This really got the old Yavana to jump from his seat and almost hit the ceiling of the carriage they were riding in. "I know Yoga. But what is *Adyātma Yoga?*"

"That is the Yoga that lets you reach your inner Self. You are not what you really see. You are not the material body that surely decays once you stop breathing. If your body is not the real You, then what is the real You? That is your inner Self or *Atman*. That is the spiritual You. Uncovering that spiritual You will lead you to Brahman since everything spiritual is ultimately Brahman. That is why Upanishads proclaim, *Thou are That.* Realizing Brahman will glide you to God and free you from Samsara. Think of Brahman as the spiritual plane that links your Soul to God Almighty."

"You mean that Brahman is the spiritual energy that permeates the entire material world and is emanating from God?" asked Demetrius.

"Precisely, once you grasp that knowledge you are free from the pull of the material world, namely, Māya. With the shackles of Māya removed, it is the beginning of a beautiful journey to God's abode," answered Kautilya.

Demetrius felt that he was now getting closer to the true meaning of the Upanishads. Their conversation around the various Upanishads kept Kautilya and Demetrius completely occupied during the entire journey. They were so deeply into the discussions that before they realized, they had almost reached Varanasi, the Holy City.

Demetrius wanted to ask Kautilya a very important question before they reached Varanasi. It had to do with the Varna tradition that had bothered him for a long time. In view of their current discussions related to spiritual aspects of life, the Varna custom struck him as counter to the spiritual tenets. How can there be divisions among men if all of us are spiritually so close to God? If all individual souls emanate from God's spiritual energy, what is the basis for the Varnas?

"Tell me, Kautilya, why do we have the Varna system? Since all our souls emanate from the Almighty Himself, doesn't it sound counter to God's will?"

Kautilya started getting uneasy. Indeed the same question had swirled in his mind many years ago. His conclusion was, while he accepted Varnas for the division of labor, he had not accepted it as some sort of spiritual ladder.

"You are absolutely right, Demetrius. The Varnas are there for the proper functioning of society. They are by no means hereditary. Nowhere in the Vedas is it specified that way," replied Kautilya.

"You are very enlightened, Kautilya. I do not find many like you these days."

"It is unfortunate, Demetrius. They all cling to Manu's interpretation of dharma."

"Oh, you mean the ancient Manu, the first man?"

"Yes. I hope some day people realize that all of Manu's interpretation of dharma is biased, and it is not God's dictum. I hope they start listening to the Lord Himself. All they have to do is to adhere to the Lord's teachings in the Bhagavad-Gita," answered Kautilya.

"I do not know what exactly your plans are in Pataliputra. Nevertheless, I hope you will do just that. Spread the teachings of the Gita."

Kautilya realized immediately that Demetrius was no ordinary Yavana. He was indeed well versed in the scriptures including the holy Bhagavad-Gita. By then, the day was ending, and it was getting colder by the minute. Fortunately, they were now inside the Holy City of Varanasi itself, and it was now time for Kautilya to part with the old man and his friends.

"I must bid good-bye to all of you now. Drop me near a guest house where I can rest for the night," instructed Kautilya.

Demetrius was sad to see Kautilya say good-bye. There was so much more he wanted to discuss with Kautilya, but he knew they had to part and only hoped that some day he would have a chance to see him again.

As they entered the main street leading to the famous Shiva temple, they saw a modest inn advertising facilities for the priestly class. The wooden sign in front of the inn proclaimed, *we have worship halls, clean rooms, and vegetarian food.*

This looks decent enough for my night stay, thought Kautilya. He then asked Demetrius's party to stop and got down from the carriage. He bid good-bye and thanked Demetrius for the ride.

"Kautilya, I should be the one thanking you. You have shown me the spiritual path in the short time we were together; I have learnt more about spirituality in the last few hours than I learnt in my entire life," replied Demetrius.

27

Demetrius and his friends then left Kautilya in front of the inn with his books and bags. A servant came and picked up his belongings and took Kautilya to the main hall of the inn.

"Welcome to our inn. We are happy that you will be staying with us during your visit to the Holy City," the innkeeper said, giving Kautilya a friendly welcome.

The clerk was a burly man and had a friendly face. He looked calm and seemed to be enjoying every minute of his life. The clerk had a permanent smile on his face that would tell the visitors that he was a man at peace with himself. His attire was simple but dignified enough for a man from the Vyshya class. His parents had named him Vishnu Gupta, but everyone just called him Gupta. Although he was a man born into the merchant class, a class so well versed in the tricks of finance and trade, Gupta was the least interested in making money. Sure, he knew all the intricacies of the accounting methods and had that innate knack for making a profit from any venture he could have bothered to enter. However, his goal was not in accumulating wealth. He had a small profit from his inn all right, but his main interest was meeting learned men who visited the Holy City, whom he would often engage in theological and spiritual discussions. He thought of his business of running the inn as a small example of doing God's work.

Kautilya looked at the innkeeper and felt like he had known him all his life. It was not often he got this sort of feeling when he met total strangers. Indeed, he had never felt like that before. He felt as if their destinies overlapped, and they were going to accomplish a lot together. For a man who never believed in premonitions or superstitions, it was an extremely strange feeling to have. Surprised by this almost irrational feeling, Kautilya took a long look at the innkeeper. The innkeeper still had that friendly smile on his face. He had somewhat long hair that made him look younger than he was. His eyes were light brown and piercing. A closer look revealed to Kautilya that there was some sadness, almost bitterness in his eyes. He knew right away that the smile was a façade that hid a painful past.

"Yes, I need a room for the night, and more importantly, I need a place to perform my evening rites," said Kautilya, answering the innkeeper.

"It will be my pleasure, Sir. There is a hall downstairs for you to perform your rites, and your room for the night will be on the first floor. The dining hall is on the west end of the building," said Vishnu Gupta. "By the way, my name is Vishnu Gupta. You can call me Gupta. Just let me know if you need any special assistance. May I know your name, Sir?"

"I am Kautilya. That will be all for tonight. I do not need anything else."

There was a twinkle in Gupta's eyes. Gupta had an enormous memory. He never forgot any name or face. He wondered if it was the same Kautilya his uncle from the Land of Five Rivers had mentioned. His uncle had talked a great deal about a scholar by that a name long time ago.

"Are you from Taxila, Kautilya?" asked Gupta.

"Yes, I am indeed from Taxila. Do you have any relatives in Taxila?"

"Not in Taxila. I had an uncle who lived not far from Taxila, and he had mentioned to me about a military scholar named Kautilya. You must be that Kautilya. It is an honor to meet you, Sir," replied Gupta very politely.

Kautilya smiled back and accepted his compliments. However, he was a little tired, wanted to go to his room, and was not in a mood for further discussion. Nevertheless, Gupta's mental wheels started turning fast. He wondered if Kautilya could be the last piece in his secret plan. Without saying much, he gathered Kautilya's belongings in one hand and led him to the room with a small lantern in his other hand. He did not bother calling the servant, as he wanted to take the opportunity to spend a few more minutes with the venerable Brahmin.

They went upstairs and entered the guest room assigned for Kautilya. The room was reasonable in size and had a small window. Gupta lit an oil lamp in the corner of the room and showed him his bed. The wavering of the lamp made Kautilya's eyes appear like a glowing sun. Gupta was awestruck by that special glow and wondered if the glow was there because he was spiritual and learned. Alternatively, was it there because he was very wise and pious? It was more than that. The glow was an amalgam of all those and something more. He could sense that he was with someone who was going to be very famous some day. Somehow, Gupta felt that Kautilya was on a special mission, and he was going to change the history of the land. It was not the first time he had sensed future events, and people often said that he was clairvoyant. Indeed, he had a premonition about King Dharma Pal's demise weeks before his death.

As he stood there helping Kautilya settle down in the room, the innkeeper wanted to know everything about him. He could sense that he was going to achieve great things, and he wanted to tell his friends that he had indeed met this important man and hosted him once in his inn. Little did he realize that Kautilya would indeed become a pivotal part of his secret plans. Indeed, he would become the owner of his plan. The coming together of Kautilya and Vishnu Gupta was pivotal to the future of dharma as future events would reveal.

As Gupta was about to leave, he turned back and tried to strike up a conversation with Kautilya.

"Can I do anything else to make your stay more comfortable?" he asked, trying to get Kautilya engaged.

"I am all right now. I will let you know if I need anything. You have been very helpful," said Kautilya.

It appeared that Kautilya was not that interested in continuing a long conversation with the innkeeper. His immediate worry was to complete his evening rites, and dinner was his next priority. Moreover, he had been on the road for several hours, and was eager to rest for the night. However, the burly innkeeper was insistent. He continued with his inquiry.

"If I may, can I enquire about your endeavor in Varanasi?" asked Gupta.

"Well, I am on my way to Pataliputra to offer my spiritual services to the royal family," Kautilya calmly replied.

Gupta felt a chill go through his bones when he heard the royal family mentioned. One gets a chill like that when one senses something ominous like an impending disaster. At the same time, Gupta was angry and could not hide it. His smile disappeared, and he started trembling. He was about to drop the lantern he held in his hand, but somehow managed to keep his balance. He stood there motionless for a long time without saying a word. Kautilya was surprised to see this and had no idea why Gupta was so disturbed.

"Please, Kautilya, do not go to Pataliputra. Do not serve the wretched Nandas. They do not deserve an eminent scholar like you. They are cruel, sinful, and have no sense of dharma."

Gupta was pleading like a child. Kautilya, unsure of what was going on in Gupta's mind, tried to reassure Gupta.

"You are not the first one to warn me about the Nandas. You need to realize that once someone has become a ruler, he has to adhere to the laws of dharma. After all, the king is the one who upholds dharma. Perhaps, the Nandas, coming from a tribal background, need to be educated about the rules of dharma. Once that is accomplished, they will change."

Gupta could not believe what he was hearing. How could an intelligent man like Kautilya be so naïve? What he did not realize was that Māya had clouded Kautilya's thinking at that moment. For Kautilya, the real threat to dharma was not the Nanda rulers, but the Yavanas. Even his encounter with Demetrius had not diluted his disgust toward the Yavana invaders. Gupta regained his senses. He quickly reasoned that Kautilya should meet the Nandas. He was bound to have an unpleasant experience, which would only help Gupta's plan. He changed his demeanor, and he wanted to encourage Kautilya in a subtle way. Despite his cunning thoughts, he wanted to forewarn Kautilya.

"Sir, I want to apologize; I do not know what overcame me. The very mention of the wicked Nandas drives me crazy. I want you to be very careful in Pataliputra. The Nanda princes can be very cruel and moody. They are famous for insulting academics, priests, and artists. Let me know if you need anything from me on your journey to Pataliputra," added Gupta.

"Do not worry good man. I am not seeking any wealth or titles. I just want to bring some spiritual light into the royal palace. A king who is spiritually inclined will do the right things to protect dharma."

Kautilya wanted to find out more about the Nandas. What happened to King Dharma Pal? Who are these Nanda princes? How did the coup happen? He wanted to know the details.

"Well said, Sir. I hope you are successful. I need to tell you how the Nandas came to power. Perhaps, you are not aware of that," replied Gupta.

"Continue, I am anxious to know the details," prompted Kautilya.

"Well Sir, the current king was only a local lord in the eastern valley before. His sons were planning a revolt when the king's men captured them. However, the elder Nanda took King Dharma Pal's personal guard and his family as hostages and used the guard to murder the king. He became

the king, and his sons, the Nanda brothers, conduct day-to-day affairs."
Gupta's facial expression had the utmost disgust, which clearly showed
how he felt about the Nandas as he continued to narrate the events.

"He then had Dharma Pal's young son put in prison and forced the
queen to marry him. She married him only to save her son's life."

Now Kautilya was getting upset and had a sick feeling in his stomach.
Should he abandon his mission and go back to Taxila? However, there
was no turning back, and he decided to visit the Nandas. What harm
would they do to a simple priest? If they refused to help him drive the
Yavanas out of Aryavarta, he would have to develop a different plan, and
Kautilya was ready for that.

"I admire your concern for me, Gupta. Nevertheless, I have to do this.
Perhaps, I can change them. Perhaps, I can make them see the divine
within all of us," Kautilya tried to assure the innkeeper.

"I hope you are right, Sir. For the sake of all the citizens of Magadha,
I hope you are successful," said Gupta.

Kautilya was not happy with his predicament. He did not want to
abandon his plans to see the Nandas although deep inside he knew it was
going to be a fruitless exercise. Gupta was not happy either. He felt guilty
that he was encouraging Kautilya to visit the evil Nandas. However,
Gupta believed that a little deceit was all right to achieve higher goals.

In spite of the awkward interaction they had over the last few minutes, both felt a special bond towards each other. Something told them
that they would need each other to achieve their goals. It was almost like
a divine signal. Kautilya looked at Gupta with a sense of fondness and
felt that he could be his confidant.

"I would like a favor from you, Gupta. I have two bags of sacred
books with me. I do not want to carry both of them to Pataliputra. I
would like to leave one of them with you."

Gupta was delighted to hear that Kautilya was seeking his help. Moreover,
the trust that Kautilya had placed in him made him feel honored.

"It will be an honor, Sir. I will keep them in my safe and protect them
until you come back," assured Gupta.

Gupta instructed Kautilya to follow him. They both went into
Gupta's office and proceeded to a small room attached to Gupta's office.
Kautilya had his bag that contained the books with hidden gold coins,

whereas Gupta carried the lantern in his hand. The room was actually a storage area with many unused items lying around the floor. Gupta locked the door that connected the storage area to his office, placed the lantern he was holding on a small table, and went on to carefully move the items aside and removed an old rug that was on the floor. Kautilya was intrigued to find a trap door that the innkeeper opened slowly. The trap door revealed a secret passage, and from the creaky sound, Kautilya knew that it was not very often that Gupta went through that passage. At the end of the passage was another room that had several safe boxes; Gupta opened one of them and looked at Kautilya.

"Sir, this is a safe that has a special lock, and you may place your books in this safe."

Kautilya placed his palm leaf books inside the safe and locked the door. He took the key out and gave it to Gupta.

"I want you to keep the key. I have complete trust in you."

Gupta was pleased with the trust that Kautilya placed in him.

Kautilya then took a close look at the rest of the room. He noticed that another passage led into the chamber. Realizing that Kautilya was staring at the second passage that led into the chamber, Gupta explained, "Sir, that second passage leads into another room in the inn. I never rent that room to anyone. The next time you are here, you can stay in that room which will give you easy access into the secret chamber."

Kautilya smiled, thanked him for taking care of his books, and followed Gupta back to his office. He then bid him good night, went back to his room, and got ready for his evening rites. After finishing his evening rites, Kautilya went to the dining hall, had a simple meal, and went to his room for some rest.

The next morning, Kautilya was up before the dawn, cleansed his body, did his yoga and meditation, and the morning rites. After finishing his breakfast, he went to Gupta to pay his dues. However, Gupta refused to accept any money.

"Sir, it is an honor to have a learned person like you in my inn. I refuse to accept any money from anyone who belongs to the esteemed clergy."

Seeing his determination, Kautilya just thanked him and was soon on his way to Pataliputra.

"May God bless you, Sir, and may Dharma be with you," shouted Gupta.

A party of merchants with several horses and carriages, with dozens of mounted guards, were traveling to Pataliputra, and they were happy to offer him a ride. Kautilya traveled with them, and spent most of his time listening to accounting matters that the merchants were discussing. While he was eager to meet the royal family and offer them his services, the merchants were busy in coming up with ways to save taxes.

"We all dwell in our own Māya plane," thought Kautilya, without realizing that he himself was a victim of Māya, his Māya being the desire to overthrow the Yavanas.

As Kautilya entered Pataliputra, he was surprised to see that it was much larger than he had imagined. It was a well-planned city with large boulevards and stately buildings. The city was bustling with commerce, and trade. There were stores stocked with expensive and fine jewelry, clothes, and furniture. Many stores were selling vegetables, grains, and wine. He could also see many dance halls, restaurants, and temples. The wealth was obvious, but somehow the citizens did not seem happy. They all looked tense and worried as if there were a cloud hanging over their heads. Kautilya noticed that there were many horse-mounted soldiers in the streets monitoring the crowds. It was as if Pataliputra was full of security men in all corners of the city. He then remembered that there was only one major fortified facility at the border of the Nanda kingdom. It seemed to Kautilya that the Nandas were more worried about an internal uprising than about an attack by an external foe.

Kautilya thanked the merchants for the ride as they dropped him off at a lodge. The lodge was crowded with all sorts of men from outside the city. There were a few clergymen like him, but mostly it was full of traders who had come to Pataliputra to sell their goods. Some had come to settle their taxes with the treasury. In addition, some wealthy men from the countryside were visiting to see medical specialists who were not available in the country. Kautilya rested that night, and the next morning, right after his religious rituals, he headed straight in the direction of the palace. There he met the guards and told them why he was visiting the Nandas. The guards sternly informed him that the Nandas would meet clergymen only on Fridays, and he should come back the next day. Kautilya was a bit disappointed and went back to the lodge waiting eagerly for the next day.

Chapter 3
Meeting the Nandas

Kautilya could hardly sleep that night. He spent most of the night tossing and turning in his bed thinking about the great plans he had for the Land of Five Rivers. Finally, when he fell asleep he had a series of dreams. He dreamt that with the help of a fair and balanced king, he was going to reestablish dharma. He dreamt of the time when Vedic traditions would hold supreme and peace and prosperity would reign in the whole continent. He also dreamt about the Nandas being cold and uncooperative. It was a strange dream in which the young Nandas kept avoiding Kautilya. When he finally came face to face with one of the younger Nandas, he smiled and pulled his skin like pulling a mask. The new face that he revealed was none other than the Greek general in Taxila. Kautilya realized that it was a nightmare. He woke up and saw that he was sweating profusely. He could not sleep any more. The night seemed too long as he worried if the dream was a bad omen. He could hardly wait for the morning sun. Finally, the morning came, and Kautilya was ready for the audience with the Nandas.

Kautilya, clouded by Māya, failed to recognize the impending danger. Kautilya being caught in his desire to reestablish the Vedic dharma was ignoring the obvious signs. In spite of numerous warning signals, he was completely oblivious to the real nature of the Nandas. He was going to do something that was unplanned, something not researched that was against his nature. It was no secret that the entire citizenry of Magadha hated the Nandas. They all knew that the Nandas had no respect for rules of dharma nor did they show any interest in art or music. Their interests were women, wine, and the perverted joy they derived in torturing others.

Not knowing all this, Kautilya proceeded to the palace hall wearing his best attire with the holy books in one hand and the letter he had written on a palm leaf in the other.

This time the guards did let him in. As he entered the palace, he realized how grand and magnificent it was; he had never seen a structure so huge and luxurious. The pillars were tall and majestic, and the walls and floors were adorned with things that displayed the best in the kingdom – silk drapes, golden moldings, carpets, various works of art, furniture, and so on. As he entered the reception hall, he was eager to meet the princes and explain to them how he planned to spread the true meaning of dharma with their help. He wanted to explain how frustrated he was witnessing the decadence in the Land of Five Rivers - Aryavarta. He had already given his letter to the guard and was confident that the Nandas would support his cause. He was soon going to find out how naïve he was in his expectations, and how wrong he was in judging the Nandas.

As Kautilya sat in the hall along with a few other Brahmins who had come seeking various favors from the royalty, he suddenly heard the doorkeepers at the entrance from the main palace building to the reception hall announcing the arrival of the Nanda princes. The announcer, glorifying princely virtues that were non-existent, recited a long list of titles. At the same time, a group of musicians played some instruments to create a regal atmosphere. As the princes entered the hall along with their entourage, the entire hall stood and bowed showing respect to them.

Kautilya sensed that the bowing had more to do with fear than genuine respect. The two princes sat in the center seats while others from their entourage sat in the smaller seats. As every one in the hall settled down, one of the princes signaled that they could proceed with the hearings.

A skinny man from the entourage stood and announced the name of one of the members of the clergy in the audience and asked him to stand up. He then proceeded in detail, "Your Highness, this priest has come to you seeking land in a nearby village. He says that the income from the land will make it easy for him to perform his religious duties. For this, he will be grateful to the royalty eternally."

The princes were pleased and signaled that they would grant his wish. The treasury officer took notes as the rest of the entourage cheered the generosity of the royalty while the musicians played the instruments again. Another poor man in thin, partly shredded clothes stood up, and the announcer gave the details.

"Your majesty, this poor man has come here to seek your help in fulfilling a religious vow. He would like sufficient money and land to build a temple in honor of the gods. He will also have a stone carving in front of the temple extolling your virtues for funding the temple. He promises to be infinitely grateful for your generosity."

Hearing that the temple would have a stone carving extolling their virtues, one of the princes immediately signaled that they would grant his wish as well. The treasury officer again took notes as the rest cheered the kindness of the Nandas.

This continued for a while, and while this was going, a beautiful female servant brought some large golden cauldrons filled to the brim with red wine and delivered it to the two princes along with some other officials in their entourage. The princes started sipping the wine as the charade continued - poor Brahmins asking for favors, getting their simple favors granted, and the entourage praising the royal princes and glorifying their virtues.

The Nanda princes were thoroughly enjoying the event as it fed into their enormous egos. As they sipped the wine, they were amazed how their fortunes had reversed in the last few months. It seemed like only a few days ago when they were in the prison waiting for the execution order from King Dharma Pal. Today, they were in power thanks to the cunning of their father. They could now do whatever they wished. They could just pick any beautiful woman of their fancy. If the woman's father or relatives protested, they would often end up in the torture chamber. The brothers especially enjoyed their visits to the torture chamber and often took part in the act. Beautiful women, wine, and luxuries they had never even imagined. For the Nanda brothers, life could not have been any better.

While this charade went on, it all seemed too unrealistic to Kautilya. At one point Kautilya was sorry that he had come there asking for a favor. It dawned on him that it was a complete mistake and he was tempted to walk away. At the very moment, he heard the announcer mention his name. It was now Kautilya's turn to ask for the favor, and he felt obliged to stay.

"Whom do we have here?" said one of the princes.

He was now in a mood to talk, perhaps, from the effect of the wine. The skinny announcer replied, "He says his name is Kautilya, and he is from Taxila."

Kautilya stood up as the skinny man was announcing his name. The prince enquired about his long journey from Taxila.

"What brings you here from far away Taxila, Brahmin?"

Before Kautilya could answer, the skinny announcer replied, "He has given a letter explaining what he wants from you, Your Highness".

"Go ahead and read it," replied the price.

As the announcer kept reading Kautilya's letter, the effect of the wine started blurring the vision and other senses of the princes. The announcer read, "I have come to Pataliputra seeking a job as a counselor in the palace. I wish to strengthen the Vedic tradition in the royal household."

However, the Nandas heard something different. For them it sounded like, "I wish to bring the Vedic tradition to the palace for you are from a backward tribe."

The announcer continued, "A king whose rule is built on dharma is sure to be loved by his subjects and is bound to extend his influence beyond the frontiers of his kingdom."

However, the Nandas heard something different, "A king who has no sense of dharma is unfit to be a ruler."

Whether it was the effect of wine or the subconscious mind that was playing tricks on the Nandas, one would never know. As the announcer continued to read the letter, the two princes started showing displeasure while they kept drinking wine from their cauldrons. Their faces started getting red. It was clear that the letter was making the two princes angry, and Kautilya was puzzled from their show of displeasure. He wondered what in his letter was upsetting them. Was it because of the way he had addressed them? Perhaps, he had not added all the royal titles in the letter. He was puzzled, but he was not scared. However, everyone else in the hall was scared; they knew very well that whenever the princes got into that sort of mood someone was going to get hurt. They all felt sorry for Kautilya.

Finally, the announcer was done reading Kautilya's letter. There was a complete silence, and the announcer looked pale and shaken. The older prince took his cauldron and threw it at the guards.

"Who let this wretched Brahmin into our court?" he shouted.

"Who does he think he is? He is the only one who knows dharma? Does he think that there is no dharma in our kingdom?" added the other.

"He wants to teach us how to be dharmic?" mocked the two in unison.

They both gave out a wicked laugh. The wine had begun to affect their logic, and their anger towards Kautilya was increasing.

The royal ranting continued. Finally, the elder of the two uttered the words everyone was expecting. He yelled at the guards with great anger, "Guards, throw this man out of my court, I cannot stand his ugly face anymore!"

There was an eerie silence as two tall guards hurriedly walked towards Kautilya. One of the guards grabbed him by the forelock that was the trademark of the clergy. Pulling Kautilya's hair not only hurt Kautilya, it unlocked his forelock. The other guard grabbed him by his legs, and the two carried him to the main entrance of the palace, threw him into the street, and shouted, "Stupid Brahmin, if you ever value your life, never set your foot in the palace again!"

Kautilya was utterly humiliated. It all had happened so fast that it seemed like a continuation of the nightmare he had the previous night. His body was aching, his clothes were dirty, and onlookers were staring at him as if he was some sort of circus animal. His anger level started to elevate. He was ashamed of himself that he had been so blind to the Nandas' evil character. It was all over the city and in the faces of the citizens, and he felt like a fool not to have realized it. Indeed, Gupta and others had forewarned him. He was upset that he had become a prisoner of Māya.

How could this happen to him? He kept asking himself, but failed to come up with an acceptable answer. Suddenly, the palace guards threw his Vedic bag that had all his books. He picked up his bag, slowly raised himself, and managed to stand straight. He tried to get the dust off his clothes and lifted his hand to touch his forelock. Realizing that it was untied, his anger increased dramatically. This was the ultimate insult to a Brahmin, someone unlocking his forelock. He was trembling with anger, and he took an instantaneous vow. He would not tie back his hair until he had annihilated the Nanda clan. Indeed, he would devise a strategy to accomplish just that. It was then and there that Kautilya, the pious Brahmin, started his metamorphosis to *Chanakya* the master strategist.

Chapter 4
Back to Varanasi

Kautilya slowly started moving away from the palace gates. He did not know where to go now or what to do. Things had unfolded so fast that it seemed like a terrible nightmare. The reality was that he knew it was all too real, and was struggling to comprehend what had really happened to him in his encounter with the Nandas. He was upset beyond imagination. Not even the Yavana general had upset him that much. It was not just the personal humiliation. It was the way they had transgressed dharma. If dharma were a fair maiden, there was a transgression. If dharma were a child, the child was now an orphan.

He had to do something. For the sake of the people of Magadha, for the sake of the Vedic religion, and ultimately for dharma itself, he had to destroy the Nandas. However, how would he achieve that goal? They had all the military might, and he was a lonely Vedic priest. He had no army and had very little money. All he had was his intellect to defeat the evil kings. He had to come up with a plan.

My temper is running too high for me to think rationally, he thought.

He started walking towards the river and decided to take a long cold dip. He walked towards the steps where other pious people were taking bath with only a token of clothing to cover their body and sat on the steps with his feet in the river. He sat there doing nothing, just staring at the river. The flowing river began to sooth him, and he soon calmed down.

An old man who had watched him sitting on the steps for a while came to him. Seeing that Kautilya had no towels, he offered him a clean new towel. Kautilya thanked him and kept it on the steps away from the flowing river. He then sat on one of the steps, and the old man walked towards Kautilya and sat next to him.

"You seem to be very perturbed, Oh Brahmin," said the old man.

"I am, I really am. Something terrible happened to me a while ago. I need to do something. I do not understand how I ended up in this predicament. I keep thinking about a monumental task ahead of me."

Kautilya was vague in his answer. He was not sure about telling the stranger about the humiliation he had just suffered.

"You were humiliated by someone very powerful. Am I right in that assumption?"

"Yes, of course. Very powerful people have humiliated me. It is not just the humiliation. It is the way they have trampled on dharma. Something needs to be done about that," replied Kautilya.

Kautilya kept realizing that all this might sound meaningless to the old man. However, the old man was patient and kept listening to every word Kautilya was saying.

"Oh, pious one, you know very well that nothing is impossible in this material world if God is with you. Maybe all this was due to a reason. Perhaps, Providence was behind all this," said the old man.

"Perhaps, Providence was behind all this. You are right. God is always there for you as long as your endeavor is to uplift dharma," replied Kautilya.

"With that in mind, the impossible that you are pondering, does it uplift dharma?" enquired the old man.

Kautilya took a long look at the old man. His body was extremely fragile, and he looked like he had been fasting for months. He looked very weak, and his face was full of wrinkles with his long flowing gray hair dancing in the mild breeze. However, his eyes were sharp, and anyone could tell that he was an alert and intelligent man despite his advanced age.

"Of course, it does. But I cannot seem to figure out where to start."

Kautilya was not trying to hide his frustration. The old man smiled.

"You know what your goal is. That is the most important piece in solving the puzzle. The other pieces will fall into their place in no time. Just keep listening to God's spiritual energy in nature, the whispering wind, or the flowing river. Every time you need a piece of the puzzle you will hear the clue."

Kautilya took solace in those encouraging words and remembered his own favorite advice to his students - "Listen to the whispering wind. You will find the answers." Kautilya smiled back.

"You are right, old man. Let me take a dip in the holy water and begin my journey towards that goal," replied Kautilya as he stood up.

As he went down the steps, the cool flowing water came up to his chest. He closed his eyes and took a dip into the river. When he got up and opened his eyes to see the old man, he was nowhere, but the clean towel was still there on the riverbank. Kautilya wondered if he was hallucinating.

Was the old man my imagination? Perhaps, he was just the personification of my inner strength, wondered Kautilya.

However, the towel was still a mystery.

Kautilya went back to his room. He did not want to stay in Pataliputra any longer. It was a dangerous place for him. However, he was not sure of his next destination. Where would he go? Whom could he trust? As he sat in his room thinking about the next moves, he thought about Varanasi and the innkeeper Vishnu Gupta. He remembered how Gupta had behaved when Kautilya had mentioned the very name Nanda. He wondered what had made him react that way. Something terrible must have happened between Vishnu Gupta and the Nandas. He wondered how bad it might have been. He also recalled that in the end, Gupta really did not want to stop him from going to Pataliputra. Did he have a reason? Did he want Kautilya to experience the evil of the Nandas first hand? Of course, he wanted that. He wanted Kautilya to be his partner in whatever plan he had been scheming for a while. Surprisingly, it did not upset Kautilya at all. In a way, he even liked it. Kautilya decided to go back to Varanasi and stay in Gupta's inn.

"Gupta's inn will be my base from now on. My journey to liberate dharma will begin from the Holy City of Varanasi," concluded Kautilya.

As soon as he found a group of merchants who were traveling west, he joined the group and reached Varanasi to find his trusted innkeeper.

Kautilya did not talk much during the trip. He kept thinking about the several books on *Artha Shastra*[19] he had read in his younger years. He wanted to revisit those books although he was certain that none of the strategies written in those books would help him to overthrow the evil Nandas. New strategies had to be developed and new methods of intelligence were required. The existing rules of diplomacy might not be good enough, and new ones might be required. In the end, revision of the whole school of Artha Shastra was required. All the new methods and strategies he would devise were to become *Kautilya's Artha Shastra*.

Kautilya thought about the daunting tasks in front of him. How would he raise an army to fight the mighty Nandas? They had a military force that exceeded one hundred thousand soldiers. They had almost ten thousand elephants, thousands of chariots, and more than thirty thousand horses. Within weeks of taking over Pataliputra, they had subjugated several smaller kings and made them their vassals. Moreover, they had secret agents planted in all corners of the kingdom, and it was almost impossible to plan an uprising. Anyone with a hint of disloyalty was subject to torture and death. They had built such a ruthless reputation that no one even entertained the thought of getting rid of them. Kautilya was, however, certain about thousands of brave ones who were ready to fight for dharma. He had to tap into that latent desire to get rid of the Nandas.

As they approached Varanasi, Kautilya came back to the present time and instructed the merchants to drop him off at Gupta's inn. He then thanked them and went inside the inn. Gupta was busy helping another customer at that time, and he gave a quick glance at the new guest that had just entered the inn. He was about to ask Kautilya to take a seat before he could attend to him when he quickly realized *who* was standing in front of his desk. He was shocked to see Kautilya with untied forelock and crumpled clothes. Without asking Kautilya for any details, he knew exactly what had happened. His worst fears had come true. However, he was glad that Kautilya himself was physically unharmed. He excused himself from the other guest and came running to Kautilya, took his bags and apologized profusely.

---

19 Texts on political and military strategies.

"I am terribly sorry, Sir. I almost did not recognize you. I will take you to your room."

He led Kautilya to a temporary room, took the bags inside, and quickly closed the door.

"Sir, for your safety, I recommend that you disguise yourself as a monk or an ascetic. I will transfer you to the room that connects to the secret chamber after dinner. That will let us get together without anyone getting suspicious of your moves."

Kautilya agreed. He himself was thinking about a proper disguise.

"An ascetic is a proper disguise for me. I do not intend to shave my head even to be a monk in disguise. Moreover, I want the untied hair to remind me of my vow," replied Kautilya.

Gupta knew Kautilya was referring to a personal vow, and did not want to pry on that.

"I agree. Shaving the head is not proper for a Brahmin priest. Please rest in the room for the time being. I will bring your dinner. You can shift to the other room after dinner."

Kautilya nodded his head in agreement. He felt at home in Gupta's inn. It was almost like going back to a relative's house.

"I have thought a lot about how I can achieve my goal in the coming years. You are going to be an important part of my plan, Gupta. You will be rewarded for your good deeds," added Kautilya as Gupta was about to leave the room.

Although it was not clear to Gupta exactly what Kautilya meant by that statement, he was nevertheless ecstatic when he heard those words. In spite of the fact that Kautilya never spelled out what his plans were, he could still guess what they were. Even without Kautilya mentioning anything about what had happened in Pataliputra, he could picture in his mind how the meeting between Kautilya and the Nandas had unfolded. Such was the spiritual connection between Kautilya and Vishnu Gupta.

"I will be back shortly with your dinner. Please take some rest. You must be very tired. After all, you had a very long journey."

Gupta closed the door and went to the kitchen to instruct the cook to prepare a special meal for Kautilya.

Kautilya sat on the bed stretching his aching arms. He decided to relax by doing a long meditation. He sat in the lotus position on the floor and closed his eyes. He inhaled deeply through his nostrils, and as he exhaled through his mouth, he repeated the sacred mantra – *Om Namo Narayana* - the mantra that expressed one's desire to reach God's abode. As he meditated, he slowly lost touch of the conscious world, and he could feel himself lifting his spirit higher and higher. The rhythmic breathing relaxed his muscles and removed all the physical stress from his body. At the same time, his mind was going through a relaxation process as well. The sacred mantra helped him cleanse all unnecessary clutter that was clogging his thinking process, and he felt spiritually uplifted. This went on for a long time. Finally, with his mind and body completely relaxed, he slowly stopped his rhythmic breathing and chanting the mantra.

Very soon, he was back into the present and saw himself sitting in the room waiting for his dinner to arrive. Soon he heard the footsteps and saw the door open with Gupta bringing his evening meal, which he placed on a small low-table that was in the corner of the room. He then placed the table in front of Kautilya and waited for him to complete his dinner.

Kautilya closed his eyes, thanked God Almighty for everything good, and asked for His strength to achieve his goals. As he was a light eater, he was finished with his dinner in no time. He drank a large cup of water and closed his eyes contemplating his next move.

Meanwhile, Gupta stood in the room silently waiting for Kautilya to speak. Kautilya realized that he owed Gupta some information about what had happened in Pataliputra and gestured him to sit on the other side of the table. Kautilya remained quiet struggling to come up with the exact words while Gupta waited patiently to hear from the master. Finally, Kautilya began to narrate his experience.

"You were right, Gupta. The Nandas are as evil as one can imagine. My whole trip turned out to be a disaster."

"No need to get into the details, Sir. What is important is you are safe and alive," said Gupta in a sincere tone.

"Yes, no need to delve into the past. What I want to focus on is the future - what *we* can do."

Kautilya paused for a while. Gupta was extremely anxious to hear Kautilya's next words. He was hoping that it would be something about overthrowing the Nandas. Indeed, it was his lucky day. He heard exactly the same words he desperately wanted to hear. Kautilya continued in a matter of fact way, "I have been thinking about a plan to dethrone the Nandas."

Dethrone the Nandas - Gupta was elated to hear that. For that, he was more than willing to help Kautilya in any way he could.

"Just tell me what you need, Sir, and I will get that done for you. I know several wealthy merchants who will be more than happy to contribute to *our* goal."

Gupta's over-enthusiasm did not surprise Kautilya. He had surmised that something terrible had happened to Gupta, and the Nandas were the reason for that. He had already concluded that Gupta was working on some plan, however amateurish it was, and desperately needed help from someone like Kautilya himself. Kautilya was ready to do just that, and he wanted to know what sort of groundwork Gupta had laid so far. He could see that Gupta was tense and was hesitant to talk about himself. Kautilya wanted Gupta to feel more comfortable so that he could be honest with him.

"One more thing as you will be my *confidant,* Gupta. There is no need to be formal with me, and you can call me just Kautilya."

Hearing those words, Gupta got almost emotional. He felt honored and at the same time was immensely happy. At last, he had found a vital piece that was missing in his plans. That piece was going to be Kautilya. Kautilya continued, "I have been thinking about what to do next. We need to raise an army to overthrow the Nandas."

Hearing this, Gupta felt that he had to tell Kautilya about his plans. He wanted to elaborate on the reasons behind his hatred for the Nandas. However, he kept quiet thinking that it was not an appropriate time to talk about his past.

"Gupta, I will give you the outlines of my plan tomorrow. Right now, I need to do some more thinking. All I want you to do now is to take me to the room that connects to the secret chamber. Tomorrow, we will discuss more of our plans."

Gupta decided that it was an appropriate time to open up.

"Kautilya, I need to tell you something very personal. I need to tell you about what happened to my parents just a few months ago."

Kautilya did not want to stop Gupta this time. He wanted to know about Gupta's wounds. While Kautilya's wounds were to his honor and his ego, Gupta's wounds were right to his heart and his soul. He knew that Gupta's wounds were very deep, and they had left a deep scar in his soul. Kautilya could sense that just by looking into Gupta's eyes. They were already moist from the very thought of revisiting that terrible night. Gupta, trying to control his emotions, addressed Kautilya in a very soft voice, "Let me take your bag to the special room. I will tell you my story once we are there."

They both left the room and quietly started walking towards the new room. It was dinnertime and most of the guests were in the dining hall, and it was safe for Kautilya to move into the new room without drawing any special attention.

Chapter 5
Gupta's Tragedy

It was just another autumn day in Pataliputra. As it was getting cold and dark, Murali Gupta was getting ready to close his shop early. Murali was a small merchant in the jewelry trade. He did not expect many customers coming to his shop that day. It was a Tuesday, and no one made any new purchase on that day. They just came to browse through the jewelry and usually made the purchase either on Thursday or on Friday.

Autumn was a good season for his business. There was the festival of nine nights, or *Dussera*, during which families spent generously on all types of jewelry. During Dussera, people of Magadha celebrated each night with dancing and singing. There were special worship services to different deities on each night. People exchanged gifts and decorated their houses lavishly. The tradition was to set up an exhibition of dolls depicting daily lives in Magadha, and people took special care and interest to have the best exhibition in their block. Autumn was also the time when people prepared for the New Year. The New Year started with *Deepavali,* the festival of lights. Deepavali came just a few weeks after Dussera. It was customary during the festival season for men to buy jewelry as gifts to their daughters as they believed that daughters were Goddess Lakshmi's blessings. Many weddings happened during that month, and jewelry was an integral part of weddings.

This year, however, was different as there was a lot of uncertainty in Pataliputra. Only a few months ago, their beloved King Dharma Pal was no more, and the Nandas had overtaken the palace. No one was happy about that and felt helpless for not being able to do anything about that. They really did not know much about the Nandas. The Nandas had made just two or three public addresses, and people were not impressed with them. Even those who did not attend the addresses had a lowly impression of them, as what they had heard about them was not very comforting. Since the assassination of Dharma Pal happened just a few weeks before Dussera, there was a kingdom-wide mourning, and no one celebrated Dussera as a way of expressing the sorrow. The merchants showed their full support for this even though it meant the loss of a great deal of business. They were hoping that the festival of lights would bring extra business to make up for some of the losses.

Dharma Pal used to visit the main temple in the capital on the first day of autumn to kick off the preparations for the Dussera and Deepavali festivities. The main deity at the temple was Goddess Lakshmi, who is the bestower of wealth. This always gave a special impetus to the public to get excited about the festivities. Moreover, the king organized special arts and crafts events and awarded prizes to artists to encourage the public to buy their works of art. He also set up funds to help people who were in need of assistance so that everyone, rich or poor, could celebrate the festivities to their liking. During Dussera, the king organized cultural events every night. There were dance performances, concerts, folk dances, plays, and so on.

The Nandas, however, did not visit the main temple in the capital to greet the arrival of the fall season. Nor did they organize the arts festival or set up the charity fund to help the needy. They did not show any interest in art or music. They just did not care about the well-being of the citizens. Nor did they have any sense of duty to perform the dharmic acts expected from the royal family. They were extremely insecure, and all they cared about was their own longevity as rulers of Magadha. Their biggest concern was the possibility of an open revolt or a secret palace coup. They spent most of their time and energy purging any one deemed anti-Nanda or pro-Dharma Pal.

Just as Murali Gupta was contemplating on closing his shop, Kapila Gupta came to his shop. Kapila was a wealthier merchant who owned several garment shops in Pataliputra. Murali Gupta greeted him with a smile, and enquired how he was doing.

"I am alright Murali, but business has been very slow as you know."

"Yes, it is very frightening indeed. I wonder if it will ever pick up."

"I know how you feel, Murali. Let us hope things improve soon. By the way, how is your son Vishnu?"

Vishnu was Murali's only child, and his hope was one day he would take over the family jewelry business. To Murali's dismay, his son was not the least interested in running the family business. Instead, he was more interested in spiritual aspects of life and spent most of his time reading the scriptures. He enjoyed spending time among pious people and always wanted to live in the Holy City of Varanasi. Murali Gupta and his wife had tried in many ways to convince him to carry on the family trade. However, in the end, seeing that he was determined, they had accepted his plans and had bought him a modest inn in Varanasi.

"Vishnu is doing well. He has made Varanasi his base and is thoroughly enjoying his stay while caring for the guests at his inn. Incidentally, he is visiting us for the New Year."

"It is good to see him well settled and happy."

Kapila was happy for Vishnu. He then paused for a moment, moved closer to Murali, and addressed him in a low voice.

"I want to talk to you about something other than our business or families. Can we go inside where we have some privacy?"

Murali Gupta knew Kapila had something serious in his mind. He was usually an outspoken one and did not worry about any one hearing his opinions. However, this time he wanted to take enough precautions given the instability in Pataliputra.

"Let me put the closed sign in front of the store and let me close the front door. We can go to the back room and talk," replied Murali Gupta as he got up to close the front door.

Murali Gupta and Kapila Gupta went to the back room once Murali had secured the front door. They both sat down on a small sofa, and Murali waited anxiously for Kapila to speak. Kapila was in deep thought as he carefully weighed his words in his own head. Finally, Kapila spoke in a soft voice.

"You know, Murali, this has been the worst time of our lives. We have the wretched Nandas ruling Magadha, and the Land of Five Rivers to the west is under Yavana occupation. There never was a time when things were so bad for dharma."

51

"Anyone who is for dharma will agree with you, Kapila. I am afraid there is nothing we can do. We are all helpless."

"That is where you are wrong, Murali. We can do something about it," added Kapila.

"Like what? We are traders, and merchants, Kapila. We do not know anything about warfare or business of the state."

Kapila nodded his head partially agreeing with Murali.

"I agree that we do not know much about warfare or affairs of the state. However, we wield enormous financial power. Every monetary transaction in the kingdom involves someone from the Vyshya class. See, Murali, we may not be able to wage a war, but we can certainly finance one," replied Kapila.

Murali Gupta was getting uneasy now. As much as he hated the Nandas, he nevertheless did not want to be involved in any coup or revolt. All he wanted was peace and quiet to enjoy his life and the talk of financing a war made him extremely nervous. He was unable to hide his thoughts as his facial expressions gave away his anxiety. Seeing his disposition, Kapila decided not to divulge any more information to Murali.

"Do not worry about anything Murali. I do not want to drag you into something that makes you uncomfortable. Nor do I need any help from you right now. I may come to you in the future for help. For the time being, let us pretend that this conversation never happened."

Kapila Gupta then quietly left the store and disappeared into the evening fog. Soon after, Murali Gupta closed his store, secured the front door, and started walking towards his home that was only a couple of blocks from his store. As he briskly walked towards his house, he had an uneasy feeling that someone was shadowing him. He was a little frightened, was afraid to look back, increased his pace, and reached his house as fast as he could. Once he was inside the house, he locked the front door and went inside to greet his wife and son.

His wife, Radha, was busy inside getting the dinner ready. She was a soft-spoken woman who took extreme care and interest in taking care of Murali Gupta. She did not pay much attention to her family business and left her husband to handle all money matters. The fact that the business was slow that year did not bother her either. Her focus was her family's well-being. She was particularly happy at that moment as her son,

Vishnu, was visiting her for Deepavali. While she was busy preparing a delicious dinner for her family, Vishnu Gupta was busy studying ancient scriptures scribed on palm leaves. He sat inside a room at the back of the house doing his study.

Seeing her husband was back, Radha started getting the dining area ready for dinner. Right at that moment, she remembered a basket full of oranges and bananas in the pantry that would complement her cooking. She called out to her son asking him to bring them to the kitchen.

"I will bring them down right away, mother" shouted Vishnu back.

He then climbed a small ladder that took him to the storage attic that was at the back of the house. His mother had organized the attic with shelves that served as a pantry. He had a small oil lantern in his hand as the attic was above the back room and was always dark even in the mornings. There were many items on the attic floor - bags of rice, flour, and sugar. He kept looking for the basket that had oranges and bananas when he heard a loud banging on the front door. He immediately knew that something was terribly wrong. No one came around banging doors at that time of the day. He quickly turned off the lamp and turned towards the front door to see what was going on.

"Open the door, or we will break it," warned stern voices from outside.

It appeared that there were at least four men outside. Murali Gupta was terrified. Nevertheless, he slowly walked towards the door, and assured the strangers.

"I am coming to open the door. No need to get impatient."

As he opened the door, four big men burst into the house. They had thick mustaches with long hair and were armed with long swords. They looked like royal soldiers, obviously loyal to the Nandas.

"What were you and Kapila Gupta discussing?" demanded one of the soldiers.

Murali Gupta tried to control his anxiety. He wanted to assure the soldiers that he was just a plain old merchant and was not involved in anything other than running his business. Just then, Radha came out of the kitchen and joined her husband. She was terrified of the soldiers and started praying to Goddess Durga for her family's safety.

"You must be referring to the visit Kapila Gupta made just before I closed my store. That was just a social call. He was enquiring about my business and my family," replied Murali trying his best to be friendly towards the soldiers.

"You are a liar. If you do not tell the truth we are going to slash your wife's throat," warned one of the men as he grabbed Radha's arm.

Radha was extremely frightened and started to cry. Murali was now worried about his wife's safety.

"Really, there was nothing more to my meeting with Kapila. All he tried to do was get me involved in some sort of scheme. I refused to take part in his plans. Please let my wife free," pleaded Murali.

"So, you know something. What is it you were trying to hide?" demanded one of the soldiers, wielding his sword.

"I really do not know the details. My guess is he has some plans and is trying to recruit people to help him. Please believe me; I did not want to be part of any of his plans."

Murali Gupta was now terrified and was extremely worried about his safety. It was obvious from their interrogation technique that they would not stop at anything to get what they were after. The soldiers looked at him in disgust as if he was some sort of an animal.

"You are of no use to us. I guess we need to use our special tricks to make you squeal."

The leader of the group was sarcastic and did not hesitate to show his displeasure. He then looked at one of his companions and signaled him to do his part of the interrogation. The second soldier grabbed Radha by her arm and pointed his sword close to her throat. He then looked at Murali, gave a sadistic smile and without showing the slightest feeling, cut her throat. As the blood started gushing out of Radha's neck, both Radha and Murali let out a terrified scream and Murali rushed to hold his wife. This upset one of the soldiers and he tried to stop Murali by pointing his sword. In the rush to hold his wife, Murali tripped and fell on the sword that went through his body. The soldier dragged his sword out and in seconds, both Murali and his wife collapsed on a pool of blood. As they lay on the floor gasping their last breaths, the soldiers looked at each other wondering about their next move without showing the slightest remorse. They concurred that it was time for them to leave the house and walked out. They soon left the area mounted on their horses, and disappeared into the darkness.

Meanwhile, Vishnu Gupta, who was in the attic, felt restless not knowing what exactly was going on in the front room. He was tempted to come down and help his parents. At the same time, something told him to stay in the attic as it was not a good idea to reveal his presence. However, the moment he heard his mother's scream, he could not stay in the attic anymore. He heard the thud from his parents' bodies hitting the floor as they both collapsed on the floor. He slowly started coming down the ladder making sure that he made absolutely no sound. He then peeped into the front room and realized that his parents were dying. He felt sick all over and tried to control his grief as much as he could. Once he was sure that the intruders had left the house, he came rushing towards his parents and saw that his father was already dead. His mother had her eyes open as he lifted her and placed her head on his lap. She slowly lifted one of her hands and touched his face as if she was giving her last blessing to her son. Soon after, she collapsed and died.

Vishnu Gupta kept weeping for hours not knowing what to do next. A festive season, a season that was supposed to be a joyous occasion, had brought him limitless sorrow.

The next morning, some of his neighbors came to see Murali Gupta and were horrified to find what had happened the night before. They helped Vishnu Gupta to cope with his sorrow and arranged for the funerals. Vishnu Gupta as the only son had to perform the last rites during the funerals.

Later on, Vishnu Gupta began to find out bits and pieces of what had happened. He came to know from another merchant about the meeting between his father and Kapila. In fact, the very same night, Kapila Gupta was found dead as well.

Vishnu Gupta felt overwhelmed to cope with multitudes of feelings that haunted him over the next few weeks. He was, on one hand, taken by guilt for having not come down from the attic in time to save his parents. On the other hand, he began to argue that this would not have happened if he had taken over the family business. His father would have been home, and the ill-fated meeting between his father and Kapila would not have taken place. He kept telling himself that there is a divine plan behind all worldly events, and nothing would have altered that fateful night. Nevertheless, he was unable to sleep for several nights and had recurring nightmares about that tragic night.

Over the next few days, with the help of relatives and priests, he performed the last rites for his parents as he cremated their bodies. He placed their ashes in an urn for later immersion in the holy Ganges River. He sold his father's business along with all of the material possessions to a relative for a nominal price. He then moved back to Varanasi with the family collection of scriptures.

Chapter 6
The Partnership

When Kautilya heard Gupta's tragic story, he was deeply touched. He now clearly understood the reason behind that deep-seated hatred Gupta had exhibited towards the Nandas. Indeed, Kautilya concluded that the humiliation he had suffered at the hands of the Nandas was trivial compared to the loss suffered by Gupta. The damage was just to his ego. His bruised ego was sure to heal, and it was something he was sure to overcome. However, for Gupta there was no way he could recover from his loss.

Kautilya saw a budding partnership between himself and Gupta. He had already concluded that Gupta had a remarkable memory. It was obvious from the way Gupta had recalled minute details of his saddest day. In him, Kautilya saw a man who could run the future secret service.

"I am really sorry for what happened to your beloved parents. As followers of dharma, they are indeed in Heaven. In the end, that is what really matters, Moksha: the eternal happiness in God's abode."

Kautilya tried to console Gupta the best he could.

"You are right Kautilya. Revenge is not worthy of someone who is seeking enlightenment. Perhaps, I should forget about that fateful night and just go back to my religious interests," replied Gupta.

"I did not say that. Revenge is not our goal. Our goal is the reestablishment of dharma. That is the only goal that matters for any one who professes to follow true dharma. One of the reasons you are here is to do God's work. Theologians would argue that this is indeed the only reason we exist in this material world. So it is imperative that you and I become partners in carrying out God's work in this world."

"Can you be more explicit, Kautilya?" Gupta seemed a little puzzled.

"Surely, Gupta, you have thought about eliminating the Nandas a million times. Elimination of the Nandas is God's work for it is the fundamental requirement for the reestablishment of dharma. You have done some work in that area. Haven't you?"

Gupta indeed had done plenty of groundwork. He had methodically researched and selected the best and most trustworthy friends of Kapila. He had met with them often incognito. The meetings took place in remote places such as the woods, the caves, and the mountains. He had taken utmost care to see that the agents of the Nandas had no hint of his nascent plans. He had now ten trusted merchants who were committed to financing an army of up to a thousand soldiers for at least a year. If that army were to make progress in making any kind of dent on the Nanda defenses, they were willing to contribute more. They had also promised to recruit more wealthy merchants should he make progress in his plans. He had also met with many Kshatriyas who were willing to fight for dharma. Some of them had even served as officers in Dharma Pal's army.

However, there was one important piece missing. There was no military strategist to guide the army. Nor did he have a Brahmin to endorse their mission on the grounds of dharma. Without the blessings of a prominent Brahmin priest, the general population would not show any interest. Gupta saw that Kautilya could fill that gap. He had all the knowledge about military strategies, and he was famous for his prowess in Vedic theology.

"Yes, I have Kautilya. I have succeeded in enrolling many wealthy men who are willing to finance an army. I have also succeeded in recruiting many young Kshatriyas who are willing to fight for dharma. All that is missing is a leader who can guide us both spiritually and militarily. You can be our leader, Kautilya," replied Gupta.

Kautilya thought about it for a moment. Indeed, Gupta had a germ of a plan that with proper guidance and planning could be the beginning of a movement to overthrow the Nandas. Who knows, with the help of God Almighty, they could even be successful in driving the Yavanas from the Land of Five Rivers.

"You know, Gupta, your hard work will not be wasted. It will be an honor to lead this movement. Let us rest today and plan the details in the next few days," Kautilya replied, agreeing to Gupta's request.

The next morning Kautilya got up, did his morning routines, and remained in his room until Gupta brought his breakfast. He was beginning to crystallize his overall plan and was already thinking about the immediate moves. His first task was to meet the wealthy merchants to evaluate their commitment to the mission. He was also going to meet some of the Kshatriya men who had committed to the cause. He also thought about the need for a military leader. He wanted a young recruit who could be the next king. His vision called for an experienced general or a warrior leader who could train the young recruits, including the future king. While he was a military strategist, he was not a warrior himself and needed someone experienced in battles who could teach the recruits. He was confident that he could find one such willing warrior if he searched hard over the kingdom.

Another vital organization was essential for his plan to succeed; it was the secret service unit. Without such a unit, they would not be able to outmaneuver the Nanda forces. Based on his observations, he had concluded that Gupta would be the ideal man to run such an organization. Indeed, he was committed to the cause, was analytic, and had an enormous memory. Moreover, he had already demonstrated the basic skills in putting together a skeleton of a secret organization.

As he finished his breakfast, he looked at Gupta, and started giving him instructions.

"I am going to grow my hair long and will soon have a beard. I will look like a *Yogi* and that will be my disguise until the Nandas are overthrown."

Gupta nodded his head in agreement. In his judgment, it was wise for Kautilya to have a low profile for the next few months.

"There is one more important thing I need to discuss with you, Gupta. In any war, covert or overt, intelligence is the most important aspect before deciding to do anything. We need to build a powerful secret service unit to counter the Nanda apparatus," added Kautilya.

"I realize that Kautilya. However, can we do that? It needs more money, and even more importantly, people with impeccable loyalty to our cause," noted Gupta.

"We will start with a very small group, Gupta. What we are embarking on is for the sake of dharma. Surely, there are thousands more who are committed to that and are willing to work for the cause and not for money. We start with the most trustworthy people. We will look for people who have suffered the most under the Nanda tyranny and start building a small but efficient network of agents," answered Kautilya.

Gupta nodded in agreement. His mental calculations were already in progress assembling a list of such individuals. Kautilya continued spelling out more details.

"I want you to be the focal point of my intelligence-gathering network. You are going to build a network that has agents from all occupations. None of your agents except for a selected few should know who the final recipient of the intelligence will be."

"What type of agents shall I employ?"

Gupta was a little intimidated that Kautilya was making him the de facto intelligence chief. After all, he was not a trained spy. He had not even seen or known a secret agent although he was aware that there were many Nanda agents lurking around in Varanasi.

"Do not worry Gupta. You shall employ men and women from all occupations, people of all Varnas. I need you to employ priests, merchants, tribal leaders, teachers, and artisans. Ultimately, there shall be agents who are currently working for the Nandas, and agents who are Yavanas. We need to infiltrate the Nanda apparatus to understand their mode of operation. We will even have agents who will appear to be Nanda agents to outsiders. There are absolutely no limits when it comes to gathering intelligence."

"But, what should be the criterion for me to recruit these agents?"

"Certainly, there are a few sacred rules you need to follow when it comes to surveillance. Men and women you recruit should be intelligent and loyal, loyal to dharma. They must be people who can resist temptations thrown at them by the enemy. In our case, this may not be that difficult. Remember, everyone hates the Nandas. Think big but start with a small network. As long as you have a clear mind and put your impeccable memory to work, you will do just fine," assured Kautilya.

Kautilya's assurance relaxed Gupta. He was a secretive person by nature and had a natural flavor for collecting and storing information. Moreover, his memory was almost legendary. His childhood friends called him *Gajendra*, meaning king of elephants for his memory prowess. Kautilya would teach him more about building the secret intelligence network in the coming days and months, but for the time being, he had told Gupta all he wanted to tell him.

Next day, Gupta had one of his trusted assistants take care of the inn while he went into the city and visited a well-known school run by scholars from all across the land. An old scholar welcomed him and asked about the purpose of his visit.

"Come in my young friend; may I ask what brings you to our school? Have you come here seeking knowledge or are you looking for some advice?"

"Thank you very much, Sir. I am looking for books that will help me expand my trade with people from foreign lands. As you can tell, I am from the merchant class," replied Gupta with a big smile on his face.

"We have plenty of palm texts on finance and rules of accounting. We have palm recordings on customs of people from countries to the west. Those texts should help you," replied the old teacher.

"Is it something I can borrow?"

"By all means my friend; after all, our goal is to spread knowledge. We always keep the original texts and make copies for daily use."

"Thank you very much, Sir. I was also curious if you had texts on rules of diplomacy and military strategies," Gupta inserted his question almost casually.

Nevertheless, the teacher was surprised that a merchant was interested in this area. Seeing the puzzled look on his face, Gupta tried to give him an answer that would not get him overly suspicious. Who knows, he could be an agent of the Nandas as well.

"That is not for me, Sir. It is for a friend who is interested in that field," replied Gupta.

His answer seemed quite convincing to the teacher, and he gladly loaned him several palm leaf texts. Gupta gave him a silver coin and thanked him for his time.

"Thank you very much, Sir. The silver coin is my humble contribution to your school. I will return these texts in a few days."

The teacher, who was extremely pleased with his generous contribution, replied, "You can keep them. That is only a copy. We have the originals, and I will have the students make a few more copies."

It was late in the evening when Gupta came back to the inn. He relieved his assistant, closed the office door, and went into Kautilya's room through the secret passage. Kautilya was fasting that day, something he did once every two weeks. Gupta brought the books to Kautilya.

"Is there anything else you want me to bring to you, Kautilya?"

"This should be plenty for the time being, Gupta. You can get back to your business, and I will tell you tomorrow how to start getting organized."

Gupta went back to his office, and Kautilya started reading the texts that Gupta had just delivered. He knew that he would not find anything he did not know, but he just wanted to confirm that. Gupta left the room quietly; he did not want to disturb Kautilya's thought process.

The next day, when Gupta came to Kautilya's room through the secret passage, he observed that Kautilya was in high spirits. He asked Gupta to sit down and appeared to be eager to give him instructions. Looking at Kautilya's growing hair and beard, even Gupta could see the disguise taking shape. Indeed, he was now beginning to look like a Yogi.

"Gupta, tell me something. If I asked you to bring the two most loyal merchants to me, who would that be? I am talking about loyalty to dharma and our cause."

Gupta thought about that and had a hard time deciding who his top two loyal backers were.

"Think about those who were most loyal to Dharma Pal. Think about those who have lost a loved one or part of their wealth because of the Nandas," suggested Kautilya.

Gupta thought about each one of his top supporters and came up with two men he could absolutely trust.

"That would be Mahendra Gupta and Rama Gupta."

"How did you come up with that decision? Can you tell me more about these two men?" enquired Kautilya.

"Well, that was easy. Mahendra Gupta lost one of his sons to the Nandas, and one of the Nanda's men violated Rama Gupta's daughter. They would like to get the Nandas thrown out as much as you and I. Moreover, they are truly dedicated to dharma."

Kautilya seemed satisfied. He was one of those who believed in building ironclad plans, and no amount of precaution was enough from his perspective.

"That is good. I want to meet these two men personally. I want to establish this rule. Each one of us will link up with a maximum number of six people we can directly deal with. This will ensure that we have minimal risk of information leakage. Everyone should strictly adhere to this principle."

"So, Kautilya, who would be the six people you will be linked with?"

"Actually, I will have only five people. You and the two merchants will be my first three links. The fourth one will be a Kshatriya who will be an experienced warrior and train our recruits."

"Who will be your fifth link?"

"That will be the future emperor!"

Kautilya continued explaining his plans to Gupta who found the whole thing gripping and was in complete fascination with everything.

"I have not found my fourth and fifth links to complete my circle. That will be my primary tasks for the next two months. Before I do that, I want to meet the two trusted merchants Mahendra and Rama. Arrange for that in the next few days. I want the meeting to be in complete secrecy, and I want them to come to the inn incognito like traveling pilgrims or silk traders," instructed Kautilya.

Gupta was all excited and went back to his office to plan his next moves. He wanted to be certain that his planned meeting with the two merchants was in complete secrecy. He thought about his planned pilgrimage in remembrance of his parents who had left this world six months ago. The next day, he told his assistant about the pilgrimage to honor his parents and spent the next few days visiting holy places. He took small breaks in between to contact the two rich merchants. He told them about his plans and Kautilya's rule of keeping their contacts to less than or equal to six. Finally, he worked out the details on how they were going to come to his inn and meet Kautilya.

Gupta went back to his inn, and it was business as usual for the next few days. He had now increased his efforts to recruit more young men for the cause. He had also selected a group of young women and men who had become his first secret service agents. He had formalized his six links and had maintained utmost secrecy in all his transactions. His first intelligence gathering assignment was to get detailed information about the structure of the Nanda military. For this, he had his agents employ beautiful courtesans in Pataliputra to glean that information from soldiers who often indulged in a little bit of extra wine and were more than willing to talk.

Exactly a week later, two pilgrims entered Gupta's inn and rented a room from him. They checked in as pilgrims who were visiting Varanasi to cleanse their sins. Everyone knew that bathing in the holy Ganges River cleansed men and women of their sins. Of course, the visitors were indeed Mahendra and Rama who had come to Varanasi for their first meeting with Kautilya.

Some time during the night when everyone in the inn was sound asleep in their rooms, the two merchants went to Vishnu Gupta's office. Gupta, who was waiting for them, let them into his office and closed the door. They then slowly crawled into the tunnel that took them into the secret chamber. Gupta went first holding a light, while the other two followed them. Once they were in the secret chamber, Gupta went through the other tunnel and knocked on the door that connected to Kautilya's room. Kautilya entered the tunnel, and soon all the four of them were sitting in the secret chamber.

Gupta introduced Kautilya to Mahendra and Rama. Kautilya asked all of them to sit down and immediately started briefing his vision to them.

"You all know why we have gathered here. I do not have to elaborate on that. What I wanted to do today is to let you know what each of us needs to do over the next two months," Kautilya began to explain his plans.

"We all agree with you, Kautilya. We are eager to hear your plans. Please go ahead and tell us about what we need to do. We are ready to support you in any way we can," replied Mahendra.

"I am delighted by your commitment to dharma. However, what we need to realize is that we are fighting an enemy that is ruthless and very powerful. My estimate, based on what Vishnu Gupta has gathered from various sources, is that they have around eighty to one hundred and fifty thousand soldiers on pay."

Kautilya then paused for few minutes to get his thoughts organized.

"As you know, a soldier costs around one thousand *Panas*[20] a year. This means that the Nandas spend at least eighty to one hundred and fifty million Panas a year on salaries and benefits for their soldiers alone. That is quite a sum of money. We cannot match them in money. Instead, what we have going for us is the commitment to dharma from every single person who joins this movement. Vishnu Gupta, can you tell us how the Nandas are deploying their soldiers?" Kautilya prompted, and Vishnu Gupta gave more details on his findings. Vishnu Gupta, through his agents, had already collected quite a bit of information about the Nanda forces.

"Well, although they have a total of about two hundred thousand soldiers on their pay list, they only have a standing army of about one hundred and fifty thousand soldiers. The rest are really reserves who are called upon in case of a war." Gupta continued to explain how the Nandas had deployed the standing army.

"What is more interesting is that they have around sixty thousand soldiers committed to defending Pataliputra. The remaining ninety thousand soldiers are all over the kingdom in ten city-forts."

Vishnu Gupta was very meticulous with his assessment. He went on and recited the names of the ten forts and their locations. He also described the main routes to each one of those forts. Everything he was telling was stored in his memory and would stay there forever. This was just one illustration of his enormous memory power.

Kautilya started to tell the merchants of his assessment of the Nanda forces.

"I am confident that we can defeat the Nandas if we initially put together a force of just around twenty-five thousand soldiers. We will have to employ a hit and run strategy to destabilize their kingdom. We will expand our forces as we start accumulating victories."

---

20 Unit of currency in ancient India (silver coin).

"How much will that cost, I mean maintaining a force of twenty-five thousand soldiers?" asked Rama.

"Of course, it will cost some money; not a great deal though. We can have our soldiers work for a tenth of what the regular soldiers are paid. That will cost around two and a half million Panas. Of course, we need weapons, horses, and other materials. That could be another million Panas," replied Kautilya.

Kautilya then paused for a while, turned towards the two rich merchants, and looked straight into their eyes. He then raised the most important question of the night.

"So the critical question for the two of you is do we have the means to raise that amount of money?"

Rama had a twinkle in his eyes that showed his confidence in meeting the challenge.

"We know enough rich merchants to raise even ten million Panas. By what time do you need that money, Kautilya?" asked Rama as he smiled back.

Kautilya was pleased. Of course, he did not need that money right away. He thought about the management of such a large amount of money. His original intent was to manage the money himself. He realized that it was probably not a wise move since monetary responsibilities would consume a large amount of his time and energy. This, in turn, could interfere with his military and strategic work. He decided to make one of the two merchants as the treasurer.

"I do not need the money immediately. However, what I need is for someone to be my treasurer. Would one of you like to be that?"

"That is an excellent idea, Kautilya. My recommendation would be to make Rama as the treasurer," replied Mahendra.

Kautilya looked at Rama, who was in agreement with that recommendation. As they were coming to the end of their first meeting, Kautilya felt that he had met the first milestone in their long journey to the eventual dethroning of the Nandas.

"That settles it, then. Rama will be the treasurer, and you, Mahendra, will be the one who brings in the funds."

They all realized that it was time to go back to their rooms. After agreeing to get together in ten days, they all quietly went back, making sure not to attract anyone's attention.

The next few days, Kautilya ventured frequently out of his room. He had slowly grown a beard and now had long hair that flowed over his shoulders. He now looked like a true ascetic. He looked exactly like one of the hundreds of yogis that wandered in the streets of Varanasi, and people did not pay much attention to him. He had gotten even more slender since he ate less and did more yoga exercises. He walked for several miles every evening along the banks of the holy river. He was very much absorbed in his plans and was busy constructing innumerable scenarios for the next few months. He simulated various hypothetical situations where things could go wrong. In every one of them, he came up with ideas and schemes to minimize the potential pitfalls. His goal was, of course, to eliminate those pitfalls. He wanted an ironclad plan. Nothing else was acceptable to him.

He was confident that Mahendra and Rama were busy on the financial side and that Gupta was busy in expanding his spy network. Indeed, Gupta's network had infiltrated the palace itself. Gupta now had one of the cooks in the palace regularly sending information about happenings inside the palace. He had also recruited a beautiful courtesan who was more than willing to spy for Gupta. It seemed that the Nandas had killed her beloved fiancé, who had been a soldier in the Dharma Pal army; she was waiting for the day that she could avenge her loss.

Ten days had now passed since their last meeting, and the two merchants checked into the inn as traveling merchants this time. They were pretending to be merchants taking fine silk from the west to Pataliputra. As planned, the four of them convened in the secret chamber in the middle of the night.

"How are we doing with our intelligence network, Gupta? Do we know anything that will help us further?" asked Kautilya as he started the meeting.

Kautilya knew things were progressing well on the intelligence front, but wanted to get more details.

"We are progressing very well, Kautilya. We are now linked with key places in Pataliputra, including the palace temple," replied Gupta.

"That is good to know. How do you think the temple link is going to help us?" queried Kautilya.

"Apparently, the Nandas have taken an enormous interest in astrology. They consult the palace priest for any important decision they want to make. That could reveal many important decisions."

Kautilya thought about that for a minute. He was not convinced that the Nandas were sincere about their intention. Not that Kautilya relied on astrology for his decisions. Gupta, as though he was reading Kautilya's mind, continued, "Of course, that intelligence is suspect. We know the Nandas are not really keepers of any tradition. Nevertheless, we never know and that source could be useful at some point."

They all agreed with Gupta on that. Gupta wanted to update on the military recruits that were willing to sign up so far.

"As of yesterday, we had commitment from slightly more than two thousand young men to join our cause as fighters. These are all men who have had good training in military skills in their early ages. They are all waiting for orders from us to get organized."

Kautilya listened to Gupta carefully. He had been thinking a lot on exactly that topic.

"Yes, I agree that we need to start organizing the men. However, we need a leader, a teacher," interjected Kautilya.

"Have you found one, Kautilya?" Mahendra asked, anxious to hear the answer. His worst fear was that without a military leader, the recruits would lose interest or even worse, they would start talking.

"Yes, I have found one," Kautilya replied calmly. That was a big surprise to the remaining three in the room. Gupta was completely surprised since Kautilya had never mentioned anyone as a potential candidate for leading their forces. He prodded his mentor.

"Who is that person, Kautilya? We would like to know more about him."

"Well, you know that I walk several miles every evening along the banks of the holy river. Every day, at the same time, I see a group of Brahmins performing religious services for common people. I have come to the conclusion that one of those Brahmins is best for the job," elaborated Kautilya.

Gupta and the other two looked surprised, so much so that they did not try to hide their disbelief.

"You want to choose a Brahmin priest performing daily religious services as our military leader?" asked Rama.

Kautilya smiled and assured them, "No need to be concerned. I do not think that he is a Brahmin. I believe he is a warrior in disguise, and there is obviously a story behind this disguise. I will talk to him tomorrow, and I know that soon we will have our military instructor. The next time we meet, he will be with us."

Gupta and the other two relaxed hearing Kautilya's assertion. They knew that Kautilya was a keen observer and that his instincts could not be wrong. It was now Mahendra's turn to update on the financial progress.

"I have already collected one hundred thousand Panas and given them to Rama. So far, I also have commitments for one hundred thousand Panas a month once we start to assemble our forces."

"That is good, Mahendra," Kautilya said. "The commitment you have received only tells me that there is an overwhelming desire for a change. If all those commitments come through, money may never be the issue for our cause. Now, Rama, tell me about your plans."

"Well, I have thought a lot about a treasury for our purpose. I concluded that using only one location for the treasury is not a very good idea. Therefore, I have decided to keep three locations for use by the treasury. I have stored the money I received in a safe place in my house. I want to have two more places like that. I am thinking of this secret chamber and Mahendra's place as the other two places to store money. I have also prepared an accounting structure to track the flow of money," explained Rama.

Kautilya seemed happy with the progress. The next move was to recruit the warrior in disguise as his military teacher. He was ready to do just that the next day. They quietly adjourned the meeting and went back to their rooms.

The next evening, Kautilya took his long customary walk along the holy Ganges River. He came exactly to the same spot where the group of priests had gathered to perform a religious service. The priests sat around a ritual fire, and several families had gathered around them. He stopped at the same place, near the trunk of a large banyan tree that was not far from where the priests and guests had gathered. From that vantage point, he could see the whole ceremony and hear the mantras as well.

Kautilya had been doing this for the last seven days, and the priests had gotten used to his presence. They had concluded that he was just another wandering Yogi.

Soon, the fire was burning brightly, and the priests were chanting the mantras in full swing. Every day, Kautilya had watched them say the various Vedic mantras. He had noticed that the youngest priest had a very subtle metric variation in his rhythm when he chanted the mantras. The variation was so minute that no one without a scholarly knowledge of the metrics of the mantras would notice it. Naturally, Kautilya, being an accomplished priest and scholar, had noticed it the very first time he saw the young priest in action. He also noticed that the young priest, while he was quite fit, had well toned muscles in his arms and thighs. Kautilya had suspected from the first day that he was indeed a warrior in disguise. Over the next few days, he was convinced about that as he had studied his movements and gestures, the way he moved his hands and walked during the ceremonies.

This time, Kautilya decided to walk closer to the group of priests and joined the families that were surrounding the ritual fire. The reciting of the mantras in unison was at its peak, when by the spur of the moment, Kautilya himself joined the priests in recitation of the mantras. His voice was clear, pronunciations were impeccable, and the metrics were perfect. While this sudden chanting by a strange yogi stunned the priests, they nevertheless found the whole chanting to be of the highest priesthood and were quick to conclude that the wandering yogi was indeed a Vedic scholar in disguise. They gladly welcomed his participation in the ceremonies.

It was getting dark as the ceremonies were completed, and all the families left satisfied that the priests had indeed helped them reach the deities of their desires. It was Varuna for the rains for the farmers, and it was Agni for those who were seeking cures from ailments. Indeed, the families were so pleased that they offered the priests some extra gifts for their services and left the banks of the holy river. It was now Kautilya and the group of Brahmins all alone in the area as most of the visitors to the riverbank had gone back to their homes or inns. The Brahmins were very curious to find out Kautilya's origins. The wanted to know his family history, the place he came from, and why he was now a wandering yogi.

"Can you tell us where you are from?" enquired the oldest priest.

"My name is Kautilya. I am a Brahmin from the west. I am just here in Varanasi for a spiritual retreat," answered Kautilya.

"You seem to have a deep knowledge of the Vedas. Surely, you could be leading any of the well-known schools in Varanasi. What drove you to this avatar of yogi?" replied the old priest.

Kautilya smiled back and was surprised that the old man was so perceptive.

"Sometimes, you need to take a break from the daily routines. Sometimes one needs to look at the big picture and ponder about his role in this universe. Am I here to change things for the better or am I here to accept just about anything that comes my way? I am on this break searching for the answers," replied Kautilya.

The priests nodded their heads as if they followed what he was saying but did not bother to press him any more. Kautilya thought that it was the right time to address the Kshatriya in disguise. He looked at him and asked him a question that made him think.

"You seem to be the youngest priest here. Surely, you must have asked yourself similar questions?"

The young priest did not want to answer right away. He was indeed attracted to Kautilya's charisma, and he himself wanted to spend some time with him in private.

"You may be right. Perhaps, we can spend some time together to ponder the answer. Do you mind walking along the river with me for a mile or two, yogi?" replied the young priest.

He then looked at the other priests and asked for their permission to leave the place.

The two of them walked away from the group of Brahmins. As they walked along the riverbank, the reflection of the moon in the river made it look much bigger and closer. At the same time, the reflection of the moonlight made the river appear to be flowing at a faster rate. As they walked alongside one another, Kautilya pointed to the holy river and asked the young priest a question to quiz his knowledge of dharma.

"Tell me, do you know why the Ganges River is considered holy?"

The young priest was surprised that Kautilya would ask him such a basic question. Of course, everyone knew why the Ganges is holy.

"Of course I do. The Ganges is the river that came from Heaven to earth all because of King Bhagiratha's penance. He did that to wash the ashes of his ancestors so that they could attain Salvation. "

"That is true. Every one knows that. However, why does washing the ashes by the holy Ganges attain Salvation?"

The young priest had to hesitate this time. He really did not know the answer to that question.

"Of course not many know the answer to this question," Kautilya interjected. "The answer is that the holy Ganges contains the spiritual energy of the Lord, which glides you to Heaven. Perhaps, I will tell you that story some other day."

By that time, they came to a secluded area where they found a large rock that was beneath a tree. The moonlight was flooding the riverbank, and it was safe for them to stop there. They both sat on the rock, and the young priest was eager to find out the real reason behind this long walk. He had a strong suspicion that it had something to do with the Nandas. Kautilya looked around and made sure that there was no one nearby and addressed the young warrior.

"So tell me young man, why the disguise of a priest?"

The young priest was taken aback. "Is it that obvious? I thought I was doing a pretty good job of imitating a Brahmin."

"You were pretty good. No casual observer would have known that you are not a Brahmin. Now, tell me why you have assumed this disguise," asked Kautilya.

"Well, my name is Chitrasena. I was commanding a small force under King Dharma Pal. After his assassination, the Nandas were purging many of Dharma Pal's military commanders, and it was not safe for my family to stay in Pataliputra."

He then paused for a few seconds. He was a little concerned that Kautilya may disapprove his disguise. He very well knew that many orthodox Brahmins did not approve of crossing over Varna lines.

"I had studied all the Vedas and the mantras," Chitrasena continued. "It was just that I had never practiced them. My knowledge of the mantras has come in handy in my disguise as a Brahmin."

"Surely, you do not want to spend the rest of your life disguised as a Brahmin. Don't you want to go back to be a warrior again?" prodded Kautilya.

"Of course, I am itching to go back to be a warrior, Kautilya. I am praying that some day, some how, the evil Nandas will be eliminated and that dharma will be reestablished," replied Chitrasena.

Kautilya was pleased inside and was amazed that Chitrasena was following his script so closely. In Chitrasena, he saw a warrior leader dying for action.

"Praying is good, Chitrasena. However, praying alone is not going to get rid of the Nandas. People like you must do the work of the Lord. Otherwise, things will never change."

"What do you mean by that, Kautilya?"

"There are thousands of young recruits who are eager to fight for dharma. There are rich merchants who are willing to finance their activities. They, however, need a leader who can be their teacher, someone who can mold them to be real warriors. I think you can be that leader."

Chitrasena had heard rumblings about a merchant looking for recruits to assemble a rebel army. He had assumed that it was just one of those baseless rumors that people of Varanasi often started to keep themselves entertained and had not pursued it any further. If it was indeed true, it was like a dream come true for Chitrasena. He had continuously fantasized about leading an army to overthrow the Nandas. He felt honored.

"What do you want me to do, Kautilya? I will gladly join your cause and train and lead the young warriors. For dharma, I am willing to do anything," replied Chitrasena with a determined voice.

Kautilya, who was more than pleased to hear Chitrasena's commitment to dharma, spent the next hour or so telling Chitrasena about Gupta, Mahendra, and Rama. He gave him clear instructions about what his role was going to be. He was going to be the military leader. His role was going to be that of a general leading a rebel army and would continue to be that way even after the Nandas were overthrown; he was not going to be the future king. Kautilya knew that he was yet to meet the future king. He also knew that he would recognize the future king the moment he saw him.

Chitrasena had no problem with any of that. Moreover, he always wanted to be a warrior and was not the least bit interested in ruling an Empire. He believed that his destiny was that of a defender, a warrior-defender of dharma.

"Chitrasena, I will send an agent and arrange for you to come to the inn in the next few days. You will meet the other three, and the five of us will then plan our moves for the next two months," instructed Kautilya.

Chitrasena agreed, and they started retracing their path back to the city of Varanasi. Before they parted their own ways, Kautilya stopped and asked Chitrasena, "Your family – how many children do you have?"

"Oh, only one child, his name is Manu, and he is just ten years old."

"That is good. Some day I would like to meet your family."

Kautilya then took two gold coins from his garment and gave it to Chitrasena.

"This is my gift to your family. I know that they will have to make a considerable sacrifice over the next few months. You know there is a lot of hard work ahead of us."

Chitrasena thanked Kautilya for his generosity, and they both parted and went back to their respective residences. When Kautilya entered the inn, it was almost midnight and everyone in the inn was asleep, except for Gupta. Kautilya was still fully awake and was in a mood to chat with his confidant. He opened the main entrance to the door with his key given to him by Vishnu Gupta. As he went into the hallway, he could see that the door to Gupta's office was closed. However, there was a faint light seeping out from underneath the door. That told Kautilya that Gupta was still awake. He quietly entered the hallway and knocked on his office door, knowing that Gupta was probably busy organizing the intelligence his agents had brought him that day. Gupta knew right away that it was Kautilya from the knock and carefully opened the door and let him into his office, immediately closing the door behind him.

"I have some good news for you, Gupta," said Kautilya in a low voice.

Gupta could guess what that news was. He knew that for the past few days Kautilya was scouting the priest and inferred that he was about to divulge his findings about him.

"Am I right to guess that it is about the Brahmin you have been meaning to talk to for the past few days?"

"Well, it is him. However, as I suspected, he is not really a Brahmin. He is actually a Kshatriya in disguise. He has agreed to train our recruits and lead the troops. He wants to be part of the dharma forces."

Gupta felt relieved. He did not know exactly why, although deep inside, he felt that it was his rigid view of the Varnas. After all, it was only appropriate for a Kshatriya to lead the rebel army – it is in the Scriptures. At least, that was his interpretation. Kautilya, being extremely astute, sensed his thoughts. He was a little worried about Gupta's narrow interpretation of the Varnas. He could not help but enlighten Gupta on what Varnas are supposed to be.

"I know you have a very rigid understanding of the Varnas, Gupta. That interpretation is indeed counter to the spirit of the Vedas. Unfortunately, you are a victim of ignorant propaganda by the deluded clergy."

"What do you mean, Kautilya?" Gupta replied rather surprised. He did not expect Kautilya, a learned Brahmin, to question his interpretation of the Varna system. He was expecting Kautilya to endorse his interpretation.

"Gupta, it is true that the Varnas are ordained in the Vedas. Varnas are there as a way to divide our collective karma. However, there is nothing in the Vedas about the hereditary nature of the Varnas. All that the Lord says is that one should choose a Varna that suits one's own nature or God given gift. Thus, someone born a Brahmin can choose to be a Kshatriya and vice versa. Similarly, one born into a Vyshya family can become a Kshatriya, or a Shudra can be any of the other three. All that matters is that one should perform God's work in the material world the best way one can. Remember, Gupta, a man's greatness is defined by his deeds and not by his birth," elaborated Kautilya.

Kautilya, although perturbed by perpetual misinterpretation of the Vedas, was calm as he explained the true meaning of the Varnas to Gupta. Unfortunately, it was something many refused to accept. The generations of ignorance were too much to overcome. Indeed, even Gupta was having a hard time accepting it and quickly changed the subject.

"You are right, Kautilya. I will try to remember that in the future."

He then brought up a piece of intelligence that he had just received that evening.

"Kautilya, I have received some interesting news from the North. It seems that the ruler of the Himalayan foothills is extremely unhappy with the Nandas. Apparently, the Nandas have looted and tortured his people for no reason."

Kautilya thought about that for a minute. He smiled as he saw an opportunity to make use of that situation. He also knew that the people from the foothills were very good at domesticating and training elephants. Trained elephants could come in handy in any major military campaign.

"That is the best piece of intelligence we have received, Gupta. We need to go and meet their leader immediately. Let us go tomorrow. Get two horses ready by the early morning, and we will ride north to meet their leader."

Gupta nodded in agreement. He could sense from Kautilya's excitement that it was indeed a major opening in their military strategy.

"I will do just that, Kautilya. You are probably tired from a long day and should be going to your room for some sleep."

Kautilya was indeed getting tired. He went into his room through the secret tunnel, and was looking forward to meeting his potential ally.

Both Kautilya and Gupta were very light sleepers, and both were up much before the dawn, energized and ready to jump on to their next mission. Kautilya quickly completed his morning routines and was ready to ride into the Himalayan foothills. Gupta had brought some fruits with him for a light breakfast for both of them, and they quickly rode into the outskirts of the city long before the first rays of light appeared from the east. They rode for almost two hours without any stop until they reached a stream. It looked like an appropriate time and place to take a break.

They ate some fruits, rested for a few minutes, and were quickly on their journey northwards. They had at least three more hours of riding before they could reach the foothills.

Finally, they reached a village that belonged to the *Parvataka* tribes. The Parvataka tribes were a feared martial tribe well known for their skills in archery. They were also experts in capturing and training elephants for military purposes. Yet, the Nandas, who had a much larger army, often made incursions into their territory and tortured their men and women. It was one such day, and the village was just recovering from an attack from the previous night. As Kautilya and Gupta rode into the village, they could see half-burnt houses still giving out dark smoke. There were broken carts, slaughtered cattle, and pets. They could see corpses of young men executed by the Nanda forces. The entire village was like a ghost town, and the few people who wandered the streets had an eerie sense of despair. Kautilya and Gupta went near an old woman who was sitting beneath a tree and crying softly.

"Can you tell us what happened here, good woman?" asked Kautilya.

The woman kept sobbing and barely had any energy to speak. She looked at Kautilya as if asking for some water. Gupta ran to a nearby well, brought some water in a container, and poured it into her hands. She drank some of it and used the rest to wash her face. She finally had gathered enough strength to speak to Kautilya.

"Oh, Yogi, how can I explain? It was all over in a few hours. Hundreds of Nanda soldiers came in the middle of the night and mercilessly attacked and pillaged our houses for no reason. They were cowardly thieves, and we had no chance even to defend ourselves. They violated our young women and killed many of our young men. There was no reason whatsoever for this rampage. Yogi, can you do something to stop these attacks?"

The woman was desperate. She was looking for any help she could get. Kautilya tried to reassure her.

"Do not worry. We are going to make sure that this will stop. Can you tell me where I can meet your leader?"

The woman pointed towards the direction of a small road that went from the village to their leader's town. Gupta offered the fruits he had to the old woman, and tried his best to console her. After spending a few more minutes with the woman, Kautilya and Gupta got back on their horses and rode towards the road that took them to the leader of her tribe. When they finally reached the town, what they saw was a charming town with houses that were neither large nor luxurious; yet it was a community that was content and at peace with nature. It was a clean town with a picturesque view of the mountains in the background. As soon as they entered the town, Kautilya asked one of the townsmen to take them to their leader. The townsman did not suspect anything suspicious about Kautilya or Gupta. Everyone assumed that Kautilya was a real Sadhu or a yogi and paid their respects to him. He gladly took them to their leader, Shiva.

Shiva lived in a large mansion that was fit for such a leader. It was not a palace, but it was big enough to house several people. There were cooks, servants, guards, and even priests in that mansion. Shiva ran that mansion more as a community center and less as a private residence. That was his style of ruling his people. He was easily accessible to his people and cared a lot about their well-being. He was not a scholar or anything of that sort, but was wise enough to understand the real significance of dharma teachings and gladly adhered to them.

Seeing that there were visitors at his gates, Shiva came out of his house and welcomed Kautilya and Gupta.

"Welcome to our abode, Sadhu. May I ask you what brings you to our town?"

Kautilya and Gupta got down from their horses when a servant took their animals to feed and rest. Kautilya thanked Shiva for his welcome and spoke to him respectfully, "Oh, great leader of the Parvataka people, we have come here seeking your alliance. My partner and I would like to speak to you in private."

Shiva was not surprised. Many people from the plains came to Shiva seeking his alliance. His people were brave fighters, and everyone sought their help. However, Shiva and his people were fiercely independent and avoided committing to any alliance. Yet, this time around, he was intrigued that a tall Sadhu riding on a horse had come with such a proposal. After all, he was used to princes and generals coming to his compound seeking alliances.

Shiva took Kautilya and Gupta to a private room where another young man who looked very much like Shiva himself joined them.

"This is my son Kumara," Shiva said, introducing him to Kautilya and Gupta.

Kautilya was ready to discuss the important matter at hand. He introduced himself and Gupta.

"I am Kautilya from Taxila. This is Vishnu Gupta from Varanasi. As you know, the Nandas are hurting thousands of men and women every day. I do not want to be the bearer of bad news, Shiva, but, we just saw one of your villages being pillaged by the Nanda forces just last night."

The moment Shiva heard the terrible news he was visibly upset. His face turned red, and his pupils expanded. He closed his eyes for a moment as if to control his outburst.

"They have done it again. They have no sense of dharma. They do not even spare children and women. They are the cruelest rulers that have ever lived in Aryavarta."

Shiva got up and paced up and down trying to calm himself down. He did not want to look like a mad man out of control in front of the guests. He was angry and at the same time extremely sad for what had happened to his people. Kautilya continued with his message.

"I think it is time for the Nandas to go. We need to eliminate them. We are building an army of able soldiers who are committed to do just that. What we need from you is your help in the form of trained elephants and Mahuts[21] to steer them. We will need them in any major battle with the Nandas."

Shiva and his son Kumara listened to Kautilya intently. Many men had walked into Shiva's compound with similar offers. Every time, they had walked away without any commitments from Shiva. Somehow, Shiva felt different this time. Perhaps, it was Kautilya's power of persuasion, or perhaps it was his magnetic aura. Whatever it was, Shiva was convinced this time and looked at his son for his response. The young Kumara was extremely polite yet very astute. He wanted to know more details.

"May I ask you Sadhu for more details? Can you tell us what is in it for our people?"

---

21 A trainer and driver of an elephant.

"That is very appropriate to ask. What we will give in return is that you will have complete sovereignty over your lands under the new ruler of Magadha. The new ruler of Magadha will never trouble you. You will be free to practice your religion and customs. The new king will protect you from any potential enemy," replied Kautilya.

That seemed very agreeable to Shiva and Kumara. They were, however, curious about the new king. Who was he going to be, they wondered.

"Can you tell us who the new king will be?"

"Actually, I do not know who it is at this time. I am still looking for a man who would be an ideal king, a ruler who will adhere to dharma forever," replied Kautilya.

The very few minutes that they had spent with Kautilya convinced both Shiva and his son that indeed they should accept the offer. Vishnu Gupta was witnessing the power of Kautilya's persuasion first hand. It was with great fascination he watched the whole exchange. He was indeed convinced that it would not be too long before Kautilya found the future king.

"Kautilya will find the new king very soon. You will meet him in the next few weeks. I can assure you that," added Vishnu Gupta. Shiva and his son nodded their head in agreement and added with a smile,

"We will join your forces, Kautilya. Your cause is our cause from now on."

Kautilya was pleased so much that he took some gold coins from inside his garment and gave it to Shiva as a token of his appreciation. He then hugged Shiva as a way of sealing the agreement.

Kautilya and Gupta spent that evening in Shiva's mansion at his request while Shiva arranged for a lavish dinner to celebrate the new alliance. The next morning, they left Shiva's mansion with clear instructions about how Gupta's secret agents would work clsely with Shiva and his son.

Chapter 7
The Future Emperor

Gupta was now so busy running the secret service matters that he hardly had any time to manage the inn. He had left most of the day-to-day running of the inn to his trusted assistant. When people enquired about Gupta, his assistant often employed the pretext that Gupta was not feeling well and needed some rest. The trusted assistant was now part of the agency and performed many important functions such as carrying messages from one agent to another. While the assistant managed the inn, Gupta locked himself inside the secret chamber and was busy recruiting more soldiers or agents. As instructed by Kautilya, he had arranged for all four of Kautilya's confidants to meet in the inn that night. Late that evening, Chitrasena checked himself as a pilgrim, and they all waited to convene in the secret chamber late at night.

After introducing Chitrasena to the remaining three, Kautilya got straight into the business at hand. He wanted to know how the recruiting was progressing.

"How many men have you signed up so far, Gupta?"

"More than ten thousand have signed up, Kautilya."

Kautilya looked at Chitrasena, wanting him to get involved in the discussions.

"How do you want to move forward, Chitrasena?"

Chitrasena was listening to the discussions so far and was getting up to speed with the accomplishments. However, he wanted more details.

"Do we know what type of skills these recruits have? Do they have some earlier training or do these men who have signed up need basic training?"

"Well almost all of them have some basic training. Some of them are experienced warriors and have received intense training in warfare," replied Gupta.

"That is good; what about weapons? Have we made arrangements for them?"

"Yes, we have made arrangements for various types of weapons. We have signed up literally hundreds of craftsmen who are making all sorts of weapons as we speak, and most of them are doing it on a loan basis," replied Mahendra.

Chitrasena thought about the most efficient way to train the recruits. He needed secluded training grounds. He began talking about the arrangements for the training grounds.

"I would like to divide the recruits into four groups of twenty five hundred men. I would like to select secluded campgrounds where these men will receive training in groups of five hundred each. We also need to set up secret places where we can store the weapons."

"That is no problem, Chitrasena. We have already spotted locations deep inside the woods that are ideal for training grounds. We have also set up several underground storage locations for the weapons," replied Gupta.

Chitrasena was getting confident now. He wanted to discuss the type of training that was appropriate for the recruits. He wanted to optimize his training to match the attack plan that was being devised by Kautilya.

"Kautilya, what type of military strategy do you have in mind? I will tailor the training to your plans," added Chitrasena.

Kautilya was silent for a while. He had not decided on the exact strategy to be used. He was not convinced that they had gathered all the intelligence about the Nanda forces to focus on a strategy.

"Well, my current thinking is to use a hit and run method. We are not strong enough to engage the Nandas face-to-face. Therefore, we can rule out direct assault on their forces. I am thinking of archery and cavalry. Anyway, our first attack is going to be exploratory in nature. Our objective will be to attack a Nanda fort and see if we can capture it."

"Well, in that case, we will start with the training of archery on mounted horses. Of course, we will also do training on lancers and hand-to-hand fighting using swords," replied Chitrasena. He then looked at Mahendra for more answers.

"Have you made arrangements to get the horses, Mahendra?"

"Yes, I have contacted several Yavana traders, and we should be getting at least five thousand horses next week."

Kautilya was getting a little worried; the expenses were mounting, and he was worried about the flow of money. He looked at Rama for the answers.

"No need to worry, Kautilya. Even with all the expenses for horses and weapons counted, we have enough money to sustain a force of ten thousand men for a year. I have also made arrangements for food for the recruits and feed for the horses with villagers near the camps we have selected," replied Rama.

Kautilya was satisfied that they had done all the preparatory work, and it was now time for some intense training of the recruits. He gave the green signal to his men to start the training immediately.

"All right, Chitrasena. Let us start the training tomorrow in the secret campgrounds. Gupta, contact your recruits and gather them at the camps. I will visit the camps in the next two weeks to see the progress."

They bid good-bye to each other, quietly went back to their rooms, and prepared for their next tasks.

Over the next two weeks, Kautilya and his confidants were busy getting the recruits trained. Chitrasena had divided the recruits into four groups and had dispersed them into four separate camps. He would ask a hundred recruits at a time to come for training and would subject them to intense training and exercises. The village leaders nearby were paid handsomely by Rama for their allegiance and were promised more rewards once the Nandas were overthrown. After training each group, Chitrasena would rank the soldiers by their skills. He was so busy training the recruits that he hardly spent any time with his wife Savithri or with his son Manu. They did not complain, for they understood the importance of his work.

Gupta was busy collecting more and more intelligence about the Nanda defenses. He did not need any more new recruits, as there were enough agents for the work at hand. He had now collected information about each one of the forts; how many soldiers were guarding those forts, how many days of food supplies were inside the forts, what was their water source, and so on. Each piece of information was subject to intense analysis for validity. He had established a ranking system for the agents, and those who brought faulty information got less important tasks later.

Kautilya regularly visited the training camps to see the progress. At nights, he and Gupta were busy poring over the intelligence they had acquired. He would use that information to come up with potential military strategies. He was very close to choosing the right one and was getting anxious to start the campaign. However, he was a little bit frustrated that he had not found someone who was, in his mind, fit to be the future emperor.

The next morning, Kautilya decided to take a tour of the countryside. This was one of the periodic sojourns he made into the countryside to assess the general mood of the citizens of Magadha. He mounted on one of the best horses that Gupta had kept and rode to the countryside. He came to a small town that was one hundred miles to the north of Varanasi. He tied his horse in a remote area in the woods, and decided to walk into the town to investigate. As he came near the outskirts of the town, he saw that a group of young men had gathered near a large tree, and it appeared as if they were practicing a play. Kautilya, who enjoyed plays, decided to stop and watch the young men. He stood beneath another tree that was not too far off, and it was easy for him to witness the play and hear the dialogue from that vantage point.

One of the young men was sitting on a rock, and it appeared as if he were a king running his court. He had a crown made up of peacock feathers. He was tall and handsome and had a glow on his face fit for a crown prince. He had long flowing hair and a thin mustache that was not yet fully grown.

One of the young men came forward and bowed in front of the king.

"Your Majesty, we have a couple who have come here seeking your help and justice."

"You may bring them in. Let me enquire about their situation."

Two others, a young man with a young woman, entered the "court." As they bowed to the king, the king enquired about their plight.

"What seems to be the problem, my beloved couple?"

"Your Majesty, we are extremely honored that you are giving us this opportunity to describe our terrible plight. Just yesterday, some armed men entered our house and took away all our cows. Our lives are ruined and we have no source of income," lamented the couple.

The couple pretended to be sobbing. The king appeared to be very upset. He got up, withdrew his real sword, and made a thundering proclamation.

"This cannot go on in my kingdom. No one who disobeys the laws of dharma shall roam freely in my kingdom. I will have them captured and punished. By the description you give, they appear to be Nanda men. We shall destroy the evil Nandas!"

He then looked at the couple, and assured them, "Do not fear, my beloved couple. I shall grant you the herd of cows that you see outside of my palace as a gift. I want you to go home and live happily."

He pointed his sword towards a herd of cows that was grazing not too far from his "court." Obviously, the king was very generous to grant someone else's herd to the couple!

Kautilya found the whole play to be fascinating. In the young man who was acting as a king, he knew that he had found the future king of Magadha. He was so impressed with his display of a sense of dharma that he decided to walk to talk to him.

As he started approaching the group of young men, one of them stopped Kautilya.

"Stop there right now, Yogi. Do you have permission to see the king?"

Kautilya was amused by that; however, he decided to go along with the play.

"No, I do not have permission. Could you ask His Majesty if he would give an audience to me?"

The king, who could hear all that was going on, turned towards them, and asked the Yogi to come to his court.

"I always have time for holy men such as the good yogi in front of us."

Kautilya entered the "court," bowed to the king, and in a very humble way proceeded to speak.

"Your Majesty, I am here on a very important mission. However, I need to talk to you in private. I need you to come out of the court, and we can discuss this quietly."

The young man looked at the yogi, a little perplexed, as if to understand if it was part of the play. On the other hand, did the yogi have some real business in mind? As he stared into Kautilya's eyes, he realized that Kautilya was indeed very serious. The intensity in Kautilya's eyes convinced the young man that he was indeed talking to someone special. At any rate, he was curious to find out what Kautilya had in mind. He decided to stop the play. He turned towards his friends, and gave them an order to disperse.

"All right, my friends. Let us stop our play for the day. I need to spend some time with this esteemed yogi," he told his friends.

Kautilya and the young man started walking towards the woods. Kautilya saw that the young man was as tall as he was but much more muscular. He figured that he was seventeen or eighteen years of age.

"What is your name, young man? How old are you?" enquired Kautilya.

"I am Chandra Gupta. I am seventeen years old."

"Very well, I will tell you why I wanted to talk to you. I am Kautilya, and I am on a mission to overthrow the Nandas."

Chandra Gupta had a twinkle in his eyes that caught Kautilya's attention. That statement only confirmed his first impression that Kautilya was not an ordinary yogi.

Chandra Gupta was not convinced, however. Several thoughts swirled in his head. How could this yogi dethrone the mighty Nandas? Even Alexander the Great abandoned his march once he found out about the Nanda might. Does he have a secret plan? Perhaps, this is just a deluded yogi who goes around making outlandish statements.

"You can do that? I have heard that the Nandas have a mighty army."

"Chandra Gupta, yes we can do that. We are building a secret rebel army. I want you to be their leader. I want you to be the future king of Magadha. Not too far in the future, you shall be the emperor of the entire Aryavarta."

Chandra Gupta found the whole thing very flattering. Like most of the people of Magadha, he despised the Nandas and wanted them deposed. At the same time, he wanted to know why Kautilya wanted him to be the future king.

"What makes you think that I can be the future emperor?"

86

"I have this vision of an emperor who is brave, strong, and one who upholds dharma. When I saw the way you ran your court, I was convinced that you are that emperor. Also, by looking at your strong body, I can see that you are a trained warrior."

Indeed, Chandra Gupta was a trained warrior although he was yet to prove his prowess in a battlefield. He was extremely ambitious and had often traveled across the land to see how he could one day be a king. His dream was so close to what Kautilya envisioned that he felt as if he had spoken to Kautilya about his vision. After all, his vision since his childhood days was to be a ruler that disposed his duties according to the laws of dharma. Moreover, he was an extremely confident individual, and he had no doubt in his mind that he could be a powerful ruler who followed the laws of dharma. As Chandra Gupta was carefully evaluating everything he had heard so far, Kautilya looked at the "crown" that Chandra Gupta was wearing, and enquired about it.

"How did you get this crown of peacock feathers?"

"Oh, this is a crown my mother made from the feathers of a pet peacock she keeps. No particular reason behind this." He then removed his crown and gave it to Kautilya.

Kautilya examined the crown as he appreciated the delicate work. Suddenly there was a smile on his face. "This is very appropriate. We will name you Chandra Gupta *Maurya* when we coronate you as the king of Magadha. Your dynasty will be called Maurya (Peacock) dynasty."

"I like that very much," replied Chandra Gupta smiling back.

By that time, they had reached the tree to which Kautilya had tied his horse. Sometimes, generations of future events are shaped by a single cosmic event. Kautilya knew that his encounter with Chandra Gupta was one such event. He suddenly stopped and looked at Chandra Gupta as if he were already the anointed one. At the same time, Chandra Gupta looked at Kautilya as if he were his spiritual teacher, his mentor. Both could sense the instant bonding between themselves.

"We need to go and meet your parents. We need to get their permission for you to join the rebel forces," added Kautilya. He did not want to waste even a single day and wanted Chandra Gupta to lead the cause immediately.

"They are my adopted parents. My real parents died a long time ago," replied Chandra Gupta.

"Sorry to hear that about your biological parents. We still need to get the permission of your adopted parents."

Kautilya let Chandra Gupta steer the horse and let him mount the horse. He then hopped on the horse and sat behind him. Chandra Gupta was so excited that he made the horse run as fast as it could, and in a few minutes, they were in front of his house. As they got down, Kautilya noticed that it was a modest house with a small garden in the front. Chandra Gupta ran inside the house to give his mother the news.

As Kautilya entered the house, a middle-aged couple came along with Chandra Gupta to greet him. They showed sincere respect, bowed in front of Kautilya, and asked him to sit on a chair. Kautilya sat down and asked them to sit as well. The mother seemed to be very nervous and was almost tearful. Kautilya could immediately tell that Chandra Gupta was an adopted child as there was no resemblance between him and the couple.

"You are probably wondering why I am here. My name is Kautilya, and for the last several weeks I have been working with a few committed men to build an army to overthrow the Nandas," Kautilya began to address the parents.

The parents sat quietly and listened to Kautilya intently.

"You may wonder what this has to do with Chandra Gupta. I have observed your son today, and I am convinced that he is destined to be an emperor. I would like him to come with me and join the forces so that he could be the future emperor," explained Kautilya.

What Kautilya just said was both happy and sad at the same time to Chandra Gupta's parents. They were proud that Kautilya had shown such an instant confidence in their son. They were sad that their only child was going to walk away from them. The mother could hardly control her feelings, and she started sobbing quietly. The father tried to console her, and after a few moments, she gathered enough strength to address Kautilya.

"From the day I found him in our farm outside the town, I knew he was very special. As he grew up, I could see that he was a warrior from birth, and he was destined to be great some day. We were childless; he was like a gift from God. I always knew that he would leave the house some day. Still it breaks my heart to think about seeing him go."

She started sobbing again. Both Chandra Gupta and his father tried to console her this time.

"I know how you feel. However, think of this as your contribution to the Lord's work. We are on our way to overthrowing the Nandas and reestablishing dharma. Can you think of any better way to make your contribution?"

She understood the significance of what was at stake. Yet, it was very hard for her to reconcile her motherly instincts.

"Who would take care of us when we are old?" asked the father in a worried voice.

"Do not worry, father. Once Chandra Gupta is the king of Magadha, there will be absolutely nothing for you and your wife to worry. Meanwhile, for your sacrifice, I will give you these gold coins."

Kautilya took ten gold coins he had hidden in his clothes and offered them to Chandra Gupta's parents. Their faces brightened a little seeing the gold coins. That was a lot of money, and the parents were indeed pleased. Kautilya, however, knew that it was an unfair exchange.

"I know no amount of money can compensate for the loss of Chandra Gupta. However, this token money is a way of expressing my gratitude for your contribution," added Kautilya.

"Yogi, could you please bless us?" asked the parents and they bowed in front of Kautilya. It was customary for families to seek blessings of learned yogis. Kautilya placed his hand on their heads and uttered a verse from the Vedas.

"God will bless you and your family. In that end it is all because of Him," he assured the couple.

Chandra Gupta then hugged his parents and left the house along with Kautilya. As they jumped on the horse, Chandra Gupta looked back at Kautilya.

"Where are we going from here, Kautilya?"

"Let us ride to Varanasi. I want you to meet Vishnu Gupta and others."

Chandra Gupta's parents stood at the door until the horse disappeared into the horizon, leaving behind a long trail of dust. His mother, who kept sobbing, knew, however, it was his destiny to rule the entire subcontinent.

Chapter 8

Preparations and a Setback

It was late in the evening when Kautilya and Chandra Gupta reached Varanasi. It was already dark, and most of the citizens had withdrawn into their houses. The inn was quiet as most of the guests were in the dining hall while some were resting in their rooms. When Chandra Gupta and Kautilya entered the inn, Vishnu Gupta saw the young man who was accompanying Kautilya and knew right away why Kautilya had brought that young man. He could see from Chandra Gupta's imposing presence that he was indeed the future king. Gupta was impressed from what he saw in Chandra Gupta – an imposing young man who was brimming with confidence. In spite of his imposing presence, Gupta could see that Chandra Gupta radiated a sense of fairness or a sense of dharma. He could see immediately that he was indeed going to be a very just ruler.

As he entered the inn, Kautilya flashed the secret sign at Gupta and quickly walked towards his room along with Chandra Gupta. The signal meant that Kautilya wanted to see Gupta immediately in the secret chamber. Gupta quickly arranged for his assistant to take over the duties and quietly went into his office. From there he was in the secret chamber in no time.

By that time, Kautilya and Chandra Gupta were already in the chamber waiting for him to arrive.

"Gupta, this is Chandra Gupta, our future emperor," Kautilya introduced the young companion to Vishnu Gupta.

Vishnu Gupta looked at him and liked what he saw. In Chandra Gupta, he saw a brave young man who was full of confidence and ready to take on the whole world. He, however, felt a little awkward not knowing how to address him. Sensing his uneasiness, Kautilya made it clear that he was not yet the king, and until then, he was just one of them.

"You can call him Chandra Gupta until his coronation," Kautilya added. "Anyway, I wanted to meet with you to discuss the next level of activities. We need to have the other three brought here as soon as possible. I want to get a report from Chitrasena on the troops."

Kautilya was having a great deal of difficulty hiding his excitement. He had never felt this good since he had left Pataliputra in utter disgrace. He felt that his vision was finally crystallizing as he had filled all the key roles in his plan, and he was eager to start executing his strategy.

"I will make immediate arrangements for the other three to meet us. We can all get together as early as tomorrow evening," replied Gupta.

Kautilya nodded his head in agreement. He was now ready to get a report from Gupta on his secret service findings.

"Tell me Gupta, have your agents recently uncovered anything interesting about the Nandas that you want to report?"

"Well, I have gotten some reports that they are planning to fortify the palace by building a gigantic fort around the entire complex. Either they have gotten very insecure or their agents have started collecting information about us."

"Well, this could be bad for us. You do not know the exact reason that they are building this?"

"Unfortunately, we do not know the reason. The Nandas are very secretive, and they simply do not trust anyone."

"When do they start building the fort?" asked a perturbed Kautilya.

"In six months. They want to wait for the rainy season to be over. Their construction engineers have informed them that the project may run from six to eight months."

This new piece of intelligence was very important as it gave a sense of urgency to Kautilya's plans. He had at the most six months to dethrone the Nandas.

"We need to act swiftly. Let us discuss the plans tomorrow. Meanwhile, Chandra Gupta needs a good rest. Let him stay in my room. Bring some extra blankets for him. Also, bring him his dinner to the room," instructed Kautilya.

He then looked at Chandra Gupta and asked him if he had any questions. Of course, Chandra Gupta had hundreds of questions, but wanted to focus on one or two key ones at that time.

"How long before we make our first move, Kautilya?"

"Well, I would like to make a move within the next four to six weeks. We will assess the situation with the recruits when we meet Chitrasena tomorrow. Let us find out how ready they are to fight a real war."

"Have we thought about our attack plan? Should something go wrong, do we have a plan to overcome that?" asked Chandra Gupta.

Chandra Gupta was no ordinary warrior. In spite of modest means, his parents had made sure that he had received the best military education from a reputed Kshatriya teacher in their town. It was not just the ways of warfare; he had received his training in the strategies of warfare as well.

"I have not made my decision on the exact offensive strategy to be used. That is something we will decide tomorrow. I am inclined to start small as there are too many unknowns at this time," explained Kautilya. Chandra Gupta nodded his head in agreement.

"Yes that is true. We need to factor in everything from size of the enemy defenses to location of their fort. Do you think that we will have some intelligence on that tomorrow?" quizzed Chandra Gupta.

Just the small exchange that took place convinced both Kautilya and Vishnu Gupta that the young man they had anointed as the future king was indeed very intelligent and pragmatic. Despite his young age, he wanted to proceed carefully. This really impressed Kautilya, as he was averse to failures. At the same time, Chandra Gupta had an instant appreciation for what Kautilya and Vishnu Gupta had accomplished so far. At the end of the discussions, he was awestruck by Kautilya's ability to make deep analysis and take decisions instantly.

The next day, Kautilya decided to take Chandra Gupta to the camp where Chitrasena was training the soldiers while Gupta arranged for agents to contact and inform Rama and Mahendra about the evening meeting. Kautilya and Chandra Gupta rode on separate horses and quickly reached the camp before noon. Seeing Kautilya with a young companion, Chitrasena stopped what he was doing and instructed the soldiers to proceed with their exercises. He then quickly took his horse to the entrance to the camp and received Kautilya and Chandra Gupta. Kautilya took his horse closer and whispered into Chitrasena's ears to move into an area a little bit far from the recruits. They immediately rode together into an area that was not too far from the camp that gave them a little bit of privacy.

As the three of them settled beneath a tree, which was a few hundred yards from the soldiers, Kautilya introduced Chandra Gupta to Chitrasena.

"Chitrasena, this is Chandra Gupta, our future emperor. He is already well versed in all matters of warfare. However, I would like you to spend some time with him in private and teach him all things about martial skills that you know." He then turned to Chandra Gupta.

"Chandra Gupta, this is Chitrasena, who will be your general after your coronation. Until we dethrone the Nandas, each of you will lead a rebel army unit. Our strategy will consist of luring the enemy into an open area by an army led by one of you, and encircling them with the second army led by the other." Kautilya then looked at Chitrasena and asked him how the training was going.

"Do you think that our soldiers are ready for a real war?"

"They are not one hundred percent ready right now. They still need two more weeks of training," replied Chitrasena.

Kautilya then wanted Chandra Gupta to meet the men. He wanted him to speak to the soldiers directly. Kautilya wanted Chandra Gupta to let them know that he was indeed the anointed crown. It was his turn to lead the warriors in the war against evil forces.

"Chandra Gupta, let us go and meet our warriors. I want you to talk to them as their future king."

Chandra Gupta was indeed anxious to meet his men. He wanted to let them know his way of doing things. He wanted to get to know them. After all, they were going to be warriors of dharma fighting against evil forces side by side. The three of them quickly turned and rode into the camp. As they entered the camp, Kautilya made this announcement to the troops.

"Men, I have an important announcement to make. I want all of you to meet Chandra Gupta, our future emperor."

The men got very excited hearing that. They all were aware that Kautilya was looking for one who could be their future king. They also knew that Kautilya was the mastermind behind all the grand plans. They had so much respect for his decisions that they immediately accepted Chandra Gupta as their future king. The imposing stature of Chandra Gupta helped his cause as well. They all shouted in unison.

"Chandra Gupta our future king! Long live our king!"

Chandra Gupta was somewhat moved by their cheerful welcome. He spoke to them as their leader and as one among them.

"Men, we all know that we live in a troubled period for the land of dharma. We all know that the Lord first revealed the rules of dharma to the people of Aryavarta so that we can spread dharma in all directions – north, south, east, and west. Instead, what we have is dharma rotting from within – right in Pataliputra. We also have dharma under siege from the Yavanas to our west. Things may look gloomy. However, believe me soldiers; we can do more than sit in despair. We can overthrow the Nandas. We will drive the Yavanas out of the land of dharma. With our lives committed to dharma, we can achieve anything. We will win. With the training of Chitrasena and with the genius of Kautilya we shall rule this land from sea to sea and from the tip of the subcontinent to the towering Himalayas. I want you to be committed to dharma forever. With the true blessings of the Lord, dharma will be with us forever!"

That was a thunderous call for action from Chandra Gupta. The soldiers were so excited from Chandra Gupta's oratory that they continued to praise him for a long time. Kautilya liked the way Chandra Gupta motivated the recruits on an optimistic tone woven around the laws of dharma. It only reinforced the belief in Kautilya that he had indeed anointed the right one. Kautilya, who himself was a man of few words, liked the fact that Chandra Gupta did not stray from the key message and touched on the critical points in a poetic way.

It was time for Kautilya to inform the soldiers of his next moves. He wanted to make sure that the soldiers were primed for the first battle. After all, it was not too far from that day. It was now Kautilya's turn to get the soldiers motivated.

"Men, we now have all the pieces of the puzzle in place. All that is left is the final preparations. We will be back here within the next few weeks ready to start our campaign. I want you all to be ready for that glorious day."

Kautilya was crisp and to the point. He then instructed Chitrasena to meet him at the inn that night, and both he and Chandra Gupta quickly left the camp and rode off into Varanasi.

Late that evening all of Kautilya's cabinet convened in the secret chamber. There was Chandra Gupta himself sitting on the right side of Kautilya, and Gupta, the man who carried the entire secret service information inside his head, was on his left side. The two rich merchants, Rama and Mahendra, along with Chitrasena, the general for the rebel army, were sitting in the front. It would be Kautilya's cabinet until the coronation of Chandra Gupta. Once that happened, it would be Chandra Gupta's cabinet.

The topics for that night were obvious. It was all about the military strategy. It was time to make a critical assessment of the training of the young recruits. It was also the time to assess the logistics for the maiden military campaign. Finally, it was time to determine the exact strategy for the military campaign, including the fallback strategy should the campaign go bad.

Kautilya looked anxious as he repeatedly ran his right hand over his long beard. As he stroked his beard, he had an ever so slight smile on his face. He thought that it was ironic that many considered it unbecoming for someone with Brahmin upbringing to be sporting long hair and a beard. However, for Kautilya, such norms did not matter at this time. Moreover, right now he was not a practicing Brahmin. He was indeed a defacto Kshatriya as he had spent the last several weeks planning his military strategy. Furthermore, he was not one of those orthodox clergymen who wanted to keep the Varna lines rigid and adhere to the definition of Varna based on ancestry. For them, one could be a Brahmin only if his father was a Brahmin. Kautilya, however, took a more enlightened attitude towards Varnas. His opinion was that one could change from one Varna to another based on one's personal situation as in the case of Chitrasena, or based on one's own intellectual desires as in the case of Kautilya himself.

"I want to begin this meeting by clearly defining what we need to accomplish by the time we leave this chamber," he began, setting the ground rules. "I want to assess the time line for starting our first campaign. I want this to be based on both internal preparedness and the latest intelligence we have about the Nandas."

Kautilya then looked at Chitrasena and prompted him to talk about the recruits.

"I have been training this group of men for almost four weeks now," Chitrasena began, giving his view of the situation. "We have around ten thousand recruits, but in my opinion only around two thousand are ready to take part in any campaign right now. However, if we wait for another two weeks, we should have at least five thousand brave men who can be part of our campaign."

"All right, that sounds good. Anyway, we are not going to start our campaign tomorrow. We can target our campaign to start two weeks from today. That should give us at least five thousand men," agreed Kautilya.

At this point, Chandra Gupta wanted to speak. He did not want to use all the five thousand men in the first campaign. The group of men had never been together as a fighting unit, and until the group got familiar with warfare, anything could go wrong. Chandra Gupta explained his reservations about that.

"I want us to come up with a plan that would involve far less than five thousand men. We do not want to risk our best troops in the first campaign."

Kautilya had no issue with that as he was thinking along the same lines and nodded his head. It was time to discuss the logistics. Of course, there was the all-important question of horses. The rebels had a few hundred horses, but for a major campaign, they needed a lot more. Kautilya looked at Rama and asked him about the situation with procuring horses.

"I have assurances that up to three thousand horses will be delivered this week, and another three thousand horses will be delivered next week. Our agents are purchasing them at various locations, some as far as Bactria. They will be coming in different routes so that no one gets suspicious."

Finally, Kautilya felt good about the accomplishments so far. It was time to discuss the details of the campaign itself. "I want to address the actual campaign itself. Of the ten forts controlled by the Nandas, I have selected the fort at Narayanpuri as our target. This fort is right on the trade route from Bactria to Pataliputra. It is only one hundred miles east of Varanasi."

"What do we know about this fort? How many soldiers are defending that fort?" asked Chandra Gupta.

"Good question. Vishnu Gupta can give us the details," replied Kautilya.

"My agents tell me that there are only two thousand soldiers protecting that fort. That seems odd, given that it is the first fort anyone invading Magadha would see. I would have expected a much bigger force defending Narayanpuri."

"Well, there is a reason for that," Chitrasena, who was familiar with the Magadha defense scheme, began to give his perspective.

"They use that more like a sophisticated observation post. The moment someone attacks that fort, intelligence agents will gather as much information about the enemy. They will then leave the fort through secret passages and go to Pataliputra to bring more reinforcements that are powerful and well equipped."

"So it is really a trap for anyone who is planning an invasion," concluded Chandra Gupta. He then looked at Kautilya wondering why he had chosen that fort. Seeing the puzzled look, Kautilya explained his reasoning.

"Let me explain why I have chosen this particular fort. First, we are not planning to occupy that fort. Our campaign is really an expedition to study the Nanda defense schemes. What we want to do is attack a vital fort on the trade route and cause extensive damage to it. This will cause a psychological blow to the enemy defenses. Moreover, this will make them commit more of their resources to Narayanpuri in the future. This makes it easy for us to capture the forts that are at the Northern edges of the kingdom."

Chandra Gupta and others began to appreciate the logic behind the selection.

"Can you give us some more details?" added Chandra Gupta.

"Well, the idea is to use a strategy similar to the one the enemy employs. We will first send a small force of around eight hundred soldiers. This would make them think that ours is a meager sized rebel army that they can handle by themselves. The fort leader may not even send for any reinforcement. Our aim is to draw them to the open. For that, we will use elephants and archers." Kautilya then continued with his logic.

"Once we succeed in drawing them outside the fort, we will trap them with a second force of about sixteen hundred soldiers."

Everyone liked the strategy. However, there was no mention of elephants until now. As if Kautilya read their minds, he began to explain, "We will use a small group of trained elephants to ram the fort gate. This will scare them and draw them to a hand-to-hand fight outside the fort."

"But, Kautilya, we have no elephants," explained Chitrasena.

"Yes, that is true Chitrasena. However, we can always get help from someone else who has the elephants."

Kautilya then turned to Vishnu Gupta.

"This may be the right time to bring our new friend, Vishnu Gupta."

The others were puzzled not knowing what was going on as Vishnu Gupta left the chamber. As they waited patiently, Vishnu Gupta reappeared, this time with a young man at his side. From the physical features, it was obvious that the young man was from the Himalayan foothills.

"This is Kumara. He is the eldest son of Shiva, the ruler of the foothills," Vishnu Gupta explained.

Kautilya instructed Kumara to join the meeting and introduced the remaining four to him. The young man was very polite and respectful in his demeanor, and he waited for permission to speak.

"Kumara, can you tell your future king Chandra Gupta, what your father has offered to bring back dharma to this land?" Kautilya encouraged the young man to speak.

"Well, my father has been very upset with the new rulers of Magadha. They make periodic attacks on our people and cause untold harm to our villages. Their soldiers are ruthless and have no shame. Rape and pillage seem to be their favorite sports. When Kautilya and Vishnu Gupta approached my father for an alliance, he was glad to agree. We will contribute a herd of five hundred trained elephants along with Mahuts to take part in the military campaign."

Everyone was pleased to hear Shiva's offer. After all, elephants were an important part of any military campaign. They were vital for carrying heavy weapons, for making the frontal attack on forts, and especially for breaking the fort's gates.

"What does your father want in return?" asked Chandra Gupta.

"Not much, Your Highness. All he wants is peaceful coexistence. He wants respect for our way of life. In return, he pledges whatever help you may need in the future."

It was a very agreeable request as far as Chandra Gupta was concerned. He looked at others for their opinion. Everyone nodded their heads in agreement and looked at Kautilya for his views.

"When a province or a nation allies with us, we will guarantee that their way of life is not disturbed. Indeed, even when we take over a nation, we will not disturb the local culture and religion. That will be the true sign of dharma – this will be a fundamental tenet under Chandra Gupta's rule," declared Kautilya. Kautilya was now speaking for Chandra Gupta more as his chief counselor.

The final plans were drawn. Kautilya and Chitrasena made a list of eight hundred soldiers under Chandra Gupta's leadership as well as the list of twelve hundred soldiers under Chitrasena. The frontal attack was going to be by a senior Mahut from Shiva's tribe leading a herd of ten elephants. The elephants were to attack the fort gate. Chandra Gupta was to follow the group next. It was Kautilya's expectation that the fort leader would come out to fight Chandra Gupta's small force rather than risking the elephants breaking the fort gate. At that point, Chitrasena was to come in to surround the forces. Chitrasena was to hide in the woods not far from the fort with some of his men watching the battle from tall trees. Kautilya himself was to be with Chitrasena if any late changes in the plan were necessary.

There was one last item to consider. They needed medical supplies and a doctor to treat the wounded, especially the leaders. Vishnu Gupta offered to take care of that.

"I have an agent who is a good doctor. He will join us with the second group and can treat the wounded," assured Vishnu Gupta.

"I want you to check his background thoroughly. He is one of the few who will know the attack plan," replied Kautilya.

In the next two weeks, everything went according to the plan. The horses had arrived, and Chitrasena and Chandra Gupta had separated the best two thousand men for intense training and planning. All rebel soldiers were now well equipped with the weapons that had been delivered by the agents just a few days ago. The excess weapons were stored in secure places. Vishnu Gupta had selected a doctor who appeared to have a clean background. Kautilya himself had made several trips to the training grounds and supervised the preparedness of the troops. Kautilya and Chandra Gupta had delivered several speeches to encourage the troops and constantly reminded them about their duty towards dharma. The troops were ready for action so much so that they were extremely anxious to get the orders from Kautilya.

Finally, the planned day arrived. As planned, they all got up very early in the morning several hours before dawn. The fort was around two hours from the camp. The two groups, the group of elephants, and the group led by Chandra Gupta, left first. The group led by Chitrasena, who were not too far behind, followed them. Kautilya, Vishnu Gupta, the doctor, several cooks, and food supplies followed Chitrasena's group.

Chandra Gupta's group along with the elephants was a few miles from the fort when he asked his men to stop. They were still inside the woods, and it was not easy for anyone to spot them.

"Let us wait here and make sure that Chitrasena and Kautilya join us," ordered Chandra Gupta.

He then selected ten predetermined soldiers and assigned them their next task.

"I want eight of you to climb the tall trees and scout the fort surroundings."

He then looked at the other two. "The two of you go towards the back of the fort. Climb two tall trees and report immediately if you see anything suspicious."

The soldiers dispersed quickly and positioned themselves in strategically placed trees. Within a few minutes Chitrasena, Kautilya and others joined them.

Kautilya rode towards Chandra Gupta and the Mahut leader and gave them the instructions.

"The elephants shall attack the gate at full speed. Chandra Gupta, you follow them with a distance of about two thousand feet. I expect them to come out of the fort seeing that yours is a small force. If anything goes wrong, I will hoist the red flag which will be a signal for you to withdraw."

"Do not worry, Kautilya. Nothing will go wrong," assured Chandra Gupta.

However, Kautilya's approach to warfare was to be ready for the worst. Anything can go wrong and will go wrong. They had to be prepared for setbacks; otherwise, they were bound to be sorry later.

The Mahuts ordered the elephants to charge. All ten elephants started romping towards the fort. The Mahuts, with the small tool poked behind the ears of the elephants to get them excited, sped towards the fort gate. The elephants were charging so fast that they built a wall of dust behind them so tall that Chandra Gupta and his men had to slow down a little to avoid the dust getting into their eyes.

It was barely dawn now, and it was difficult for anyone to see beyond a few feet. However, the guards who were on the watchtowers of the fort could see the group of elephants charging toward the gate. They were charging so fast that it almost scared them.

"Here they come. I think they are Chandra Gupta and Kautilya's men," observed one of the guards calmly. It was as if they were anticipating the attack.

"What do we do now?" asked the guard turning towards their leader, who had just joined them.

"You stay here. I will go down and instruct the soldiers to open the gate. After all, we have to go along with their anticipated plan. We will have our soldiers face them in the open," explained the leader with a smile on his face. He then signaled his men to open the gate and charge into the open space in front of the fort.

"Open the gate and charge outside. Do not attack the rebels. Just take your positions and wait for me to give the orders," he shouted towards his men.

The charging Mahuts could see that the fort doors were slowly opening. They remembered the instruction to stop charging and steer the elephants towards the sides as soon as the doors opened. Promptly they brought the elephants to a stop with great difficulty, and then they split into two groups and they steered them towards the sides.

Chandra Gupta and his men now had a direct view of the fort. They saw the doors opening and a large group of soldiers pouring out of the fort on their horses. Chandra Gupta ordered his men to take their positions. He noticed that the enemy force was slightly more than his was. He was, however, not too concerned about it as he knew that there were additional men on his side who were soon to join him along with Chitrasena.

Chandra Gupta slowly formed a "V" formation with his soldiers staggered in front of him on both sides. When the enemy attacked, they planned to split into two parallel units with Chitrasena and his men joining them at the center. This would virtually encircle the enemy, and if all went as planned, the defeat of the enemy forces and the capture of the fort was not too far behind.

The scouts, who were watching all this from the trees, got down and informed Chitrasena that it was time for him to proceed. Chitrasena gave the orders to his men, and they charged towards the battlefield and joined Chandra Gupta and his men. A fierce battle followed. It now appeared that Chandra Gupta and Chitrasena had overwhelmed the enemy numerically and were winning.

The battle had proceeded for about five minutes when one of the soldiers who was stationed behind the fort came galloping towards Kautilya as fast as he could. He was so excited he could hardly breathe. He stopped right in front of Kautilya, gathered his breath, and exclaimed,

"We are going to be surrounded. A large Nanda force is coming towards the battlefield from behind. What do we do now?" He looked extremely worried and was sweating profusely.

"How big do you think the force is?"

"I do not know, Kautilya. Maybe five or six thousand men; it is hard to say. I do not think we have enough men to fight them."

Kautilya had to think fast. He knew they had been betrayed. Somehow, the Nandas were aware of their plans. How did that happen? However, that was not his immediate problem. He had to do something to save his men, especially the lives of Chandra Gupta and Chitrasena. He decided to retreat. He asked his men to hoist the red flag from the trees. He also asked the men who were with him to play the instruments to signal the withdrawal. He immediately sent a few more men towards the battlefield to announce the withdrawal. The men galloped and shouted at the troops.

"WITHDRAW! We are going to be surrounded soon," they kept shouting in their loudest voices. Now, all of Kautilya's soldiers started shouting, "Withdraw! Withdraw!"

Chitrasena and Chandra Gupta looked back and saw the hoisted red flags. They knew it was a signal that there was imminent danger, and it was time to withdraw from the battlefield. They did not know the exact problem, but were sure that Kautilya had made the right decision. They immediately turned back and started galloping away from the fort. However, the enemy started chasing them, and many of their men were either slain or wounded. The Nanda forces surrounded the elephants and the Mahuts. Chandra Gupta knew that they had lost the elephants. Fortunately, Kumara, Shiva's son, who was riding one of the elephants, had realized this and had jumped from the elephant onto one of the horses. Kumara and his soldier companion rode the horse as fast as they could and joined Chandra Gupta.

When Chitrasena, Kumara, Chandra Gupta, and his men joined Kautilya, he ordered them to disperse into the woods in different directions.

"Let us go in eight directions. We will soon convene in a safe place."

They were soon dispersing into the woods, making it difficult for the pursuing enemy to home in on any one group. Moreover, the Nanda forces were elated that they had driven away Chandra Gupta and his men. They were too excited that they had captured the elephants and did not bother pursuing the rebel forces.

Chapter 9
Kautilya's Triumph

Kautilya, Chandra Gupta, Chitrasena, and their men had fled from the fort of Narayanpuri as fast as they could. They dispersed in all directions into the woods to avoid the Nanda soldiers who were in hot pursuit. However, the Nanda soldiers were not really committed to catching the rebel soldiers and soon gave up on their pursuit. Some of the rebel soldiers were hurt in the battle and became prisoners of the Nandas. Kautilya knew very well that those captured soldiers were going to be subject to intense torture and the Nandas would soon find out all the details - about their training grounds, their allies, and so on. There had to be a new plan, new training grounds, and a new strategy. It was definitely not a good idea to go back to any of the previous secret spots.

Even in those chaotic conditions, Kautilya and Vishnu Gupta had stayed together. Two other young soldiers had stayed with Kautilya to ensure that no one harmed him. Even after they had avoided the enemy soldiers, the four of them kept moving north just to make sure that they were safely outside the territory controlled by the Nandas. They finally reached an area that had many trees with a small stream near by. They decided to stop there for some rest.

Kautilya looked to his young companions and gave them an urgent assignment.

"Go back to the training grounds and make sure that no one gathers there from now on. Tell the soldiers that we will contact them as soon as we have decided on the new secret place to train."

The soldiers wasted no time and galloped in the direction of their hidden training area.

Meanwhile, Vishnu Gupta felt utterly embarrassed. He knew as well as Kautilya that someone had tipped the Nandas about the planned attack. He felt that he had failed his first major test. Kautilya had relied on Gupta for all intelligence. Indeed, Kautilya had full confidence that Gupta would not only bring good intelligence about the enemy, but would protect top-secret information about their own plans. Vishnu Gupta knew that he had failed that trust, and he was not ready to forgive himself. He felt miserable.

There was a long silence as neither Kautilya nor Gupta spoke. The silence was killing Gupta, as he did not know what was going on in Kautilya's mind. Was he upset? On the other hand, was he disappointed? Gupta tried to read Kautilya's mind. He stood still leaning on the stem of a large tree while Kautilya kept pacing up and down not too far from him.

Kautilya was neither upset nor disappointed. One thing he had learnt about warfare was that there is no foolproof plan. Things could always go wrong. The important thing was to learn from the mistakes and not get discouraged. His immediate worry was to make sure that the Nanda soldiers did not discover their stored weapons. He had to get them transferred to a safer place. Kautilya stopped pacing and walked towards Gupta.

"Gupta, we need to find a safe place to get those weapons transferred. Can you check with Rama and come up with a list of safe places to hide them?"

"I will do that Kautilya," replied Gupta in a somewhat subdued tone. He then added, "Are you not bothered about what happened at the battlefield? You seem to be too calm about it."

"Yes, I was terribly bothered for a few minutes. What happened there a while ago was disastrous. Somehow, the enemy knew our plans. It makes me wonder if we have a Nanda agent who works in your network."

"I have thought about that. However, no one knew the whole battle plan. It was just the four of us. It was Chandra Gupta along with Chitrasena, you, and me. No one else knew the entire plan."

"Are you sure Gupta? Had you mentioned the two-pronged attack to anyone else? Did you tell anyone else about the time and day of the attack?"

"Come to think of it, I mentioned the time and day of the attack to the doctor. I had checked on him, and he seemed reliable."

It suddenly struck Gupta that he had not really done a thorough investigation on the doctor. Gupta's technique was to collect information about important people from several sources and corroborate the findings. For some unknown reason, for the doctor, he had not done that. He was satisfied with the first report, which had suggested that he was a reliable man who cared about dharma. That was a terrible mistake. Gupta, who was obsessed with thoroughness in everything he did, had lapsed in meeting his own standards. The more he thought about this, the more he was convinced that the doctor was indeed the enemy agent. He felt sick in his stomach and started wringing his hands in frustration.

"Kautilya, I take full responsibility. It was my blunder that I did not do a thorough check on the doctor. I am convinced now that he is the enemy agent."

Kautilya looked into Gupta's eyes, and he could see that Gupta was completely distraught. Gupta felt humiliated that he had failed his first major test. On the other hand, he was also very angry with himself for being careless. His carelessness could have altered the future. It could have cost the lives of the entire leadership of the dharma forces. He tried to reassure Kautilya, "I will get all the information about this traitor. Once I have proof that he is indeed the enemy agent, we will have him executed."

He was so angry that his face radiated utter disgust towards the doctor. Kautilya tried to calm him down, "There is no need to take such drastic actions. The doctor may come in handy in the near future."

Gupta tried to understand what Kautilya had in mind. Whatever it was, for Gupta it was inconceivable to continue to use the doctor in their future endeavors. However, Kautilya was not in a mood to discuss that any further and indeed did not want to talk about their failed first battle anymore. What followed was a long silence creating an invisible ravine between the two.

Kautilya walked towards the stream, washed his face with the cold water, and sat on a nearby rock. He folded his legs in the lotus position, closed his eyes, and in minutes he was in a deep meditative state. While he was meditating, Gupta sat underneath the tree wondering what was going on inside Kautilya's mind. His biggest fear was that Kautilya would get discouraged or lose interest in the cause and walk away from it all.

However, deep inside, he knew that the odds of such a thing were next to nothing. Still, he was deeply disturbed by that recurring thought. Since the murder of his parents, Gupta had felt so insecure that he hardly slept during the nights. For him, Kautilya had become a mentor, a teacher, and the source of his security. The very thought of Kautilya walking away made him immeasurably insecure.

As Gupta stared towards the horizon in the south direction, he noticed a group of approaching soldiers. They looked like enemy soldiers, and the group got bigger by the minute. He saw hundreds of soldiers galloping towards him, leaving a large cloud of dust behind them. They all had their swords drawn out, pointing them in his direction, and shouting out something that was hardly audible to him. As they got closer, he tried to understand what they were saying. He could now see their faces, and they all looked the same. They were all looking at him in a fearsome manner and yelling at him, "We will get you Gupta. You are a traitor, and we will give you the same treatment we gave your parents."

As the soldiers came closer, Gupta froze. He could not say anything although he tried his best to call out to Kautilya, and he started trembling uncontrollably. He fell on his knees and put his head down with his hands covering the back of his neck. He kept crying out for help, "Kautilya, help me please. Save me from these evil soldiers."

Kautilya had just finished his meditation, got up, and looked in the direction of Gupta. He saw that Gupta had fallen down on his knees with his head touching the ground. He knew immediately that Gupta was suffering from a hallucination. The battlefield retreat was too much for him.

He quickly walked to Gupta, shook his shoulders, and tried to assure him, "You are having a bad dream, Gupta. You must have fallen asleep. There is nothing to worry. We will overcome this setback."

He then took him by his arms and made him walk slowly towards the stream where he splashed his face with cold water. Gupta slowly came back to his senses and realized that it was all his imagination, and he was safe next to Kautilya.

Kautilya waited a while for Gupta to recover completely. They were now ready to travel further north. He had concluded that the safest place for them right now was to be in the Parvataka territory.

"You need some rest, Gupta. Let us travel north and meet Shiva. That is where we can regroup and get back to action. We need to get Chandra Gupta and others to join us soon."

"I will get back to Varanasi in a couple of days and get the others informed about what is going on," replied Gupta who now looked energized.

Indeed, Gupta was now relieved that Kautilya was not thinking about abandoning their goal of annihilating the Nandas. As they traveled north towards Shiva's town, Gupta posed Kautilya a basic question that had bothered him since the retreat from the battlefield.

"Kautilya, is God really on our side? I am getting discouraged that perhaps we may never overcome the Nandas."

Kautilya, of course, had no doubt that God was on their side. After all, the Lord Himself had stated that in the Bhagavad-Gita.

"Of course the Lord is on our side, Gupta. After a setback, it is not rare to get such a feeling. You know the assurance He has given us – whenever dharma declines and adharma (unrighteousness) rises, He will appear."

It was one of those situations when one needs reassurance. Gupta knew that verse, but he wanted to hear it from Kautilya himself.

"Of course, we are not talking about His physical appearance. What we are talking about is His presence in the hearts of all good people that will drive adharma away," explained Kautilya.

They were now very close to Shiva's town, which was named Giripuri. Shiva was in his front garden at that time enjoying the beauty of the flowers along with the mild breeze. He looked into the horizon and recognized that the two riders who were approaching his mansion were none other than Kautilya and Gupta. He knew immediately that something was wrong. He knew that the battle was that morning, and he did not expect to see them for at least a few more days. As they entered Shiva's house, he came hurriedly towards them to find out what had happened. His immediate worry was the well-being of his son.

"What happened? Is Kumara all right?" he said with a worried look.

"Kumara is safe and unharmed. He will be here soon. Unfortunately, we lost your elephants and the Mahuts. Let us go inside and discuss the details," replied Kautilya.

Losing the elephants was the least of the worries for Shiva. His men had the skills to capture hundreds of elephants at a time. Moreover, he still had several hundred trained elephants that could come handy in future battles.

"Did Chandra Gupta come out unharmed? Is he all right?"

"Yes, Chandra Gupta was able to make a quick escape. We will have him join us in a few days."

Shiva took them to the back of his house, and they all climbed up a ladder that took them to the attic. From the attic, they went through a passage and went to a small room hidden behind the attic. This was Shiva's secret place where he planned important matters.

As they settled in the room, Shiva enquired about their fatigue.

"You both must be tired from the long journey. Can I bring you something to drink?"

"We are all right, Shiva. Let us talk about what happened in the battlefield. We can attend to other things later."

"All right, then. Tell me, did you run into unforeseen traps or surprises?"

"Well, there were surprises," replied Gupta. "You always expect that in a battle. The real surprise was that we had a Nanda agent in our own network."

"Do you know who it is? What are you going to do about him?"

"We know who it is. I will let Kautilya decide what he wants to do with him," added Gupta.

"We made a mistake. We had a small setback," Kautilya started. "The important thing is that all our leaders are all right and that most of our forces are intact. What we need from you is to show us secluded areas where we can train our troops. The ones we were using are no longer safe. We would like to use your mansion for our meetings."

"I will gladly give you all the help you need, Kautilya. You can certainly use this chamber for your meetings. I will also provide you rooms in the house for your stay whenever you are here," replied Shiva.

Gupta was relieved that Shiva had embraced them full heartedly. Indeed, he was more than relieved that Shiva was now becoming a full pledged partner for their cause.

"You both must be tired. I would like you to have something to eat and take rest for a while," suggested Shiva.

Kautilya and Gupta had a long deserved rest and were up early the next day, eager to plan the next steps. Gupta, who was in a hurry to reach Varanasi, left right after breakfast. He had to reach Rama and Mahendra as soon as possible. It was important for Rama and Mahendra to know what the next steps were in their plans. It was also very important to move the stored weapons to new locations. All of this required a lot of coordination among his agents. From now on, he was going to be extremely careful. He was not going to allow for any sort of complacency in his network. He felt as if he had never been so determined in his life.

This gave Kautilya some time to spend in solitude and plan his next moves. Although their first battle was a failure, he had learned a great deal from the fiasco. He had learned about the speed of their cavalry. He had also made mental notes on types of weapons Nanda soldiers carried. He was now ready to use even the minute details he had collected to their advantage.

The next day, Chandra Gupta, Chitrasena, and Kumara came to Giripuri. It turned out that they had a rougher time reaching Giripuri. It was obvious that they were worn-out and tired. They had gathered in the front yard on their horses, when servants came running towards them to help them get down. As soon as they got down from their horses, the servants took the horses away to feed and clean them. Shiva and Kautilya came, enquiring what had happened to them since they had fled from the battlefield.

"You must have taken a longer route to come here. Did the enemy soldiers follow you?" enquired Kautilya.

"Well, we initially thought that we had lost them for good. That turned out to be false. Some hundred or so of the enemy soldiers kept chasing us. They were chasing us almost the whole day. We were just thirty in total, and we had to keep running."

"So, how did you overcome them?"

"We were lucky. We got into an area where we had a terrain advantage. We were at a higher location, and we stopped to face them," explained Chandra Gupta.

"Moreover, we were lucky. We had several master archers, whereas they had none. This helped us kill or wound many of them even before they came close to us," added Chitrasena.

"We finally had a hand-to-hand fight, and we were able to kill many of them. The remaining survivors just ran away."

Chandra Gupta was almost exhausted when he finished narrating their adventure. They all went inside the mansion to get some well-deserved rest.

Meanwhile, in Varanasi, Vishnu Gupta was busy with his mission to find out every minute detail about the doctor. His name was Vaidya Nathan. It turned out that he had many avatars in his life. He had traveled all over the kingdom and had never settled in any place for more than a year or two. He was never married and frequented courtesans. It turned out that in one of his avatars, he was a Brahmin priest, while in another avatar he was a Jain priest. He had even wandered in the kingdom for a few months as a Buddhist bikku. Vishnu Gupta tried to find out what his weakness was. It was certainly not women as he had no committed relationship, he had no family except for his aging parents, and he had no sense of dharma either. After a little bit more research, he uncovered one weakness, however. It turned out that he was addicted to gold. He had a habit of buying gold from the money he earned, and he would hide it in his parents' house. His appetite for gold was insatiable – the more he collected, the more was his desire to acquire gold. It was no wonder that he had become an informant for the Nandas. It was all because of gold. He was now staying in Pataliputra, worried about his safety. That was fine with Vishnu Gupta since he really did not know what to do with him. Indeed, a thought had crossed Vishnu Gupta's mind to send his agents to catch him and take him to Kautilya. In the end, he reasoned that it was unnecessary; he knew Kautilya would have a better plan.

Gupta wasted no time in arranging a meeting with Mahendra and Rama to update them on the plans. He had the weapons transferred to a safe location deep inside Shiva's territory. He was constantly in touch with Kautilya and Chitrasena through trusted intermediaries and had received the location of the new training grounds. He made sure that the rebel soldiers received information about changes in the location of training grounds. He had taken care of everything he could, and was ready to head north and join Kautilya and Chandra Gupta. He patiently waited for the message from Kautilya for the next move.

Back in Giripuri, Kautilya and Chandra Gupta, along with Chitrasena had spent innumerable hours going over their battle plans. The plans were subject to repeated analysis to ensure a flawless plan. Shiva provided an independent assessment of the plans and played the role of the enemy in their war games. Chitrasena had resumed his training of the rebel forces in the new location. It was now time for Vishnu Gupta to join them. Kautilya wanted to assign his agents an important task and sent out for Gupta.

The next day, Kautilya, Chandra Gupta, Chitrasena and Shiva, along with Vishnu Gupta had convened in the secret chamber. Kautilya wanted to discuss the role of the secret agents in his plan.

"We all know what went wrong in the previous battle a month ago. We know that there was an enemy agent who knew our plans too well," Kautilya began his deliberations.

"We know who he is. Why do we not just get rid of him? He is after all a dharma traitor," added Chandra Gupta.

Chitrasena and Shiva nodded their heads in agreement while Vishnu Gupta sat quietly knowing Kautilya's inclination on that subject.

"Let us not do anything emotional like that. The doctor is truly valuable to us. He is going to play a key role in our next battle."

"But how?" wondered Chitrasena.

"It will become obvious in the near future. Right now, we need to bring him back to Varanasi where Chandra Gupta and I will meet him. Gupta, do you know where he is right now?" added Kautilya turning towards Vishnu Gupta.

"Yes, we know where he is. He is in Pataliputra right now. We can surely throw bait and have him meet us in Varanasi. I will arrange for that very soon," assured Gupta.

Over the next few days, an agent of Vishnu Gupta who was also a gold trader traveled to Pataliputra and met with the doctor. The trader informed him that Vishnu Gupta had a very important mission, and he would receive a rich compensation for his part. He also told the doctor that the compensation would be in the form of gold coins. He was also told to come alone, and if he brought any one else with him, his life

113

would be in danger. In advance, the doctor was given a few gold coins. Lured by the reward in gold, he agreed to meet Gupta in Varanasi in a secret place, which was a small house that belonged to a local priest.

When the doctor came to the secret place, the priest took him inside to a small room that was in the back of the house. He then closed the door and left. The doctor saw Vishnu Gupta along with Kautilya, and Chandra Gupta waiting for him in that room. The presence of Kautilya and Chandra Gupta told him at once that he was on to something very important.

"Come in Vaidya Nathan. Please join us. You have met Kautilya and Chandra Gupta before." Gupta gave a warm welcome to the doctor.

Vishnu Gupta wanted to make sure that he was comfortable. Vaidya Nathan sat next to them eager to understand his mission.

"Vaidya Nathan, we want you to take part in an important mission. You know that we had a small setback last time we attacked the fort at Narayanpuri. I think that we misjudged the strength of the Nanda forces. So this time we have decided to attack the same fort with a much bigger force – around thirty thousand rebels," explained Kautilya.

"When do you plan to attack?" replied the doctor.

"Exactly one week from today," added Chandra Gupta.

"So what is my mission? What do you want me to do?" The doctor was eager to know his assignment.

"Your assignment is very simple. We want you to infiltrate the Nanda network, and tell them that we are planning to attack exactly *two* weeks from today. This way, our job will be easier when we attack the Narayanpuri fort. Since you are a doctor, it will not be difficult to infiltrate the enemy network," explained Kautilya.

"There will be a reward of one hundred gold coins for your hard work. Here are ten gold coins in advance," added Chandra Gupta as he placed ten glittering gold coins in Vaidya Nathan's palms.

Vaidya Nathan was extremely pleased with the assignment. That was the easiest ten gold coins he had ever made. His wicked mind saw an opportunity to make even more gold coins. He saw an opportunity to use the information he just had received and make a lot more money from the Nandas.

"We want you to come to Narayanpuri in ten days. By that time, we will have overtaken the fort. That way you can get your remaining gold coins and be safe under our protection," added Kautilya.

"Do not worry Kautilya. I will do exactly as you told me. I will be careful and will meet you in Narayanpuri in ten days."

The doctor then hid the gold coins he had received from Chandra Gupta inside his clothes and quietly departed from the house. He was soon on his way to Pataliputra and was giddy with the thought of the additional gold coins he was going to profit from the intelligence he had just received.

After making sure that the doctor was no longer anywhere close to the house, Kautilya and the others thanked the priest for his help, and traversed north back to Giripuri. On their way to Giripuri, Vishnu Gupta tried to understand Kautilya's clever plan.

"We are not going to attack Narayanpuri again, right?" asked Gupta.

"Of course we are not going to do that. Our plan is to attack smaller forts in the North. Let us talk about that when we get back to Giripuri," replied Kautilya.

"What do you think the doctor will do next?" asked Chandra Gupta.

"You know that there is no limit when it comes to greed. He is sure to sell the intelligence he has just gathered for a higher price. He will try to get two hundred gold coins for that piece of intelligence from the Nandas. Māya has struck him in the form of gold."

"Now I understand. When the Nandas find out that the intelligence he has brought is useless and misleading, they will kill him on the spot," commented Chandra Gupta

"That is the right punishment for him. He certainly deserves it," observed Vishnu Gupta. Vishnu Gupta now saw the genius of Kautilya in dealing with a traitor like Vaidya Nathan.

Once they reached Giripuri, they spent the next few days making final preparations for the attack. Kautilya, Chandra Gupta, and Chitrasena finalized their plans. Vishnu Gupta kept refining the intelligence he had gathered so that Kautilya knew even the minute details of the Nanda defenses. There were five important forts on the northern side of the river Ganges. Kautilya and Chandra Gupta wanted to capture them in a matter of seven days. Their plan was to capture them with such speed that the Nandas would have very little time, if any, to react. The plan was for Chandra Gupta with his forces to attack two of the forts while Chitrasena with Shiva would capture the other two. Kautilya was to stay with Chandra Gupta while Vishnu Gupta accompanied Chitrasena. Both Chandra Gupta and Chitrasena commanded a rebel army of about six thousand. Vishnu Gupta's intelligence had gathered that each of the four forts had three thousand soldiers protecting the structures. Kautilya was confident that with six thousand soldiers, he could overwhelm the fort defenses. Moreover, they had assembled catapults drawn by elephants. They were going to deploy them to break the fort gates.

As planned, exactly one week after the meeting with the doctor, Chandra Gupta and Chitrasena led their respective armies towards the target forts. Kautilya had a third force of about three thousand soldiers marching towards Narayanpuri. That force was just a decoy to confuse the Nandas. They were to march close to the Narayanpuri fort to make the Nanda forces believe that they were under attack. However, that unit was going to remain several miles from the fort and would not attack the fort. Kautilya wanted that force to stay in the vicinity for a day or two so that Chandra Gupta and Chitrasena had an easier time attacking the northern forts. Shiva's son Kumara was leading that force.

Back in Pataliputra, as Kautilya had suspected, Vaidya Nathan had sold the intelligence he had gathered to the Nandas for a lot more gold than what Kautilya had promised. The Nandas trusted him having benefited from his earlier intelligence. Promptly, they assembled a large force and sent it to Narayanpuri for fortification. They also kept a very large force in Pataliputra on alert in case additional help was necessary. They also stationed scouts in the woods to provide early warning about the approaching rebel forces. The scouts spotted the approaching enemy force led by Kumara and promptly reported that to the top general inside the fort.

"We have spotted the enemy force. They are fast approaching our fort. We estimate that force is about five thousand men," reported one of the scouts. The other scouts nodded their heads in agreement. Obviously, the expectation that Chandra Gupta was going to attack the fort with a larger force had colored their estimation.

The general was anxious to know more details.

"Was Chandra Gupta leading the force?" he enquired.

"We did not spot him in the lead position. Another young man who looked like Shiva's son was leading the forces."

"That is interesting. There must be another force led by Chandra Gupta on the way. This group may be the advance group. I expect more reinforcements soon. We need to be very vigilant," explained the general. The general was relying too much on the intelligence he had received from Vaidya Nathan.

"It is not wise for us to face them outside the fort. Let us wait for them to attack the fort. We will hold them off and send for reinforcement from Pataliputra." The general ordered his men.

He had a straightforward defensive scheme. After all, that scheme had worked every time they had employed it.

Meanwhile, Kumara and his soldiers camped a few miles outside the fort without any intention of advancing further. The Nanda forces stayed inside the fort waiting all day for the rebels to attack the fort. They anticipated that the attack would commence once Chandra Gupta joined the advance group. However, the rebels showed no sign of moving even as night descended over the fort. Nor was there any sign of Chandra Gupta joining the advance group. Meanwhile, inside the fort, the general got a little worried and started wondering if Chandra Gupta was planning to attack in the night. He ordered his soldiers to light extra lamps and stay extra vigilant all through the night.

On the northern edge of Magadha, Chandra Gupta and Kautilya had reached the fort they had planned to attack. The scouts saw the approaching army, quickly closed the huge gates to the fort, and completely sealed off all entrances to the fort. Chandra Gupta surrounded the fort and ordered his soldiers to start bombarding the entrance with heavy boulders. Once the soldiers started launching the boulders, the enemy soldiers guarding the fort were terrified. They had never seen such a large catapult showering heavy boulders. The boulders made a lot of noise as they struck the gates, terrifying the occupants inside the fort.

Within minutes, the gates fell down and Chandra Gupta's men charged inside with the elephants leading the attack. The Nanda soldiers tried to defend themselves by resorting to archery, which was futile as thousands of Chandra Gupta's men poured into the fort. What followed

117

was a furious hand-to-hand combat with both sides losing many of their men. However, in the end, Chandra Gupta and his men had either killed or captured all the enemy soldiers. The remaining soldiers soon surrendered and agreed to lay down their arms.

It was Chandra Gupta's maiden victory and it was indeed a proud moment for Kautilya as he watched the entire battle from a distant vantage point. Chandra Gupta personally went to the top of the fort and hoisted the saffron flag that had a peacock symbol at the center. The peacock was going to be his royal symbol and the royal emblem of his future Empire. Kautilya had chosen the saffron color as it represented peace and prosperity.

As the victorious rebels brought the prisoners to Chandra Gupta, he gave them a clear choice. "I will spare your lives if you agree to join the dharma forces. This way you can live and be part of a worthy cause. We will get rid of the Nandas in a few months. We will reestablish the rule of dharma and bring prosperity to all the citizens. Do you want to be part of the dharma force?"

"We do! We do want to be part of the dharma force!" All the prisoners shouted in unison.

The prisoners were relieved and gladly agreed to join Chandra Gupta's forces. No one had any love left for the Nandas.

"That is good. My men will give the instructions on what to do next," replied Chandra Gupta.

"Long live Chandra Gupta. He is our king!"

The situation was not very different at the other fort. Chitrasena and his men had captured the fort in a matter of hours, just like Chandra Gupta. Chitrasena made it clear that the captured soldiers had two choices. "You can be prisoners and be locked in the dungeons, or you can commit your allegiance to Kautilya and Chandra Gupta and join the dharma forces," Chitrasena said, giving a stern message.

Here too the enemy soldiers gladly deserted the Nandas, and were more than happy to commit their allegiance to dharma. It all happened so swiftly that Vishnu Gupta who was witnessing the battle from a distance was amazed at the disciplined way Chitrasena and his men had captured the fort. He immediately sent an agent to Kautilya to update the progress.

Meanwhile, as the night gave itself to early morning, the general in charge of Narayanpuri was getting very anxious. He sent a scout to check on the rebel forces stationed a few miles from the fort. He paced impatiently as he waited to find out about the rebels. He could sense that something was not right. Within a few minutes, his scout came galloping back to the fort.

"They are gone, general. There is no one there," the scout shouted as he entered the general's chamber.

The general was very angry and felt like a fool for having listened to Vaidya Nathan. His immediate conclusion was that Vaidya Nathan was an agent of Kautilya who had misled the Nandas. He ordered his soldiers to bring him. Vaidya Nathan who had accompanied the general from Pataliputra was sleeping in a comfortable room inside the fort. Two soldiers came to his room, ordered him to open the door, and immediately dragged him to the general. As they made him stand in front of the general, Vaidya Nathan looked at the general who had a nasty frown on his face, and he knew immediately that something was terribly wrong.

"Whatever happened to your friends Kautilya and Chandra Gupta? They never showed up," stated the general with a rigid voice.

"I do not know, general. As far as my information goes, it was their plan to capture this fort. They told me that personally."

"I will not believe you even for one second, doctor. You are not telling us the whole truth. If you value your life, you are not going to hold back anything."

Vaidya Nathan started perspiring profusely, as he searched for a proper reply. He knew that Kautilya and Chandra Gupta had used him, and he could only blame himself for his predicament.

"General, I am being honest. I have told you everything I knew. Our enemies have tricked us, and for that you cannot be angry with me."

The general looked at him in disgust as he ordered his soldiers to put Vaidya Nathan in a dark room in the dungeon. He would address his plight later; he was more concerned about important things that needed his immediate attention.

He asked his guards to bring three of his best agents and assigned the first one his mission.

"I want you to go back to the Nandas and report on what has trans-pired so far. Bring me back any intelligence they may have received about Chandra Gupta."

He then looked at the other two and gave them specific instructions.

"I want you two to travel north, and find out everything about what Kautilya and Chandra Gupta have done so far. I suspect that they may have attacked our forts in the north. I want the answer within the next twenty four hours."

Back at the northern forts, Kautilya and Chandra Gupta had put the conquered forts under the control of trusted men from their army. There was always a risk of a change of heart among those who had surrendered, and it was important to keep a close watch on them. Kautilya knew very well that how his forces managed the situation post conquest was as important as executing the attack itself. The remaining soldiers, along with Kautilya, Chandra Gupta, Chitrasena, and Vishnu Gupta went back to Giripuri where Kumara was already waiting for them with his men.

Having succeeded in conquering the first two forts, Kautilya did not want to let up on his attack plans. He had a series of meetings with Chandra Gupta, Chitrasena, and Vishnu Gupta on the next battle plans. They were now confident that they could take the remaining three forts on the northern side of the Magadha kingdom easily. This time Kautilya devised three forces, led by Chandra Gupta, Chitrasena, and Kumara respectively. Each targeted a fort, and within days of conquering the first two forts, they were marching towards the other northern forts. The battles went similar to the other two, and the three forts fell under Chandra Gupta's control without any major problem. Chandra Gupta now had complete control of the northern edges of the Magadha kingdom.

Kautilya's plan was to attack the southern forts next. However, he wanted to increase the troop size before they decided to commence the southern expedition. Towards that goal, Vishnu Gupta, Rama, and Mahendra were working diligently as they recruited several thousand more young men willing to join the dharma forces. Now that Chandra Gupta's reputation as a conqueror was spreading fast among the citizens of Magadha, many more men were willing to join his force. It was also getting easier for Rama and Mahendra to raise the funds to buy more weapons and horses. Chitrasena and Chandra Gupta were busy training the recruits while Kautilya kept fine-tuning his battle plans. Kautilya and Vishnu Gupta spent several hours every day going over the latest intelligence reports.

"It has been two weeks since we took control of all the northern forts. How are our preparations coming, Chitrasena?" Kautilya asked about the new recruits. He was anxious to launch the next phase of his plans, but at the same time did not want to launch an expedition not being completely prepared.

"Well, it is going very well, Kautilya. We almost have sixty thousand troops ready to go on the next attack. They are all eager to get your order to march soon," replied Chitrasena.

Kautilya looked at Chandra Gupta and Kumara and wanted to know their opinion.

"Are you and Kumara ready for a southern expedition?" he queried Chandra Gupta. There was a sense of uneasiness as he looked at him.

"We are all ready Kautilya. Give each of us twenty thousand men. We will overwhelm the southern forts in no time. However, you do not seem to be so sure, Kautilya. Is something about the plans bothering you? You seem to be worried about something," asked Chandra Gupta.

He could sense that Kautilya was uneasy about launching an attack right away.

"We have two choices at this point. We can attack the southern forces one by one just as we did in the northern side. However, it is very possible that the Nandas will anticipate this and will be prepared to defend the forts aggressively. They could even surround us by bringing more reinforcements," Kautilya began, elaborating his concerns.

"So, what is your suggestion, Kautilya?"

"Well, we need to change our strategy on the southern side a bit. We will use our agents who have infiltrated the Nanda intelligence apparatus to plant the exact same plan Chandra Gupta just described. That is, we want the enemy to think that we are attacking the three southern forts simultaneously with three forces led by Chandra Gupta, Kumara, and Chitrasena. We will even plant the information through our agents that each force is fifteen thousand men. I expect the enemy to be waiting for us with a much bigger force at each fort. This time they will be ready to face us outside the fort."

"However, since we will not follow that plan, what are we going to do?" asked Kumara.

"This is what we will do. We will use all the forces on one fort. We will overwhelm them. This time, the enemy will come at us even after we have occupied the fort; they will be desperate. We need to be ready for a major battle. We will have a chance to crush them and plant fear in their hearts."

Everyone loved Kautilya's plan; however, Chandra Gupta had some questions.

"How wedded are we to this plan, Kautilya?"

"You can never be wedded to a single plan, Chandra Gupta. The greatness of any military strategist lies in how flexible his plans are."

"But you must like this plan for some specific reason," stated Chandra Gupta.

"Well, we have certain advantages being the ones attacking the Nandas. The more unknowns there are the more difficult it is for the enemy to defend. The whole idea of planting faulty intelligence is to cause confusion in the minds of the enemy planners. I like this plan because we can easily adapt our strategy based on what we see on the ground," explained Kautilya.

Vishnu Gupta, who had been quiet all through the meeting, knew very well that it was now time for his spies to do exactly what the plan demanded. His agents were going to give the false intelligence to the enemy, and one week later Kautilya wanted to start his campaign.

"I will get my agents to plant exactly what you want, Kautilya. We will do it so that no one in the enemy camp will ever uspect even the slightest deceit," confirmed Visnu Gupta trying hard to control his excitement.

Chapter 10
The Nandas Must Pay

W hile Kautilya and Chandra Gupta were busy devising their clever plan, the situation was very different back in Pataliputra. Indeed, the situation was outright tense. It was just a few hours before that, the Nandas had received the bad news about the loss of their northern forts. Dhana Nanda had called an urgent meeting with his sons and his trusted generals. He knew that the situation was grave, and a single misstep could lead to a total disaster. However, his younger sons were overconfident and considered Chandra Gupta and his band of soldiers a mere nuisance.

"I want to know everything about this Kautilya. It looks to me like he is the mastermind behind all the trouble," stated the elder Nanda.

"We have collected sufficient intelligence about him, Your Highness. He is a Brahmin who for some strange reason is upset with the royal family. He apparently has taken a vow to overthrow the regime. He surely must be deluded. You do not have to worry, Your Highness. We will have him captured and tortured in no time," a general assured.

"What about this Chandra Gupta? What do we know about him?"

"He is just a troublemaker from the countryside, father. He is a simpleton and is not good at any thing. We will have him captured and roasted," boasted one of the Nanda brothers.

This made Dhana Nanda extremely angry. He wanted to give his sons a piece of his mind. "Listen to me, you two. Never underestimate your enemy. If he is no good, how is it that he is capturing forts one after another?"

The Nanda brothers did not answer him, as they did not want to make their father even angrier.

"Do we have any intelligence about their next attack plans?"

"Yes, Your Highness. We have had some of our best agents go into the countryside to get more information. They now have an army of more than fifty thousand men. Our agents are telling us that they plan to attack the three southern forts simultaneously. They have two other rebel leaders in addition to Chandra Gupta. One is Chitrasena, and the other one is Kumara."

Dhana Nanda did not say anything for a while. He was digesting all he had heard and was trying to come up with a plan to counter Kautilya's strategy. All of the others kept quiet lest they disturb his thought process. Moreover, they all knew that Dhana Nanda was the smartest one in the room.

Dhana Nanda wanted to send twenty five thousand troops to each fort. He did not want to lose the southern forts, as it would lead to enemy encroachment from both north and south. Moreover, those forts were extremely important for controlling commerce with southern kingdoms. He even considered sending more reinforcements to protect the southern forts. However, committing seventy five thousand troops to protect the three forts would leave just one hundred twenty five thousand soldiers including the reserves to defend Pataliputra. He was not willing to dilute the defenses of the capital any further. Finally, he spoke as everyone listened intently to his plan.

"All right, here is my counter plan. We will put twenty five thousand men in each fort. Since they have huge catapults with elephants and several thousand expert archers, it is not wise for us to defend the forts from inside. We will face them outside the forts, and defeat them before they enter."

The generals agreed. They were confident that Dhana Nanda's plan would work. However, Dhana Nanda himself was not one hundred percent sure about his plan. He knew that he was up against Kautilya and Chandra Gupta who were sure to have more surprises. He kept pacing, trying to construct multiple scenarios. Can the intelligence be faulty? Perhaps, they will attack a single fort with an overwhelming force. In such a case, having twenty five thousand troops each to protect the forts will be useless. He soon realized that he was at a disadvantage. If he decided to commit his troops to one fort, the enemy will skip that fort and attack other forts; it seemed like he was constrained and unable to make any major maneuver. He began to admire the cunning nature of Kautilya's plans albeit grudgingly.

Chandra Gupta and his men launched the plan exactly as Kautilya had planned. They set out as three independent forces led by Chandra Gupta, Chitrasena, and Kumara. However, they stayed close to each other with the intention of merging into one army as they came closer to the first fort. The intention was to mislead the enemy scouts.

On the other side, the Nandas had placed twenty five thousand men at each of the three southern forts. The forts were vital for the Magadha economy, and they were committed to defending them. Dhana Nanda had instructed his scouts to contact the generals if they saw any changes in the enemy routes.

At the right moment, Kautilya sent agents to the three rebel groups instructing them to converge on the first fort. In no time, the three rebel forces merged into a single force and launched a major attack on the Nanda forces defending the first fort. It was no match as there were sixty thousand rebels against a force of twenty five thousand men. In a matter of minutes, Chandra Gupta and his forces decimated the enemy, and the first fort fell under the control of Chandra Gupta. It was no time to celebrate, however. As Kautilya had anticipated, the enemy agents quickly went to the other two forts to inform the generals about what had just transpired at the first fort. The enemy was bound to attack Chandra Gupta and his men. This time, they had to be in a defensive position that was flexible enough to fight a major battle against an army of fifty thousand men.

Kautilya formed a linear formation with three segments with Chandra Gupta in the center segment. Chitrasena and Kumara led the segments at the two ends. Inside the fort, he kept a small force of around five thousand men for backup. He himself stayed at the top of the fort so that he could get a good view of the battlefield.

Within two hours, the enemy forces were approaching Chandra Gupta and his men. The two armies came face to face, and there was a tense moment as they all remained silent. Kautilya signaled his men to start charging towards the enemy, and soon the soldiers were in fierce hand-to-hand fights. Bodies fell, and blood flowed all for the cause of dharma.

There was deafening noise caused by the clash of metal weapons; there were men screaming as they fell down, and horses and elephants making strange noises in fear and excitement. Nothing really mattered for Kautilya as he completely focused on assessing the enemy strengths and weaknesses. As soon as he concluded that the enemy's right side, which was facing Kumara and his men, was the weaker side, he sent a sizable reinforcement from inside the fort to augment Kumara's forces. The soldiers spilled out of the fort in a hurry, joined Kumara, and gave him the message to start advancing towards the center in the form of an arc. The Nanda generals realizing the breakdown of their forces on the right side started moving more of their men to that side. This gave one more opening, and Kautilya sent his remaining soldiers inside the fort to augment Chitrasena's side.

Kumara and Chitrasena systematically started dismantling the Nanda defenses and within a matter of one hour, Chandra Gupta, Chitrasena, and Kumara had surrounded the enemy on all three sides. It was as if the enemy was in the grips of a huge nutcracker. They had nowhere to go but fight for their survival. It was all in vain, as what followed was a complete rout of the Nanda forces as they started falling at an astonishing speed. The few that survived saw no hope of wining and quickly withdrew from the battlefield and fled into the woods.

This battle was indeed the turning point for Chandra Gupta and Kautilya. They could now sense that total victory was not too far away and the only thing left was the conquest of Pataliputra itself. Kautilya, however, did not want to rush into attacking Pataliputra. He knew very well that the Nanda army defending the capital was formidable. They still had one hundred twenty five thousand troops defending the capital city. Moreover, they had a rich treasury that enabled them to add more soldiers at will.

As Kautilya stood on top of the fort surveying the battlefield filled with dead soldiers and animals, he had some momentary self-doubt. Was it all worth it for the sake of restoring dharma? What had he done? Had he gone mad and forgotten that he was a Brahmin who was supposed to uphold non-violence? His face flinched in disgust. Just then, he saw an old man walking towards him. He wondered how that old man had reached the top of the fort. He looked very familiar, and as he came closer, it all came back to him. He was the same man he had met on the banks of the river. He had been humiliated the very day by the Nanda brothers. He wondered why he had come here.

"Do not doubt your mission, Kautilya. You are on the right path. Believe me, you are doing the Lord's work," he spoke as he came closer to him.

"Are you sure about that? Sometimes I feel like I have lost my spiritual bearings."

"Nonsense, never have such self-doubt," replied the old man.

Kautilya was not so sure, however. He closed his eyes as if asking for forgiveness. When he opened his eyes, the old man was gone, and all he could see were white clouds in the distant sky. Just then, someone touched his shoulder, and he looked back. It was his friend Vishnu Gupta.

"Whom were you talking to, Kautilya? Are you feeling all right?" enquired Vishnu Gupta.

"I am all right. There was a moment I was imagining things. Nothing to worry," assured Kautilya.

Vishnu Gupta was worried, however. He wanted to make sure that Kautilya got good rest that day.

"Let us all rest in this fort for a couple of days before we proceed any further."

Kautilya agreed, as it was sound advice. For the next two days, Kautilya, along with his trusted companions, stayed in the fort as they planned their next moves.

In their next planning meeting, Kautilya was already thinking about the neighbors of Magadha. He knew that once Chandra Gupta became the ruler of Magadha, it was important to know who his potential allies were and who were going to be his competitors. His conclusion was that the time was right to make that assessment.

"Vishnu Gupta, I am going to assign an important mission to you. I want you to send your best agents as emissaries to the surrounding kingdoms. Ask them to contribute forces for our final assault on Pataliputra. For those who cooperate, tell them that they will be rewarded in the future," instructed Kautilya.

"For those who do not cooperate, tell them that there will be a steep price to pay," added Chandra Gupta.

Both Kautilya and Chandra Gupta were thinking beyond Magadha. However, neither of them had lost track of the magnitude of the immediate task in front of them.

Chandra Gupta's reputation as a ferocious warrior was now legendary all over the continent. Indeed, many kings wanted to be part of that legend and almost all the neighboring kings, except for two, agreed to join forces with him to overthrow the Nandas. Even Yavana mercenaries wanted to be part of the attack on Pataliputra. When Kautilya and Vishnu Gupta counted all the troops committed to them, there were more than three hundred thousand of them. Kautilya again divided the troops into three parts, one led by Chandra Gupta, and the other two led by Chitrasena and Kumara. The final battle plans were drawn, and it was just a matter of getting all the logistics aligned. Kautilya held his final meeting with all the leaders before the start of the battle for Pataliputra. He knew that if they failed to capture Pataliputra, the newfound allies would hesitate to help them the next time. He carefully drew the battle plans and explained that to Chandra Gupta, Chitrasena, and Kumara.

"We will take three distinct routes, each led by one of you. I want Kumara to attack from the north and Chitrasena to attack from the south. Vishnu Gupta will accompany Chitrasena, and I will accompany Chandra Gupta. We will attack Pataliputra from the west."

"What about Narayanpuri? That fort is still under the control of the enemy."

"It won't be under the control of the enemy for a long time, Kumara. We will make a brief stop there on our way to Pataliputra," explained Kautilya. Kumara smiled in satisfaction.

"After we siege Pataliputra, there is a good chance that the Nandas will try to escape through one of the secret passages that run from the palace to the outskirts of the city. We need to be very vigilant about that," cautioned Chandra Gupta.

"We have made sufficient arrangements for that, Chandra Gupta. My agents know all of the escape routes, and we will be waiting for the wretched Nandas at the end of the tunnels. This time there shall be no escape for the enemy," explained Vishnu Gupta.

One could sense that Vishnu Gupta had reached his limit of patience, and he was not going to let any one of them escape alive.

"All right, all is settled then. Let us start our expedition. We will do this for the sake of people of the Magadha, and *for the sake of dharma!*" proclaimed Kautilya.

There was an immeasurable excitement as soon as the soldiers heard that marching order. It caught on like a fire as each soldier repeated that statement at their highest pitch, and it became their war cry as the three forces started their march towards Pataliputra.

Chandra Gupta and Kautilya made their first stop at Narayanpuri where they sent a small group of advance scouts to see what was going on at that fort. When the scouts reached the fort, to their astonishment, they found the fort gates open. They carefully went inside the fort, and realized that the enemy had abandoned it. As they examined the fort, it felt as if they had entered a ghost town.

They did not want to waste much time; however, they decided to look inside the rooms and passages to make sure that there were no surprises.

"There is absolutely no one here," said one of the scouts casually.

Right at that moment, another scout called out.

"Come and look over here," shouted the scout in an excited voice.

When the other scouts went there, they saw the body of a man hung from a ceiling beam. One of the scouts, a close agent of Vishnu Gupta, recognized the body.

"Oh, that is the doctor, Vaidya Nathan. He deserves it," he stated in disgust.

The scouts did not want to waste any more time and soon went back to Chandra Gupta and Kautilya.

"The fort had been completely abandoned, Sir. There is no one but the dead doctor," one of the scouts reported.

"That is good. I want a small group of our soldiers to go there and occupy the fort. The rest of us will march to Pataliputra," announced Kautilya.

Within twenty-four hours, the three wings of the dharma forces had Pataliputra under siege. The enemy, who were in a defensive posture, had completely closed off the city and had their best archers at the top of the fort showering sharp arrows at the rebels. Kautilya's forces were ready for this. Their response was to use a herd of large elephants to attack the gates. The Mahuts riding the elephants were in metallic armor and escaped the sting of the arrows. The sharp arrows only got the elephants overexcited as they charged towards the gates with utmost ferociousness. As they kept ramming into the doors, the main gates could not bear the impact anymore, and the attacking soldiers poured into the city. The situation was not much different on the other two sides as the Nanda defenses had completely collapsed. As his forces pierced into the walled city, Chandra Gupta felt as if he was a Vedic god. He felt as if he was Indra destroying the evil dragon Vritra.[22] He had never felt so high in his life. The feeling of destroying evil for the sake of restoring dharma was too intoxicating for him, and he kept reminding himself that restoring dharma went much beyond killing the evil Nandas and liberating Magadha.

As the soldiers poured into the city, royal forces engaged them in a ferocious battle. Both sides lost many men as blood stained each building in the capital. The roads became rivers of blood as the rebel soldiers kept pushing the Nanda forces slowly but surely to the palace complex. The palace complex was a fort within the city with iron gates securing the entrance. This time it was a combination of catapults and elephants as the iron gates collapsed making a loud thud. As Chandra Gupta and Chitrasena rushed into the palace mounted on their horses, they came face to face with the two Nanda brothers. What ensued was an intense sword fight. Within a few minutes, the two brothers were dead by severe sword wounds as they were no match for the invaders. Seeing their princes dead, the remaining royal commanders and soldiers surrendered to Chandra Gupta. Right at that moment, Kautilya came and joined Chandra Gupta who was indeed very pleased to see the Nandas dead.

"You can now tie your forelock, Kautilya," Chandra Gupta said in a respectful way.

"That can wait, Chandra Gupta. We need to find the old man, Dhana Nanda. Let us get inside the palace and search for him," replied Kautilya.

Chandra Gupta and Kautilya carefully entered the palace with Chandra Gupta holding his sword in front of him. There was an eerie silence, as they could find no one. They kept going from room to room hoping to find Dhana Nanda. As they entered the royal chambers, they saw two dead bodies; one was that of the queen, wife of Dharma Pal who

---

22 Rig Veda 1.32.

was a hostage of Dhana Nanda, and the other was that of her young son. By the fresh blood on the floor, it was obvious to Kautilya and Chandra Gupta that Dhana Nanda had just committed that horrible crime. As they looked around, they noticed that a trap door was open which led to an escape tunnel. Quickly, Kautilya asked a soldier to bring him a torch, and they both entered the tunnel to catch Dhana Nanda before he escaped too far.

Meanwhile, outside Pataliputra, Vishnu Gupta and his men were going from one tunnel to another tunnel trying to catch anyone who was attempting to escape from Pataliputra. All they had caught so far were low-level commanders who were unwilling to fight for the Nandas. His soldiers brought one such commander to Vishnu Gupta.

"If you value your life, take us to the tunnel that is connected to the palace," demanded Vishnu Gupta.

"I will happily do that. Please do not kill me," begged the enemy commander. He then took Vishnu Gupta and his soldiers to a tunnel that was at the north end of the city where they patiently waited. Finally, their patience paid off as Dhana Nanda slowly emerged from the tunnel, not knowing that Vishnu Gupta and his men were waiting at the end. Dhana Nanda knew very well that Kautilya and Chandra Gupta were right behind him, and he was completely preoccupied with losing them. However, when he came out of the tunnel, he was extremely surprised as one of Vishnu Gupta's soldiers jumped at him and pointed his sword at his throat.

"Drop your weapon. We want to take you to Kautilya and Chandra Gupta," the soldier said tersely.

Before anyone realized what was going on, Vishnu Gupta had drawn a sword from the soldier that was standing next to him and thrust the sword deep into Dhana Nanda's chest. In no time, Dhana Nanda collapsed into a pool of blood right as Kautilya and Chandra Gupta emerged from the tunnel.

"That was for my parents, for Dharma Pal and his family, and for thousands of innocent peope who were killed by you,"proclaimed Vishnu Gupta.

Chapter 11
The Birth of the Empire

Victorious Chandra Gupta went from one corner of Pataliputra to the other to meet the citizens with the intention of assuring them about the future. He was not afraid of anyone and told himself that he was not going to be a monarch hiding inside the palace. He wanted to be a monarch who was always in touch with his subjects. Nevertheless, Kautilya had made sure that his bodyguards were nearby to protect him in case someone had any schemes. To his disappointment, there were very few who came out to greet him. Citizens were still tense and were worried about their safety. For them, Chandra Gupta was still an unknown leader.

He understood why there were not many to greet him, but was anxious to make them feel better in whatever way he could. The future he envisioned was one where the laws of dharma ruled supreme, and no one would be above dharma. For him, ruling Magadha was a divine duty, and he planned to execute that duty with greatest care. His intent was to perform that duty flawlessly. Toward that goal, he was going to rely on Kautilya's wisdom and skills. He knew that there was a lot more to do; Kautilya had continuously warned him that defeating the Nandas was the easy part. Winning the hearts of citizens of Magadha was going to be the difficult part. Of course, there was the need to establish all branches of governance to ensure proper running of the kingdom. He had to establish all departments of the government for day-to-day functioning of the state. All this was new to young Chandra Gupta. However, he was not worried, as he was confident that Kautilya was going to take perfect care of those needs. Kautilya was going to be his prime minister and others like Vishnu Gupta, Chitrasena, and Rama were all going to have important roles under his rule.

He reached a residential part of Pataliputra when an old woman came to him. Unlike the others he had encountered, she seemed not the least bothered by him or his bodyguards. She slowly walked up to him and looked straight into his eyes. Meanwhile, his bodyguards soon surrounded her to make sure that she was not hiding any weapon.

"So, you are Chandra Gupta, the conqueror of Magadha? Are you going to be any better than the Nandas?" she enquired.

She completely ignored the bodyguards, and it seemed like she had no fear whatsoever. Chandra Gupta looked at her face that was full of wrinkles, and she reminded him of an old woman he used to see every day on his way to school when he was a little boy. He admired her courage, was eager to answer her question, and signaled his bodyguards to step back from her.

"Yes, I am Chandra Gupta, my good woman. My intention is to follow the laws of dharma as specified in the sacred texts. I want to assure you and others that under my rule you will have a bright future. I want you to feel safe and protected. Kautilya has taught me that serving my people is serving the Almighty," replied Chandra Gupta with utmost sincerity.

The old woman was pleasantly surprised. She could not remember the last time anyone from the royal establishment had even mentioned dharma to her. Here was a young warrior who cared about dharma just a few hours after conquering Magadha. He was handsome, had a pleasant outlook, and above all had a presence that made everyone around him feel secure. Right at that moment, her skepticism gave way to respect. She folded her palms together and bowed.

"Your Highness, what you just said is music to my ears. May I humbly request that you make a proclamation and invite people to the city center tomorrow just to repeat what you just told me? That will win their hearts instantly," she said politely.

Chandra Gupta thought that her suggestion was an excellent one and agreed with her.

"I will do just that, good woman. Now go home and be rest assured that better days are ahead," he declared and went back to the palace to meet Kautilya.

As he rode back to the palace, he saw many dead soldiers with bloodstains on the streets. He also saw many doctors helping wounded soldiers. There were cleaners who were washing the streets and moving dead bodies to carts that were to take them to crematoriums. Kautilya wanted to make sure that each of the dead soldiers received proper funeral services. After all, dharma specified that what happens to one's soul after departing from the material world was something only the Lord would decide. The only thing that was possible in the material world was to ensure that the loved ones had a proper closure irrespective of what sort of life the departed soul had led. Even the Nandas deserved a proper cremation.

Nothing he saw bothered Chandra Gupta. The misery and gore were soon going to be distant memory. He was determined to maintain peace and prosperity for his subjects. In his mind, the gore and misery he had just witnessed was a small price to pay for that.

When Chandra Gupta walked back into the palace, he was surprised to see that things were organized and orderly with his men already positioned at key locations. Kautilya had collectively rounded up Nanda loyalists, and Chandra Gupta's men had taken over the security of the palace.

Kautilya was having a meeting with Chitrasena, Vishnu Gupta and others when Chandra Gupta walked in. They all got up and bowed to him as he entered the hall.

"Chandra Gupta, this is the last time I will address you by your name," said Kautilya. "Soon your coronation will take place. The coronation will declare you as Chandra Gupta Maurya - the king of Magadha. From then on, we will only address you as *Your Highness*."

"Remember Kautilya, even after the coronation you are my teacher. One thing I have been taught is to always hold my teachers at the highest esteem," replied Chandra Gupta as he sat next to Kautilya.

"Let us start planning our next steps. What are the important things that we need to do next?" Chandra Gupta looked at Kautilya for an answer.

"There is an endless list, Chandra Gupta. The first important thing is to select an auspicious day for the coronation. I have already arranged for priests to come and read your horoscope to select the day and time. Once we have the day fixed, we need to get the capital decorated and ready for this important event."

"What will be the next event once the coronation is over?"

"Well, your coronation is going to be the first step in expanding the boundaries of Magadha. We will invite the surrounding kings to attend the coronation. After the coronation is over, we will have a meeting and give them a choice: become a satrapy of Magadha or face the mighty Magadhan army. We will spend the next twelve months consolidating power all along the plains of Ganges."

Chandra Gupta liked it. He was not going to be satisfied until the entire Aryavarta was under his rule. Although Kautilya never explicitly talked to him about the Yavana occupation of the Land of Five Rivers, he knew from his instincts that Kautilya was eager to get rid of the Yavana rule.

"Yes, once we do that we will march towards the Land of Five Rivers, and get rid of the Yavanas," Chandra Gupta added in a matter of fact way.

Kautilya looked at him to gauge his seriousness and could instantly see the burning desire in his eyes to rule the entire continent that stretched from the Himalayas to the tip of the land and from sea to sea. Kautilya was gratified to see the passion in Chandra Gupta, as he realized that the day when Aryavarta was free from the Yavana rule was not too far off.

As they were about to conclude the meeting, Chandra Gupta remembered what the old woman had recommended.

"I want a royal pronouncement asking people to gather in the market square tomorrow morning. I want to address them about the Mauryan creed," announced Chandra Gupta.

"That is a good idea. I will make arrangements for that," replied Vishnu Gupta.

The priests who came to read Chandra Gupta's horoscope gave several auspicious days for his coronation. Kautilya personally selected a day that was just one month away. This gave him time to get everything organized. First, he had to rewrite the rules for taxation as the treasury was running almost empty and needed new sources of revenue. The army was in need of reorganization as they were no more a rebel force. There was also a need to formalize Vishnu Gupta's secret service and even expand it further. All this meant intense work ahead for everyone in the inner circle. Of course, there was the additional work of getting the city ready for the coronation.

The next morning, Vishnu Gupta had arranged everything for Chandra Gupta's maiden address to his subjects. The podium was set, secret agents were in place for Chandra Gupta's safety, and there were soldiers mounted on horses for crowd control. Indeed, the market square was overflowing with people and no one could remember the last time there was such a large crowd in the square. The crowd was full of energy and anticipation as rumors had swirled about Chandra Gupta and Kautilya. Chandra Gupta is the bravest, he is the most handsome prince, Kautilya was the genius behind Chandra Gupta, and Vishnu Gupta was the secretive one and so on. Who are going to be there? Will Kautilya come with Chandra Gupta? There were many questions as the crowd eagerly waited for their new ruler to appear on the podium.

A soldier entered the podium and announced the entry of Chandra Gupta and Kautilya. The crowd went hysterical as they saw their new king. They all cheered at his appearance. Of course, their thinking was that anyone would be better than the cruel Nandas. However, would he be as good as Dharma Pal? That thought lingered in the minds of many in the crowd.

Kautilya spoke first, as a way of introducing Chandra Gupta.

"Good citizens of Magadha, we all know the misery and suffering you have been through under the cruelty of the Nandas. I want to tell you that a new era has come, and all the suffering is a distant memory. What you have in front of you is the future king of Magadha who will soon be ruling the entire continent of Aryavarta. He is Chandra Gupta Maurya, the first ruler of the Maurya dynasty that will be wedded to the laws of dharma."

That was enough to get the crowd excited.

"Long live Chandra Gupta!" the crowd bellowed.

Finally, Chandra Gupta stood up and waived the crowd to calm down. He then delivered his maiden address to his future subjects.

"My beloved citizens of Magadha, just like esteemed Kautilya spoke, the Mauryan rule will be based on the laws of dharma where dharma will reign supreme. I cannot promise rain and harvest every year, nor can I promise you that mother Ganges will not flood the city of Pataliputra. However, I will promise you that under my rule there will be peace and prosperity, and there will be no place for tyranny. We will reestablish dharma in all corners of Aryavarta."

When the crowd heard Chandra Gupta, they shouted in unison as his promise deeply touched their feelings.

"Chandra Gupta, we are with you forever!"

Kautilya, after arranging for several key administrative tasks that afternoon, left the palace to go towards the northern side of the city. That was where the cremation of the dead soldiers from the war was taking place. There were literally thousands of dead bodies and the priests were busy cremating them as the families offered the last rites. There were women and children sobbing uncontrollably. The misery and pain on their faces was obvious as they were now orphans with no one to support them. As he watched the scene with flames burning ferociously, Kautilya was unable to control his feelings. He felt sick all over his body and wondered about the whole purpose of his mission. He could not stay there anymore and forgot about the very purpose of his visit - he had come there to provide some solace to the families and offer them financial help from the treasury. He mounted his horse and rode eastward along the mighty Ganges. He had traveled for several hours when he decided to stop underneath a banyan tree. He tied his horse to one of the trunks supporting the tree and sat on a small stone bench. It was one of several stone benches erected by some ancient king to help travelers like him. He sat there, tired and wondering about the whole purpose of it all. Of course, he knew the answers, but the doubts kept lingering in his head. It was as if a torrential rain of emotions was constantly drenching him. It was a feeling he had never felt before. It was the thought of those children growing fatherless that had completely upset him. Kautilya remembered the closeness he felt towards his father as a child growing up in Taxila, and could not control the downward spiraling of emotions.

Soon Kautilya was sleeping on the stone bench as he was very tired. He had been sleeping like that for almost an hour when a strong breeze woke him up. The fluttering leaves in the breeze made a constant noise that sounded like the beating of drums. He woke up, sat on the bench, and looked towards the river when he noticed that there was another traveler sitting on a different bench not too far from him. He immediately knew who it was. He had encountered the same old man every time he was in angst. The old man smiled at him.

"You seem troubled again, Kautilya," asked the old man.

"You always know what is going on in my head. It is the plight of the children. I understand that it is an inevitable part of war. Indeed, I also know that this war was for the reestablishment of dharma. Still I am troubled," replied Kautilya.

"Kautilya, for a man of your intelligence, I am surprised that you have not thought of an answer."

"What do you mean?"

"This was a necessary war. You were just doing the Lord's work, getting rid of those who went against the basic tenets of dharma. As far as children are concerned, give them a gift no one can ever take away from them. Give them the gift of knowledge – there is no gift better than that. Build schools that will take care of these children," the old man explained.

It seemed perfectly logical to Kautilya. He felt reenergized, was eager to go back, and set some money from the treasury just for that purpose. He looked up to thank the old man, but all he saw was an empty bench.

The next few weeks were extremely busy for Kautilya as he spent time with Chandra Gupta organizing the military and treasury. They had decided to divide the army into five units. There was the central command that was part of Pataliputra, and the other four commands were to be in four large forts in the west, north, south, and east. Chitrasena was to be the commander of the central forces while Kumara was to lead the northern forces. Young warriors who had fared very well in their attacks on the Nandas led the other forces. Vishnu Gupta and Kautilya chose these young men after a thorough check on their loyalties. Rama became the treasurer, and Mahendra became the chief tax collector. Kautilya abolished taxes that were unfair or unwise. He also made sure that merchants who owed past taxes paid their share by removing penalties for late taxes. His goal was to establish a tax regime that was fair so that people would not cheat on their dues. To ensure this, Mahendra and Vishnu Gupta established a branch of the secret service that reported on cheating merchants.

It was now time to decide on the list of attendees for the coronation. Vishnu Gupta had a list based on those who had helped them in the months of preparations trying to overcome the Nandas. So did Mahendra and Rama, while Chitrasena had a list based on merit. He wanted to invite those warriors who had done the best in the battlefield. He was going to use the same list for promoting the warriors to important positions in the Mauryan army. Kautilya took the entire list and combined it so that it was reasonable in size to manage. Vishnu Gupta and he then sat down with Chandra Gupta and Chitrasena to discuss another list he had in mind.

"Chandra Gupta, we need to invite the surrounding kings to the coronation. There are eight of them, and we want to invite all of them."

Chandra Gupta knew very well that Kautilya had a particular agenda in bringing up that list. He looked at Kautilya, wanting to know more.

"We will send them a special invitation. We will select some of our brave warriors and ask them to personally deliver the invitation," explained Kautilya.

"What will that invitation say?" Chitrasena asked, curious about Kautilya's plan.

"They are invited to attend the coronation as new partners in the Mauryan kingdom. By accepting the invitation, they cease to exist as independent kings but become satrapies of the Mauryan Empire. If they refuse, they will have to deal with the might of the Mauryan army," added Kautilya.

It sounded perfectly logical to everyone in the room. Vishnu Gupta had already prepared a file on each of those eight kings. His expectation was that at least four of them should accept the proposal without any hesitation. He expected some resistance, perhaps a military resistance from the remaining.

"Are we prepared to wage wars against these kings, if they refuse to accept?" asked Chandra Gupta.

"We are, Chandra Gupta. We do not believe that all of them will refuse. At least half of them should join Magadha. We have an army that is too big for our kingdom. We need to expand to maintain such a large army," replied Kautilya.

139

Chandra Gupta was satisfied and gave a go ahead to the plan. Eight warriors were sent to the surrounding kingdoms to deliver Kautilya's message.

The coronation day finally arrived, and the entire city of Pataliputra was in a festive mood. Citizens were wearing their best clothes and were eagerly waiting for the procession that would bring Chandra Gupta after the ceremonies. Skilled artisans had repaired the damages to the buildings and palaces from the battle. There were colorful decorations on the streets and buildings to celebrate the event. People had decorated streets with garlands of flowers and mango leaves. There was music played by visiting artists on street corners to augment the festive mood. Priests were busy building a large fire for the sacred homa. The palace decoration was impeccable, and the goldsmiths had prepared a large golden throne. The new throne was created by melting the older throne where the elder Nanda sat and adding many more diamonds, and gems to make a new design. Kautilya had personally supervised and approved the design. There was also a new golden crown studded with diamonds created to fit Chandra Gupta's head. True to the name of his Empire, a peacock feather was at the top of the crown.

The priests started the sacred chanting at the right moment, and the homa started with all the royal pomp and circumstance that made the occasion glorious yet sacred. The homa was for the prosperity of the Mauryan dynasty and for the prosperity of the people of Magadha. The entire aristocracy of Magadha was there as well as six of the surrounding kings. They were no longer independent kings, but satrapies under Chandra Gupta. They were wise enough to accept Kautilya's invitation. After the chanting and sacred hymns were completed, the chief priest took Chandra Gupta and placed him on the throne. He then took the crown, blessed it with the holy water from River Ganges, and placed it on his head as the other priests continued to chant the sacred verses from the Vedas.

Chandra Gupta stood up and started walking towards the palace front door to join the procession that was waiting for him. Chandra Gupta looked even taller wearing the new crown. There were hundreds of elephants and horses in front of the procession. There was also a brand new chariot for Chandra Gupta to ride. Instead, he chose his white horse, jumped on it, took his crown into his hand, and commanded the procession to proceed. As the procession progressed with artists performing entertainment in the front of the procession, Chandra Gupta smiled and waved at his new subjects. The Empire finally had a crowned monarch committed to dharma.

Chapter 12

The Western Expedition

It had been only a few months since the coronation of Chandra Gupta Maurya. Kautilya and he were busy incorporating the adjacent kingdoms to the Mauryan Empire. The kings were now satrapies, and their loyalists were part of the Mauryan army. To make sure that the satrapies would continue to be loyal to the emperor and would not fancy any misadventure against the Empire, Kautilya had shuffled the satrapies; kings who were ruling kingdoms in the south became satrapies in the west, and kings from the west became satrapies in the south. Even the generals of the incorporated kingdoms were shifted to Pataliputra so that Mauryan agents could keep a close watch on them.

Of course, there was the question of the two kingdoms that had refused to accept Mauryan supremacy. One of them was the kingdom of Vanga, which was a small kingdom to the east, around three hundred miles from Pataliputra. The other one was the kingdom of Karnataka to the south, which was almost a thousand miles from Pataliputra. As the new monarch, Chandra Gupta was not pleased with this. Although, everyone now referred to him as the Emperor of the Mauryan Empire, he was not pleased that the two belligerent kings had refused to surrender, thus limiting his ambition of extending his Empire from sea to sea and from the tip of the continent to the mountains of the Himalayas. Of course, there was the irritation of the Yavana rule in the western part of Aryavarta. He wanted to deal with that once the status of the two non-cooperating kingdoms was resolved. Chandra Gupta called his first meeting as the emperor with Kautilya, Vishnu Gupta, and Chitrasena to discuss exactly those issues. Chandra Gupta was sitting on his royal chair while the others sat in the chairs assigned to ministers around a large table. Chandra Gupta did not want to waste any time and went straight to the point.

"Kautilya, I have called this meeting to discuss what we are going to do about those two kingdoms that refuse to join the Mauryan Empire."

"Your Highness, we have had our agents infiltrate those kingdoms to understand what is behind their refusal. After all, both those kingdoms are small and weak," explained Kautilya. He then turned to Vishnu Gupta.

"What have we found so far, Vishnu Gupta?"

"The two kingdoms seem to be worried about their cultural identity. Vanga people are Goddess worshippers. They worship the deity of Goddess Durga. People of Karnataka follow the Jain tradition. Both are worried that if they become satrapies of the Mauryan Empire, they may not be allowed to keep their traditions," reported Vishnu Gupta.

"That is nonsense. Under the Mauryan rule, everyone is free to practice their faith. Don't they know that it is the basic tenet of my rule?"

"That is true, Your Highness. However, the kings of Karnataka and Vanga do not know that."

"So what is your suggestion, Kautilya?"

"We will send a large force of around fifty thousand men to Vanga. We will not attack their capital. We will merely surround them and ask them to submit with the assurance that we will honor their tradition. Once they are brought into the Mauryan fold, Karnataka should follow soon," explained Kautilya.

Having seen the misery a war can bring to families and children, Kautilya was not the least eager to wage wars. From now on, he was going to use a show of force reinforced with diplomacy to achieve the same goals that a military campaign yielded. Moreover, wars were expensive and taxing on the entire state. In his mind, a financially weakened state was eventually going to be sitting prey for a waiting enemy.

"That is good. I will lead that expedition," replied Chandra Gupta.

"That is a small expedition, Your Highness. I think Chitrasena can take care of the expedition. Moreover, we have an important campaign coming soon," Kautilya said, trying to convince Chandra Gupta not to lead the Vanga campaign.

Chandra Gupta knew what Kautilya was talking about, and he agreed that Chitrasena should lead the Vanga campaign.

The Vanga campaign went exactly as Kautilya had planned. There was no bloodshed as the king of Vanga, facing the mighty Mauryan force, agreed to become a satrapy of the Mauryan Empire. He saw the wisdom of not fighting, and the offer of keeping their tradition as they pleased finally swayed him to submit to Mauryan supremacy. The news of the Vanga surrender traveled fast to Karnataka, and the Jain king of Karnataka too was eager to make peace with Chandra Gupta.

When Kautilya heard this, he was not surprised. He remarked to Chandra Gupta something that became a nugget of wisdom for the future generations.

"Your Highness, the fragrance of flowers spreads only in the direction of the wind. However, the goodness of a person spreads in all directions."

Indeed, Chandra Gupta was genuinely good. In exchange for the peace offer, Chandra Gupta asked the king of Karnataka, who was now his satrapy, to send a Jain scholar to his court with the intention of having a balanced representation of all faiths.

Less than twelve months after taking over Pataliputra, the Mauryan Empire stretched from the tip of the Indian continent to the Himalayas and from sea to sea. The only land that was not under the control of Chandra Gupta Maurya was the western part of Aryavarta, which included the Land of Five Rivers. It was still under the rule of Stallios. A lot had changed in the Yavana power structure since Kautilya had left Taxila. However, Stallios was a smart man and had become a satrapy under the rule of Seleucus, who had served as a general directly under Alexander the Great. Alexander had died only a few months back, and Seleucus now ruled the eastern part of his Empire. Seleucus ruled the territory that included Persia, Bactria, and western Aryavarta.

It was a routine Mauryan court session that Chandra Gupta conducted to let his citizens meet and appeal their concerns directly to him. This was something that Kautilya had encouraged him to do, as he believed that even the king could learn something important from a common citizen. Moreover, Kautilya always felt that it is important for the king to display his power to reinforce his control over the kingdom.

"Are these sessions really necessary, Kautilya?" Chandra Gupta often questioned.

"Your Highness, they are not only necessary, they are your duty. Remember, you are the first servant of dharma. As protector of dharma, you need to show your wisdom as one who is energetic about the tenets of dharma."

"What do you mean, Kautilya?"

"Your Highness, everything you do should radiate dharmic values. When a king is energetic about dharma, his subjects will be equally energetic. His subjects will love him and his enemies will think twice before attacking him. If a king is reckless, so will his subjects be, and he will easily fall into the hands of his enemy. Besides, it is an opportunity for Your Highness to be ever awake and aware of what is going on in the Empire," explained Kautilya.

During these court sessions, common citizens could directly approach the emperor and ask for favors or speak about matters that troubled them. The screenings of citizens for security purposes was mandatory and were subject to a friendly interrogation by a trusted minister to ensure that they brought questions or issues that were really worth the emperor's attention.

The court session was in full operation with Chandra Gupta surrounded by his counselors. The golden throne studded with diamonds and gems signified Mauryan might. The royal court was brimming with several representatives from the surrounding vassal states. It seemed that the entire aristocracy of Pataliputra was in the court.

A citizen who appeared to be a well-to-do merchant entered the court with permission to speak to the emperor. He was tall, well built, and his attire suggested that he was a wealthy man. His clothes were of the finest silk, and he was wearing many ornaments of gold with gems and diamonds embedded in them.

"Your Highness, I am a man who is committed to dharma, and I always conduct my trade according to the laws of dharma," he began.

"In my years as a trader, I have traveled all across Aryavarta and beyond, reaching as far as Bactria and Persia. What pains me in these journeys is the fact that part of Aryavarta is still under the Yavana occupation."

"How does that pain you, merchant? Can you elaborate it to the people in the court?" asked Chandra Gupta.

145

"Your Highness, whenever I am inside the Mauryan realm I can see and feel dharma, which makes me happy and content. The moment I enter the Yavana realm, all I see is greed and violence. There is no peace, and what I see is never ending warfare for no rhyme or reason. It makes me sad that dharma is an enslaved woman in our own land - the western part of Aryavarta. Can you not do something about that?"

Everyone in the court was touched by the merchant's monologue. It brought back bad memories for Kautilya and made him think about the real reason he had started his long journey out of Taxila.

"What do you want the emperor to do, my good man?" asked Chandra Gupta.

The rich merchant hesitated for a minute not knowing exactly how to respond to that question. After a moment of silence, he spoke softly trying to explain what was in his mind, "I know it is not my place or function to advise the emperor about the affairs of the state. However, I am speaking for thousands and thousands of followers of dharma who would want the emperor to cleanse the western end of Aryavarta. Your Highness, may I beg you to free the land for dharma's sake?"

The passionate appeal made by the merchant had an effect on Chandra Gupta. Indeed, the thought of the western end of Aryavarta under the control of Yavanas had continued to be a nuisance in his mind. He also knew that Kautilya was still waiting for the right opportunity to make a military move against the Yavanas.

"Well spoken, my good merchant. I assure you that someday we will have the entire Aryavarta liberated and dharma will flourish all over the continent," replied Chandra Gupta.

During the next royal meeting, everyone knew what was going on in Chandra Gupta's mind. Vishnu Gupta, anticipating the questions from Chandra Gupta and Kautilya, had collected detailed intelligence about the Yavana occupation in the Land of Five Rivers.

"You all know what is at the top of my mind these days. What are we going to do about that?" Chandra Gupta thus began the meeting.

"We are going to start a major expedition. I will not be satisfied until the entire Aryavarta is under Maurya control," he added without any hesitation.

There was a moment of silence as he went around the room, looking for ideas from his counselors.

Kautilya spoke first. Obviously, he had gone through mental simulations of that expedition thousands of times. He knew all the strengths and weaknesses of the Yavanas. He also knew the hurdles that they faced in a direct onslaught of the Yavanas. "First, we need to assess what we are up against. Vishnu Gupta, can you update us on the Yavana rule in western Aryavarta?"

"There have been a lot of changes in the last few years. Alexander the Great died in Mesopotamia after a major injury in a battle in lower Aryavarta. His generals partitioned the Empire with Seleucus ruling the eastern part, including the Land of Five Rivers," explained Vishnu Gupta.

"What other changes have taken place?" asked Chandra Gupta.

"Well, the general who was in charge of Taxila is now the satrapy of the Land of Five Rivers. His name is Stallios," added Vishnu Gupta.

Despite his efforts to conceal his feelings, Kautilya's face turned red when he heard that name.

"What about their military might? How is it these days?" asked Chitrasena.

"They are very powerful. Stallios has an army of almost one hundred thousand men under his control, not to mention thousands of elephants and chariots. There are also the reinforcements he can get from Seleucus who rules from Mesopotamia. Our agents tell me that Seleucus has an army of more than two hundred thousand men," Vishnu Gupta explained.

Chandra Gupta and Kautilya listened carefully to all the details. Nothing Vishnu Gupta mentioned bothered them, as the Mauryan army now numbered more than five hundred thousand soldiers. However, Kautilya was reluctant to start a major campaign since it was going to cost an enormous amount of money to the treasury.

"A successful military campaign could last three to four months. In the event Seleucus decides to come to his satrapy's rescue, it could require three hundred thousand soldiers from our side. When we add thousands of elephants and chariots needed for the campaign, we cannot even begin to calculate what it will cost the treasury," observed Kautilya.

Chandra Gupta understood Kautilya's hesitation in starting a major military campaign. He looked at Rama for an answer. "Rama, do you have an estimate for the amount of money it is going to cost the treasury if we were to start such a campaign?"

"Your Highness, it could cost nearly ten million Panas a month. So when we add up everything, it could cost us about fifty million Panas. However, once victorious, we can recoup more than twice that in just one year from all the additional revenue we will get from the Land of Five Rivers," replied Rama.

Chandra Gupta got up and started pacing up and down the hall. On one hand, he was eager to free the whole of Aryavarta from the Yavana rule as soon as possible. He felt that his job was unfinished until he accomplished that. On the other hand, he did not want to do anything reckless. Kautilya could read his mind and offered some more factors to consider.

"Your Highness, as you know, a weakened treasury could be an invitation for our enemies to attack us. Furthermore, we cannot even begin to put a material value for the men who will die in the campaign."

"So what do you suggest Kautilya?" Chandra Gupta knew that he could rely on him for the best advice. No doubt, deep inside Kautilya was eager to rid the Yavanas more than anyone else in the room.

"Your Highness, my suggestion is to use the diplomatic path and see if that works. I really doubt that we will be successful diplomatically, but at least it gives us some time to prepare for a military campaign. Meanwhile, Vishnu Gupta's agents will be in an intense intelligence-gathering mode and find out everything we need to know for the military campaign. I suggest that we send Shiva as our ambassador to the satrapy asking him to accept Mauryan supremacy. We will give an explicit message that if he refuses he will have to face the Mauryan military might," replied Kautilya.

"All right, I am in agreement with that. Let us send Shiva, and meanwhile I want to know everything about their military. Their strengths, their weaknesses, how committed is Seleucus to his satrapy, and what is the best place for a battle if we chose to go that path," commanded Chandra Gupta.

While Shiva was on his mission, Kautilya, Chandra Gupta and Chitrasena were busy planning the military campaign. Because of the planned absence, Kautilya wanted to ensure that a trusted viceroy would be in charge of Pataliputra. They had concluded that Kumara was the right person for that purpose because of his unquestionable loyalty to dharma and Chandra Gupta. Kautilya had devised a strategy that involved a three-stage attack on the Yavanas. At first, a weaker force with Chandra Gupta's double was to lure the Yavanas deeper into the Mauryan side. At that time, a strong reinforcement with Chitrasena as its commander was going to intercept them as a second step. Kautilya, not satisfied with that plan, wanted to add one more element of surprise in the battle plans. He had chosen a battlefield on the east side of river Indus that was open and large, but at the same time secluded because of large vegetation to the north. Just like Alexander the Great, Seleucus was bound to cross the river to attack the Mauryan army. The large vegetation to the north allowed Chandra Gupta to cross the river to the other side to disrupt the supply lines of the Yavana forces. He could also use the same bridges built by the Yavanas to sandwich them between the forces led by Chandra Gupta and Chitrasena.

Chandra Gupta and Chitrasena liked Kautilya's plan, and it was now a matter of deciding on the size of the army for the expedition. As expected, Shiva got a haughty reply from Stallios mocking the Mauryan might as a military illusion. Kautilya was pleased to hear that as he always believed that an overconfident enemy was the best enemy to face. The agents were successful in getting all the military details Chandra Gupta wanted. They had even intercepted an exchange of messages between Seleucus and his satrapy. Indeed, Seleucus was furious when he heard that Chandra Gupta was planning to invade the Land of Five Rivers. He was not willing to lose that territory, as it was the richest land under his control.

Vishnu Gupta had requested an urgent meeting with the emperor to report the latest intelligence he had gathered from western Aryavarta. He was worried that if the Mauryan forces did not invade on time, Seleucus would fortify his forces significantly; it might be very difficult to dislodge the Yavanas from the plains of five rivers. As it was an impromptu meeting, only Chandra Gupta and Kautilya attended the meeting.

"Your Highness," Vishnu Gupta addressed Chandra Gupta, "I am very concerned that Seleucus is preparing for a massive build up on the banks of river Indus. If we delay our expedition any further, we may have a very difficult time dislodging the Yavanas from Aryavarta."

"What exactly is the information you received that bothers you so much?" asked Chandra Gupta.

"Well, Your Highness, we believe that he is preparing for a six month expedition," explained Vishnu Gupta with a worried look on his face. "He is bringing a force of one hundred thousand troops from Persia to reinforce his satrapy. We also know that he will be bringing at least one thousand elephants."

"What is your assessment, Kautilya?" Chandra Gupta replied, turning to Kautilya who had been quiet until then.

"Your Highness, I do not think we need to panic. The next three months are rainy months, and there is no point in starting the expedition now," continued Kautilya, "Moreover that gives us enough time to plan our expedition. I will stay with our original plan of invading his territory in the early months of winter."

"That is good. Let us accelerate our preparations and launch our expedition right after the rainy season. Do we need anything else from Vishnu Gupta?" Chandra Gupta seemed to be confident and looked at Kautilya for suggestions on last minute intelligence.

"Yes, there are a couple of things. Vishnu Gupta, I want you to gather everything about the Yavana preparations. In addition, you need to get two or three doubles for Chandra Gupta who will accompany us to the war."

The next three months were quiet but intense preparations for the war. Kautilya had made every arrangement in Pataliputra to ensure that there was not going to be any subversion during Chandra Gupta's long absence. Vishnu Gupta's agents had compiled a list of potential rivals to Chandra Gupta, all of who were assigned positions in the expedition. A large force of about one hundred fifty thousand men with thousands of elephants and chariots left Pataliputra with much fanfare.

Chandra Gupta gave the soldiers his speech on liberating Aryavarta from the clutches of Yavanas. His speech was always inspirational as he was now adept in linking his expeditions to the duty of dharma.

"Men, we are embarking on the most important mission of our lives. The battle that awaits us is nothing but a war of dharma," he proclaimed sincerely. "The enemy is strong and motivated," he continued, "However, dharma is on our side, and we shall triumph for dharma is always victorious in the end."

His men could see his zeal and his conviction. They were ready to do anything for dharma. After all, in their minds they were warriors ordained by the Lord Himself to protect dharma. They all cheered Chandra Gupta. At that time, he turned his horse around and galloped forward when he came behind a large elephant that allowed him to exchange his horse with that of his double who was waiting for him. Chitrasena and Chandra Gupta's double continued to lead the force.

Several days later, Chandra Gupta, along with a force of almost sixty thousand cavalry men mounted on fast horses, took a northern route. They had many war machines with them, like catapults that threw rocks at astonishing rates. They traveled mostly during the nights so as not to attract too much attention. While Kautilya accompanied the first force, Vishnu Gupta accompanied the second force.

Seleucus was also feverishly preparing for the war. Of course, he was also continuously receiving intelligence about the Mauryan forces. When he heard that Chandra Gupta was marching towards western Aryavarta with a force of about one hundred fifty thousand men, he was amused at what he thought was Chandra Gupta's audacity. How could he be so sure that he can drive the mighty Seleucus from the land of Indus? Surely, he is immature in warfare. He had also brought several master bridge builders to cross the Indus, as his plan was to crush Chandra Gupta in a strategy similar to the one used by Alexander the Great.

The Mauryan forces landed five miles east of the river Indus and set up their military camp getting ready for Seleucus and his men. Meanwhile, Chandra Gupta and his men reached a place that was twenty miles north of where the Mauryan camp was, and they set up their camp not too far from the river. The two camps were in continuous communication waiting for the Yavana forces to make their move.

Seleucus arrived on the west side of the Indus eager to face Chandra Gupta and the Mauryan forces. For him Chandra Gupta was an immature ruler who was crossing an invisible line. There was, after all an unspoken understanding that for a peaceful co-existence, Chandra Gupta was to stay east of the Land of Five Rivers. Seleucus was irritated that Chandra Gupta had broken that unwritten understanding. Moreover, his adventure had drawn Seleucus away from Persia where there were other urgent matters to attend. One could see from the expression on his face that he was getting impatient to crush the Mauryan army.

Seleucus, who was with his daughter in the camp, asked the bodyguards to bring his satrap Stallios to his tent. Stallios, a short, slender man, came to his tent and greeted him with utmost respect, "Your Highness, you wanted to see me?"

He stood in front of Seleucus waiting for him to speak.

"What do we know about these Mauryan forces?" asked Seleucus. "How much intelligence do you have on them, Stallios?"

"We know all about their numbers and weaknesses, Your Highness," replied a confident Stallios.

"Do you have more details? Can you be explicit?"

"Yes, we do, Your Highness. We have more men than they do, and their soldiers are not as disciplined as ours are. Theirs is a rag tag army that is fit for a rebellion and not a major battle," Stallios boasted with confidence.

Seleucus agreed as his own intelligence officers had concluded the same about the Mauryan army. He gave his orders to Stallios.

"Have the men start building the bridge in the middle of the night. We will storm across and crush the Mauryan army," Seleucus continued. "I want you to lead the first wave, and I will be right behind you to finish the work."

Stallios grinned and saluted, as he was extremely confident that they were going to defeat Chandra Gupta, which would further expand his territory.

That night, Yavana soldiers started building large bridges over the river Indus which had receded as the rains had stopped almost two months ago. Kautilya had scouts monitoring their progress just to make sure that he had the right formation ready to receive the Yavana forces. By dawn, the bridge was ready, and Stallios charged towards the Mauryan troops. Kautilya had a weaker force in the front side to receive Stallios and his men. Chandra Gupta's double led the weaker force, and Stallios and his troops were able to make a substantial advance against this weak force. As they kept advancing deeper into Mauryan formation, Kautilya had the two flanks maneuver to encircle Stallios and his men in a semi-circle.

Seleucus, watching this from the other side of the river, soon realized that his satrapy was in danger of being sandwiched unless he went to his rescue. He immediately ordered his troops to follow him.

Meanwhile, Chandra Gupta and his men had built a bridge across the northern side and crossed to the western bank of Indus. They proceeded to march southward towards the Yavana camp. Chandra Gupta divided his troops into two sections – a small force to attack the Yavana supply lines and the large one to cross over the same bridge over which Seleucus had rushed to save his satrapy. His small force equipped with catapults completely disrupted the supply lines and soon encircled the tent that housed Seleucus's daughter who had accompanied her father on the mission. She was now a Mauryan prisoner.

On the east side, Seleucus and Stallios kept fighting hard when an arrow struck and downed Stallios. The Yavana soldiers were dying in rapid succession as intense fighting continued. Seleucus seeing his forces surrounded on all four sides realized that he had no way out but to surrender. He signaled a general nearby to fly a white flag indicating his desire to seek peace.

Chandra Gupta ordered his troops to stop fighting as the Yavana soldiers began to drop their weapons. Chandra Gupta went towards Seleucus to demand that he surrender the entire western Aryavarta to the Mauryan control. He, however, waited for Kautilya to join him and do the treaty negotiation. Seleucus surrounded by Mauryan soldiers saw Chandra Gupta and Kautilya approaching him. Seleucus who was already impressed by Chandra Gupta's military skills was further impressed by his tall stature. He went to Chandra Gupta and offered him peace, "Chandra Gupta, as the Emperor of the eastern Greek Empire, I want to seek peace with you. There is no point in us fighting any more. Let us make a long lasting peace," Seleucus made his peace offer.

"You may be correct. I do not seek war either. However, the entire Aryavarta belongs to the Mauryan Empire. For any lasting peace, you and your troops will have to retreat from Aryavarta. I will let Kautilya do further negotiations," Chandra Gupta added.

Seleucus looked at Kautilya who looked more like tall, skinny ascetic than a royal counselor. Nevertheless, one stare from Kautilya convinced him that this was no ordinary ascetic. That deep penetrating stare which was the trademark of Kautilya, now a legend all over Magadha, signaled to Seleucus that there was going to be some hard demands from the ascetic. He waited patiently for Kautilya to spell out the Mauryan demands. Kautilya spoke in a deliberate way just to make sure that there was no ambiguity about the Mauryan demands.

"Not only that, the emperor wants the Yavanas to surrender the territories of Panjashir valley and move your troops out of the territory of northern Bactria," added Kautilya who wanted to make sure that there was a buffer zone between the Mauryan Empire and the Empire of Seleucus.

When Seleucus heard this he was irritated that Kautilya was demanding too much, but saw that he was in no position to negotiate a treaty that was favorable to him. As he was grudgingly agreeing to Kautilya's conditions, Mauryan soldiers brought his daughter Laodice in a chariot who had been a prisoner since the sacking of Seleucus's military camp. She got down from the chariot, rushed to her father, and was relieved that he was safe.

"Father, you are safe. I was so worried about your health," she commented in a worried voice as she hugged Seleucus.

She then looked at the Mauryan nobility that had surrounded her father. It was as if it was her destiny - all she could see was Chandra Gupta. Everyone else seemed like an irrelevant blur. She saw in Chandra Gupta an extremely handsome emperor and her heart started beating fast as if she knew what was about to happen. Even though she tried to look away from him, she was unable to do so as if a spell was binding her to stare at him. She knew she was instantly in love with him, and she blushed realizing the sweet feeling of being in love with a young emperor. It was as if it was a destiny blessed by the gods as Chandra Gupta had similar feelings towards her, and he could not take his eyes away from her.

Kautilya immediately realized that Chandra Gupta and Laodice were in love and proposed that Seleucus seal the treaty by marrying his daughter to the Mauryan Emperor. In return, Seleucus was to receive five hundred war elephants as a gift from Chandra Gupta. It was Kautilya's idea to make sure that Seleucus was not tempted to cause any more hostilities in the future. Seleucus turned to his daughter and asked for her opinion.

"Are you in agreement with that proposal, my dear Laodice?" he asked his daughter.

Laodice was too shy to reply but nodded her head in full agreement. Kautilya himself performed the sacred wedding ceremony as an ordained Vedic priest. Soon, Seleucus and his generals left Aryavarta with five hundred elephants as wedding gifts while Chandra Gupta returned to Pataliputra with his new wife, and his victorious army. A lavish royal wedding ceremony was to take place in a later day in Pataliputra.

Kautilya, however, decided to remain in the Land of Five Rivers along with Chitrasena and Vishnu Gupta. A small Mauryan force stayed behind to secure the remaining forts and cities.

"Chitrasena, it is time for us to visit each fort in the Indus plains to ensure continuous subservience to the Mauryan might," commented Kautilya.

"How do we do that, Kautilya?" enquired Vishnu Gupta.

"We shall appoint commanders of the forts to the Mauryan court. Let us move the leaders to Pataliputra and appoint them to important positions. At the same time, Mauryan loyalists will take over the forts as viceroys of the Empire," explained Kautilya.

"We will do that, Kautilya. An enemy is like a weed that needs removal from its very roots," said Vishnu Gupta.

In the next few months, while Chitrasena and Vishnu Gupta visited each fort from Indus to Bactria to ensure Mauryan loyalty, it was time for Kautilya to visit his beloved school in Taxila. He decided to go alone to his school and meet his pupils. When he reached the school, he stopped his horse and took a long look at the main building. He was pleased that the school was intact, and that the garden was in a good condition. As he sat on his horse staring at the school, his eyes got moist with a torrent of nostalgic feelings about the early school years. Bhima Sen, who had just stepped outside the main building, recognized Kautilya, and came rushing to receive him. He helped Kautilya to get down from the horse as they both stared at each other. Then without saying anything, Kautilya hugged the caretaker, and they both walked into the school.

The students were ecstatic to see their teacher back at the school. Many of them assumed that he was back for good. They wanted to know everything, how he had reached Pataliputra, how the Nandas were overthrown, and how the Yavanas were defeated. They wanted to know about Chandra Gupta. Was Chandra Gupta the greatest ruler Aryavarta has ever seen? How grand was Pataliputra?

Kautilya patiently answered all the questions and enquired about their studies. He was pleased that Vasudeva and Mukunda were now accomplished scholars who were doing a very good job running the school. After a while, Kautilya decided to walk to the garden for a small break. He sat on his favorite boulder and recalled the day he had decided to leave the school. As he sat on the boulder enjoying the mild breeze, Mukunda joined him.

"Sir, may I ask you something?" Mukunda said in a polite manner.

Kautilya nodded his head to go ahead with his question.

"Now that the Yavanas have left, and the entire Aryavarta is under dharma, are you satisfied?"

"Of course I am satisfied, Mukunda. If the Yavanas had gotten pow-erful and occupied Magadha, dharma would have disappeared forever," replied Kautilya.

Mukunda thought about the answer, and there was a long silence as neither of them said anything.

"Sir, was it all worth it in the end? The wars and the battles?" asked Mukunda.

Kautilya thought about the question. The deeper he pondered, the more difficulty he had in finding the right answer. Mukunda, realizing that Kautilya was struggling for the right answer, wondered if he had overstepped his bounds.

"Sir, I know you are not going to stay here. I want to come with you to Pataliputra," Mukunda added trying to change the topic.

Kautilya thought about that request and had no problem with Mukunda coming to Pataliputra. Indeed, he was looking for some one who would document his thoughts about affairs of the state. He wanted to call that work *Artha Shastra* and even wanted Vishnu Gupta to contribute to run-ning the secret service organization.

"That is all right with me. You can come with me to Pataliputra. I may even give you a project," answered Kautilya.

Mukunda's face lit up. He was so happy that his grin seemed to stretch from ear to ear, and he ran back to the school.

Kautilya closed his eyes trying to find an answer to Mukunda's question – was it all worth the efforts? He failed to come up with a satisfactory answer, opened his eyes, and rubbed his face in frustration. He was surprised to see that the old man was standing a few feet away right in front of him. It was as if he always knew when Kautilya was struggling for answers.

"You did not answer your pupil. Was it all worth the efforts in the end, Kautilya?" the old man repeated the question.

"I do not know old man. I cannot seem to find an answer,"

"Of course it was. Were you not doing the Lord's work? Destroying enemies of dharma and reestablishing dharma?"

"I suppose so. But, what about the thousands of young men who sacrificed their lives?" asked Kautilya.

"Think about the lives that were saved. Without these battles, thousands more would have perished. As long as you are convinced about that, it was all worth the effort – for the sake of dharma," replied the old man.

Kautilya was happy with that explanation just when Mukunda came out of the main building to tell him that the dinner was ready.

"I will be with you in a minute, Mukunda," Kautilya replied.

He then turned towards the old man to thank him but saw no trace of him. As always, he had vanished without any trace.

Meanwhile, Chitrasena and Vishnu Gupta were busy visiting all the forts in the new territories added to the Mauryan Empire. They received warm welcome wherever they went and had no problem carrying out exactly what Kautilya had suggested. That was until they reached a small fort called Gandharapuri. Chitrasena and Vishnu Gupta were surprised to see that the fort was not flying the Mauryan flag. In fact, the fort was flying no flag at all. Chitrasena sent a group of soldiers to go inside the fort and find out what was gong on.

When they came back and reported their findings, Vishnu Gupta was very perturbed.

"What is their reason for not flying the Mauryan flag?" questioned Chitrasena.

"They say that they mean no harm, but they are a community that does not belong to any one. It is a community, which has Aryas, Yavanas, and even Persians. They claim they are peaceful and want to be left alone," explained the soldier.

Vishnu Gupta did not like that at all. In his mind, any refusal to submit to the Mauryan authority was unacceptable and deserved a harsh treatment.

"Go and tell them that they have exactly ten minutes to fly the Mauryan flag. If they refuse to do that, tell them that we will attack them immediately," Vishnu Gupta gave his answer to the soldier without even waiting for Chitrasena's consent. Although Chitrasena felt that it was an unnecessary fight, he agreed to go along with Vishnu Gupta.

As expected, the fort leader refused to fly the Mauryan flag and decided to fight. Chitrasena ordered a small contingent of his forces to attack the fort. What followed was a ruthless attack that made the earlier battle between Chandra Gupta and Seleucus almost look civilized.

Part 2
Manu

Chapter 13
Chitrasena and Savithri

It was several months after the end of the western expedition. Finally, both Kautilya and Chandra Gupta had a sense of accomplishment. For Kautilya, his favorite Land of Five Rivers was free of Yavana rule while for Chandra Gupta, he had finally established the Empire from coast to coast and from the tip of the continent to the highest mountains just as he had always dreamed. More importantly for him, it was an Empire built on the laws of dharma, and as long as he lived, dharma was to rule supreme in his Empire.

There was peace and prosperity all over the Empire and commerce flourished. Kautilya and Vishnu Gupta had built a web of intelligence agents that blanketed the entire Empire and kept a close watch on every potential threat to the state. Kautilya had spent a few months after the western expedition streamlining the bureaucracy. He had set several new departments to manage tax collection, land distribution, and agricultural activities. He had set up a council of learned men to draw the new laws that were true to the spirit of dharma. He did not neglect the military area either and had set up a separate department that was responsible for evaluating and managing procurement of weapons for the military.

As far as the military itself, Chandra Gupta was the commander-in-chief. Chandra Gupta at the suggestion of Kautilya reorganized his forces into five commands and anointed Chitrasena as *Senapati*, or chief general, in charge of all the forces. However, Chitrasena had to stay back for several months in western Aryavarta to ensure that all the forts were under complete Mauryan control and a western command of the Mauryan forces was established. For Kautilya and Chandra Gupta, this was the most important command, as they very well knew that future threats were likely to come from the west, which had narrow mountain passes that made it easy for invaders to enter Aryavarta. Therefore, Chitrasena's long absence from Pataliputra was acceptable to both Kautilya and Chandra Gupta. Indeed, Kautilya himself made several visits to western edges of the Empire to monitor the progress made in reinforcing that part of the Empire.

Although Chitrasena was still absent from the capital for several months, Kautilya had made proper arrangements for his wife Savithri and son Manu to settle down in a lavish house fit for the top general not too far from the palace complex. The mansion, exquisitely decorated, was big enough to house several families, and there were several servants and workers to assist Savithri in the day-to-day management of the mansion. However, for Savithri, this did not make her happy as she was extremely worried about Chitrasena's well being. His long absence from Pataliputra bothered her so much that there was never a moment when she was not worried about his safety. Furthermore, the ugly rumors she had heard about him made her extremely tense. When Chitrasena did come back to Pataliputra to assume the position of chief general no one was happier than she was. She hoped that the rumors would die, and she could go back to caring for Manu and Chitrasena.

To her dismay, the ugly rumors kept circulating, now with a different twist. All the pomp and glitter that surrounded her as the wife of the most important general meant nothing to her. Indeed, she could not bear that burden any more. She kept praying to Goddess Shakti to give her strength to face what was obviously the most difficult time in her life. Even the times when they were on the run from the Nandas living on meager means seemed like a picnic to her.

It was just another spring day in Pataliputra, and Savithri went through the day wondering what the purpose of her life was. Should she confront Chitrasena and ask him directly about the rumors? Would that only drive her husband away from her? Perhaps that was the only choice left to her. That night, before she went to bed, she decided to bring her frustration into the open. She knew Chitrasena was a man of dharma and was not going to do anything to hurt her or Manu. Yet the ugly rumors kept circulating that made her lose sleep for weeks. She had to find the underlying cause of the rumors.

"Chitrasena, I hope I am not overstepping my limits to talk to you about these ugly rumors I hear," she began awkwardly.

Chitrasena knew what was bothering her. Indeed, he was ashamed of what had happened and had made a commitment that he was going to be free of the temptation that had driven him to do just that. He felt awkward as well and did not know how to answer her. Finally, after a long silence, he mustered enough strength to address her question.

"Savithri, I know exactly what those rumors are. Before we discuss that, I want to tell you that I have always loved you, and I will love you till the day I die," replied Chitrasena.

His reply brought tears to Savithri, and she did not know why she was really in tears. Was it the fact that he was reaffirming his love to her or was it the fact that he was indirectly admitting that the rumors were true? Seeing her in tears made Chitrasena extremely emotional and even ashamed. He felt like he had broken the first rule of dharma – not to hurt anyone, especially the ones he loved. He held her soft hands and tried to console her.

"I was lonely and overcome by desire. Please forgive me for breaking the sacred trust. It is only better if we do not go into all the details. All I can tell you is that it is over, and I promise you that I will do anything that will make you happy," added Chitrasena.

Savithri stayed on the bed and kept sobbing, not knowing what to say as Chitrasena sat at the edge trying to console her. He was sensitive enough to know that anything he said now could only hurt her further and kept quiet. It was as if there was an invisible ravine between them, and the long silence made it seem like it was getting wider by the minute. However, Savithri was a woman of strength and conviction and was thinking hard to find a solution to their divide.

"So she is in Pataliputra now?" she asked Chitrasena.

"I understand so. I mean, I have been told so," he replied.

"You mean to say that you have not seen her in Pataliputra?"

163

"I have not seen her since coming back, nor do I want to see her. I do not want to do anything to hurt you any more." Chitrasena replied looking into her eyes as if begging for her forgiveness.

Savithri sat there with her head down not knowing what to say. She had never been so angry with him and kept wondering if he was telling the truth. When she finally looked up, all she could see was a foggy image of her husband, reflecting how her mind felt: confused and foggy, not knowing what to say or do next. She slowly wiped her tears and looked into Chitrasena's eyes; she was somehow convinced that he had indeed stopped seeing the other woman. She felt enormously relieved as if she had found something she thought she had lost forever, the trust between the two of them. She did not know who the other woman was, nor did she care to find out any details about her anymore. All she wanted was to find a way to ensure that Chitrasena would never go back to her again. Suddenly, Savithri had an idea that seemed like the Goddess herself had revealed it to her.

"Chitrasena, I want us to go back to Chitrapuri. I do not want us to stay in Pataliputra anymore," she said, expecting an affirmative answer from him.

When Chitrasena heard her demand, he had mixed emotions about what to do. After all, being the top general under Chandra Gupta was the highest honor a warrior could have. Being in Pataliputra, which was the center of power in the entire Aryavarta, was everyone's dream. On the other hand, what was more important to him than his wife's happiness? If it meant that he had to give up all the power and glamour, he was willing to do it. For Savithri's happiness, nothing seemed like an unreasonable demand.

"We will do just that, Savithri. Nothing is more important to me than your happiness," assured Chitrasena.

Savithri smiled with approval, and it was as if the dark spell melted right in front of her; they fell into an embrace that felt sweeter than the first time they had embraced.

It was not easy for Chitrasena to convince Kautilya and Chandra Gupta about his decision to step down from the Senapati position and move back to Chitrapuri. He mustered enough courage the next morning and went into a meeting with Chandra Gupta and Kautilya. At the appropriate time, he announced his intention to step down from his position. Both Chandra Gupta and Kautilya were shocked to hear his intention.

"What seems to be the issue, Chitrasena? I will give you anything. Is it more money you want?" asked Chandra Gupta as Kautilya stood next to him.

"Your Highness, I am really sorry about my decision. Nothing material would make me happier than serving under you as your Senapati. It is not more money or anything material," he assured Chandra Gupta.

"Then what is bothering you so much, Chitrasena? Have you really thought about the implications of your decision? Why this sudden decision?"

"Your Highness, I have to do this for my family's happiness," he replied. He did not want to elaborate any further.

Kautilya understood what was going on. He indeed had seen reports from Vishnu Gupta about Chitrasena's recent romantic interlude. His deeper understanding of human behavior under the influence of Māya told him exactly what was going on. He decided to come to Chitrasena's rescue.

"Your Highness, the foremost dharma for a married man is to ensure his wife's happiness. If Chitrasena's move to Chitrapuri is essential for his wife's happiness, we indeed need to honor his request. That would be dharma for us," explained Kautilya.

Chandra Gupta nodded his head reluctantly and agreed with Kautilya's assessment although with a heavy heart. He could only think of all the gallant things that Chitrasena had done until now, and could have done for the Mauryan Empire.

"That is all right, Chitrasena. I will approve this, as it is my dharma to do so. We will appoint Kumara as the next Senapati, and you will be in charge of a small force that will form the northern command."

Chitrasena was relieved immensely when he heard that. He thanked both Chandra Gupta and Kautilya for their understanding, and left hurriedly to give the good news to Savithri.

Chapter 14
Manu

Chitrasena had stayed with his wife Savithri and son Manu in Pataliputra for a few more months until he was able to make all the arrangements for his move to Chitrapuri. Once the transition of his duties was completed, he had moved with Savithri and Manu to Chitrapuri. That was five years ago when Manu was only thirteen years old. In Chitrapuri, Manu had studied basic military techniques under his father, and for the last two years, he had been at the military academy in Pataliputra. It seemed like only yesterday when Manu went to Pataliputra to join the military academy. It was not just any ordinary academy - it was the prestigious *Chanakya Military Academy*. Chanakya, meaning genius, was the title bestowed on Kautilya by Chandra Gupta himself.

It was only fitting that Manu had gone to the academy to become an elite soldier ready to serve the emperor. Getting into the academy was no small feat. After all, every Kshatriya boy in the Mauryan Empire dreamt about graduating from the academy. It was a natural stepping-stone to becoming a future commander or a satrapy in a distant province. Naturally, the citizens of Chitrapuri were extremely proud of their beloved son Manu. After two years in the famous academy, Manu had graduated with the highest honors, and today was the day he was coming back to Chitrapuri. Chitrasena himself had gone to Pataliputra to bring him back to Chitrapuri. There was a large crowd that had gathered at the entrance to the city-fort to welcome Manu. Everyone in Chitrapuri was eager to see him. People of Chitrapuri loved him; after all, he was the perfect Kshatriya boy - brave, courageous, and strong - just like his father - but he also showed compassion that he had inherited from his mother. People predicted that one day Manu was going be a high commander and perhaps one day he would attain the position of Senapati just like his father had.

It was getting late, but the people of Chitrapuri did not mind waiting for Manu. It was late summer, and the temperature was more moderate and bearable. The sun was almost setting, and a cool breeze was keeping the crowd huddled in their seats. The entrance to Chitrapuri looked festive – decorated with garlands of flowers, colorful cloth banners, and mango leaves. For people of Aryavarta, flowers and mango leaves signified auspicious occasions. There were temporary tents built where the city leaders had gathered. There were the temple elders, Manu's mother Savithri, Soma Verma the city administrator, Lakshmi his wife, and their daughter Leelavati, all seated in the main stand. Chitrasena had gone to Pataliputra with a group of elite soldiers to bring back his son to Chitrapuri. The plan was for them to be back before sunset, and the fact that there was no sign of Chitrasena's entourage made Savithri a little anxious.

"They should be here any minute," said Savithri, trying to hide her anxiety.

She was excited at the very thought of her son coming home after a long stay in Pataliputra. Was he taller now? Had he grown his hair longer? Was he now more muscular after the rigorous training at the academy? The delay in Manu's arrival was making her nervous for she knew that unexpected hazards could befall anyone, especially a military leader like her husband. Although there was peace and prosperity in the Mauryan Empire, there were always natural hazards such as unexpected thunderstorms or lightning.

"I just cannot wait to see Manu. It is so exciting that he is coming home with the highest honors from the academy," whispered Lakshmi.

Manu was an exemplary student. He had mastered all the military techniques and skills in no time and had impressed all the teachers at his academy. Indeed his reputation as an unmatched swordsman and archer had reached the great Kautilya himself. On the day of his graduation, Manu was the lead soldier and received the honors first.

The crowd got a little excited when they saw two soldiers galloping towards the city. The soldiers had come ahead of Chitrasena to announce Manu's arrival. Every one was relieved and happy to see that Manu was going to be there in few minutes, and the musicians in a nearby tent started playing their instruments. This really excited the crowd as they started cheering for Manu's arrival. Very soon, Chitrasena, Manu and the small group of soldiers who had accompanied Chitrasena were at the main entrance. Chitrasena greeted the crowd, and Manu waived at the crowd from his horse. Manu looked bigger, stronger than ever, and indeed had grown long hair just as his mother had imagined. He looked more handsome than ever.

Manu got down, greeted the elders, and bestowed his respects to the priest, his mother, and Leelavati's parents. He then enquired how Leelavati was doing.

Chitrasena who was hungry from the long travel announced to the crowd that there would be a dinner celebrating Manu's homecoming in the temple banquet hall. The crowd cheered, and a little boy yelled, "Thank you Manu, it was worth the wait."

The crowd burst into laughter. Even Chitrasena smiled as they all proceeded to the temple hall, which was at the center of the town.

The next morning, the very first signs of dawn woke Manu up. He just could not sleep well that night and did not know what was troubling him. Was it the travel or was it the excitement of being back at home, he did not know. I should be excited, having just graduated from the most prestigious military school in the entire Empire - thought Manu. After all, he had graduated with the most honors from the most prestigious academy. Thousands of Kshatriyas from all over the Empire aspired to go there every year but only a few hundred made it. Manu had a smile when he remembered the day when the academy honored the graduates with a state dinner. That was his first encounter with Kautilya.

"So you are Manu," said Kautilya looking straight into his eyes.

Kautilya was a tall, lanky man, and Manu, who was equally tall, stared right back straight into his eyes. Like thousands before him, that eye contact confirmed to Manu all he had heard about Kautilya. His father had told him repeatedly that Kautilya was the most intelligent man ever born. After all, he was the kingmaker. He had made Chandra Gupta Maurya what he is today – the emperor of the largest Empire since the days of Alexander the Great. Manu felt hypnotized, and he was eager to hear Kautilya's words.

"Yes, Sir. I am Manu. I am honored to meet you," answered Manu.

"Chitrasena must be proud of you. You have the same good looks and apparently even better military potential according to the teachers," complimented Kautilya.

Manu smiled at Kautilya, as he savored the compliments coming from the legendary Kautilya. He was also aware of his father's accomplishments in the battlefields and knew that his comments were the highest compliments indeed.

"Thank you, Sir. I hope to contribute to the Empire soon and live up to your expectations," replied Manu.

Kautilya smiled, patted him on his back, and walked away. Kautilya, not known to smile a lot, had shown an instant liking to Manu, and young Manu was delighted.

Manu woke up from the daydream and slowly walked to the washroom. A Kshatriya should never start his day unclean Manu murmured to himself. His mother and his teachers had taught him well about the daily duties and routines. As he took a leisurely bath, his mind wondered about what was in store for him for the next few months. Before he could plan the rest of his day, he decided to complete his daily meditation to increase his spiritual energy. Manu finished his bath and promptly went into the meditation room. This was his favorite room in the mansion since it was where he found the most solace. As he started to meditate focusing on the image of Goddess Shakti, his wandering mind slowly settled clearing all the mental clutter that was disturbing his serenity. As he took deep breaths, he could feel the power of meditation at work. It was almost as if meditation were washing away his worries. Slowly his mind entered into a sedate state while his inner conscience kept rising higher. He could sense the slow release of the spiritual energy that revitalized him. In the next few minutes, he felt like he was getting lighter and lighter. Finally, he felt so light that he felt like he was at the top of the Himalayas, and soon entered a state of trance, which the wise called *Samadhi*.

His teachers marveled at the fact that he could meditate like a seer at such a young age. Manu was an exceptional student, not just in the martial arts that are so central to a Kshatriya upbringing, but in the spiritual and theological aspects as well. He had mastered all the Vedas and Upanishads, the art of music, and was even sought out by temple priests to recite the Vedas on auspicious days.

Almost an hour had passed when he got out of the meditation room. He slowly walked out of the room into the garden and sat beneath the large *neem* tree at the center of his garden. Chitrasena's house was the biggest in Chitrapuri. It was a large mansion with several quarters for servants, guards, cooks, and many others whose tasks were unknown to him. There were stables for horses, elephants, and state chariots. It was a mini-palace in grandeur, and yet it had a woman's touch one finds in an ordinary house. That was all because of Savithri, his mother. She was a noble woman who had never lost touch with common people or common feelings. She was very devout, was always kind to her servants and strangers, and was ever ready to help anyone who came to her with a request; above all, she was a wonderful mother. As Manu walked towards the garden, Savithri could see him from the worship room window where she was getting ready for the morning worship. As she looked at his tall handsome body and his extraordinary looks, her heart filled with joy, and she closed her eyes and thanked Shakti for the blessings.

Manu was exactly the son she always wanted - handsome, intelligent, and kind. In her mind, the only thing left was for him to get married before he moved to Pataliputra. Just the thought of Manu's wedding made her dizzy with excitement!

Manu surveyed the garden and admired the beautiful flowerbeds neatly arranged like gems in a piece of jewelry. The early morning breeze made the large mango and neem trees in the garden sway gently. After just a few minutes, he felt relaxed enough to take a stroll towards the small river Sita that was not too far from his house. He marveled at nature's rhythm as he sat on a rock near the riverbank listening to the flowing river. After a while, he wanted to go back to his house to do some intense exercise.

The exercise room, which was at the other end of the garden, was Chitrasena's favorite room. The morning exercise was a regular part of Chitrasena's routine, and a trusted soldier guarded the entrance to the room. As Manu walked towards the room, the guard at the entrance to the exercise house saluted Manu and let him into the room. His face brightened as he scanned all the swords, lancers, arrows, and bows displayed on the walls. He practiced with each one of those weapons until he was soaking with perspiration, when he decided to go back to the main house for another leisurely bath. He was quite relaxed after the bath, and sat on a chair in the main hall trying to plan the rest of his day.

"Are you coming to eat your breakfast, Manu?" he heard his father call.

"I will be there in a minute, father," Manu replied, walked towards the dining hall, and sat at the table right in front of his father.

Savithri had already placed the breakfast on the plates, and he was eager to start. He waited for his father to signal him to proceed. He was so hungry from all the intense exercise that he immediately forgot that he was with his father and found himself engrossed in eating his breakfast. Both Chitrasena and Savithri found that amusing; Savithri was pleased that her son was indeed eating well. For Manu, it had been a long time since he had tasted home cooked food, and everything in front of him tasted irresistible. Sensing that his mother was watching him, he looked up and smiled.

"Do you have any special plans for the day?" asked Savithri.

"Not really mother. I may walk along the river or go into the woods on my horse," replied Manu.

"If you have nothing planned, why don't you go and visit Leelavati?" she added in an encouraging voice.

Manu knew what was going on. He had the suspicion that his parents and Leelavati's parents hoped for the two to be bride and groom some day. It was as if they were praying that the two would fall in love and get married. Of course, Manu liked Leelavati a lot. She was extremely intelligent and a beautiful girl. However, at the same time, his feelings towards her were more as a friend and he was not the least bit interested in marrying her. Luckily, for Manu, Leelavati had similar feelings towards him. Nevertheless, he was more than willing to go and spend some time with Leelavati. He did not mind chatting with her about the things that had happened since he had left Chitrapuri.

"I will just do that mother. I will go for a walk along the river with her," Manu replied.

"Do not go too far, and make sure that you have your sword with you," added Chitrasena.

Manu took a leisurely stroll along the main street of Chitrapuri and came to the front of Leelavati's house. A guard went inside and announced his arrival, and in no time, Leelavati came outside to greet him.

"Manu, I am so happy to see you. Come and spend some time with us, and mother will prepare a special lunch for you." Leelavati did not attempt to hide her excitement.

"That is very nice of you Leelavati. I actually wanted to go for a walk along the river and was wondering if you wanted to join me?" replied Manu.

Leelavati liked the idea. That was something they often did before Manu went to Pataliputra.

"I like that. Let me tell my mother and join you." She went inside to inform her mother.

As they walked along the river underneath tall trees, the shade from the trees kept the afternoon heat bearable. They both marveled at the beauty of the forest on the far side of the river, which looked like a chain of rolling green hills from their side of the river. The locals called the river Sita, which was a small tributary that flowed into a river that eventually joined the Ganges. As they walked along the riverbank, Manu admired the rhythmic sound that was coming from the bottom of the river. That sound blended with the singing birds in the forest made the whole experience almost spiritual for Manu. He had always loved walking along the river for he considered the river a friend and a teacher. He visited the river when he was happy, and was there when he was sad. Every time he went there, he had felt happier, and more spiritual.

He thought about the days when he and Leelavati were kids plucking *Jambu* fruits. He turned to Leelavati.

"Do you remember when we used to come here to pluck fruits from the wild trees?" asked Manu.

"Of course I do. I remember the time there was a heavy rain, and we had to take shelter underneath that banyan tree," she said, pointing towards a large banyan tree just a few hundred yards from them.

"Yes, I remember that. I was worried about a sudden flash flood, and we both climbed the tree and waited for the rain to stop. That was some adventure," Manu laughed.

Leelavati looked at him affectionately as if his laugh took her back in time. Manu tried to read her mind, trying to understand her feelings towards him. He decided to be brave and bring the subject out into the open.

"You know something; my mother has some strange ideas about the two of us," said Manu.

"I know what you mean. She has hinted at that many times," she replied.

There was a momentary silence. She then smiled and looked at him.

"Doesn't she realize that we don't have such feelings towards each other? We are almost like brother and sister," she added.

Manu was infinitely relieved when he heard that. He was happy that Leelavati had the same feelings for him. His immediate worry was how to break the news to his mother. However, he did not worry about that too much. He knew she was going to be disappointed. Nevertheless, she would understand and look forward to other possibilities. She was not a woman who would delve into things that were out of her control.

"Do not worry about her. She will understand once I explain it to her," assured Manu.

Manu and Leelavati reached an area where the river had made a natural pool, and there were stepping-stones around the pool. It was a place where children from surrounding villages congregated for recreation. A group of young women had come there to relax. The girls smiled at them, and Leelavati walked towards them to chat while Manu rested below a tree.

Leelavati came back in a few minutes towards Manu.

"You know those girls?" asked Manu.

"Yes, I come here often, and we chat about all sorts of things. They are from the village just a few miles from here."

Manu looked at the group of girls. One of them looked very pretty. He wanted to get to know her.

Leelavati noticed that Manu was having difficulty in taking his eyes off from the girl. She decided to tease him.

"You like her, don't you? Her name is Kusuma. Would you want to meet her?"

Manu smiled back, and felt a little awkward that his attraction towards Kusuma was so obvious. As he hesitated to answer her question, she prodded him some more.

"Are you that shy, Manu? Or are you speechless because of her beauty?"

Leelavati took his hand and tried to nudge him to make a move. Manu nodded his head in a confused way. He did not know what exactly to say. Of course, he was eager to meet her and they both walked towards the girls.

"Kusuma, this is Manu, my friend," Leelavati introduced them. "He just finished his military training in Pataliputra. He is here just for the summer," she added.

Kusuma had heard a lot about Manu, she had once seen him from a distance in the market, but had never met him. Many from the surrounding villages talked about Chitrasena's accomplishments and often mentioned Manu in those conversations. They never forgot to stress that Manu was a very handsome warrior. She, however, had no idea how he looked now; but this unexpected encounter made it very clear to her that not all she had heard about him was doing enough justice to his handsome looks. She too had difficulty in taking her eyes off Manu. It was as if they were trying to communicate through their eyes. It became obvious to Leelavati that Kusuma liked Manu as well.

"Kusuma, do you come here often? Do you like the river?" Manu tried to start a conversation.

"I do. My friends and I come here almost every day. We love walking in the shallow waters," Kusuma replied.

Manu found her voice mesmerizing and just wanted to hear it continuously. For the next few minutes, he kept talking about mundane things just to listen to her voice. Her voice was so amazing that it was as if she could reach out and touch his inner most feelings with her voice. He kept looking into her beautiful eyes and could not resist his love for her, which kept making him dizzy. Soon it was time for Kusuma to go back to her village with her friends, and she left the pool area along with her friends.

As Manu and Leelavati started going back to Chitrapuri, Manu could not stop thinking about Kusuma. For him, she had the sweetest voice he had ever heard, and it kept ringing in his mind. He could not erase her smile from his mind nor could he stop thinking about her beautiful eyes. He wondered how he could meet her again.

"You're in love with her, aren't you, Manu?" asked Leelavati.

"I do not know about that, all I know is that her face is engraved in my mind. It is a weird feeling," he replied.

He was trying to hide his feelings but with little success. He knew very well that he was madly in love with her.

"That is love, Manu. There is nothing wrong with that," observed Leelavati.

Manu noticed that Leelavati's voice had changed. It was as if she was worried about something.

"Are you trying to tell me something, Leelavati?"

"You know, Kusuma's people are outside the Varnas. I do not think your father is going to be pleased about your love for her," she said it in a sad voice.

Manu was thinking about the same thing. He knew from Kusuma's attire and the dialect she spoke with her friends that she belonged to the hill tribe. Of course, the tribe was outside the four Varnas, and his parents, especially his father, would not approve of his love for her. Why should that matter? No other girl ever had an effect on him the way she had. To him, she was like a gift from heaven, and he could only thank Leelavati for bringing them together.

"I know what you mean, and I do not know how I am going to deal with it," he replied in a voice that echoed the sadness in his heart.

Of course, there was no problem in dealing with his feelings; his sadness was with the social barriers. He did not know how he was going to overcome those barriers. What was even more troublesome was that many had twisted dharma to make those barriers look like God sanctioned divisions. As he thought about that, the ancient Manu came to his mind.

Chapter 15

Kusuma

Manu could not stop thinking about Kusuma the entire day. He could not eat well, nor could he sleep well that night. Savithri noticed the change and wondered what was bothering Manu. Nevertheless, she left him alone for the fear of seeming too intrusive.

He kept tossing and turning in his sleep wondering what he was going to do next. It should have been a pleasant experience for him; after all, she was the first one who had aroused feelings of love. Instead of that, he was worrying about the consequences, what impact it would have on his parents. He thought that it was silly that he was worrying about them; he was not even sure if Kusuma liked him. He finally fell asleep as he was getting too tired thinking about the future.

The next morning, he got up early and finished his routines – meditation, yoga and other exercises. He then sat with his parents for his breakfast and kept to himself during the breakfast. His silence was utterly bothering Savithri.

"Is everything all right, Manu? You are being very quiet since last evening," she asked.

"Please do not worry, mother, I was just a little tired. Moreover, there are too many things in my head; I am thinking about what I am going to do after I go back to Pataliputra," replied Manu. He knew he was not being completely honest, but did not want to alarm his mother with his feelings for Kusuma. It was, however, true that he was thinking a lot about his next assignment in Pataliputra.

"So, do you have any idea what Kautilya has in mind for you?" asked Chitrasena.

"Not really, father. All I know is that I will be leading a small group of elite soldiers in charge of special tasks. I am hoping that my first assignment will be something thrilling," Manu answered.

Military topics were something he was always comfortable discussing with his father. Chitrasena was open and flexible when it came to discussing military strategies and methods. In spite of all his accomplishments, he never had preconceived rigidity. That was something he had learned from his association with Kautilya. A good military leader will listen to everyone and will formulate methods that are best for a given situation.

However, when it came to matters of dharma, he was as rigid as Vishnu Gupta. They both were firm believers in the laws of ancient Manu. Ancient Manu was the first man God created and assigned him the role of specifying the rules of dharma. To them, dharma was adherence to the *Laws of Manu*. Ancient Manu had defined the Varnas, and the way one dealt with those divisions had to be in accordance with the laws of Manu. Indeed, both of them were somewhat unhappy that Kautilya had taken a very enlightened view of Varnas.

"It will be, Manu. You do not have to worry about that. As long as you remember that a Kshatriya's duty is to protect dharma fully, you will do fine. Do not worry too much about that. Just enjoy your free time," Chitrasena gave his fatherly advice to Manu.

"Your father is right. Just relax and enjoy your free time. Go and visit the temple and chat with the priest - Shotri. He always enjoys talking to you," added Savithri.

That seemed a good suggestion to Manu. Soon after he finished his breakfast, he started his leisurely walk to the temple.

He always enjoyed talking to the priest – the conversations were always spiritually uplifting. He helped Manu see things in a way that always added a spiritual dimension to his questions. When Manu entered the temple, he saw that the priest had just finished the morning services and was getting ready for the evening services. Shotri smiled when he saw Manu. Shotri also enjoyed talking to Manu and saw a bright mind that could one day achieve great things spiritual or otherwise. Manu went inside the main hall, prayed for a while, and then walked to the place where Shotri was sitting.

"How is everything Manu? Are you enjoying your break from the school?" asked the priest.

"Yes, I am indeed enjoying my break," Manu replied but hesitated to add more. The priest could see the unusual level of anxiety in Manu's face.

"Something seems to be bothering you, Manu. Is it something you can share with me?" asked Shotri, trying to help him out.

"Tell me about the Varnas. Why is it not right for a man of Varnas to be in love with some one outside the four Varnas?"

Shotri took immediate notice that something was bothering Manu. Indeed, he knew the exact nature of Manu's anxiety. However, he was somewhat taken aback from the bluntness of his question.

"Yes, it is not right according to laws attributed to ancient Manu. However, there is nothing in the Vedas that forbid love with someone outside the Varnas," replied the priest.

"Then, why do these rules – as those specified by the ancient Manu - even exist?" asked Manu in a painful voice.

"I really cannot answer that, Manu. They are there because we are all drowning in the sea of Māya," observed the priest. He paused for a minute and then added his honest opinion on that subject.

"Anyone who has mastered the scriptures knows that these divisions are only delusional."

For Manu, it was soothing to hear that. He was, in fact, surprised that many enlightened souls did not care about the laws of ancient Manu. Unfortunately, for him, his father was not one of those enlightened souls.

He always had enormous respect for the priest, and this exchange only reinforced his respect for Shotri. He had one more question he wanted the priest to clarify. "What makes one a priest – a Brahmin?"

"That is pretty easy to answer, Manu. It is knowledge that leads one to priesthood, specifically the knowledge of God. However, that is only the beginning. There is a lot more to becoming a Brahmin," replied Shotri.

"Becoming a Brahmin?" Manu was surprised to hear that phrase. Being a Brahmin was hereditary – at least that was what he knew.

"Yes, anyone can be a Brahmin. It takes control of the mind, control of the senses, penance, forgiveness, compassion, and above all dedicating your present life to service of God," the priest added.

"So, can I be a Brahmin?"

"Certainly, anyone can be a Brahmin. Even a hunter who lives in the woods can be one. For all we know, he is already one if he has all the qualities I just described." Shotri had a pleasant smile as he gave his views.

That was something for Manu to ponder. He was thankful to Shotri for throwing a different light on the Varnas. It relaxed him a little, and he felt like a burden of guilt had melted away.

He did not want to discuss that subject any more. Moreover, his mind was somewhere else now. He wanted to go back to the place where he had seen Kusuma the day before. He thanked Shotri for the enlightening discussion and quickly started walking towards the river.

As he kept walking along the riverbank, he wondered why Kusuma had touched him so much and what made him so worked up. Maybe it was all unnecessary and she may not even feel for him the way he felt about her. He finally reached the same place where he had met her and sat underneath the same tree. It was late morning and the river pool was completely deserted; there was not even an animal near the river pool, and he felt lonely like he had never felt before.

Kusuma's village was on the other side of the river, and a trail ran from the village to the pool. The trail forked as it reached the pool area with one side leading to the stepping-stones, and the other side went over a bridge on the narrow neck of the river that led to another trail on Manu's side of the river. As he sat beneath the tree playing with pebbles he wondered if he was wasting time. Just then, he saw three women approaching towards the river pool, and his heart started beating faster as he realized that it was Kusuma with her friends. He got up and started walking towards the bridge, and to his surprise, he saw that Kusuma kept walking towards the bridge while her friends went towards the pool. They both reached the bridge at the same time, and he slowly went towards her and smiled. He held her hands as he looked into her amazing eyes.

"I cannot stop thinking about you. I don't know why, perhaps it is your amazing eyes or maybe it is your sweet voice," Manu said almost sheepishly wondering what had driven him to say those words.

Kusuma blushed when she heard that. "If it makes you feel any better, I did not sleep very well last night either, maybe it is your smile that kept me awake," she replied.

Manu was ecstatic when he heard her say that. He wanted to take her to a place where they had more privacy so that he could talk to her about his feelings.

"Can we walk towards the woods? I would like to talk to you where there is some privacy," Manu pointed towards the woods.

She nodded her head in agreement, and they both started walking towards the woods and sat on a boulder underneath the trees. The trees and shrubs gave them enough privacy to talk freely.

"So what is that you wanted to tell me, Manu?" asked Kusuma.

"Well there were so many things I wanted to tell you, but I cannot remember anything now; all I want to do now is look at you and listen to your voice," Manu replied.

He could not resist laughing at himself for his predicament.

"You are being silly; you must have something important to tell me. Otherwise, you would not have brought me here," added Kusuma.

"Of course I do. I will remember that soon. You know, I am a simple man, and simple things like looking into your eyes will make me happy," he said almost teasingly.

"You know Manu, it is usually complex people who claim to be simple," Kusuma shot back.

Manu realized she was right. He was not really a simple man; he often himself had trouble understanding his spiritual bearings. He was convinced that in his earlier life he was a seer or a Sadhu; he often thought that he was a spiritual seeker caught in a Kshatriya body. Somehow, for some reason, he was now in deep love with a beautiful mountain girl sitting in front of him.

"You are right; I am not a simple man. However, this is true though. Simple things can make me very happy," he added.

"Simple things like what?" asked Kusuma.

"Like a sweet kiss from you," replied Manu.

Kusuma felt shy although deep inside she had the same urge to kiss him.

Manu leaned forward, took her beautiful face in his hands, and bent over and started kissing her. She did not resist; indeed, she kissed him back passionately.

"I love you," he proclaimed and moved his head away from hers.

His deep kiss sent electrical waves through her, and it was a feeling hitherto unknown to her. His declaration of love for her made her almost ecstatic. She moved close to him, hugged him tight, and placed her head against his strong shoulder. This made Manu immensely happy and relaxed. They both remained in that position for a long time completely oblivious to the march of time. Suddenly, she realized that her friends were looking for her as she heard them calling out her name. She freed herself from Mau and looked at him with her face filled with sadness to leave him there.

"I need to go. My friends are looking for me," said Kusuma.

Before he could say anything, she was running towards the bridge to meet her friends.

"Can we meet again tomorrow?" Manu shouted at her.

She looked back, smiled, and nodded her head positively, which made him ever so happy.

Manu was extremely happy and in high spirits the rest of the day. Savithri noticed the change in him and wondered about the reason. She also noticed that he kept humming some melody which she had never heard before. What she did not realize was that it was a poem which Manu had written in his own mind for Kusuma. He could not wait to meet her and recite it the next day.

Manu had never been so happy before; at least in this way. He had discovered brand new emotions, which he liked. Nevertheless, they had brought other anxieties to him. The biggest question that swirled in his mind was what was going to be the next step. He was now certain that both he and Kusuma were in deep love. Certainly, for the next two months while he was in Chitrapuri, he wanted to spend every possible minute with her. He wanted to open up, as he had never done before, and at the same time, he wanted to know everything about her. Of course, the fact that she was outside the four Varnas was a recurring anxiety for him. How would his parents take the news once they found out about it? He knew his mother would be understanding and was not going to come in the way of his happiness. He was, however, not certain about his father's reaction. He knew that his father would not approve of it, but would he give in if Manu insisted?

The next day, Manu decided to ride his favorite horse to the river pool where he saw Kusuma waiting for him.

"Would you like to join me? We can go for a ride into the woods," asked Manu as she walked towards him.

She hesitated for a minute not because she was afraid of riding the horse; she was concerned about the safety in the deeper parts of the woods. Every one knew that tigers roamed that part of the woods.

"Are you afraid to ride the horse?" Manu prodded her.

"Not really, Manu. I am concerned about wild animals in the deeper part of the woods," she replied.

"You do not have to worry about that. They will only bother you if you disturb them. Moreover, I will be with you," he smiled and pointed at his sword.

She nodded her head in agreement, jumped on the horse, and sat behind him. She held him tight as the horse galloped into the denser part of the forest. Kusuma found the ride exhilarating; she could feel the strong muscles in Manu's body rubbing against her as they both rhythmically moved up and down along with the horse's strides. The closeness of his warm body coupled with the summer breeze generated an intense feeling that was hitherto uncharted for her. She closed her eyes, placed her face against his strong back, and felt immensely secure.

She opened her eyes only after realizing that Manu had stopped the horse. They were near a stone structure that looked like a resting area for hunters. Manu got down, tied the horse to a tree nearby, and helped her get down. As she glided down, he brought her close to him and soon they were in a kiss that seemed like a continuation of yesterday's first kiss. They had no idea how much time had passed when they finally sat on the edge of the stone structure.

"We can relax here and talk. No one is going to bother us here," commented Manu.

"What do you want to talk about? You want to tell me how you spent your time since we parted yesterday?"

"Well, I spent the whole time thinking about you. You were everywhere. It was like you controlled my mind," he answered.

It was no different for Kusuma and she completely resonated with what he was saying. She kept looking at him as she admired his openness.

"You want to know something else, Kusuma?"

"Sure," she replied.

"I will tell you if you promise not to laugh," added Manu.

"I won't laugh. I promise you that," she tried to assure him.

"I have been composing a poem; do you want to hear it?" Manu was anxious to recite the poem he had hummed all night long in his mind.

Kusuma was now eager to hear his poetry. She knew very well that even an ordinary poem could reveal hidden emotions. She coaxed him to recite it. "Go ahead Manu; do not keep me waiting for a long time."

Manu garnered enough courage to reveal his words. He was a little shy as it was the first serious poem he had constructed.

Growing up in a fort,
With four colorful walls,
Mother three times sweeter,
Father strong as an army
In a royal picture.

I had everything I ever wanted,
Protected just like the prince,
Who became the Enlightened One.

Suddenly a flower dropped next to me,
Like a sign from the heaven;
As I lift that flower to soak its beauty,
All I see is the bondage of invisible chains,
With the fort becoming a painful prison.

Indra, the mighty one, where are you now?
Free me from this bondage with your thunderbolt,
When I reach Him, I want this flower by my side.

Kusuma had tears in her eyes, as she understood the meaning of his poem. It was all about him and her; after all, "Kusuma" meant flower. She knew the four walls were the four Varnas, and Manu felt imprisoned since she was outside the Varnas.

"Does it bother you that much that I am outside the Varnas?" she asked.

"No, but it bothers me that such false divisions continue to exist among men and women," he replied. "The Upanishads are right when they say that the Varnas are for deluded men. I wish my parents were that enlightened."

Kusuma got worried. Did he bring her here just to tell her that theirs could never be an acceptable relationship? Did he bring her here to give her the bad news? The romance was going to die even before their love blossomed.

Manu saw her worried face and wanted to assuage her worry the best he could.

"Nothing is going to prevent us from being together. Neither the Varnas nor the ancient Manu will come between us. This is my promise, I will love you for the rest of my life," Manu said, making a bold declaration.

That is all she wanted to hear as she was in tears again; however, this time they were tears of joy.

"You know Manu, I always saw you once a week before you went to Pataliputra," she began, as she wanted to tell him about her own feelings.

"Where did you see me? I do not member knowing you before last week," Manu was curious.

"In the weekly fair where my family sold all sorts of fruits and vegetables," she explained. "You came with your mother every week to buy fruits, and I think I was secretly in love with you ever since I saw you for the first time."

There was a sense of excitement as she spoke; it was a feeling one gets when they reach their long sought-after goal. It was at that moment he realized how deeply she was in love with him. Manu remembered those days when he always accompanied his mother to the weekly market. Hearing her tell about her love at first sight, he wondered if it was past karma that had brought them together.

The next few days, their daily encounter in the woods continued, and Manu had never been so happy before. It did not take much time for Savithri to realize that Manu was in love with a young woman. It did not bother her except that she wanted to know more about the woman. She sent a trusted servant to find out more about the girl who was secretly meeting her son, who came back to her after a few hours with detailed information.

"I know who Manu is meeting every day, mother. I am worried that you may not like the details," the servant began.

"You do not have to worry about that. Nothing is going to bother me as long as Manu is happy," she assured the servant.

"It is a girl from the village across the river. What you may not like is that she is outside the Varnas," the servant hesitated as she gave the details.

Savithri had a sudden worried look on her face. It was not that she did not approve of Manu's newfound love. She was worried about Chitrasena. As a staunch believer in the laws of dharma as specified by ancient Manu, Chitrasena would never approve of that relationship although she herself had never been a supporter of those rules. She never had an occasion to express her views on that, and now she was afraid that she had no choice but to express her strong views, which was bound to cause friction with her husband. That could wait, she thought; her immediate goal was to find out more about the girl who had stolen her son's heart.

"I would like to see her some time. How can I meet her?" she asked the servant.

"That should not be any problem, mother. She goes with her family to the market every week. You can see her next week when we go there," replied the servant.

"Do you know her name?"

"Yes, her name is Kusuma," the servant replied.

"We will do exactly that. Next week when we go to the market, show me Kusuma," Savithri added.

The next morning, right after he finished his meditation, Manu went inside the *pooja*[23] room just to offer a flower to his chosen deity, Goddess Shakti. This was something he did on special days. Although, it was not any special day, he somehow felt drawn to offer the flower. He stood in front of the image of Shakti as if asking for Her blessings in what he was about to do that day. As he looked around the room, his attention fell on a box that was next to the deities – it was the family jewel box. The family jewel box had all the golden jewelry that Savithri had collected over the

---

23 Pooja is the Sanskrit term for worship service.

185

years. He opened the box and took out one particular necklace. It was a simple gold chain with a small golden pendant. It was no ordinary pendant though, as it had the sacred Om inscribed on it. He held it in his right hand, and slowly touched his eyes with the pendant not knowing what was making him do that. He then put that in his pocket and walked away from the pooja room. He then realized that it was indeed a special day; he was going to give the necklace to Kusuma as a token of his love.

Manu decided to take Kusuma to the same place in the woods where he took her every day. They reached the same stone structure where they spent most of the afternoons. As they both got down from the horse, Kusuma realized that Manu was somewhat in a somber mood.

"Is something bothering you, Manu? You seem to be very serious today," she enquired.

"Yes, but don't say anything. I want you to close your eyes and don't open them until I say so," he said gazing into her eyes.

She was eager to oblige, wondering what he had in mind. Manu took her face in his palm, and slightly lifted it and looked at her face as if he was seeing her for the first time. He felt immensely happy just looking at her face. He then took the necklace out of his pocket and put it around her neck. He was now even happier seeing the beautiful necklace around her neck.

"You can open your eyes now," announced Manu.

Kusuma opened her eyes, touched the pendant, and looked down at it. She was ecstatic when she saw it and did not know what to say. She was overcome with emotions, hugged Manu with tears in her eyes, and stood like that for what seemed like eternity.

After she had calmed down, Manu held her hands and proclaimed his intentions.

"Kusuma, I have realized that I cannot live without you even for a day. Being away from you makes me feel empty. It is as if I am barely alive, and I just do not like that feeling. I want our love to be eternal," he continued ever so slowly that made Kusuma wonder what he was getting at. "I want you to marry me and come with me to Pataliputra. Will you marry me, Kusuma?" He finally gathered enough strength to declare his intentions for her.

She had dreamt those words for the last several days. Indeed, it was even better than what she had imagined. She was so happy that she felt increasingly weak in her legs, and fainted as Manu held her from falling down. He then sat on the stone structure holding her with her head resting on his lap. Her reaction was much unexpected, and he was now worried, but waited patiently for her to wake up. She slowly came out of her reverie, sat down, and started sobbing.

"I do not know what to say. I have never been happier than this," she spoke softly.

"You can say yes," Manu said prompting her, as he was anxious to hear her answer.

"Of course, my answer is yes," she replied as she held his face in her hands and stared into his eyes.

"Have you discussed this with your parents?" she asked in a worried tone.

Manu knew she was bound to ask that question. He himself had thought about that a thousand times, but had never garnered enough courage to face his father to break the news.

"No, not yet; don't worry about that. Let me face that problem," he assured her.

Meanwhile, Savithri could not wait for the day when she could meet Kusuma. Finally, when the market day came, she and her servant were one of the first ones to go to the market. Another servant took them to the market in a horse drawn carriage that was only appropriate for a woman of her status. A countless number of traders from surrounding villages and towns had gathered at the fair. Some were selling vegetables and fruits, while others were selling handicrafts and jewelry. Savithri pretended to be a serious customer and bought many items that she did not really need. They finally arrived at the area where Kusuma and her uncle and aunt were selling some handicrafts. At that moment, the servant quietly whispered into Savithri's ears about Kusuma's presence. They both walked to the stall and pretended to be seriously interested in items that were on sale. At the same time, Savithri looked at Kusuma, who smiled back. That smile was enough for her to reveal all the reasons why her son had fallen for Kusuma. It was the sweetest smile she had seen. Kusuma knew it was Manu's mother, and she realized that Savithri was aware of what was going on between Manu and her.

While she was a little nervous, the serene look in Savithri's face completely calmed her, and she was completely relaxed. What Savithri saw in her was not just a girl with a beautiful face but also one with a pure heart. Suddenly, the long piece of cloth that was around Kusuma's neck slipped and revealed her new necklace with the Om pendant. That together with the glow in Kusuma's face told the whole story to Savithri. She knew at the very moment that Manu intended to marry her, which gave her goose bumps. She was excited and happy for her son knowing what was going on. At the same time, Kusuma realized that Savithri had seen her necklace and looked up at Savithri. Her face was full of anxiety not knowing what Savithri would say about her necklace. Savithri saw that anxiety in her face and wanted to remove it instantly. She looked into Kusuma's eyes and smiled at her in an approving way. That smile was all that Kusuma wanted to see as it told her exactly how Savithri felt about her. There was sincere warmth in that smile which was a silent welcome signal from Savithri. Kusuma felt infinitely relieved. She, however, knew that there was one more hurdle to cross which was Chitrasena.

As Savithri went back to Chitrapuri along with the servant, she sat quietly in the carriage thinking about Kusuma. She was now more worried than Manu about Chitrasena. She knew very well that there would be overwhelming opposition from her husband to Manu's intentions. She was going to do her best to see if she could change his mind, but she was not very hopeful. She, however, wanted to tell Chitrasena about Kusuma as soon as she could. She wanted to tell him in such a way that he would not lose his temper and hurt Manu's feelings. Even worse, she was worried that Manu might just walk out of the family. She knew her son was deeply in love with Kusuma, and he might do just that.

The next morning, during breakfast, Manu observed that both his parents were unusually quiet; neither one of them was in a mood to talk. Manu looked at his mother's face and realized that she had not slept well that night. He then looked at his father and knew what was going on; obviously, they were involved in some serious argument. Chitrasena looked angry and tense. It was as if he was extremely unhappy. What he did not realize at that moment was that it was about his unfolding plans. Savithri had tried the whole night to convince Chitrasena to support Manu's intentions. However, Chitrasena was stubborn; he did not intend to be the first one in his family to break the laws as laid out by ancient Manu. To his mind, they were non-negotiable; to him they were indeed sacred.

Chitrasena kept fuming inside while he had a semblance of outward serenity that was nothing but a façade. He was disappointed at his son – he was struggling to accept that his own son was going to break the sacred laws. He kept asking where he had gone wrong. Did someone against dharma influence his son in Pataliputra? He knew there were many such elements in Pataliputra, despite Vishnu Gupta's constant vigilance. He was even more upset at Savithri who was ready to accept Kusuma as their daughter-in-law. Even more serious was that she had questioned the very laws of ancient Manu. To Chitrasena, that bordered on blasphemy.

"Manu, what are your plans when you get back to Pataliputra?" Chitrasena finally broke the silence.

"I really do not know, father. It all depends on what assignment they give me," replied Manu quietly.

"You do not have much time left. Have you started mentally preparing for your future assignments?"

Manu did not know why his father was asking those questions. It looked as though Chitrasena was looking forward to his departure. That seemed very odd to him, and he merely shrugged his shoulders. A long silence followed, and Manu kept wondering if it was the right time for him to mention Kusuma. He had to do that some time, and he very well knew that no time was going to be the right time for that.

Manu looked outside through the window as a long shadow fell on the backyard garden. From nowhere, dark clouds had moved in, and he knew it was going to start raining soon. He knew that the wind was blowing from the north, which meant that the clouds had taken a detour as they encountered the towering Himalayas. That always meant torrential rains that often flooded the river Sita. He was now a little worried as he remembered that he had promised Kusuma to meet her at noontime right over the bridge.

"Is there something you want to tell me, Manu?"

He came out of his thoughts as he heard Chitrasena. That question told him everything about his father and mother. The unusual silence, seemingly odd questions, and now this – it all came into focus. He looked at his mother again and realized that her eyes were red from crying. They must have found about Kusuma, and the argument was obviously about him. It was like a confluence of forces coming together, and it was probably the right time to tell the whole truth. He was amazed that there was neither fear nor hesitation in him; indeed, he felt relieved that his father had brought up the topic. He looked outside through the window and observed that the rain had started coming down hard as he carefully prepared to answer his father's question.

"I have met a girl named Kusuma," he replied.

"What can you tell me about her?"

"She lives in a village across the river," Manu said cryptically, knowing where his father was going with that question.

"I mean what is her Varna?" asked Chitrasena seemingly irritated.

"She belongs to the hill tribe," replied Manu calmly.

Chitrasena stood up and started pacing in the dining room as Manu sat quietly expecting him to explode. To his surprise, Chitrasena was calm and did not say anything for a few minutes, which seemed like an eternity to Manu. He just wanted to be done with the discussion; he knew very well that it was going to end up on an unpleasant note.

"What are your intentions with this girl?" asked Chitrasena.

Manu did not like that question the least and was even surprised that his father would question his integrity.

"Of course, I love her, and I intend to marry her," replied Manu without losing his patience.

Chitrasena, already knowing this, was still very upset and did his best to control his anger. After all, Manu was his only son and he did not want to do something that would drive him away.

"Manu, you are too young to understand all the implications of such a union. For your sake, and for our family's honor, I forbid you to marry her," replied Chitrasena as if he was commanding Manu to follow his orders.

Manu looked outside and saw that the intensity of the rain had increased several fold. His frustration with his father was rising with the storm's intensity. Yet, he did not want to be disrespectful to his father.

"May I ask you why you forbid this union, father?" asked Manu calmly.

The way Manu was handling the situation surprised his mother who stood in the corner trying not to get involved. She felt proud of the way he was dealing with a difficult and emotional situation.

"It is all in the ancient laws specified by Manu, the first man God created. I named you Manu hoping you would uphold those laws. Instead, you bring me this awful news." Chitrasena looked saddened, and even bewildered.

"Father, the laws of ancient Manu are misguided. Everyone knows he was deluded when he compiled those rules. You know that the Vedas state that God is in all of us, and we are all at the same spiritual level. Do you really want me to be truthful to the one who was deluded or to the Vedas?"

As Chitrasena heard Manu's arguments, he knew deep inside that his son was right. Yet, for some unknown reason, he refused to accept the thesis. He was now beginning to lose his sense of reasoning. He uttered something that he was going to regret for the rest of his life.

"I do not know who is feeding you all this nonsense. As your father, I forbid you from marrying her. If you want to continue to be part of this family, you will heed my advice," he replied in a very stern voice.

Those were the harshest words either Savithri or Manu had heard from Chitrasena. Savithri felt like something very sharp pierced her heart, and she could not take it anymore and started sobbing. Manu did not want to stay there anymore and felt unwelcome. He started walking to the door that led to the backyard. Savithri hurried towards Manu, still sobbing, trying to stop him.

"Where are you going in this storm, Manu? Please stay here and give your father some time. I know he will come around."

She tried to do her best to stop Manu from doing something dangerous or even irrational.

"Do not worry about me, mother. I will be all right. Right now I just want to be away," he replied and rushed into the shelter that housed the horses.

He was soon riding his favorite horse towards the bridge where he was planning to meet Kusuma.

The rain kept pounding so hard that even the horse had difficulty moving forward. The visibility was very poor, and the river level kept rising. As he started getting closer to the bridge, he noticed that Kusuma was standing on the bridge waiting for him even in that storm. He knew that it was very dangerous for her to stay on the bridge as the river level kept rising. He tried to shout in his highest voice, "Kusuma, get off the bridge. Move to the hills."

He kept shouting repeatedly. The storm, the howling wind, and the pounding rain all made his warning worthless. Suddenly, in the distance, behind the bridge, he saw a large wall of water moving rapidly towards Kusuma. He realized it was a flash flood.

"Kusuma, run to the hills, please run to the hills," he kept yelling as loud as he could.

It was all futile as the wall of water engulfed the bridge along with Kusuma. Manu himself had to maneuver the horse towards a higher location. The storm was so strong that he could hardly see anything for several minutes. Finally, when the intensity calmed down and he looked at the bridge, what he saw made him cry uncontrollably. It was as if the floodwaters had washed away all his dreams. All he saw was a broken bridge with no sight of Kusuma anywhere.

Chapter 16
The Eastern Expedition

S everal weeks had passed since Manu's return to Pataliputra. He had completely engulfed himself in his military routine and was doing his best to forget what had happened in Chitrapuri. It was not easy for him to forget Kusuma, however. The more he tried to forget the tragedy, the harder it was for him to erase the memories of Kusuma. What made it so difficult was that her thoughts occupied most of his non-military mind, and all he could see was her lovely face moment after moment. It was as if he lived two lives; in one life, he felt a constant pain in his heart and nothing seemed to interest him anymore. His other life, the military one, was not in bad shape. He took even more interest in his military routines and worked harder than ever to be the best Kshatriya man. He had decided to commit his life to the protection of dharma – whatever it really was. At least in his mind, it was not the dharma according to ancient Manu; he was, however, ever so hopeful that someday he would find the true meaning of dharma.

Manu was now spending a considerable amount of time with Ravi, another elite soldier in the Mauryan Army. Ravi was one year older than Manu and had graduated from the academy a few months ahead of him. He was jovial in his attitude and had a somewhat casual outlook towards everything. It was as if he never took anything seriously and wasted no time in cracking jokes about any situation. For him, life was always about the present; there was no point in thinking about things that were beyond the limits of one's control. Live for the moment and just enjoy every moment of your life whatever it may bring was his motto. He was, however, an excellent warrior, and for some unexplained reason Manu liked him and was drawn close to him.

Manu and Ravi spent several hours together each day – in the exercise room, in the dining hall, and riding horses. They talked about many things, and Manu tried his best to see the man behind that jovial mask.

"Why are you never serious about anything, Ravi?" asked Manu.

"It is not true that I am not serious about anything. You know very well I am quite serious about my military training," he said in defense.

"I mean about other things in life. You seem to be so casual about everything else."

"Well, Manu, this world needs people like me to compensate for people like you who are very serious about everything," replied Ravi.

"Maybe that is true. Still, it does not explain your outlook."

"You know, spiritual people like you tell me that the world is an illusion. So, just live for the moment, enjoy life, and just do not let anything bother you."

"You mean everything in this world is driven by Māya, and one should not take anything seriously?"

"Something like that. But then again, I do not think about those things like you do, Manu," replied Ravi, smiling.

Manu kept quiet. He wondered if Ravi was right. Why worry about anything? Just live for the moment and do not worry about anything. Indeed, everything in this material world is illusionary. At least it was temporary, and everything was bound to perish someday. Ravi looked into Manu's eyes, and he knew that there was something untold, perhaps a sad story. Manu felt uncomfortable and tried to turn away. Ravi could at once see the hurt Manu was trying to hide. He decided that it was now his turn to ask the questions.

"You know, Manu; I think that there is a sad story behind those eyes. Is it something you can tell me?" asked Ravi.

Manu was in no mood to discuss that with anyone. The wounds were much too fresh to visit that tragic night or, for that matter, to talk about anything concerning Kusuma.

"I am not ready to discuss that, Ravi. I hope you will understand that," replied Manu.

"That is alright. Is it about a girl you loved? Your parents do not approve of her. Is it something else? You can tell me whatever it is. I will protect your family honor." Ravi knew that Manu's father was Chitrasena, one of the most powerful generals in the Mauryan army.

Manu was not surprised at Ravi's statement; he would have guessed the same thing as well. Perhaps, it was time for him to open up and release the feelings he had imprisoned in his own heart, he thought. Maybe it would make him feel better.

"My story goes beyond that," Manu added quietly.

Ravi did not say anything realizing that Manu was trying hard to open up, and he did not want to do anything to stop that.

"If it was just that, I would not have cared. I was ready to marry her despite my father's opposition," he continued.

"What went wrong then?" asked Ravi in a sympathetic tone.

Manu recalled that fateful day. The rain was pouring so hard that he could hardly see five feet in front of him. He had done his best to steer his horse to a higher elevation. Yet at the same time, he had turned back several times to see Kusuma. All he could see was a huge wall of water crashing on the bridge. He saw Kusuma engulfed by the surging floodwater within seconds, and that was the last time he saw her. He waited for the rain to recede before he could do anything to track her. To his agony and frustration, the rain kept pouring all day and all through the night. It was the next day, around mid morning, when the rains finally stopped. The river was flooded beyond imagination; it looked like a vast lake. Manu was tired and hungry yet he kept navigating his horse through the storm and flood debris, his mind focused on one thing, to locate Kusuma. He kept looking for her along the riverbank, hoping she had somehow miraculously escaped any harm and had washed into the banks. There was no such miracle. He kept looking for her all along the river Sita until it joined the mighty river Ganges.

His search kept him away for two full days during which he had hardly eaten anything. Yet he was not hungry or tired. He was sad, angry, and frustrated. He had never felt so helpless. In the end, he had to accept that she was no more and went back to his house, remained in his room and cried for hours.

Several hours later, Savithri and Chitrasena walked into his room. Chitrasena looked worried and had an apologetic look on his face. He wanted to apologize to Manu for all he had said. As he stood there hesitating to say anything, worried that he may further upset Manu, Savithri gently nudged him to say exactly what he had in his mind.

"Manu, I am sorry I said those things to you. I have thought about it long and hard and have changed my mind. I was wrong in my interpretations of dharma. You can marry Kusuma or for that matter, any one you desire. I am not going to be in your way."

Chitrasena had never sounded so apologetic in his life. Manu did not know why his father had changed, nor did he want to know. Everything looked meaningless to him at that time. Within a few days, he decided that it was unbearable for him to stay in Chitrapuri and left for Pataliputra.

When Ravi heard the story, he felt terrible for Manu. He put his hands over his shoulder and tried to express his sympathy.

"I am sorry to hear this. I am sorry that I was sometimes tactless, and inconsiderate towards your feelings," Ravi expressed.

Manu sat on his chair with his head down with tears flowing on his cheeks. He lifted his hand as if to say it was all right. Ravi quietly left the room to let Manu recover from his grief.

The next few days went by fast with Manu feeling better as each day progressed. He was now completely into his military routine and was even more dedicated to his duties as a warrior than ever. He increased his meditation and yoga routines to strengthen his focus that made him even stronger inside. Suddenly, he felt like he was no more an eighteen year old caught between adolescence and adulthood. It was as if he had reached full adulthood overnight. He was now ready to face any adverse situation and was ready to take on the whole world.

As Manu and Ravi finished their dinner and walked towards their rooms, a royal agent came towards them from nowhere. Manu, impressed by his stealthy appearance, looked at him in anticipation. He knew that the royal agent must have a good reason to come to him and wondered if he had brought him an important message.

"Manu, I want you to come with me. Ravi, you proceed to your room and keep this encounter a top secret," he commanded them as he flashed his secret code only elite soldiers knew.

Ravi was hesitant to leave, as he wanted to make sure that the agent was genuine, and not an enemy spy. He insisted that he would walk with them until the entrance to the royal quarters. Because of Ravi's rank as an elite soldier, the agent obliged, and they quickly went towards the entrance to the palace quarters. The guards greeted the agent and Manu, and asked Ravi to leave immediately. Ravi convinced that the agent was indeed genuine, left for his quarters knowing Manu was safe.

The agent took Manu to a corner of the complex, went behind a shrub, and opened a trap door that led them to a tunnel. Manu and the agent went inside the tunnel, as the agent quickly closed the trap door and locked it. Outside, the guards quickly covered the trap door with sand. The dark tunnel was one of several secret entrances to Vishnu Gupta's office, and both Manu and the agent carefully threaded their way until they came to the part of the tunnel that was lit with oil lamps. Then they briskly walked towards a passage that led them to Vishnu Gupta's office where Gupta himself was eagerly waiting for them.

"Come in, Manu. We are so glad to see you," welcomed Gupta with a big smile and asked the agent to take leave.

Manu looked around for signs of anyone else. He knew Gupta was not alone, as he had alluded to someone else joining them. Gupta, noticing his puzzled look, smiled and explained.

"Give us a few minutes. Kautilya himself will be joining us shortly," he said and led Manu to a table that was surrounded by several chairs.

"Please sit down, Manu," he directed, sitting in a chair opposite to Manu.

Manu sat quietly, not uttering a single word, wondering all along why he had been summoned to the secret chamber. The fact that Kautilya was going to join them soon made it very clear to his mind that indeed something very important was in store.

"Manu, you are probably wondering what this is all about. We will get to that soon. Before we do that, tell me, how are things with you?"

"I am doing fine, Sir. I am eager for some real assignment."

"Do not worry about that. That will happen sooner than you think. By the way, about what happened in Chitrapuri, are you doing alright?" asked Gupta.

Manu was a little surprised that Gupta knew about his tragedy. Then again, he realized that he was talking to the master spy, and nothing escaped his wide net of informants. Was Gupta really concerned about his well-being? Manu knew it was a result of Gupta's relentless devotion to the state, and that his concern for him was one of not wanting to lose a prized warrior. It had nothing to do with how he really felt about Manu or how Manu felt about Kusuma for that matter. Therefore, it did not bother Manu. He was now immune to the selfish behavior of people all under the guise of dharma.

"I am all right now, Sir. I would appreciate if we do not dwell on that," Manu replied politely.

Just then, Kautilya walked into the room looking even taller than the last time Manu had seen him. Maybe he is getting thinner by the day, Manu mused. He had heard reports that Kautilya fasted more than half the time these days. He worked such long hours that he hardly had any time for eating, which perfectly suited him. Both Gupta and Manu stood up to greet Kautilya.

"No need to get up. Let me join you both, and let us not waste any time and get down to business right away," Kautilya urged, joining them.

"Manu, let me explain why we brought you here this evening. We have received some disturbing intelligence, and we are concerned about potential instability in the eastern border," Kautilya began. He then looked at Gupta to give the details about the intelligence reports. "Gupta, please update Manu on the intelligence report you have received."

"I will be happy to, Kautilya," replied Gupta as he stood up and started pacing. Kautilya did not mind that, as he was fully aware of Gupta's condition that made him nervous if he sat in one place.

"Manu, we have received intelligence that a rebel group is undergoing intense training in the eastern valley. We estimate that there are around two thousand of them," he started.

"What is their ultimate goal?" asked Manu.

"They do not seem to have any particular goal. They may start destabilizing the eastern border region, hoping to carve out a small kingdom. Should they succeed, it could encourage other elements that are opposed to the Mauryan rule," replied Kautilya.

"Surely, the Mauryan army can crush such a group in a matter of minutes," Manu observed, as he did not see any urgency to squash the rebels.

"You are absolutely right, Manu. However, that would cost the treasury quite a bit of money. Moreover, there are ways we can eliminate this problem without having to mobilize a large army unit. That is where you come in," explained Kautilya.

"What do you want me to do?" asked Manu. He had a vague idea what was in Kautilya's mind but wanted a confirmation from the genius himself.

"I want you to lead a small group of elite soldiers that will go and annihilate that group," Kautilya replied and waited for Manu's reaction.

"You want me to lead a group that secretly attacks the rebels? You want us to carry out a covert attack?" Manu replied in an almost objecting tone, as he wanted to confirm.

"Precisely, that is what we want you to do, Manu. I want you to be the leader of the group that will carry out this important covert operation."

"With all due respect, Sir, is it all right for us to attack them with no warning? Is this not against the tenets of dharma?"

As Manu looked troubled by the assignment, Kautilya understood his concerns. After all, Manu was still a young idealistic warrior, and such questions were not completely out of the realm. He deliberated to provide the best answer to Manu's question. However, Manu's question had an immediate impact on Vishnu Gupta. He did not like Manu's line of questioning at all, and started developing bizarre thoughts in his mind. Whenever someone questioned his own interpretation of dharma, Gupta felt like dharma itself was under attack by evil forces. He felt claustrophobic as if caught in a shrinking room with walls slowly encroaching on him. He started sweating, and trembling, and closed his eyes. He tightened his fist and somehow managed to control the desperate urge to scream. When he finally had his senses under control, he tried to suppress his anger at Manu. The only thing that prevented him from doing anything irrational was the presence of his mentor Kautilya.

Manu was somewhat perplexed by the bizarre convolution of emotions on Gupta's friendly face. Nevertheless, Kautilya who understood what was going on inside Gupta's head better than any one else tried to calm him down. However, for all those who were unaware of Gupta's past, he appeared to be just an unstable man who often had unexplainable emotional bursts.

"It is all right, Gupta. There is nothing wrong with Manu's question. Let me handle that," Kautilya assured.

"Manu, there are times when a covert action is preferred to an open war. It will save lives of innocent citizens. Moreover, we have verified the authenticity of intelligence reports several times. These rebels are just thugs, and they have no morals. Do not think about them. Think about saving thousands of innocent lives. It is your brave action that will save those lives," Kautilya assured Manu.

Manu accepted Kautilya's argument as it made a lot of sense. He was not going to question Kautilya, someone who had mastered the Vedic scriptures. Moreover, he was itching for a military adventure anyway.

"I am with you now, Kautilya. Tell me how you want me to carry out the mission," Manu replied, bringing a sigh of relief to Gupta.

"I want you to lead a small group of soldiers, not more than four hundred or so. I want your forces to surround the rebels in their hideout and eliminate them. I do not want any one of them escaping and causing more trouble in the future." Kautilya was very clear about what he expected from Manu.

"In that case, I will take two hundred of the best archers and two hundred swordsmen. I will need at least a week to get the plans solidified," Manu said, more enthusiastically this time.

"That is very good. Let us reconvene in four days to discuss the plans. I want you to personally select the soldiers that are going to be part of your expedition," replied Kautilya.

As Manu was about to leave the chamber, Vishnu Gupta had some special advice for him. "Manu, once you have finished your job, as you are leaving the battlefield, do not ever look back."

That seemed like strange advice to Manu, and he did not hesitate to question Gupta. "May I know the reason behind that logic, Sir?"

"You may have mixed emotions. You may feel guilty or you may feel overwhelmed by gore. Those emotions are nothing but Māya trying to take you away from your warrior duty," Gupta eagerly advanced his argument.

Manu nodded his head as if he was in agreement with Gupta and quietly left the chamber.

Manu was extremely busy for the next two days. He had selected all the soldiers that he wanted in his expedition. He, of course, had chosen Ravi as one of the lead soldiers. He and Ravi had worked on the battle strategy for several hours and had come up with a plan they thought was solid. The plan was to divide the force into two groups with one group approaching the valley from the north, and the other group approaching the valley from the south. The archers would make the surprise attack on the rebels in the middle of the night while the other soldiers attacked them from the sides. They also planned to keep the archers moving so that it was impossible for the rebels to guess their location.

Kautilya and Vishnu Gupta reviewed the plans and endorsed them without many modifications. The next night, Manu divided his men into two groups. One group under his command would enter the valley from the north, and the other group led by Ravi was to enter the valley from the south. They left Pataliputra in the evening, just as night was falling on the city. They traveled all night and got very close to the valley several hours before dawn. There, they slowly encircled the valley and hid behind rocks and bushes. There was hardly any light except for the twinkling of the stars. It took them a while to focus on the rebels who were all sleeping on the valley floor with their horses tied to trees. There were so many rebels that it almost looked like a military camp, and for a moment, Manu worried that Vishnu Gupta had underestimated the rebels. He surveyed the valley and tried to get a quick count, but he was relieved as he realized that there were actually fewer than two thousand rebels.

As they settled in their positions, one of the archers released an arrow into the woods to signal the other group that they were ready to launch the attack. Within a few minutes, the other group launched an arrow to signal their readiness. Manu gave his men the signal to start the attack.

The archers immediately started showering arrows at the rebels. The arrows came so fast and with such force, that every rebel hit by the arrows fell down instantly and was rendered motionless by the poisoned tips attached to the arrows. The flood of arrows struck many horses, which made them cry out in pain, waking the rebels. The rebels, realizing they were under intense attack, tried to gather their weapons to fight back. As they reached for their weapons, arrows came down upon them, stopping their defense. Manu instructed his men to stop shooting arrows, as they were now ready to descend into the valley. As the showering of arrows ceased, Manu and his men cautiously descended into the valley from the sides and ambushed those that were trying to escape by horse. The hand-to-hand fighting quickly ended with all the surviving rebels being killed by the soldiers. Of course, the rebels were no match for Mauryan soldiers, who had received intense training. Within an hour, all the rebels had been killed, and Manu and his men stood in the valley, amazed at the speed at which they had accomplished their mission. What was even more amazing was that Manu had not lost a single soldier in the encounter.

Manu and Ravi made one more round through the valley just to make sure that there were no surviving rebels. Satisfied that they had accomplished the mission to Kautilya's specifications, they collected their arrows and quickly left the valley without a trace. As they started galloping away from the valley, Manu was tempted to stop and look back at the fallen rebels. He immediately remembered Gupta's advice and resisted the temptation to look back.

The soldiers got back to Pataliputra and quietly went back to their rooms as if nothing had taken place that night. They rested for a few hours and were back to their normal routine. That night, right after dinner, the same royal agent came to see Manu and took him to Gupta's chamber. This time, Gupta was by himself. He was relaxed and had a big smile on his face.

"Congratulations on the job well-done, Manu. Kautilya sends his congratulations as well," Gupta welcomed, patting him on his back.

"It was nothing, Gupta. As you explained last time, I was just performing my dharmic duty," Manu replied.

"Do not be so modest Manu. I have reports that every one of the rebels is dead, and no one in the valley has the foggiest idea how it all happened. This will make future troublemakers think twice before any misadventure." Gupta seemed very proud of Manu's accomplishments. "Anyway, the reason I brought you here is to tell you that there will be a secret party to honor the leaders. We will let you know the details soon. There will be entertainment, food, wine, and dance. I want you to select forty of your top soldiers to come to the party," explained Gupta.

Manu knew that all his men had done very well, and it was going to be a challenge for him to select the best forty. Nevertheless, he was happy that Gupta and Kautilya appreciated his work.

Chapter 17
Chitralekha

Manu had just finished his morning rituals. He came back to his room and sat on a chair trying to get his thoughts together for the rest of the day's activities. He had to do his morning exercises and the afternoon drills. There was the strategy session he had to go to in the afternoon when senior intelligence officers would brief him and his peers about any upcoming secret missions. He tried to concentrate on his exercise routine and found it almost impossible to do that. Manu was missing his usual sharp focus that morning; and he knew very well what was distracting him. The beautiful dancer he saw last night was fogging his mind.

It had been almost three weeks since Manu was back from the eastern expedition. However, it was all a distant memory to him, and all he could think of was the dancer at the celebrations the previous night. The celebration arranged by Vishnu Gupta was a token of appreciation for the good work Manu and his men had done on their mission. There was good food, music, and even a dance performance. A woman whose beauty seemed divine to Manu led the dance troupe. She had amazing eyes, and an exotic look, and Manu could not resist looking at her admiring her beauty.

All he could think of was her beautiful face and her tantalizing smile. Her name was Chitralekha; he had found that out from his friend Ravi. Manu thought that she was divine; he had not seen any one as beautiful as her. He had noticed that she had glanced at him several times during her dance performance. On one such occasion, Ravi had teased Manu, "Manu, have you noticed that she keeps looking at you? Maybe she wants to tell you something."

Manu ignored him. He did not want to give an impression that he was interested in her, although it was impossible to hide that from his face. Despite his façade of aloofness, the desire was too obvious in his eyes. Ravi did not want to stop.

"She has glanced at you three times in the last five minutes. Do you know what that means?"

"What does that mean, Ravi? Please enlighten me," Manu said, somewhat sarcastically.

"It can only mean that she wants you. You have studied *Kama-Sutra* by *Dattaka*. Haven't you?"

Manu knew Ravi was being silly. "There is no such thing in Kama-Sutra. Stop being silly, Ravi."

"All right, maybe it is not a statement attributed to *Laws of Love*, but it is certainly my experience."

"And you are very experienced in such matters? You can read the mind of a beautiful woman?" Manu teased him back.

"Yes indeed, my friend. One day I will chronicle all my experiences and call it *Adventures in Love*," replied Ravi.

They both laughed. Manu felt more relaxed to ask Ravi about the dancer.

"What is her name, Ravi?"

"See, you are interested in her. Her name is Chitralekha. She is half Arya and half Yavana. The rumor is she is some general's mistress. Maybe you should forget about her Manu."

Manu did not like what he just heard, especially the part about her being someone else's lover. Why did everything have to be so complicated? He wondered. "You are right, Ravi. Let us forget about her. Just enjoy the party."

That was the end of their conversation about Chitralekha. However, she had penetrated Manu's mind, so much so that it was as if there was an imprint of her face etched in his mind.

Manu tried to shake off thoughts of her and decided to go into the exercise room. There he saw Ravi already well into his exercise routine. After his warm-up, he started his martial arts routine with Ravi. They both enjoyed that routine so much so that they had not realized how fast time had slipped. It was almost mid-morning when they stopped and walked into the garden. They sat on a bench trying to relax before they went to the bathroom to clean their sweaty bodies. Ravi was up to his old tricks.

"I see those red marks from the arrows shot by Kama, god of love," he began wanting to continue the previous night's conversation.

"Will you stop it, Ravi? Let us forget about Chitralekha."

"Seriously, why should you forget about her? She likes you, and I know you are crazy about her. Perhaps there is no general involved at all. Maybe it is all a false rumor. Why don't we go to the dance hall after dinner tonight and see if you can meet her."

Manu liked what Ravi said and indeed wanted to believe Ravi. He reluctantly agreed to visit the dance hall, although he knew that it was not something he was going to enjoy. He did not want to get into the habit of enjoying drinks that would hinder his thinking. After all, the dance hall was one place where men went to enjoy food, drinks, and entertainment and forget about the world outside. However, the main reason they went there was for a chance to spend time with lovely courtesans.

As dusk approached, Manu was eager to visit the dance hall. He could not concentrate on anything else, not even his dinner. He just went through the motions, went back to his room, put on the clothing that he thought was appropriate for the evening. As elite soldiers, they did not want to appear in public with any hint of military connection.

When Ravi and Manu reached the dance hall, it was quite dark except for the two burning oil flames on the two sides of the door. Manu noticed that the door was almost twelve feet tall with ornate designs. There were carvings of dancers in various poses inviting visitors to the hall. There were two tall guards with swords and lancers guarding the gates. Manu noticed that they had royal emblems on their attire which meant that they were actual employees of the Mauryan state.

The guards stopped them and made sure that they had enough credentials to enter the hall. The guards opened the door that led them to a reception area where a lovely courtesan greeted them. Ravi took out some coins and gave them to her. Manu realized that it was the entry fee to the hall. The fee went to the state, as did one third of all the revenue generated inside the hall. Kautilya believed in taxing at the end-point rather than at the point of production. For example, farmers and artisans did not pay any tax, but merchants who sold their products paid a tax on a graduating scale with tax going up from basic commodity to luxury items. Naturally, visiting courtesans for entertainment, considered a luxury, had hidden taxes at all stages.

As they entered the main hall, Manu was awestruck by the lavish decorations. There were colorful draperies on the walls made up of the finest silks in red, blue, and green. There were decorative oil lamps on the walls. There were mirrors, false windows, and all sorts of paintings on the walls. There was also a big stage where musicians and dancers were performing delightful routines. There was an intoxicating aroma in the hall, so delightful that it almost made him feel light headed. Manu liked what he saw; maybe this is not a bad place, he thought.

As they sat at their table that gave them a good view of the dance floor, an attractive girl came to them holding several drinks on a plate. Ravi took a glass filled with wine, but Manu made sure that all he took was a glass of fruit juice. As they sat at their table enjoying the entertainment, a middle-aged woman came towards them. For Manu, she looked more like a state official than some one taking care of visitors in the dance hall. What Manu did not know was that she was indeed a state official who made sure that the establishment paid its fair share of taxes. She smiled at them, as she got closer to them.

"Hello, young men. Are you here to enjoy just the music and dance? Or would you like to spend some time with our lovely courtesans?" she asked in a matter of fact way.

"I may want to do that later. However, my friend here is not interested in that. He wanted to know if you can arrange a meeting with Chitralekha."

Manu kept quiet as Ravi did the negotiations. He was a little embarrassed for having to use a stranger as an intermediary to meet his heart's desire.

"Young man, you must be dreaming, right? She does not mingle with ordinary traders or soldiers," the woman was terse in her reply.

She then smiled at both of them, and said, "Why not let your friend take a look at one of our beautiful girls?"

Ravi looked at Manu for an answer, and Manu shook his head indicating his non-interest in any such thing. It did not matter as the woman had already walked away from them.

Within a few minutes, two beautiful young courtesans came towards them and sat next to them. One of them held Ravi's hands, and started whispering something into his ears. Ravi smiled, and they both stood up.

"I will see you tomorrow, Manu. Maybe you should do something wild tonight. At least spend some time with her, and talk to her. It will help you overcome your anxiety."

Manu smiled, and did not say anything as Ravi walked away with his courtesan partner. The other courtesan girl sat next to Manu and held his hands. Manu noticed that her hands were tender and beautiful. Her touch relaxed him, and he smiled at her. She smiled back at him and asked in a sweet voice, "Is something bothering you, young soldier?"

"Why do you think I am a soldier?"

"Your body, your muscles, and your alertness all tell me that you are an elite soldier. Can you tell me your name?"

Manu looked at her and realized she was very attractive indeed. She had a delightful round face, and the fragrance and the jewelry she was wearing made her look even more inviting. Nevertheless, he was not interested in spending the night with her, and he wanted to tell her just that in such a way so that she would not feel hurt. He then wondered if courtesans would really feel hurt by his words. They must; after all, they were God's creations just as he and Ravi were, he reasoned. As he looked into her eyes, he wondered why an attractive girl like the one in front of him would become a courtesan. What is her story? Is she an orphan from a war? Perhaps she is a love child from an affair between a traveling merchant and another courtesan. He was tempted to find out more about her but decided against it.

"Don't you want to talk to me? Don't you find me inviting?" The girl's questions broke his chain of thought. He took her hands, held them softly as he spoke to her.

"It has nothing to do with you. I came here to meet someone. It seems that she is beyond an ordinary person like me. Anyway, as far as we are concerned, you may be better off throwing your love darts at someone else."

The girl smiled. She was not hurt or anything. Indeed, Manu's sensitivity pleased her. "I know. You came here to see Chitralekha, right?"

"How did you know that? Did the woman who was here earlier tell you that?"

"Not really. Many young men like you come here to meet Chitralekha. However, she is not interested in any of them. I do not know why. I really do not know much about her. She is a mystery to most of us."

Manu wondered if she was telling the truth when she said she did not know anything about Chitralekha. He wanted to pry some more. "Does she have a lover? Is there some powerful general who visits her?"

The girl looked at Manu as if he was a hopeless case. "Won't you forget about her, soldier? Why not relax and spend some time with me? I will teach you things you have never even imagined."

Manu could not resist smiling. She certainly knows how to charm a man, he thought. Nevertheless, he got up, and started to walk away from her. "Thank you any way. I hope you will meet some one to spend your time with tonight."

Manu bid goodbye to her and walked towards the main door. As he walked out of the hall, he saw a shadow move behind the curtains at the other end of the hall.

Manu did not give up on his quest to find out more about Chitralekha. Indeed, he was now obsessed with the desire to find out everything about her. To his astonishment, he felt like he had known her for a long time. There was an unexplained connection, which was generating inexplicable desires in him. Deep inside he wanted to embrace her. However, the desire to know her was almost as strong as the desire to embrace her. He decided to do some of his own investigations.

To his dismay, it was as if she was a woman with no history. No one seemed to know where she came from or how she came to Pataliputra. He could never get a satisfactory answer to whether she was some general's mistress or not. Some people thought that her lover was not in Pataliputra any more. Some people thought that she still had a lover high up in the ranks of the military. No one could confirm it. The mystery surrounding her made him covet her company more than ever.

Manu tried his best to focus on his work and other daily duties. Somehow, deep inside, he was confident that he would meet Chitralekha one day and would be able to unearth her story. Meanwhile, he and Ravi kept going to the dance hall almost every night. The outcome was always the same. Ravi ended up spending the night with some lovely dancer and Manu rejecting yet another beautiful courtesan and walking out of the hall. Every time he walked out, he saw a shadow behind the curtains watch him leave.

This had gone on for a week, when on the seventh night Manu decided to stay in the hall until Ravi came out of the interior rooms that were reserved for men to have private moments with the courtesans. He sat at his table drinking fruit juices and enjoying the entertainment when one of the girls came to him with some wine and enticed him to try it. He decided to try it without even thinking about his own commitment. He had committed to stay away from drinks like wine or Soma.

As he sat there drinking wine and enjoying the entertainment, he wondered if he was now a slave of Māya. He did not understand why he was so attracted to Chitralekha. Was she a magician who had put a spell on him? How can he break out of her spell? Should he just forget about her and spend a night with some beautiful courtesan? Ravi had been suggesting just that every night. He would then be just another pleasure-seeking soldier like Ravi. Is that what he wanted?

Just then, Ravi came out of the interior rooms, entered the main hall, and was surprised to see Manu. "I am surprised you are still here, Manu. Did you spend any time with one of the girls?"

"No, Ravi. I just wanted to relax and enjoy the entertainment. Can we get back to our rooms now?"

As they walked towards their rooms, Manu wanted to understand what drove Ravi into his pleasure-seeking behavior.

"Tell me Ravi. Do you have any feelings towards the courtesans you meet every night?'

Ravi laughed. He thought Manu was strange.

"No Manu. It is just a transaction for me. It is like going to a massage expert and getting a good massage or like going to a barber and getting your hair groomed."

"You find that fulfilling?"

Ravi laughed again. He had no idea where Manu was going with his questions. Manu continued, "Seriously, do the courtesans provide you the love you are seeking?"

"You are confused, Manu. You do not go to any dance hall seeking love. You go there for pleasure, to forget your troubles, or to quench your desires."

"The whole thing is just that? It is nothing but a mere transaction to you, and you don't see any other connection cosmic or otherwise?"

"I find it cosmic all right. It is a cosmic accident that I am with a certain courtesan on a given night," Ravi started laughing at his own description. Manu did not laugh but continued to push Ravi to think about his encounters in a different light.

"Next time you are with a courtesan, making passionate love to her, look into her eyes. Do you see joy? Do you see sadness? Even worse, do you see emptiness? Tell me what you see."

Ravi found the entire conversation somewhat strange but was not surprised knowing Manu; he knew Manu came from a different realm when it came to inner feelings.

"How does that matter Manu? After all, the courtesans are there to serve men like us – soldiers, merchants, and travelers. If you start going beyond that limited partnership, you begin to complicate things."

"Ravi, you need to go beyond those conventional boundaries and rules even if it means complications in life. Remember that courtesans are God's creations as well."

"Are you trying to be a Buddha, Manu? You know, the more you think beyond the present and the more you attach meaning to things that go beyond what they really are, the less you will enjoy life. In the end, I am afraid that you will be an old man still searching for the elusive answers. You will not be happy or content, but confused and frustrated. I do not want you to be someone like that."

"Firstly, I am not trying to be like the Enlightened One. You know, unlike him, I am a firm believer in God. Secondly, my friend, those who find the answers are going to have eternal happiness that goes beyond this world. Believe me, I will find the answers!"

There was a sudden silence as both of them wanted to pause. By that time, they had reached their quarters, and Ravi did not wish to continue the discussion. Moreover, Manu's discourse was wearing Ravi down.

Why does he have to complicate everything? Manu takes everything too seriously. He cannot help it, and it is just his nature, Ravi reminded himself. As they were both tired, they went back to their rooms without further discussions.

The next evening, Manu decided not to visit the dance hall, and instead he decided to go to the banks of river Ganges. As he walked towards the river, he had a strange feeling that someone was trailing him. It did not overly bother him, as he knew that secret service agents often monitored the movement of elite soldiers. He was never disloyal to the Empire and being monitored by agents never bothered him. Nevertheless, he was curious to know who was following him. He stopped abruptly and looked back. To his dismay, there were too many people in the market place, and even his trained eyes could not identify who was shadowing him. There were merchants, women, children, soldiers, and even holy men. The market place seemed too normal.

Frustrated, Manu walked briskly, made a random turn into an alley where he found a place where there was a vegetable cart. He looked around, and, realizing that there was no one nearby, he quickly climbed into the cart and hid himself behind the large baskets full of produce. He remained there for almost ten minutes, which seemed like an eternity. Convinced he had successfully tricked the agent, he slowly came out of the cart, went back to the main street, and resumed his walk towards the river.

When he reached the river, he saw hundreds of men and women bathing in the holy river. He kept walking along the bank until he reached an area that was somewhat secluded. He saw many ascetics and holy men who were sitting in that area; some were meditating, and some were sitting next to a fire reciting scriptural verses scribed on palm leaves. He decided to sit beneath a tree nearby and tried to relax. He sat in the lotus position, closed his eyes, and tried to meditate. Several minutes had gone by, and he was unable to focus on his internal spiritual bearings and felt frustrated. He opened his eyes, buried his face in his palms, and tried to decide what to do next. Just then, he heard some footsteps and looked up to see who was approaching him. An old yogi was walking towards him. He smiled at Manu, and sat next to him. Manu was not the least bit surprised by this as he had experienced strange yogis approaching him many times.

"You look troubled, young man," the yogi tried to strike a conversation.

"You do not have to be a great yogi to decipher my situation," Manu said to himself. He, however, was polite to the yogi, and smiled back.

"I can tell it is a woman who is bothering you. I can even tell you that she is a beautiful courtesan who is beyond your reach," the yogi continued. This time, Manu was a little bit impressed, and wanted to hear more.

"You may be right there," Manu replied.

"I know I am right. It is written all over your face," the yogi continued.

"I do not have a magic potion to solve your predicament. Nevertheless, here is my advice. Make sure that she is as beautiful inside as she is outside. It is her inner beauty that will make you happy; not her external appearance."

Although the yogi's advice was too obvious, Manu was nevertheless thankful to him. As he looked closely into the yogi's eyes, suddenly, he had a suspicion that the yogi had trailed him. He was sure he had seen that face in the market place. He wondered if he was an agent who masqueraded as a yogi, or maybe he was a real yogi who just happened to be an informant to Vishnu Gupta's network. He also wondered if this yogi had any connection to Chitralekha. Maybe he was an agent who worked for her?

The yogi then stood up and kept walking towards the woods that were further down stream. The encounter with the yogi added more mystery to Chitralekha's intent. If she were the least bit interested in him, why would she have someone follow her? He had to know her intent. The thought that she might have employed an agent only made his desire to be with her swell like the Holy Ganges after the rainy season.

His desire was manifold; he not only wanted to know Chitralekha's story, he now wanted to know her as a lover, as a friend, and as a spiritual partner. Manu decided to go back to the dance hall, and wanted to try one last time to meet her. When Manu reached the dance hall, he received friendly greetings from every one at the hall. To them he was now a regular visitor albeit a visitor who just came for the music and dance.

As Manu sat at his table enjoying the music and dance, a young courtesan came to him with some drinks. He smiled at her and asked her to sit with him. She was more than pleased to do so as every girl in the hall admired his handsome body, and his pleasant nature.

"Can you do me a favor?" asked Manu.

"Certainly, just tell me what you want me to do," the girl replied.

"Well, this may be my last visit to the hall. Can you tell Chitralekha that I really need to see her? If she does not meet me tonight, I am not coming back ever."

The girl did not mind doing that. As she got up to go to the back rooms, Manu added, "Tell her I just want to talk to her."

Manu sat at his table listening to the music and drinking his wine. He waited anxiously for the girl to come back hoping for an affirmative answer. While the anxiety level was high, he also felt confident that he would meet Chitralekha that night. It was not the first time he had gone through such diametrically opposed feelings. He had gone through a similar experience when he was waiting for his final assessment at the military academy. It seemed like hours had gone by while he waited for the girl to come back. Finally, he saw the girl coming back towards him. He tried to anticipate the answer by looking at her face, but the girl had such a blank stare that Manu could not guess Chitralekha's answer.

The courtesan smiled as she approached Manu's table, which made him experience a gush of happiness through his veins. He knew the answer right then. "Yes, Manu, she wants to see you. She will be happy to spend the whole night talking to you. Just follow me. I will take you to her room."

Manu was delighted and relieved at the same time. He followed the girl to an area behind the hall that connected to courtesan rooms. The girl stopped and took a blindfold out from her handbag.

"I need to do this before we proceed any further. Let me put this blindfold on you. I hope you do not mind this," the girl said apologetically. She seemed embarrassed to be doing it.

Manu did not mind that at all. He was ready to go through any sort of humiliation just to have an opportunity to speak to Chitralekha. The long wait had exhausted him so much that he was now free of any pretense. His feelings for Chitralekha were so intense that he felt that it was his destiny to be the one with her.

What he did not know was that Chitralekha had developed similar strong feelings towards him from the day she had seen him in the palace. She had watched him every night from behind the curtains as he was leaving the dance hall. She was torn between her loyalty to the Mauryan state, and her growing feelings for Manu. She did not know if getting too close to Manu would cause complications in her life. She was a key agent in the Mauryan spy agency run by Vishnu Gupta, and any relationship with a man that involved passion or love would complicate matters for her.

Manu kept walking blindfolded holding the courtesan's hand. He had walked for at least five minutes when the girl stopped and took off his blindfold. Manu knew that he had reached Chitralekha's room, and he started rubbing his eyes to get into focus as the girl left the room. Manu looked around and saw one of the most elegantly decorated rooms he had ever witnessed. The room had the finest furniture, the best silk drapes, and the most beautiful silver and brass lamps, which made the main dance hall look almost ordinary. He then focused on Chitralekha who was sitting on a chair holding two cauldrons of wine. Having not seen her so close by, he was stunned by her beauty; her exquisite features, her dove-shaped eyes, her long silky auburn hair all made her look divine to him. To him she was indeed a goddess. She looked like one of the nymphs who had just dropped from Indra's court. She smiled at him and gave him a gracious welcome.

"Won't you please sit down?"

Just hearing her voice made him feel happier than ever before; it was like sweet nectar to him. As he sat down, she handed him one of the wine glasses. Manu started sipping his wine and was lost for words. Now that he was in her room with complete privacy, he wondered what he was going to say. Realizing he was at a loss for words, he was somewhat embarrassed.

"Now, tell me Manu, how does it feel to be a hero? Even Kautilya considers you to be a hero."

"Oh, that was nothing. All I did was my duty as a Kshatriya. I was just doing my part in protecting dharma," Manu tried to sound modest.

"You take your duty very seriously," Chitralekha replied.

"Of course, one has to. Protecting dharma involves everyone. Even dancers like you."

Chitralekha laughed. As she focused on his face, she saw the same face, the same long hair, high forehead, and intense eyes. The only difference was that Manu was a little taller.

"Now, surely you must be jesting. What can a dancer like me do to protect dharma?"

Manu was not naïve. He knew there was more to her than what was obvious to naked eyes.

"Tell me Chitralekha, what is your role in the grand scheme of things?"

"What do you mean? I am just a simple dancer."

Now it was Manu's turn to laugh. The same laugh had echoed so many times in her heart that it almost made her cry.

"Look at your room. Look at the protection you get. Surely, you are very important to Vishnu Gupta."

She did not even try to answer that question. She was in no position to talk as she tried to suppress the memories. It was now Chitralekha's turn to break down, with all her guard melting like the Himalayan snow in the summer months. It was as if she wanted to make up for the lost time.

By then, both had finished drinking their wine, and she got up and bent over to get the empty cup from Manu. As she bent over, she looked into his magnetic eyes. Manu sensed the desire in her, which encouraged him to do the unthinkable. Overcome by the desire to hold her, Manu drew her close to him. Instantly, both dropped their cauldrons, stared into each other in silence, and were kissing each other endlessly.

It was like there was an avalanche of Himalayan snow. It was like a sudden onslaught of torrential rains in the plains. Manu, surprised by Chitralekha's embrace, felt like they were two lovers that had come together after a long separation. For her it was like going back in time. For Manu, it was as if he had reincarnated ino a future life, for he had always assumed that it was impossible for him to meet her in the current life.

Chapter 18

Bliss

M anu was very happy. Indeed, he was beyond happy. He kept searching for the right word to describe his feelings. He realized that he had never been that happy in his life; blissful was the word that aptly described his mental state. He had forgotten about all his worries, and his recurring existential questions had just vanished. He had forgotten all about Chitrapuri, and Kusuma was a distant memory. He spent the whole night in Chitralekha's room, which was like entering an unknown realm. Indeed, there were so many things she had taught him that night which only reinforced that he was still an amateur in matters of love and passion. Of course, he did not progress much in finding out about her past; those questions remained dormant somewhere in the back of his mind. They did not talk much either, and Manu kept wondering if the whole thing was real. He felt like the lost warrior in an ancient story he had read in his childhood. In that story, enemies chase a handsome prince who is on a hunting expedition. He enters an abandoned mansion and hides behind a pillar. After a while, satisfied that he had tricked his enemies, he leans on the pillar with a deep sigh of relief. Just then, two soft hands start massaging the prince's back. Startled, he jumps and demands that whoever was hiding inside the pillar come out. To his astonishment, an amazingly beautiful woman walks out of the pillar, and he instantly falls deeply in love with her. It was quite a fairy tale, but Manu had always liked that story. He was tempted to tell that story to Chitralekha, but he resisted that temptation.

For Chitralekha, it was like going back in time; at last, she had found the love she had longed for. She was not sure if she was doing the right thing, although she had agonized about it for many days. Now that she was with Manu, she really did not care if it was right or wrong. She felt immensely secure in his arms, and blissful was indeed the word that aptly described her emotional status as well.

Before long, Manu was exhausted and fell into a deep sleep. He did not realize how long he had slept that night. Finally, he could vaguely feel soft hands trying to wake him up by shaking his body. He also heard a voice that seemed to be coming from a distant place.

"Wake up Manu, it is almost morning and time to go back to your place," Chitralekha said.

Manu opened his eyes and did not know exactly where he was. It took him a few minutes to realize that he was in Chitralekha's room, and he jumped up and sat on the bed when he realized that it was getting late. He had to be back in his room before dawn, or otherwise, he could be in trouble.

"I need to get back before dawn. Is there a way I could leave your room without drawing much attention?" he asked Chitralekha.

Chitralekha smiled, sat next to him, and started moving her fingers through his long hair.

"Do not panic, Manu. You will be out before dawn, and I will make sure that no one sees you," she assured him.

He gazed into her beautiful eyes, and he knew deep inside that getting out of that room and leaving her alone was the last thing he wanted to do. However, his warrior duty came first, and he was not going to walk away from that. Chitralekha had tears in her eyes as she concentrated on Manu's eyes. There was a resurgence of magical feelings every time she looked into his eyes. She put her arms around his neck and started kissing him passionately.

"I will be back in the night. Rather, can I see you again tonight?" Manu replied awkwardly. On one hand, he was trying to make her feel better, and on the other hand, he was trying to see if she was serious about their love.

"Of course. I mean, I want you to be here every night from now on," she replied, wiping her tears.

Manu smiled feeling immensely happy. He knew right at that moment that their love was not a "celestial accident" as Ravi had referred to his affairs. It was indeed their destiny together.

Chitralekha went to a corner of the room and opened a trap door covered with a decorative rug.

"Go down this passage, Manu. It will lead you to a chamber at the other end. When you get out of that room, you will be behind some tall curtains in the main hall. You can sneak out without drawing any attention from anyone," she explained.

They hugged for a long time, and as he released her, he entered the passage reluctantly and slowly walked into the dark passage that led into a chamber just as she had described. He opened the door from the chamber, entered the hall behind the curtains, and quickly went into the hall and was back in his room a few minutes before the dawn.

In the morning, he got into his routines without showing any signs of fatigue. To his surprise, he was not distracted any more. He was really into his warrior duties, and he felt that his life was all coming together nicely. He now felt like a real warrior having successfully accomplished his first mission. What's more, he was now in love with a woman who understood his work and really appreciated the importance of his work. For him, their first night together was really the beginning of his new life.

As Manu took a break from his routines, and sat on a bench outside the exercise room, Ravi walked to him with a big grin on his face.

"So did you finally get to meet her?" he asked Manu quietly as he sat next to him.

Manu did not say anything but smiled back.

"Good for you Manu. I am so happy for you that you finally found the love you so much longed for," said Ravi. He waited for a few more moments for Manu to say something. The silence was killing him, as he was anxious to know more.

"Was she everything you had imagined, Manu?" Ravi prompted Manu, trying to make him open up. Of course, he was immensely curious to know more.

"She was beyond anything I could imagine, Ravi. It was as if I had died and gone to heaven and met one of Indra's nymphs," Manu finally replied as he could not hide his joy.

The next few weeks, both Manu and Ravi visited the dance hall regularly. Every night it was the same routine. Ravi would select a girl of his fancy to spend the night, and a different girl would take Manu secretly to Chitralekha's room.

The moments they spent together seemed like they were beyond this realm. He did not know exactly what it was about her that made him feel that way. Was it the tender touch, or was it her embrace? Was it the way she looked into his eyes and ran her soft fingers all over his face? It really did not matter to him. All he knew was that all of it made him feel infinitely closer to her. It was a feeling of closeness that took him into a higher plane. Was it Māya? If it was Māya, he loved every minute of it.

As Manu got comfortable with Chitralekha, he asked her the question he always wanted to ask her. "Chitralekha, tell me about your past. Tell me how you ended up working as a spy for Vishnu Gupta?"

"Manu, you know what they say. Never try to dig into a Sadhu's or a dancer's past. It is never going to be pretty," replied Chitralekha trying to steer him away from the subject.

"I know what they say, Chitralekha. Nevertheless, it does not matter to me. Nothing about your past is going to upset me," Manu tried to reassure her.

"If you really want to know, I will tell you, Manu. I am an orphan of war, and I was fortunate that Vishnu Gupta took an interest in me. It was pure accident, and since then he has protected me like a daughter," Chitralekha replied.

Manu noticed that her eyes were teary, and she had started crying. It was obviously painful for her to go back in time to those terrible days. Manu felt very bad that he had broached that subject.

"I am sorry, Chitralekha. I did not mean to upset you," Manu apologized.

She kept crying which made him even more uneasy, and he finally got out what was really bothering him.

"I was hearing all these rumors about you being a general's mistress, and it kept bothering me," Manu said, relieved that he finally got it off his chest.

Chitralekha stopped crying. She looked at him as if she was surprised that Manu had even brought it up. There was even a tint of disapproval in her look.

"You believe everything you hear, Manu. There are probably hundreds of rumors about the emperor himself. But you know they are all just that, mere rumors," she tried to play down the rumors.

"So you are not seeing any general, right?" Manu still wanted reassurance.

"Of course not, and don't be silly. There is no one else but you," she reassured him as she passionately kissed him.

Manu felt relaxed. Everything was perfect now, except for one thing. He was not too happy with their meeting arrangements. The fact that he had to meet every night in a secretive way made him feel uncomfortable. If there was no one else, why should the meetings continue to be so secretive? He knew there was some security risk in Chitralekha being seen with Manu in the open. He also knew that Vishnu Gupta was not going to approve of such an open relationship. Manu kept thinking for a way out of his situation before it became too unbearable for him. There was only one way out in his mind and that was for him to marry her. However, would she marry him? He had to find out.

In the next few days, Manu and Ravi could not visit the dance hall as Vishnu Gupta had them on a mission to rescue a rich merchant kidnapped by a group of bandits from the jungle. The bandits were demanding a ransom, and the merchant's family was in such a state of emotional despair that they were more than ready to give in to the demand. However, Vishnu Gupta's agents got wind of this, and they had promptly informed him. This was simply not acceptable to Vishnu Gupta for two reasons. Firstly, it was against dharma to reward lawbreakers, and secondly, it would only encourage other bandits to resort to more kidnapping which would ultimately weaken the economy and the Mauryan Empire itself. He promptly had his agents stop the family from paying the ransom and assured them that the royal agents would resolve the crisis. Of course, there was a fee for the service, which went into the treasury.

This was a minor operation for Manu. He selected a few of his best soldiers including Ravi and had a nighttime raid into the bandits' camp, and in a matter of minutes had freed the rich merchant. The intelligence data that Vishnu Gupta had provided was of course, a major reason for a flawless execution of their plan.

All through the campaign, Ravi had noticed that something was bothering Manu. He knew it was something to do with Chitralekha but kept quiet waiting for the right moment to enquire about Manu's well being. Manu and Ravi personally escorted the rich merchant to his mansion, and were on their way back to military quarters when Ravi decided to break the silence.

"What is the matter, Manu? You seem to be in deep thought," asked Ravi.

"Not just one thought, Ravi. A whirlwind of thoughts is going through my mind. It is like I am lost in a jungle and I cannot find my way out," replied Manu, somewhat sad.

"What is this change of tone I see? You were the happiest man a few days ago, and now you sound like you are in some sort of deep crisis. It is Chitralekha isn't it?" Ravi was genuinely concerned about his friend.

"Yes it is. I am so happy when I am with her that I cannot even begin to describe it to you. I cherish every moment with her, and I find it impossible to be away from her even for a few hours," Manu said. It was hard for him to explain his mental state.

"So what is the issue then? All I can tell is you have fallen deeply in love with her."

"I know that. That is the issue. I cannot be her lover the way it is now. I cannot be seeing her the way I do every night. I am getting tired of these secretive meetings," Manu looked sad as he explained what was bothering him.

"There is only one way out, Manu. You need to marry her," was Ravi's prompt answer.

"I know that is the answer. However, will she marry me? You know the obligation she has to Vishnu Gupta. What if he does not approve of it and she does not go against his will? She treats him like her own father," Manu was indeed very sad. "Why do things have to get this complicated?" Manu added as if he was looking for some help from Ravi.

"Isn't it all Māya, Manu? I remember reading that Māya is like air. One cannot escape from it. One has to swim in it, breathe it, and learn to love it. Isn't it part of one's karma?" It was Ravi's turn to get serious.

Manu had never seen that side of Ravi. He was pleasantly surprised and smiled back knowing that he was getting the type of advice he was freely dispensing to others.

"You are right, Ravi. It is my karma. I need to take care of it myself," replied Manu.

The next time Manu was going to be with Chitralekha, he was going to ask her to marry him. He was going to tell her how difficult it was for him to continue the way they were carrying out their meetings. The time was not far off.

It was one of those tender moments. Manu was on the bed next to Chitralekha who was leaning over him, and exactly at that moment he decided to ask her. She would run her finger over him, starting over his forehead, slowly moving over his eyebrows, then down his nose, and finally across his lips. When her soft finger was on his lips, Manu opened his mouth and caught it with his teeth biting as softly he could. Chitralekha pretended to be in pain. Manu released her finger, and grabbed her. Chitralekha thoroughly enjoyed it and started tickling Manu to escape from him. When that silly moment was over, Manu brought up the question.

"Tell me Chitralekha, are you happy with the arrangements we have? Do you want to continue to meet secretively like this?" Manu asked her.

"Why are you asking that, Manu? You are not happy to see me like this?" replied Chitralekha. She was hoping that he would not want them to change the arrangement they had.

"Don't misunderstand me Chitralekha, I do enjoy every moment with you. It is the time when I am not with you that makes me miserable," Manu replied as he kept feeling her soft, long hair.

"What are you getting at Manu?"

"Well, I want us to be able to spend time together whenever we want and wherever we want. I want our love to be in the open, not some state secret," Manu replied in a frustrating tone.

"I cannot be seen in public with any one. That is too risky, and you know that," Chitralekha pushed back.

"Well, there is a way out. You can stop being a spy, and you and I can get married," Manu could not believe how easily he proposed marriage to her.

Chitralekha's demeanor changed immediately. Manu stared hard into her eyes trying to read what was going on in her mind. Her facial expression went through so many transformations at such an astonishing speed that Manu felt like she was not one person but several personalities trapped in that beautiful body. She was happy for a moment as she smiled at Manu almost like a shy virgin, and immediately she was serious as if she were frowning at Manu. That did not last either, as her eyes got teary and she started sobbing as if she were deeply hurt. Manu was at a loss for words and did not know how to react. This was far from the reaction he had expected. Right at that moment, she did something that continued to confuse Manu. She hugged him tightly, resting her head over his chest. They stayed in that position for such a long time that it seemed like an eternity to Manu. Manu did not mind this and kept quiet, waiting for her to come back to her normal state. At last, she finally started to reply to Manu's proposal.

"You know Manu; I am the happiest when I am with you. I am so deeply in love with you that nothing would make me happier than being with you forever. It hurts me so much that I cannot marry you," she cried.

Manu was deeply puzzled from her answer. "Why can't you marry me, Chitralekha? What is preventing you from that?"

"You know, I belong to the Mauryan Empire. A few years ago, a rich merchant saw me and wanted to marry me. He even approached Vishnu Gupta. Vishnu Gupta told him that the price for taking me away from the state was fifty thousand Panas."

"Fifty thousand Panas is what Vishnu Gupta wants? That is the salary of the top General," exclaimed Manu realizing that such a large amount of money was out of his reach.

"Do not blame Vishnu Gupta, Manu. He has set these rules for the integrity of his secret service network. The money goes to the treasury. You know that," replied Chitralekha.

Manu realized that there was no way he was going to raise fifty thousand Panas. He wondered if his father had that much money. However, he was not going to ask him for help. Manu wanted a clear assurance.

"So tell me Chitralekha, if I somehow brought fifty thousand Panas, you will marry me?"

"Of course, I will Manu. You know I love you more than anything in the world," replied Chitralekha with a teary look.

Manu was happy again. Indeed, he had never been so happy before. He was in a blissful state, and he wanted to be like that forever.

Chapter 19
Ravi's Destiny

Manu now had a new challenge, which was something completely new to him. He had never shied away from challenges, but all his previous ones were military challenges, which were easy for him. The present challenge was of a different nature, it had to do with money. He had never paid much attention to money matters all his life. When he was growing up in his father's home, his parents took care of all the financial business. All he had to do was let them know about his wishes, and they were always ready to fulfill his wishes. As an elite soldier, he earned a decent salary that was more than what he needed for his day-to-day needs. Indeed, he had even saved some money over the last few months, but nothing close to the money he needed to secure Chitralekha. However, deep inside he had the confidence that he would acquire fifty thousand Panas. Nonetheless, he did not have the slightest idea how he was going to do that.

Not surprisingly, Ravi had noticed the change in Manu's disposition. He knew Manu had talked to Chitralekha about his desires. He had also guessed that there was some progress but did not know all the details. He did not want to appear to be too inquisitive and waited for Manu to open up on his own at the right time.

A few days after that important conversation he had with Chitralekha, Manu decided to discuss his latest hurdle with Ravi.

"I did have that conversation with Chitralekha about the current arrangement, and it made me uneasy," Manu began.

"Did you ask her to marry you?" Ravi replied, curious to know what had happened.

"I did, Ravi. I told her about all my heart's desire. I asked her to get out of Vishnu Gupta's spy network and marry me so that we could be like any other normal couple".

"You did the right thing, Manu. Did she say yes?"

"It is not that clear cut, Ravi. Chitralekha owes a lot to the Empire for providing her protection all these years. She cannot get out of Vishnu Gupta's network unless I come up with fifty thousand Panas," Manu explained.

Ravi was a bit disappointed when he heard that but he was not surprised. He even wondered if it was just an excuse on Chitralekha's part. "Are you so naïve, Manu? I cannot believe her excuse. It is not as if she is anyone's slave. There must be something more to it, something mysterious," Ravi expressed.

"Maybe so; but I trust her, Ravi. I have to for my own sanity. As far as I am concerned, I need to find that money. She has promised me that she will marry me once I find fifty thousand Panas." Nevertheless, deep inside, Manu had his own questions; he just did not want to focus on them for the time being.

"All right, in that case, that is good news. But how are you going to get that much money?" Ravi knew that it was almost impossible to get such a large amount of money unless someone stumbled across a hidden treasure. Manu had a similar thought at the same time.

"You know the story in which a poor Brahmin helps a tiger trapped in a well, and in return the tiger leads him to his cave that is full of treasure? I hope something like that happens to me." Manu reminded Ravi about a story from Pancha Tantra. Ravi laughed at it; it was a laughter mixed with sadness, as he knew deep inside that it was a hopeless fantasy.

"Yes, I know that. We all know that it is a fairy tale, and that is not going to happen to you Manu," Ravi replied.

"Do not say that, I am desperate," Manu pleaded.

Ravi now felt terrible that he said that. After all, as a friend, he should be providing him support, not making fun of Manu's situation.

"I am sorry, Manu. I did not mean to discourage you. You will find that money soon. I will help you in any way I can," Ravi assured Manu.

The days kept rolling on with Manu finding no possible way to discover the money he needed to marry Chitralekha. He even thought of giving up his military career and becoming a trader or a merchant of some sort. However, that was not an option for him; he knew nothing about running a business and was quite certain that he would not succeed as a trader. He was beginning to accept that the only way he could be with Chitralekha was the current arrangement they had. Over the weeks, he got so comfortable with the whole thing that he even rationalized that it was his karma to have such an unusual relationship with her. His love for her was beyond this world, and he was ready to go through any sort of trouble to see her as often as he could.

A few weeks later, Manu was on one of those monthly secret expeditions that he and Ravi were required to take as elite soldiers. It was something that Vishnu Gupta had mandated for his elite soldiers in order for them to get a different perspective on what he called the health of the Empire. While he and Kautilya continuously gathered intelligence about what was going on around the Empire from an army of secret service agents, Vishnu Gupta never relied entirely on that source. He wanted to get a different perspective from his soldiers who had better training in spotting any military abnormalities. He would randomly select a city or town and ask his elite soldiers to spend some time in that town to spot anything that was unusual.

"I do not like these random trips we need to make," Ravi complained.

"I know how you feel, Ravi. But, you know as Kautilya says, no intelligence is useful unless corroborated. His disciple takes it to the limits. This is Vishnu Gupta's way of cross-checking on his reports. Let us at least humor him."

This time Vishnu Gupta had selected a small town called Ratnapuri that was right on the banks of river Ganges between Varanasi and Pataliputra. Manu and Ravi left Pataliputra in the early morning towards Ratnapuri in a horse drawn wagon. The wagon was fit to look like any ordinary one used by merchants of the time. They even had some silk and spices in their wagon to convince anyone that they were indeed serious traders. As soon as they reached Ratnapuri, they checked into an inn and decided to spend a day or two in Ratnapuri.

After hours of random strolls through the streets of the town, they did not find anything unusual about Ratnapuri. In fact, it was a quiet town where people went about their business in an unassuming way, and where everyone seemed to be at peace. Ravi was immeasurably bored, and even Manu felt that he was wasting his time in that town. He would have left after spending just a few hours, but decided to spend more time only to fulfill Vishnu Gupta's desire for never-ending intelligence.

It was late evening that day, and Manu and Ravi decided to take a stroll near the banks of river Ganges. It was a cool evening and many families had congregated on the banks of the river to enjoy the sunset. There were many children playing in the sand dunes near the riverbank as their parents and caretakers sat on the steps immersed in their conversations. Manu and Ravi sat on a stone bench not too far from the river, and decided to observe the movement of people for anything unusual.

Moments went by and everything seemed to be in order. The sky turned orange in color as the sun slowly disappeared into the horizon. Suddenly, there was a loud scream from a woman who stood not far from where Manu and Ravi sat. The woman was pointing towards the river and screaming for help. "My child is drowning. Please, someone save her," she screamed and cried.

Before Manu realized what was going on, Ravi had dashed towards the river and was quickly swimming towards the drowning girl. Like all soldiers, Ravi was an expert swimmer, and Manu was confident that he would save the child. However, Manu felt chills go down his spine when he heard an old man say, "He is a foolish man; doesn't he know that there are crocodiles in the river?" The old man seemed extremely concerned. Manu closed his eyes and started praying for Ravi's safety.

It was as if by providence that the crocodiles did not make a move towards Ravi, and he was able to hold the girl and quickly swim back to the shore. Perhaps the scary beasts were not hungry, and they left Ravi alone.

Within moments, Ravi had saved the child and had her safely on the banks. He carefully placed her on a sand bed, with her face down, and pressed her back to get all the water from her body. The girl started coughing and crying as the water came out, and her mother rushed to hold her in her arms. She tried to calm the child, and reassure her, and at the same time looked at Ravi to thank him for saving her daughter. At that time, Manu witnessed an extraordinary exchange of looks. Anyone could decipher that look. It was as if there were instant love signals exchanged between Ravi and the woman. They were falling in love. For Ravi, it was all new. For him, love was always a physical experience, and suddenly it was beyond that and he knew all too well that he was charting into an unknown territory. He looked at the child who was still scared from the trauma of drowning and slowly touched her cheeks to reassure her that everything was going to be all right. The girl smiled back ever so faintly as if she understood him. The woman thanked him profusely and walked back with her servant.

A few moments later, the servant came back to Ravi to extend an invitation to him for a dinner the next day. She even asked Manu to join them, but he politely excused himself saying that he had to be back in Pataliputra the next morning.

Manu could see that Ravi was completely lost in love. He knew exactly how he felt; after all, he had been in a similar state of mind when he first met Chitralekha. He only hoped that Ravi would have an easier task in advancing his feelings for her.

Ravi wanted to find out everything about her. Who was she? Was she married? Manu did not think she was married as there was no *Mangala Sutra*[24] around her neck. His guess was that she was probably a widow who had lost her husband in a war.

Ravi looked at Manu as if to ask for his permission to go on an exploratory trip. He was going to do a fact-finding mission of his own to find out more about the woman who had overwhelmed his feelings. "I will do some research on her, Manu. I will see you later at the inn," Ravi said, eager to proceed with his exploration.

"That is all right. We can talk later," replied Manu and went back to the inn.

The next day, early in the morning, Manu was curious to learn about Ravi's findings. "What did you find out about the lady who has captured your fancy?" Manu enquired.

"It is not just my fancy, Manu; she has overtaken my mind. I cannot stop thinking about her. Now I know how you felt when you were desperately seeking Chitralekha," Ravi expanded.

"That is good, Ravi. To be truly in love with someone is a precious feeling. So what did you find out about her?" Manu tried to be supportive.

---

24 Mangala Sutra is a pendant that indicates if a woman is married or not.

"I have found out a great deal about her. Her name is Sulata, and she has lost her husband to the Nandas. He was a very rich merchant who was a victim of Nanda agents when they had found out that he was helping Kautilya and Chandra Gupta."

"The wretched Nandas; I just cannot imagine how many lives were ruined by them." Manu felt terrible just thinking about all the evil deeds committed by the Nandas.

"Anyway, she has now inherited the business and is running it successfully on her own," added Ravi.

"I hope you will have better luck with Sulata, Ravi. Let me know your plans after you come back to Pataliputra," Manu replied.

As planned, Manu went back to Pataliputra in the carriage while Ravi stayed back. He knew that Sulata would arrange for Ravi's travel back to Pataliputra, and he did not have to worry about that.

Manu got back to Pataliputra and gave his report to Vishnu Gupta. He reported to him that they had found nothing noteworthy in Ratnapuri. He also told him that Ravi would be taking a week off from his duties for personal reasons. Vishnu Gupta did not say anything. He just smiled back, and Manu had an eerie feeling that Vishnu Gupta already had reports about what had transpired in Ratnapuri.

Days passed and Manu had not heard from Ravi. He was getting a little anxious about Ravi's well being. However, he was happy to be back in Pataliputra and to be with Chitralekha. It was as if nothing bothered him when he was with her.

Just as Manu had anticipated, Ravi appeared in Pataliputra exactly a week after he had left Ratnapuri. He looked very different, and Manu noticed that he was wearing rich silk clothes and had the look of a wealthy merchant. Moreover, there was a special glow in his face, which told Manu that he was not going to stay in Pataliputra any more.

"How was Ratnapuri, Ravi? You look very happy and relaxed."

"I have never been this happy Manu. I finally understand what love is. I am so much in love with Sulata, I cannot imagine being away from her," replied Ravi.

"So are you going back to Ratnapuri?"

"Yes, I am going to do just that. I am going to resign from my duties as a warrior. I am going to see Vishnu Gupta and inform him of my decision."

"He probably already knows that Ravi. Nothing escapes him," Manu smiled. Ravi smiled back and hesitated as if there was something else he wanted to discuss. "Is there something more you want to tell me?" Manu added. Although Manu knew what was coming next, he wanted to hear that from Ravi himself.

"Yes there is something important I want to tell you. I am marrying Sulata and adopting her daughter," Ravi replied trying hard to control his excitement.

Manu was very happy for Ravi although he knew very well that he was going to miss their friendship.

He had to accept that. After all, changes come, some planned, and some unexpected. There was no reason to complain about changes. Moreover, he still had Chitralekha. What more could he ask for?

"I am very happy for you, Ravi. I want you and Sulata to have a good life. "

"We will be very happy, Manu. However, I worry about you all the time, and I want you to achieve your desire as well. I am sure that you will come across fifty thousand Panas soon and will be able to marry Chitralekha," Ravi replied with utmost sincerity.

Ravi and Sulata had a simple wedding in Ratnapuri that Manu attended. Of course, Ravi had to pay a hefty fine for leaving his military position in the middle of his tenure. Manu went about doing his routines wondering if he was ever going to see Ravi again. Manu reasoned that Ravi, having settled into a comfortable life style as a wealthy merchant, probably had no room to think about Manu or Pataliputra. He was convinced that he was right, as he never heard from Ravi for the next six months.

However, he was wrong, as Ravi never forgot Manu or his predicament. One day all of a sudden, Ravi appeared in front of his room. He looked somewhat heavier for the lack of intense physical routines. His sedate merchant role had made him gain some weight. Manu was surprised to see him and greeted him with a smile.

"What brings you to Pataliputra?" Manu enquired.

"Oh, I was here to make a business deal. When you are a merchant, you are always looking for opportunities to make a profit," replied Ravi.

Manu felt weird discussing business with Ravi. It was not something that interested Manu. He was more interested in telling Ravi about his recent project, but Ravi seemed less interested in that. It was altogether a different man that was standing in front of him. Manu was surprised how a woman could change a man so easily in such a short period.

"There is one more reason that I came to Pataliputra," added Ravi.

Manu wondered about the reason and gave Ravi a puzzled look.

"Manu, your troubles are all over from now on. Here is a gift from Sulata and me to you. This bag has fifty thousand Panas."

Ravi handed a bag full of gold coins to Manu. Manu was speechless and did not know what to say. He tried to control the confluence of emotions that overwhelmed his feelings. On one hand, he was extremely happy that he now had an opportunity to marry Chitralekha. On the other hand, he was not ready to accept such a large amount of money as a gift.

"Ravi, I am really grateful for your generous gesture. However, I cannot accept it. I do not deserve such a gift," Manu replied.

"That is nonsense. You deserve every bit of it. Nevertheless, if it makes you feel better, you can take this as a loan. You can pay it back to me over a twenty-year period," Ravi insisted.

That seemed like an acceptable compromise to Manu. He was so happy that he wanted to dance. Manu accepted the compromise without hesitation. "It is a deal then. I will take the money as a loan. I do not know how I will ever pay you back for this generosity," Manu replied.

Ravi was happy to hear that. All he wanted to do was encourage Manu to see Chitralekha as soon as possible.

"Do not worry about that Manu. There will be plenty of time for you to repay the loan. What are you doing here talking to me, anyway? You must be with Chitralekha right at this moment," Ravi teased.

Chapter 20
Her Burden

Manu had never been so excited in his life. He now had the money, all of fifty thousand Panas, to achieve his heart's desire. The very thought of being free from any restrictions, and to have Chitralekha as his wife made him feel ecstatic. He drifted into a daydream as he thought about that. Finally, when he came back to the present, he thought that Ravi was right; it was no time to be wasting even a second. He quickly kept the money in a safe that was given to all elite soliders for their valuables. He then hurried towards the dance hall. It was still daylight, and Manu knew that entrance to the dance hall would be closed. It did not matter to him, as he knew the secret passageways to Chitralekha's chamber.

Manu had reached the entrance chamber from where a passage took him to Chitralekha's chamber. There, he ran into a dancer who was surprised to see Manu during the daytime. By now, all dancers knew about Manu and his relationship with Chitralekha. They all liked him and even admired his devotion to her. The dancer came to him and smiled, "You are early today, Manu. You know, Chitralekha is not there in her chamber right now. If you want, I can take you to her chamber, and you can stay until she comes back," the dancer suggested.

"That should be all right. I will just do that. Do you know where she is right now?" asked Manu just out of curiosity. He knew she was not out of town on any assignment.

"I think she has gone to meet Vishnu Gupta. She always visits him to give her weekly reports on Saturdays," the young dancer replied.

Manu knew that of course. He remembered that it was Saturday and decided to relax in Chitralekha's room as the dancer led him to the chamber and closed the door. He had never been alone in that chamber and it was a strange feeling waiting for Chitralekha. It was always the other way around with her waiting for his arrival. As he looked around the room, the luxury and grandeur of the decoration was obvious. It was clearly a reflection of her taste and special touch. A large marble framed mirror that hung on one of the walls attracted him. The frame was of pink marble that seemed flawless, and there were many precious stones inlaid that made the mirror exquisite. He was surprised that he had not spent any time looking at the mirror during his previous visits. Of course, with Chitralekha in the room, her beauty masked everything else around her. He wondered how she had acquired that treasure. Was it a gift from someone, rich and powerful, who had loved her in the past? He did not want to think about it.

His attention moved to his own image in the mirror. What he saw was a tall handsome warrior with immaculate looks. He focused on his chiseled facial features and his long flowing hair. His strength was obvious from his toned muscles. He felt good and infinitely confident. He was sure that there was nothing now that was going to let Chitralekha resist him. Just then, the door opened as Chitralekha walked in.

"Is everything all right Manu? I came as soon as I could when I heard you were waiting to see me." She had a worried look on her face as she closed the door.

"There is nothing to worry about Chitralekha. I have a pleasant surprise for you. Indeed, what I have is the greatest news you ever imagined," replied Manu.

Chitralekha flinched to hear that although she had no idea what the surprise was. She carefully hid her feelings and silently hoped that Manu's surprise was not what she feared the most. "You seem to be overly excited, Manu. Can you give me some hints about what it is?"

"I will tell you all about it very soon. First, let me take a close look at you," Manu replied as he held her close to him.

He looked into her hazel eyes, which always made him so happy that he wanted to freeze time every time he held her that way. The effect was even more dramatic on Chitralekha. Every time he held her that way gazing into her eyes, she always felt so weak in her knees that she had an uncontrollable urge to kiss him passionately. It was no different this time. There was absolutely no question about how much she loved Manu. Unfortunately, her past had prevented her from accepting his proposal.

Several moments later, Manu opened up to give details about his newly acquired wealth. "Chitralekha, you remember that insurmount-able barrier that kept us from being a normal couple? We do not have to worry about that any more," Manu began.

Chitralekha listened silently worrying about how she was going to deal with the situation. She was now certain that Manu had somehow acquired fifty thousand Panas. He was going to ask her to marry him again, and she was going to say no. This time, however, Manu deserved to know the true reason.

"Do you remember that I told you a few weeks ago about my dear friend Ravi marrying Sulata, a rich widow?"

"Yes, I do remember that very clearly. You were proud of Ravi and would not stop talking about it," replied Chitralekha.

"Well, Ravi and Sulata have given me a loan of fifty thousand Panas. I can repay it over several years," Manu said. He could not hide his excitement as he explained his newfound wealth. "You know what it means, Chitralekha? You are completely free now and do not have to worry about any sort of obligation, not even Vishnu Gupta. You are free to marry me. Will you marry me?"

Manu went down on his knees as he held her hands. Chitralekha was extremely saddened as Manu completed his story. In spite of the fact that she loved him immeasurably, she had to say no to his request. She knew deep inside that there was no way she could marry him given her past. It broke her heart to say no to Manu. Chitralekha stood silently, almost motionless, wondering how she was to give the negative answer to Manu. The long silence was killing Manu, and he could take it no more.

"Chitralekha, please answer my question," pleaded Manu.

Chitralekha gently urged Manu to stand up and led him to her bed. As they sat next to each other staring at one another, she began to explain her side of the story. "Manu, you know how deeply I love you. You need to understand my past before I can even try to answer your question. Perhaps, my story will tell you about my predicament better than any explanation I may give you," added Chitralekha.

"There is nothing to fear Chitralekha. Nothing in your past, however dark it might be will stop me from loving you. Please say yes," pleaded Manu again.

"No Manu, I am not going to give you an answer right now. You need to hear my story first," insisted Chitralekha.

Her story was very long and sad, and, given Manu's sensitivity, she knew it was not going to be easy on Manu. Furthermore, when Manu found out about the other man, she had no idea how he would deal with that. Nevertheless, she continued with her story.

Her youth was a happy childhood growing up in Gandharapuri. Her mother was a Yavana and her father was an Arya. They had met when her father had traveled to Bactria during his trading trips. Gandharapuri was a fort community situated right at the edge of the Land of Five Rivers that had people from several territories. There were Yavanas, Aryas, and even Persians who all lived happily in the fort. They had enriched each other culturally and had no quarrel with each other. Even Alexander's forces had left them untouched. As an only child, Chitralekha had everything she ever wanted and was well versed in all aspects of Arya traditions, including the Vedic religion. Nevertheless, she had grown to respect aspects of other traditions as well. Everything was going very well until one day the Mauryan forces led by Chandra Gupta and Kautilya came storming into the Land of Five Rivers. The Mauryan forces overwhelmed the Yavana forces under Seleucus, and the entire Land of Five Rivers including Gandharapuri came under the Mauryan rule. People of Gandharapuri were unconcerned by all this since it never mattered to them who really controlled the Land of Five Rivers. They always considered Gandharapuri an independent fort unaligned with any specific ruler.

Chitralekha remembered the day when there was a lot of commotion in the fort. A small Mauryan force had surrounded the fort, and a messenger had come to the gate they had closed in a hurry. He had brought a specific instruction from the Mauryan leader.

"You have exactly ten minutes to fly the Mauryan flag and surrender. If you do not abide by that order, we are going to attack with no mercy." The message was very stern.

The leaders of the fort had a brief discussion about what to do and sent back the messenger telling him that they would fight until the end rather than submit to the Mauryan might. Chitralekha's father had thought that it was not a very smart decision. Indeed, the decision was suicidal.

Within minutes, the Mauryan force was at the fort entrance with large elephants barging on the door. In a few moments, the doors fell, and the entire Mauryan force was inside the fort. The forces of Gandharapuri were no match for the well-trained Mauryan forces, and in a matter of minutes, most of them perished. The Mauryan forces did not stop there; they started going from residence to residence looking for any resistance.

Chitralekha's mother, fearing that the soldiers would come to their residence, quickly hid Chitralekha beneath a bed. Her fears came true when two soldiers who looked intoxicated broke into their house. The soldiers were so inebriated they began a rampage inside the house, which Chitralekha's parents tried to stop. This infuriated the soldiers who wasted no time in slaying her parents.

Chitralekha who witnessed all this from beneath her bed was mortified. She was only sixteen years old and was an orphan in a matter of minutes. She silently cried underneath the bed not knowing what was going to happen to her. She had stayed there for almost two hours when she heard someone going from house to house witnessing what had happened. From his voice, she could tell that it was a man of authority like a general. He was very upset that many civilians were victims of the rampage.

"What has happened here is unacceptable in the Mauryan army. You have not only broken the basic rules, you have also broken the basic tenets of dharma," he yelled. There was a long silence as all the soldiers had now realized that they had crossed the limits. "I want you to go from house to house and provide medical treatment to the surviving civilians."

Chitralekha was still afraid to come out and stayed underneath the bed motionless. Finally, a soldier noticed her when he was searching underneath the beds. "Come out, young woman. We are not going to hurt you," the soldier assured.

She slowly crawled out from underneath the bed and was sob-bing quietly, still worried that the soldier might kill her. The soldier was awestruck by her beauty and decided to take her to his general. He slowly guided her to the tent where the general, none other than Chitrasena, was resting.

Chitrasena looked at Chitralekha and found her beauty to be breath-taking. He had never seen anyone so beautiful in his life. He reminded himself that he was a married man and loved his wife, and he suppressed his awkward feelings. He then asked the soldier to leave.

"I see that you are sobbing endlessly. Something must have happened to your parents. Are they hurt or were they killed?" Chitrasena enquired.

Chitralekha did not reply and continued to sob. Chitrasena felt help-less not knowing what to do.

"Can you at least tell me your name?" asked Chitrasena.

There was a long silence again, and finally she replied in a very low voice, "Chitralekha."

Realizing that she was too horrified to go back to her residence, Chitrasena asked one of the soldiers to set up a small tent for her at-tached to his tent. He also asked the soldier to bring her some food, as she looked tired and hungry. She was, however, in no mood to eat as she drifted periodically between shock and grief. Finally, when she did feel very hungry she ate the food and soon fell sleep.

The next day, Chitrasena went about his business of getting the fort organized while Chitralekha stayed in her tent. In the evening, he came back to her tent to see how she was doing. Chitralekha was still grieving but had accepted that her parents were no more, and she had to think about her future. Her immediate worry was how she was going to survive the next few weeks let alone the next few years. From her perspective, Chitrasena's kindness made her feel a little secure. His strong physique and good looks made her develop a sense of affection for him.

That night when everyone was asleep, dark clouds started gather-ing over the fort, and a torrential thunderstorm started blanketing the area. Suddenly, a massive thunderbolt woke up Chitralekha. She was frightened beyond her senses and did not know what to do. All she could think of was Chitrasena, and she rushed into his tent. Soon she was in his arms feeling secure and protected.

She was now Chitrasena's wartime wife. No one said anything about this as everyone realized that Chitrasena had been away from his wife for months, and the long separation had driven him into that relationship. However, it was Chitrasena himself who was most uncomfortable with his relationship with Chitralekha. He knew he had broken his own commitment to Savithri and was not sure how he was going to deal with that.

"Manu, you now realize why I cannot marry you," explained Chitralekha.

As Chitralekha explained her past to Manu, he felt as if the massive thunderbolt in her story had hit him. He was horrified to think that the woman he wanted to marry was once his father's mistress. He remembered the time when his mother was tense and worried during his father's absence. His immediate thought was that he had committed a grave sin by loving the woman who had caused endless anguish to his mother. He felt angry and dirty; and in a way, he was disgusted at himself. He felt misused now that he knew that the fifty thousand Panas was just an excuse. His face was red, and he was trembling. As Chitralekha witnessed the fast change of emotions in his face, she was worried that Manu might do something terrible in his anger. True to her fears, Manu stood up and drew his sword, which frightened her. Manu did not want to do any harm to Chitralekha, but he had to do something to let out his anger. He looked around the room and focused on the mirror.

"So you got this from my father?"

"Yes, it was a gift he got for me in Taxila," she quietly replied.

"So when did the whole affair end?" Manu wanted to know how the whole thing had ended; he wanted to know that for his own serenity.

"I was his mistress for six months until your father realized that he loved your mother more than anyone in this world. He brought me to Pataliputra and asked Vishnu Gupta to protect me. Ever since, Vishnu Gupta has been like a second father to me," replied Chitralekha.

Manu was still angry. He did not know what he could do to control his anger. Deep inside he was worried that he could do something terrible like hurting Chitralekha, which was against his upbringing. He even had a dejected smile as he thought about how his upbringing, the rules and all the conditioning over the years, had brought him nothing but misery. He did the least destructive thing he could do to quench his anger. He drew his sword, tore the drapes that were decorating the walls, and walked out of her chamber as Chitralekha kept sobbing. She had lost the man she had loved for the second time in her life.

Chapter 21
Bikku

Manu quietly sat in his room not knowing what to do next. Within a few hours, his life had turned from what seemed like total bliss to endless misery. It was as if whenever he got close to ecstasy, agony was just around the corner. He looked at the safe and wondered what he was going to do with the fifty thousand Panas Ravi had given him. He had to return it to Ravi and Sulata for he had no use for any more. A break from routine work would be good for me, he mused. He thought of taking a small break and visiting Ratnapuri to return the money. The more he thought about it, the more he realized that he needed a break from the whole civilization. He did not want to live in Pataliputra any more. Everything there reminded him of Chitralekha. He even considered going to Vishnu Gupta and asking him for an assignment far away from the Capital. He was struggling to find a purpose in his life. Why was he in this material world? Was he here to do something universally good? What is real happiness? Would changing his profession make him happy? Would it give him a real purpose in life? He wondered if he should seek a very different profession like becoming a teacher. The more he thought about life, the more he became confused.

For a long time he was very angry with Chitralekha. He felt used and deceived. However, as time progressed, his anger subsided a little. He remembered that it was he who was desperately in love with her. It was he who had pursued her endlessly. He was now more forgiving; after all, everything is Māya, he thought. There was no reason to be upset at Chitralekha when he should really be upset at Māya. Suddenly it occurred to him that the cure to all his problems was very simple; just overcome Māya. However, how would he achieve that? He had to find the answer to that question. That was going to be the quest for the rest of his life. He now had a real purpose in life. At that very moment, he knew exactly what he was going to do the next day. He was going to tell Vishnu Gupta that he was going to resign from his military post and head towards Ratnapuri. He was going to return the money to Ravi, and would be on his way to overcoming Māya. He was going to conquer it.

Manu was so tired from the restless agitation in his mind that he did not know when he fell asleep. When he woke up, the sun was already out. He collected his belongings from the safe, and he quickly headed towards Vishnu Gupta's office. As a top-level soldier, he had quite easy access to Vishnu Gupta and was immediately in his office.

"What brings you to my office so early in the morning, Manu?" enquired Vishnu Gupta.

"I want to resign from the military post. I will pay whatever is the fine I am required to pay," replied Manu hesitatingly.

Vishnu Gupta looked at Manu somewhat sympathetically. He had the look of someone who knew exactly what was going on in Manu's head. Nothing surprised Manu when it came to Vishnu Gupta's intelligence prowess. He did not even care if he knew all the details about his previous evening's nightmarish encounter with Chitralekha. This was his first test as far as conquering Māya.

"What is going on here, Manu? I seem to be losing my best soldiers every few months. First it was Ravi, and now it is you." Vishnu Gupta was visibly frustrated.

Manu did not want to say anything and kept quiet. After a long pause, Vishnu Gupta broke the silence. "Do not worry about the fine. You are a free man, Manu. You are free to pursue whatever other interests you may have. You do not owe anything to the Empire," responded Vishnu Gupta.

Manu nodded as if he was thanking Vishnu Gupta and quietly walked out of the office.

"You can keep your horse, Manu. There is no need to return it to the royal stable," Vishnu Gupta added as Manu was about to walk out of the door.

For some strange reason, he was in a generous mood that day. Perhaps, he was happy to see that the relationship between Manu and Chitralekha had ended.

Manu did not waste any time in Pataliputra anymore; within hours, he was in Ratnapuri to meet Ravi. He returned the money to Ravi, thanked him for his help, and left Ratnapuri as soon as he could. Ravi, realizing that Manu was deeply hurt, did not press him for any details.

Manu did not know where his next stop was going to be. He kept riding south of the river Ganges looking for a place to make a stop. None of the villages looked interesting to Manu as he kept riding further south. Suddenly, he noticed the tall tower of a temple in a village that was straight ahead. The temple looked very interesting to Manu and he decided to make a stop. The temple built of red sandstone with a tall tower capped with a golden ornament at the top had a large compound around it. There were even several trees inside the compound and a stable outside for tying horses. He got down, tied his horse, and walked into the temple compound. Several people had congregated inside the temple and were getting ready for the evening worship. However, what attracted him was a Sadhu who was meditating beneath one of the trees. The Sadhu was a barely clad old man with various *mudras*[25] on his body. He had mudras in different hues on his shoulders, chest, and forehead. He had long flowing gray hair with a long gray beard and a mustache. Manu thought that the old Sadhu was at least ninety years old, or perhaps he was approaching the century mark. What attracted Manu was the Sadhu's face. Although the Sadhu kept his eyes closed, Manu could see that the strange looking Sadhu had the most peaceful face one could ever imagine. "Here is a man who has conquered Māya," he immediately thought. That thought energized Manu enormously as he realized that with the Sadhu as his guru, he could be on his way to conquering Māya. He went near the tree and waited silently for the Sadhu to complete his meditation.

As Manu stood close to the Sadhu waiting patiently for him to open his eyes, a stranger came to him and tapped on his shoulder. "Walk with me to that tree. I will tell you something about that Sadhu." The stranger addressed Manu in an almost whispering way as he pointed to another tree inside the compound.

Manu walked with the man without any hesitation, as he wanted to know more about the Sadhu.

---

25 Religious or spiritual symbols

"You are going to be disappointed when he opens his eyes," the man began to explain.

Manu had a puzzled look on his face, as he was unsure about what the stranger meant.

"I know you are a little puzzled. Let me explain; the Sadhu has taken a *Mauna Vrata*[26] and has not spoken a word in several years. If you want him to be your guru, you are going to be disappointed," elaborated the man.

For Manu, that was very disappointing to hear. Could he still be his guru? Perhaps, he could use some sort of sign language or he could write notes on palm leaves.

"He looks like such a wise man. It is a shame that he has entered this vow of silence," Manu replied without trying to hide his disappointment.

"No doubt about him being wise. Even if you went to the Himalayas, you will not find someone wiser and more learned than this Sadhu," replied the man.

"What is the use of his knowledge and wisdom if he cannot share it with the rest of the world?" Manu said in a dejected fashion and walked away from the stranger towards the temple entrance.

The temple that housed an image of Goddess Mother had a simple yet elegant architecture. The image of Goddess Mother was in white marble with exquisite decorations. Devotees continuously entered the temple and offered flowers and fruits to the Goddess. Manu sat inside the temple and closed his eyes to pray to the Goddess. He prayed to Her to give him strength to conquer Māya knowing very well that the Goddess represented Māya itself. The whole temple reminded him of his childhood days at Chitrapuri. After he was done with his prayer, he got up and was about to leave the temple when a woman walked to him and offered him some fruits as *Prasada*[27]. He ate the fruits as he was now very hungry, drank some water from the temple well, and walked toward his horse outside the temple. At that moment, it occurred to him that he should donate his horse to the temple. He wanted to disassociate

---

26 Vow of silence.

27 Prasada is the food offered to the deity that is distributed to worshippers as a blessing after the religious service.

with anything that reminded him of his life in Pataliputra. He went back inside, talked to the temple administrator, and convinced him that he should accept the horse as a donation to the temple.

When he was about to leave the compound, he saw a group of people near the tall pillar at the center of the temple quadrangle. There was a priest, along with a man dressed in silk with his wife and a few other relatives. The priest was helping the man place a silver replica of the Goddess's feet at the bottom of the pillar. Curious to know what was going on, Manu asked a stranger the significance of the ritual that was taking place.

"What you see there is a wealthy merchant who had a vow that he would get those silver feet placed at the bottom of the pillar if he had a successful year," explained the stranger.

"What is the significance of the silver feet?" Manu asked, still puzzled.

"It is like this," the man continued, somewhat surprised at Manu's question, "those who are outside the four Varnas cannot enter the temple. This gives them an opportunity to pray to the Goddess without violating the rules laid down by ancient Manu. All they have to do is touch Her silver feet to pray to Her."

Manu felt very sad that a place of worship would discriminate against anyone who wanted to pray. Why would their standing in the society matter? The way Manu understood it, the Varnas were a mere symbol of one's position in the society. Why should that matter in accessing a place of worship? He knew that the Goddess did not approve of that grotesque practice. Manu felt dejected and quickly walked out of the temple.

The only thing he was carrying now was his bag that had a few of his possessions. He kept walking further south in the hot sun not knowing where he was going. He felt lost and thought that he was now a drifter unsure of his next steps. He kept walking in the hot sun for miles and miles without any sight of a village or a town. He had now walked for almost four continuous hours, and he started getting tired and weak. He realized that he was very thirsty and had no water to drink. All he had was his small bag that contained no fruit or water. As he kept walking, he saw a group of buildings in the distance. In the late afternoon haze, he was not certain if it was real, if it was a mirage or if it was his own imagination. The buildings were in the shape of *Stupas*, and he wondered if the buildings were a Buddhist monastery. He started feeling extremely weak and started wobbling; he could not walk anymore, however hard he pushed himself. Finally, unable to walk, he collapsed on the ground.

What he saw was not a mirage; indeed a Buddhist monastery was just ahead of him. Just outside the monastery was a large tree, beneath which sat Chit-Ananda. He was the most senior monk in the monastery who delivered once a week sermons to the public beneath the same tree. Every afternoon, he came and sat underneath the tree to prepare for his evening meditation. As he sat underneath the tree getting ready for his meditation, he saw a man walking towards him at a distance. Suddenly, he noticed that the man was wobbling and struggling to proceed. Within a few seconds, the man collapsed on the ground. Alarmed, the old monk called out to his assistants who came out as fast as they could. He asked them to rush to the man and bring him to the monastery.

The junior monks brought Manu inside the monastery and placed him in one of the rooms. They placed him on a simple bed made out of ropes and gave him some cold water to drink. Manu slowly swallowed the cold water, as he was barely conscious. Then they carefully loosened his garments and sprinkled some cold water on his face. This made Manu come back to his conscious state, and he slowly opened his eyes. As he opened his eyes, he realized that he was in a strange place surrounded by people he did not know. They were all wearing orange robes and had their heads shaved. They were all staring at him as if he was some sort of object of interest. That was not a surprise, given that not many warrior men walked into the monastery. Manu noticed that he was in a small room that had a tiny window, and the door to the room was open. He looked out through the door, and realized that the building had many rooms like the one he was in with an open quadrangle at the center. The quadrangle had manicured walkways with many flowerbeds and trees. There were even several stone benches underneath the large shade trees. The shaved heads of the monks and the structure of the building told him that he was indeed inside a monastery. Manu wondered how he had ended up in that room.

"You will be all right, young man. There is nothing to worry," the elder monk smiled as he assured Manu.

"How did I get here?" Manu blurted out.

"We saw you collapsing on the road. We brought you here to make sure that you would be all right. As the great Buddha once said, - there is nothing more important than helping a soul in trouble,'" explained the old monk.

By that time, another monk came in with a bowl of hot soup. He made Manu sit on the edge of the bed and fed him the warm soup ever so slowly. The soup was bland, but Manu was so hungry that it tasted very delicious. The soup really helped him as he could slowly feel the blood circulating through his body again.

"What is your name? Where are you from?" asked Chit-Ananda.

"My name is Manu. I am from Pataliputra," replied Manu.

"You must be a royal soldier. Are you on your way to some place?" enquired the monk.

"Not really, I am not sure where I am going," Manu replied somewhat hesitatingly.

"You look very tired. You are welcome to stay with us as long as you want. By the way, my name is Chit-Ananda. You may have realized that this is a Buddhist monastery. Anyone who needs help is welcome to stay with us," explained the old monk. The old monk saw a bright young man in Manu and hoped that one day he would join his order as a monk. He was always looking for a few good men who were ready to accept the teachings of the Enlightened One. Once trained in the monastery in the teachings of the great Buddha, they would be ready to spread his teachings to newer villages and towns. Chit-Ananda dreamt that some day Buddha's teachings would reach all corners of the world.

As Manu stared at the old monk, he tried to analyze his inner spirit. What he saw in Chit-Ananda was an old man who was completely content. It was different from the face of the old Sadhu he had seen at the temple. The Sadhu was, indeed, in complete peace. But it seemed as if he were detached from this world. It was different with the old monk. Manu could see that the monk had reached a state where one can be still in this world but yet completely content. He was certainly a man of the present. Manu was not very familiar with the Buddhist thoughts although he had heard many good things about the Buddha. He was not sure if the monastery was the right place for his spiritual quest. Nevertheless, Manu nodded his head indicating his willingness to stay at the monastery.

Over the next few days, Manu slowly got used to the life at the monastery. He got up very early in the morning along with the other monks and practiced yoga and meditation with them. He attended the spiritual classes delivered by Chit-Ananda. While the monks took turns going into surrounding villages seeking alms, he stayed back in the monastery lending a helping hand either in the garden or in the kitchen. He did the heavy jobs such as bringing water from the well or bringing firewood from the forest nearby. Very soon, everyone in the monastery was fond of Manu, and he developed a special bond towards them.

One evening, Chit-Ananda was delivering the lesson on Four Noble Truths. These were the truths that Gautama had realized when he attained enlightenment. From that day, he was the Buddha, or the Enlightened One. For a student of Buddha, it was important to know that the Four Noble Truths were essential in understanding the path to enlightenment.

"Let us focus on the first noble truth," Chit-Ananda started. "The first noble truth is suffering," he declared.

Suffering as a "truth" seemed somewhat obvious to Manu. However, what was "noble" about that truth was not obvious to him. As if Chit-Ananda had read his mind, he continued, "Birth is suffering, so is death. Sickness is suffering, so is aging. Union with something you detest is suffering, whereas separation from something you love is also suffering. In other words, suffering is everywhere and is timeless. It is inevitable. We are ignorant of that truth. As long as we are ignorant of this noble truth, there is no peace, there is no Nirvana."

Chit-Ananda's precise logic was overwhelming to Manu. His argument seemed faultless to Manu.

"What causes suffering?" Chit-Ananda continued. "Suffering is caused by desire or craving. This desire propels us into the endless cycle of birth and death or Samsara. 'Desire is the root cause of suffering' is the second noble truth."

"So how does one overcome this endless suffering?" Manu interjected. He found the logic to be simple, yet infinitely elegant.

"That is the beautiful third noble truth, Manu. All you have to do to stop suffering is cessation from desire or craving," replied the monk.

Manu was not naïve when it came to desires. He had enough experience in life to understand how desire caused pain and suffering. At the time, he knew very well that it was not easy to walk away from desire. After all, it was desire that was the driving force of the material world.

"So how does one walk away from desire?" questioned Manu.

"You are a very good student, Manu," replied the monk, "That is the fourth noble truth. All you have to do is follow the noble eight-fold path to overcome desire. We will learn about that tomorrow. Let us now start our chanting and meditation."

Thus, Chit-Ananda completed his lesson for the day. He was deeply satisfied that the teachings of Buddha were beginning to have a profound impact on Manu.

Manu did not sleep very well that night. He could not wait for the next lesson from the old monk. He, indeed, had a copy of the eight-fold path like all other monks. However, he wanted to hear the teachings from the master himself.

However, the next day, when he sat with the other monks for the lesson on the eight-fold path, Manu had a strange feeling that he was an outsider. Although he had lived in the monastery for more than a month now, he still felt different. It suddenly dawned on him that the feeling was a result of his attire. As he looked around, he was the only one clad in a white robe while the others were all clad in orange robes. At the same time, he also realized that he was the only one with long flowing hair while the other monks had their heads clean-shaven. He knew at that point that it was time for his initiation into the Buddhist path to become a monk. It was not from a desire to conform to the rules of the monastery; rather it was a desire to follow the teachings of Buddha. Manu did not want any sort of distraction that delayed his chances of achieving Nirvana. He thought that it was strange that he was thinking about Nirvana. After all, he was not completely aware of the real meaning of Nirvana.

The next day, the old monk continued his spiritual lesson on the eight-fold path. Chit-Ananda started with the first part of the lesson. That had to do with *Shila* or character. He spelled the first three rules within the eight-fold path that belonged to this group.

"Shila is the way you conduct yourself in this world. Your conduct is essentially defined by three aspects: speech, actions, and livelihood," the monk began. "When I say speech, I mean the right speech. When I say actions, I mean the truthful actions, and when I say livelihood, I mean livelihood that does not hurt anyone."

"But, all these are relative; I mean the right speech, the right actions, and the right livelihood?" asked Manu.

"Right is never relative, Manu. Right means you are doing things that hurt no one. Not hurting anyone, including oneself, is the fundamental tenet of Shila," replied Chit-Ananda.

Manu had to agree. Indeed, that was the basic principle of his up-bringing. His mother always warned him to think of others in whatever he did. For him, adhering to the first three principles of the eight-fold path was not a concern at all. The old monk began his sermon on the next phase of the eight-fold path, which was *Samadhi*. This part was how a seeker would develop his mastery over his mind.

"Samadhi is right exercise," Chit-Ananda explained, "It is the right meditation which is the exercise for the mind. The right exercise for the body is yoga. Yoga and meditation will develop perfect balance between body and mind. With this balance, one perfects one's aware-ness. Perfect awareness is to see things as they really are with correct consciousness."

This part of the eight-fold path was new to Manu. He did practice yoga and meditation on a regular basis. However, it was the teaching of Buddha that connected the power of yoga and meditation to awareness that was new to him. He was now determined to practice the Samadhi part of the eight-fold path with more vigor and energy.

Chit-Ananda then came to the last part of the eight-fold path, which was the most difficult part of the eight-fold path. "The last two steps are developing right understanding and right thoughts. These two together are referred to as *Prajna*," concluded the monk.

As Manu listened to the whole sermon, both the simple logic and the complex steps of the eight-fold path bewildered him. He knew that while it all sounded simple, it was not going to be easy for him to master the eight steps. The old monk read his mind as it was the first reaction most of the young monks had towards the noble eight-fold path.

"Manu, I know exactly what is going on in your mind. Yes, it is not simple to master the eight steps. Fortunately, there is a way to accomplish this which becomes the foundation for your spiritual quest," observed the monk.

"Chit-Ananda, can you explain that to me?" enquired Manu enthusiastically.

"All you need is to take refuge in the three noble jewels. The three jewels are the Buddha, the Dharma, and the *Sangha*,"[28] explained the monk.

"I have indeed done just that, haven't I?" asked Manu.

"You are right, Manu. With your dedication and enthusiasm, I do not see why you cannot be on your way to achieve Nirvana," answered the old monk.

All other monks sitting in the room knew that this was the highest compliment the old monk bestowed on his students.

That was just the beginning of his lessons from Chit-Ananda. Manu was so enamored with the four noble truths and the eight-fold path that he was now committed to follow the teachings of Buddha. The next time the village barber came to the monastery, Manu was the first one in line to get his head shaved. The same evening, Chit-Ananda officially welcomed him to the Buddhist order.

Over the next several months, Manu practiced the principle of the eight-fold path with all his dedication. He was now a strict adherent of the monastic life style. He was always the first one to rise in the early morning. He did hours of yoga each morning to increase his focus and dedication followed by hours of meditation. This together with a strict vegetarian diet made Manu very lean and slim. This made him look even taller, almost like a pillar.

The monastic life style had completely changed Manu. He did not even think about anything in his past. The mundane things in the outside world were of no interest to him anymore. His interest in the external

---

28 Sangha means Congregation.

world was always how he could help others so that they could achieve their spiritual goals. His father, Kusuma, Chitralekha, Kautilya, and Vishnu Gupta were all a distant memory. Nothing bothered him any more although he continued to think about his mother. He was now immensely happy; more than that, he was content. The only question in his head was what was next?

One winter afternoon, when he was taking a long walk with Chit-Ananda, he asked him a simple question, "Chit-Ananda, now that I have dedicated my life to the noble eight-fold path, where do I go next?"

Chit-Ananda looked at Manu as if he was trying to read his mind. Was Manu getting a little bored? Was he asking that question out of some worldly expectations? "You are on your path to Nirvana, Manu. One day you will have reached the state of enlightenment just like the Buddha himself," replied the old monk.

"How would I know that? Moreover, what does it really mean to reach Nirvana?" replied Manu, still not sure of what Nirvana really meant.

"I can only tell you from what I have read from the books on dharma. We all hope to reach Nirvana some day, Manu. It is when you are devoid of any craving, there is no suffering anymore, and there is no cycle of birth and death," explained Chit-Ananda.

"Why do we go through the cycle of Samsara, Chit-Ananda?" Manu was still a curious student, albeit an advanced student.

"The cycle of birth and death is intrinsically related to your karma, Manu. Karma is not just the actions you perform. It is also the intent behind it. As long as the intent is not pure, we will come back to the material world as a consequence of our actions," replied the monk.

"How can we escape from that cycle?" asked Manu.

"The only way to escape is to reach the state of enlightenment or Nirvana. The eight-fold path will help one to discriminate between the karma that leads to Samsara and the karma that leads to Nirvana. As the intent behind your actions becomes pure, you will reach enlightenment," replied the monk.

They were back in the monastery by that time, and they stopped the discussions and went into their respective rooms. They both, however, knew that the dialogue had to be continued. Manu still had many unanswered questions and was eager to find the right answers for them.

Now that Manu had a clear understanding of Nirvana, he did not feel like he was unaware of his spiritual bearings. He felt like he knew exactly where he was going. However, it was not that he was looking for a signpost telling him that he had reached Nirvana. He knew very well that it would just happen provided he did all the steps right. What he did not realize was that his feelings of spiritual certainty were only temporary.

Months went by and winter was now spring. Spring was like heaven in the plains of the Ganges. Days were neither hot nor cold, trees and shrubs were full of new leaves and flowers, and there were no threats of rain either. As Manu sat just outside the monastery savoring the sweetness of spring beneath the tree where Chit-Ananda often practiced meditation, Manu realized that he had never felt so much at peace with himself anytime before. The effects of his dedication to the teachings of the Enlightened One were obvious to every one in the monastery. Indeed, many younger monks had started coming to Manu for spiritual discussions. The practice of Buddha's teachings had purified his heart and mind in a way he had never imagined. Before he came to the monastery, he did not even know that one could reach such a peaceful state so easily. Manu even wondered why so many little things had bothered him so much before he had accepted Buddha's teachings. Things that seemed like the end of the world just a year ago were trivial now from his new vantage point. As he mused about life in general, for some unknown reason, his mind went back to the days he was with Chitralekha. He felt neither anger nor passion towards her. Instead, to his surprise, his feelings towards her were of tender affection. He felt that his feelings were similar to the one the old monk had towards his students. At the same time, he even felt ashamed that he had erupted in such uncontrollable anger the day he walked away from her. Now that he understood what real suffering was, he realized that it was Chitralekha who had suffered the most. He only hoped someday he would meet her again and could ask for her forgiveness. It occurred to him at that point that he was not too far from Nirvana. He remembered that Chit-Ananda had once told him that there would be hints of enlightenment before he reached Nirvana.

Manu was now visiting surrounding villages on a regular basis and was answering any question a common person would have on the Enlightened One. He had now read almost all the writings on Buddhist scriptures and was comfortable in discussing these with anyone: scholar or common person.

Soon, spring became summer, and village leaders often requested Manu to come to their hamlets to deliver a sermon on Buddha's teachings. These sermons took place in village squares in late evenings. Manu gladly went to the villages to give his sermons; his enthusiasm for the teachings of the Enlightened One was limitless. How beautiful it was to be free of any spiritual doubts, thought Manu. Chit-Ananda who had taken keen interest in Manu's progress was extremely pleased with this development. He was happy to see the transformation in Manu from a young student to an admired teacher.

Just when Manu was confident that everything was moving flawlessly, it happened again. In spite of all the readings and discussions, one day, Manu had a very fundamental question about Nirvana itself; he wanted to know about what happens after Nirvana. That evening during his walk with Chit-Ananda, he brought up that question.

"Tell me, Chit-Ananda, what happens to the ones who reach Nirvana?" asked Manu.

"At that point, the soul is liberated, Manu. It is free from the cycle of birth and death. You, of course, know that," replied the old monk.

Of course, Manu knew that. His question was much deeper.

"Does it mean the soul has reached God Almighty?" asked Manu.

That question really surprised the old monk. He was even a little frustrated by that question. Did Manu not know that Buddha denied the existence of an omnipotent God? It was as if all these months of scriptural study by Manu were wasted.

"Manu, I am really saddened by that question. I know my sadness stems out of my desire that you see the teachings of the Enlightened One in a proper light. The feeling of sadness makes me realize that we still have a long way to reach Nirvana. Nevertheless, you know that the Buddhist religion is non-theistic," replied the old monk visibly hurt.

"I am sorry that I caused those wrong feelings in you, Chit-Ananda. I know what the scriptures say, but I am having a real problem in accepting that," replied Manu apologetically.

Manu, of course, knew that Buddha denied the existence of God. However, his followers had built temples and Stupas with images of Buddha all over the Mauryan Empire and prayed to him. That needed an explanation.

"Chit-Ananda, why then do we pray at the image of Buddha? Isn't there an implied divinity in Buddha?" asked Manu.

"You, of course, know this Manu. We pray at the image of Buddha to focus on his teachings. It is reverence, not implied divinity," replied the old monk.

Manu was still not convinced about the non-existence of God. He was also struggling to accept Nirvana as the end-point in his spiritual journey.

"Then, according to the teachings of the Enlightened One, who is the creator of this world?" Manu brought up the question that the monk always avoided answering.

"It is humans who have created God as a result of ignorance. It is a notion created out of fear and is an imperfection that attaches you to something that does not exist. Clinging to this non-existent 'God' becomes a mere impediment to reaching Nirvana," explained Chit-Ananda.

Chit-Ananda had cleverly avoided the question of how Creation had happened. Of course, the Buddha had said, "with our thoughts we make the world." That was, of course, too complex to discuss in a casual setting.

Manu was still not satisfied with the answer. He knew that there are many "gods" in stories told in the Buddhist scriptures. These stories were often part of Chit-Ananda's sermons. Manu wondered why they existed in Buddhist scriptures if the Enlightened One did not acknowledge the existence of a Supreme Being.

"Don't the gods in *Sutras*[29] imply a certain level of divinity?" questioned Manu.

---

29 Buddhist scriptures.

"The gods in Sutras are not divine, Manu. They are mere mortals who have gained a superior power because of good karma. They can only influence events in the material world. They can in no way influence how and when you reach Nirvana. For that, the noble eight-fold path is the only way," declared the old monk.

Manu knew right at that point that he had come to the end of his spiritual journey as far as his stay in the monastery was concerned. He was not sure if he could accept the non-existence of a Creator. Suddenly, for Manu, Nirvana was not everything. It seemed only like a partial answer to his spiritual quest.

Chapter 22
Yaksha

Manu was tired and was eager to fall asleep, but the theological argument he had with Chit-Ananda kept him awake until it was midnight. He was finally exhausted with all the arguments swirling in his mind about the existence of God. Who is our Creator? Why are we here in this material world? What is our purpose here? Can I see God? Can I realize Him? So on and so forth. His questions were endless, but he saw no path to the right answers. He had followed the *eight-fold path* with all sincerity but the devotion to the teachings of the Enlightened One had not brought him any of the answers he was seeking. He felt like a traveler lost in a dark forest, anxious but not hopeless. He somehow felt that his quest would not be fruitless.

Before he knew it, he had fallen asleep. Only when he woke up in the early morning did he realize that he had had a decent sleep that night. He had slept that night in the monastery garden like most of the bikkus did on hot summer nights. He had slept on the same bed made out of ropes and had covered himself with a light cotton sheet as protection from the insects. He felt calm and rested, and he felt energized by the serenity of the early morning. As his mind was blank, he stayed on the bed searching for his next move. He stared at the stars as if looking for a divine guidance. The sky was completely clear as the rainy season was a few weeks away. He was not sure if he wanted to be a bikku the rest of his life. Should he stay in the monastery as a bikku or should he move on with his spiritual quest? The time spent with the other bikkus had indeed helped him to get over the trauma of breaking up with Chitralekha; his early experience was indeed pleasant as he was learning many new things, including a different approach to spirituality. He even felt that he had seen glimpses of Nirvana. However, after last night's discussions with the old monk, he was convinced that Nirvana was not his final goal. Now it was becoming very clear that the path laid down by the Enlightened One was not for him, as he was unsure where it was taking him.

As his mind came to focus, Manu decided to leave the monastery. He knew that his decision was the right one. He argued in his own mind that the decision was good for him and for the monastery. His prolonged stay would only cause him increased frustration, and the other bikkus may start regarding him as a troublemaker.

The sun was not yet out; there was not even any hint of the fast approaching dawn. He looked around and saw that all the bikkus were fast asleep. He wanted to leave the camp before any one of them woke up for their morning routine. He got up and walked towards a rock that was at the edge of the garden far away from where he was sleeping. He took out his old bag he had carried with him all the way from Pataliputra. He had kept it in a brass box given to him by Chit-Ananda that was hidden underneath the rock, well protected from the elements. It contained all the worldly "possessions" he had brought with him. As he opened the box and took his bag out, he noticed that the bag was dirty and wrinkled. However, what was inside the bag appeared well protected as he slowly opened the bag and sat there for a while staring at the contents. There were a few gold coins, which he never needed. There was also a palm text that had the sacred Scripture, and the golden bracelets he had bought to give as a token of his love to Kusuma. He thought about Kusuma and wondered what had happened to her. It took him back to Chitrapuri, which made him almost cry. He could not forgive himself for not being able to stop her from drowning in the flash flood. He thought about his father; he was surprised that he was not angry with him any more. He had realized that his father was being a traditionalist and was just following the rules handed down by the ancient Manu. He was pleased at himself for not getting angry as he remembered his father. There was a smile on Manu's face; the sort of smile one gets having accomplished something important. Perhaps, this is one of the fruits of months of training as a bikku, he mused.

The palm text was the holy Bhagavad-Gita, given to him by his mother during the initiation into the Vedic tradition - his *upanayana*. According to the laws of ancient Manu, only the top three Varnas were initiated to study the Vedas. That was when he had gotten the sacred thread that went across his shoulder, which he had removed after entering the monastery. Of course, Buddha did not believe in the Vedas or the Vedic traditions. The tradition of initiation to learn the sacred texts was not foreign to them. Their spiritual masters always initiated bikkus just like his initiation into the Vedic tradition several years ago. After all, Chit-Ananda himself had initiated Manu when he joined the monastery more than a year ago. However, to the followers of the Enlightened One, carrying a thread across one's shoulder to symbolize the first step towards the spiritual path seemed unnecessary. Moreover, they could not accept the Vedic tradition of granting only the first three Varnas the right to initiation. The Enlightened One had forbidden any such discrimination when it came to the question of spiritual quest. Manu agreed with that; he had never felt comfortable about the Vedic tradition of Varnas. He remembered all the arguments he had with his father when he wanted to marry Kusuma. He then thought about his mother Savithri and her perennial kindness. His eyes got moist, and he wanted to see her again. He was trying hard not to cry. The words of Chit-Ananda echoed in his head: misery comes from attachment – free yourself from attachments to the material world. He realized that he had failed to get rid of all his past attachments. Why should he get rid of the feelings he had for his mother? The more he tried to stop from sobbing, the more uncontrollable it became. He kept crying ever so quietly until he was exhausted, and his eyes were almost dry. When he finally stopped crying, he recalled that he had never cried after joining the monastery. Living with bikkus had given him a different perspective on his own spiritual journey. He was now certain that desire and agony were connected. He was also certain that leading the life of an ascetic was good for his soul. He always liked meditation and yoga. His main frustration was their non-theistic approach to spirituality.

How could you believe in spirituality if you do not believe in God? He never found a satisfactory answer to that from any of the sacred Buddhist texts, not even from Chit-Ananda. He felt sorry for the bikkus, as he was certain that the other bikkus were all destined to get frustrated just like him. The path they had chosen may or may not be leading them to Nirvana. Sure, it made them mentally tough and gave them the ability to reject worldly comforts. By his casual observations, not all of them had succeeded in getting rid of the noose of desire. Those who had conquered desires, material or otherwise - they indeed had achieved peace of mind in a way. They were indeed content with whatever little they had and had found solace in their simple way of life. However, for Manu, that was not enough. He was not seeking just peace of mind; his goal was to reach God Almighty Himself. All the talk about the existence of just a supreme state (Nirvana), and God being just a creation of deluded men, frustrated him a lot. Perhaps there is a supreme state where one is devoid of suffering. However, what is the source for that supreme state? After all, everything including the supreme state owes its existence to God. Therefore, in Manu's mind reaching Nirvana was only half the journey. Why should he aim for something that is not the source but just an effect? In the end, he realized that Nirvana was not what he was seeking. Being content and at peace with his feelings, was not what he was seeking; he felt like he had taken an unnecessary detour in his spiritual quest.

He looked at the palm text – the Bhagavad-Gita. He got nostalgic about his Upanayana. True to her nature, Savithri had made grand arrangements for his Upanayana. Hundreds of guests had come for the initiation ceremony. There was even an envoy from the emperor himself; he had come to the ceremony bearing gifts. His father was very proud of that day. His only son was entering the path laid down by the ancient Manu. He would become a real warrior and would be the pride of the Kshatriya race. He would be a protector of dharma and bring honor and fame to his family. He was even busy discussing how Manu would one day join the Mauryan army and how he would be a star general. Savithri was different; she understood the true meaning of Upanayana. She new it was the first step in her son's spiritual journey. Her wise words were still vivid in his mind.

"You need to memorize all the seven hundred verses of Gita, Manu," Savithri advised as she gave him the palm text.

"I will mother," Manu promised.

"It is not enough to memorize the verses. You need to understand them and capture the true meaning," added his mother.

"Mother, I have been told that it is not easy to grasp the true meaning of the Gita," Manu replied, daunted by the task of understanding the true spirit of Gita. He knew that even scholars struggled to grasp the true spirit of Gita.

"Yes, that is true. Read it once, twice, ten times. You will finally begin to understand the true meaning. But you need to read it again and again until one day the Truth will hit you."

Manu had indeed kept his promise. He had memorized all the seven hundred verses. He had read the Gita hundreds of times, but always would be stuck at some difficult verse. No doubt, he had understood the literal meaning of all the verses. He knew, however, that Gita is not about the literal meaning of the verses. There was that hidden Divine knowledge - the secret he was after, which always seemed so elusive. Manu wanted to read the Gita again. He wanted to find a guru who would show him the hidden meaning of the sacred Scripture. He was now confident that he would grasp the true meaning of the sacred Scripture.

It was as if the right time had come for his enlightenment. Like his childhood teacher, Shotri used to say, "There is a right time for everything. Until that time comes, you need to be patient!" Perhaps, the right time is just around the corner, thought Manu.

As he walked away from the monastery with his wrinkled bag, he felt relieved that he had taken the right step. Nevertheless, he was not sure what that next step was. Where was he going to find his guru who would show him the path to the Lord? How was he going to discover the bridge to the Lord? Would he meet him today or tomorrow or next month? What would he do if he never found such a spiritual master? He felt dizzy and stopped thinking. He felt weak, abandoned, and lost. He could not move any more; he stopped for a minute, closed his eyes, and focused all his energy on God Almighty. He stood there still with his eyes closed until he regained his composure.

Suddenly, he had a surge of excitement go through his body and soul. All the answers are in the Gita, he assured himself. He thought about setting up his own ashram to study the Scripture and unearth its meaning. He knew that there were many ashrams if he could travel a few hundred miles to the south of river Ganges. He could just join one of those ashrams.

The region south of the Ganges was full of dense forests. There were lawless thugs who randomly raided unsuspecting travelers. The royal army made periodic raids into the woods to catch the thugs. Over the years, the woods had become reasonably safer; however, there was always the risk of attacks. There were other dangers too. Many dangerous wild animals like tigers, bears, boars, and cheetahs freely roamed in the woods. In spite of such inhospitable surroundings, many learned seers had built ashrams deep in the woods teaching young students the secrets of Vedic scriptures.

Manu's immediate plan was to join one of those ashrams. Perhaps, he could join one of the ashrams, become a resident helper, and use the time to study the Gita. He could discuss the secrets of the Gita with the seers. He could even start his own ashram one day. Manu could not control his excitement about the endless possibilities. Suddenly, he was confident that he was on the right path this time. The self-doubt was gone.

He kept walking away from the monastery as briskly as he could. The sun was not yet out. Any minute now, the sun should start peeking out, and the chirping of the birds would wake up the bikkus. He wanted to be as far away as possible before any one of them woke up. He did not want to explain his decision to the other bikku friends especially the old monk Chit-Ananda. He did not want any of them to feel bad although he was certain that as learned ascetics they would not be hurt. At most, they would be disappointed and may even feel sorry for Manu. There was no need for any of that. It would be wasted emotions and thoughts from Manu's perspective. He stopped and looked back at the bikku monastery for one last time. It appeared almost like a miniature camp from that distance. He silently bid his final goodbye to his dear bikku friends and started walking south.

He must have walked eight or ten miles when he started feeling weak and wanted to rest. Manu saw a large tree with a stone bench beneath it. He sat underneath the tree to relax. Manu was indeed very tired but had never felt so energized before. As he sat there staring at the horizon, he saw a cart drawn by two horses approaching him. As it came closer, he saw a farmer who was carrying some vegetables and milk in the back of the cart. The farmer was on his way to a nearby town to sell them. The farmer recognized the bikku and slowed his cart. He stopped the horses, got out of the cart, and bowed in front of Manu, a symbol of reverence. Common people always respected bikkus, and Manu was not the least surprised by this. The farmer addressed Manu in a humble manner, "Oh Bikku, I am very pleased to see you. May I offer some fresh milk to you?" asked the farmer.

"Thank you very much for your kindness. I am not hungry right now. I may want to go to a nearby village for afternoon alms," replied Manu.

"You look tired. Please have at least a cup of milk," the farmer insisted.

"All right, I will take a cup of milk," Manu agreed.

The farmer got excited. Everyone in his village believed that feeding a bikku was good for the soul; it was good karma. He briskly went back to his cart and brought a cup of fresh milk. Manu felt refreshed as he drank that milk.

"May I ask you where your village is?" Manu enquired as he finished drinking his milk.

"My village is just four miles south of here. Please do visit my village. They are always eager to hear words of wisdom from bikkus like you," he eagerly replied. There was a sense of reverence in his request.

"I will do just that. I can have some rest before I proceed on my afternoon journey," assured Manu.

The farmer felt good about the fact that a bikku had accepted his milk. Many in his village believed that bikkus brought good luck. Manu thanked him once more and continued his southern journey as the farmer went back to his cart.

Manu kept walking in the morning sun until he had entered the farmer's village. He wanted to stop in the village for a drink of cool water as the summer morning was becoming warmer by the minute. As he entered the village, he saw that a group of villagers had gathered around a large tree and were relaxing after the morning work. There were children nearby who were playing with toy carts. On the other end of the road, he saw two young boys chasing a rooster. The houses looked modest, but one look made it clear that it was a village full of life and bustle. One of the men who had gathered around the tree saw Manu, rushed to him, and led him to the group.

The village elder came to Manu with his hands folded, and asked Manu to sit on a stone bench that was underneath the tree. As Manu sat on the bench, the crowd gathered around him. They seemed to be full of curiosity. Each one of them seemed eager to talk to him, but waited for Manu to settle down. Finally, the village elder spoke, "Bikku, my name is Veera Sena. I am the village head here. We are very happy that you have entered our village to share your wisdom. Welcome to our village and please consider this as your home. We would be very pleased if you would accept alms from us," the village elder welcomed.

"I am delighted to be in your village, Veera Sena. Indeed, it will be an honor to accept your alms. Any village that respects men of religion is my home indeed. However, all I want is some fruits for my lunch and some cold water to take a reprieve from the summer heat," replied Manu.

The elder was pleased, immediately summoned a servant, and asked him to bring fresh fruits from his house. As the young servant ran to his master's house, Veera Sena turned towards Manu and looked at him with respect. The intense staring by the old man made Manu wonder what he wanted from him. The old man's face looked wrinkled, yet it had a mysterious charm. He still had a full head of hair that had turned completely gray, yet his eyes were sharp and exhibited intense energy almost like that of a young warrior. The way the other villagers treated him made it obvious that he was an accomplished warrior, a rich merchant, or a wealthy landowner. Perhaps, the advancing age had made him look into the spiritual aspects of life. He appeared to have the curiosity of a seeker; he did not look like any of the common citizens that Manu had met in his daily routes who were interested in blessings for the sake of material gains in life. Even his questions were thoughtful.

"Would you be kind enough to share your words of wisdom with us? We know that bikkus are great reservoirs of wisdom. You surely look like one who has discovered the secrets to enlightenment. Can you reveal some of it to my people? Please tell us about the path that leads to Nirvana."

Manu was embarrassed. He did not think that he deserved all the praise that Veera Sena showered on him. "I will do my best. I am still a seeker. Nirvana has eluded me for a long time, but I have learnt to distinguish between what is real and what is a mirage. I will speak from my own experience," explained Manu.

Before Manu had realized, there was a sizeable crowd that had gathered around him. The boys had stopped chasing the rooster, and the group of children had abandoned their toy carts and had come to see Manu. Even some women had joined the men who were already there. Many of the women had fruits in baskets and were eager to offer them to Manu. Children watched him with curiosity as he ate some of the fruits and drank cold water.

All this fascinated Manu. He felt important, and it made him feel good. He was sure that the villagers were dharma conforming citizens; their eagerness to learn more about dharma made him develop a bond towards them. He felt like he belonged to that village as the crowd waited patiently for Manu to finish his meal.

The crowd could not hold back anymore. They were darting questions at him like eager children in a school. Every one wanted to know about the four noble truths. Some wanted him to explain the eight-fold path. Some wanted to know about God. One man even asked if Buddha was an incarnation of God. When Manu explained that the Enlightened One did not believe in God, there was a loud gasp. A child asked him if he had met the Buddha, and the adults started laughing. To add more levity to the atmosphere, Manu added, "Do I look three hundred years old?"

That really made everyone laugh including the children. After a while, a middle-aged woman got up and spoke. She was dressed in a bright green sari and had a motherly appearance. Manu thought about his own mother. Her eyes were red either from crying or from lack of sleep. She looked worried and had an anxious look. Anyone could tell that she was in some sort of crisis.

"Bikku, do you have the magic powder?" pleaded the woman.

"What type of magic powder?" Manu asked as he was not sure about her question. Manu could only guess where she was going with that question. He felt uncomfortable knowing he was going to disappoint her, whatever the reason behind that question.

"My little girl is very sick, and I have heard about the magic powder which cures illness in children," the woman replied.

Manu felt bad for the woman. He did not think such a powder existed. At the same time, he did not want to disappoint her. He suddenly remembered that he had some sacred ashes in his bag that was given to him by the Shotri in Chitrapuri. For some unexplainable reason, he had always carried it with him. He remembered what the Shotri had said, "It is not the ashes itself but the faith in God that will help you." He took it out from his bag and gave it to the mother.

"Smear this over your child. This will protect her. However, promise me that you will take her to a doctor in a nearby town. Have absolute faith that God will protect your child," he assured her as he placed a pocket of ashes in her hands.

The woman's face brightened up. She was now convinced that Manu was the answer to her prayers, and that the sacred ashes would indeed save her child's life.

Manu did not want to spend more time in the village. He started to feel uneasy that the villagers had unreal expectations about him. They even assumed that he had some sort of divine power, which made him very uncomfortable. He knew very well that he had no such power in him. He took some of the fruits they had brought to him and put them in the bag.

"I want to thank you for all your hospitality. Nevertheless, I must be going. My journey has just begun," explained Manu.

The crowd felt disappointed. However, Veera Sena understood Manu.

"We thank you for gracing our village. We would want you to stay a few more days, Bikku. However, we realize that it is not possible, and we wish you success in your spiritual journey. Let me walk you to the gate," the village elder thanked Manu sincerely.

Veera Sena kept walking alongside Manu, as it was the customary way to bid farewell to important guests. They had walked a few yards from the crowd, when an old woman came walking from one of the side streets. She had ruffled hair, rags for clothes, and had her hand stretched out. She kept humming a melody while staring at her stretched palm and almost bumped into Manu. Manu stopped and held the woman as she looked up at him and smiled.

"It flew away," she said.

"What flew away?" queried Manu. Manu realized that she had a troubled mind, and was searching for some thing she had lost, perhaps a loved one.

"My pet parrot is gone. The one that I loved so much, which danced on my palm. Sometimes it danced on the back of my hand. I had it in a cage, and when I came home, he was gone," she said. She kept sobbing as she told her story to Manu. Manu tried to console her, but was unsure how. What could he say? Tell her that the parrot was safe somewhere?

"I think the cat ate him. Do you think so, Bikku? I know that is what happened. My sweet parrot, can you please bring him back?" she continued to sob.

"Why do you think that the cat ate your parrot? Did you see any feathers? Perhaps, it just flew away to be free in the wilderness. Wouldn't that make you happy?"

The old woman stopped sobbing and slowly looked up at Manu. This time her eyes did not seem that sad; instead, there was a twinkle in her eyes.

"Oh, Bikku, do you really think so? You think he is happy where he is. Is he safe?"

"Yes, indeed. I think he is free and safe in a far away forest. There is nothing for you to worry about. He is free, flying from tree to tree, and playing with the other parrots. That is the way it should be."

The old woman felt like she had received another life. It was not just the lost parrot; she indeed had lost hope itself. She had been lonely and unhappy for a long time. People wondered why she was upset so much about a lost parrot, and everyone had only treated her as if she were mentally unstable. No one was willing to listen to her story, and no one seemed to care about how she felt. However, here was a young bikku, a total stranger who was willing to listen to her, and even astonishing for her was the fact he had shown her a way out of her misery; indeed, he had given her peace of mind.

She looked at her palms as she brought down her stretched arms. She looked up in the sky, and tried to focus hard on the birds in flight as if to spot her parrot. She then looked at her own clothes and felt somewhat ashamed. She bent down and touched Manu's feet, which embarrassed Manu infinitely. She then got up and started walking towards her house, slowly at first, but briskly as she approached her home.

Veera Sena was immensely pleased with what he had just witnessed. He knew at that moment that Manu was special.

"Please come back and visit us soon, Bikku," said the elder as he bid farewell to Manu at the village gate. His eyes were almost moist as he saw Manu walk away from the village. Manu's intelligence, honesty, and wisdom had overwhelmed the old man.

Manu had walked several miles south when he noticed that he was entering a wooded region. As he followed the trail, the vegetation was getting thicker by the minute, and soon he was inside a dense and lush forest. The forest was so dense that even with the sun out it seemed dark and eerie inside. He kept hearing strange sounds of animals and birds. The forest was getting scarier by the minute, and he wanted to reach a safe place before it started getting too late in the evening. Sensing that it was dark all of a sudden, he looked up and noticed that dark clouds were gathering in the sky. There was a storm brewing, and soon there would be torrential rains. He knew it was going to be a wild night; he started walking briskly towards a small hill that was a mile or so from where he stood. At least, he wanted to be on higher ground to avoid the flash floods that the rain would bring. As he started walking briskly towards the hill, the wind was picking up and the swirling wind made unbearable noise. At the same time, he saw the bright patches of light from the lightning streaks, and the thunder that followed those streaks was deafening to Manu. It started raining hard, and the raindrops were soaking the forestland so much that the forest floor was getting slippery by the minute, and it was impossible to walk briskly.

All of a sudden, Manu felt something hit him on the head. Before he could realize what had happened, he had fallen flat on his face on the wet forest floor. He stayed motionless on the ground for several minutes trying to recover from the jolt. Finally, he tried to get up and felt like he had an unbearable headache. He wondered how long he had passed out. He slowly got up and managed to walk with great difficulty. The rain was coming down so hard that he was beginning to lose his bearings as he could hardly see ten feet in front of his nose. The rain kept pounding incessantly, and the wind made such an unbearable noise that he had to cover his ears as he walked slowly in the storm. He was extra careful this time, as he did not want to fall and get hurt again. Nevertheless, it happened again. Before he knew what happened, he had slipped again, and this time he was sliding down the hill towards the bottom of a valley. As he slid to the bottom of the hill, he was relieved that he had not hit any large tree or a thorny bush. He sat at the bottom of the valley trying to regain his senses.

It must have been hours before he garnered enough strength to stand up and look around. He noticed that the rain was easing and at the same time, the wind was dying down. He looked up and realized that he had entered a long and narrow valley that looked very idyllic. There was a large lake at the center of the valley. The lake water was as clear as crystal; there were hundreds of lotus flowers – pink, white, and yellow flowers floating on the surface of the lake. He noticed that the storm had completely stopped, the clouds had moved out, and the sky was clear. The filtered sun light made the trees and the flowering vines that hugged them look heavenly. The grass was so green and dense that the waves caused by the mild breeze made it look like a flowing green river. The shrubs were blooming with colorful flowers and added more beauty to the backdrop. The air was misty; adding a sense of mystery to the entire valley.

"Where am I? Am I dreaming?" Manu wondered. He could still feel the pain in his head from the fall, which assured him that it was not his imagination. He thought that he had discovered some sort of hidden playground for the gods! Nevertheless, Manu sensed a kind of eeriness. There was silence everywhere. He could not hear even a bird or an animal. All he could sense was the fragrance that filled the air. The fragrance that radiated from the water lilies was so pleasing it made Manu almost light-headed. Perhaps because of the aroma in the air, Manu felt like he had been to that place before; it seemed so familiar that it was as if he were in a time warp. Suddenly, out of the mist, he saw a mysterious figure emerging. As he focused on the approaching figure, he noticed that it was a tall man who was staring at him as he walked towards Manu. "Perhaps he is another traveler who is lost just like me," thought Manu.

As he came closer, Manu noticed that the man looked like no one he had seen before; he had glowing skin and long hair. He was wearing clothes decorated with golden embroidery.

"Perhaps, he is a prince who has lost his way around the forest. Perhaps, he was here on a hunting expedition," reasoned Manu.

"I was expecting you, Manu. What took you so long to come here?" asked the mysterious man.

Manu was baffled. "How does this prince know my name? Is he a relative of the emperor? Does he know Kautilya or my father?" Manu immediately thought.

"Who are you? How do you know my name?" Manu enquired the stranger.

"Oh! I am a Yaksha. I have been sent to show you the path to ultimate Truth," replied the mysterious man.

"You are a Yaksha? Who sent you here?" asked Manu sounding a little nervous. At the same time, there was total disbelief in Manu's voice. Manu had read about Yakshas in ancient stories, but he never believed that they really existed. He had heard that they lived in the high Himalayas and had mysterious powers, but he always thought that was just in ancient tales. If they did exist, was he here to ask him questions? He remembered the episode in the *Mahabharata*[30] – called "Yaksha Prashna" or "Yaksha's Questions" – the episode in which a Yaksha had come to test the five Pandava brothers. He recalled the four questions in that episode posed to the eldest Pandava prince.

The Yaksha had asked, *"What is this world covered by?"*
The eldest Pandava replied, *"This world is covered by ignorance."*
"What makes it invisible?"
"It is invisible because of the dark qualities in humans."
"Why does a man abandon his friend?"
"A man abandons his friend because of greed."
"What prohibits a man from going to Heaven?"
"Attachment to the material world prohibits a man from going to Heaven."

---

30 Ancient Sanskrit epic that addresses four goals of life: dharma (righteousness), kama (pleasure), artha (wealth), and moksha (liberation).

After reading that episode, Manu had thought that the eldest prince's answers were very enlightening. He was nevertheless dissatisfied with both the questions and the answers. He felt that the questions and answers revealed only the partial truth. Of course, Manu wanted to know the whole Truth, and he was not willing to settle for partial answers.

Manu came back to the present thinking that he was not worthy of such a special treatment. Indeed, he knew that a Yaksha would descend from his realm to help a mortal being only if the human were special. At least, that is what he had read in ancient stories. He wanted to find out more about this Yaksha's intentions. He wanted to know what had brought the Yaksha to him or what had made him stumble across this mysterious being.

"What do you mean by the path to ultimate Truth?" enquired Manu.

"Are you not a seeker? You have indeed searched for the Truth all your life. I want to show you the path that takes you there," answered the Yaksha.

"How do you know I have been a seeker? Is it my bikku robe? Besides, I have never believed in the existence of Yakshas. Are you real or are you some kind of spirit that has descended to torment me?" Manu asked nervously. Manu was also aware of the bad spirits in ancient stories that often came down to torment humans. The Yaksha was somewhat amused by Manu's questions as he smiled.

"Relax, Manu; I am not going to hurt you. Indeed, I am a Yaksha, and we are real. I know everything about you. I have been watching you ever since you were a baby. We only appear to answer difficult questions when someone deserving needs help. Haven't you read about the story of a Yaksha who came to help a prince who was madly in love with a village girl?"

Manu did not know that story. Nevertheless, he liked the theme. "Then, where were you when I needed you years ago?" Manu retorted.

"You mean when you wanted to marry Kusuma?"

This astonished Manu. It seemed that the Yaksha indeed knew everything about him. His apprehension about the Yaksha disappeared. Instead, there was enormous respect for his powers. He noticed that he suddenly felt comfortable being near him. Manu was no longer fearful of the Yaksha's powers, and indeed started believing in him. He now wanted to know more about the Yaksha himself. He mellowed and asked softly, "Do you have a name, Yaksha?"

"Yes I do. My name is *Siddha,* and you will be happy that you met me," replied the Yaksha continuing to make Manu feel comfortable. "Manu, you are destined to reach a higher spiritual plane. The hurt and disappointment that you have experienced in your life so far were all part of a larger plan. I am here to reveal that plan to you."

Manu found the whole encounter with Siddha very intriguing. What was the grand plan he was talking about? He got very curious. How was he going to reveal that plan?

"What is this plan you talk about, Siddha? How are you going to reveal it? Can you explain all this to me? I am really lost here," replied Manu, almost pleading.

"Well Manu, we will go on a journey back in time. We will witness sacred events as they unfold. They will lead you to the Truth. It will become clearer as we travel back in time. Just hold my hand and we will begin our journey."

Manu hesitated. Nevertheless, he was attracted to Siddha's mysterious powers and felt hypnotized. He could not help but want to do exactly what he was told. As if under the Yaksha's spell, he slowly lifted his hand and held Siddha's palm, which seemed unbelievably soft. Manu felt like a marionette controlled by a puppeteer.

Chapter 23
Mysterious Journey

Manu held Siddha's palm tightly not knowing what to expect next. He was anxious and even worried about his well-being. Suddenly, he could see Siddha and himself lifting up into the sky at an astonishing speed. He felt like he was traveling faster than Indra's thunderbolt. He had never experienced such a high speed; even the fastest steed he had rode was nothing compared to what he was experiencing now. The sucking sound generated by the wind was deafening. He was afraid that he would burn or even worse, that he would fall into a valley or a river and die. He started feeling dizzy and felt that he was losing his grip; he could feel his sweaty palm slowly slipping away from Siddha's grip.

"Help me Siddha, I am slipping. I am going to die," shouted Manu, hoping Siddha would hear him.

"Nothing to worry about, Manu; you will be all right. It is just a few more minutes," assured Siddha.

He looked up and saw that the Yaksha was firmly holding his hand and knew immediately that it was all his imagination. He started to feel a little better, but the thought that he had to go through the journey for a few more minutes made him sick to his stomach. He closed his eyes and started to meditate to calm his senses. Slowly, his meditation calmed him down, and the nauseating feeling he was experiencing subsided. Now that he felt a little secure, he started wondering about Siddha. Why was he taking him on this mysterious journey? Was he someone who had come back from the past, perhaps, a famous Yaksha he had read about in ancient stories? He thought about Kubera, a famous Yaksha who had an air-chariot that traveled at astonishing speeds. Perhaps Siddha was Kubera in disguise. Why would Kubera, the richest being in the entire universe, take him through this journey to help him see the Truth? His curiosity would not go away.

Manu did not know how long he was lost in his thought. He suddenly felt that they were descending. The wind was decreasing, and it now felt like a pleasant breeze in the spring. As they both touched the ground, he was scared that the momentum would throw him into a tree or a large rock causing him some serious injury. To his surprise, he landed very softly and barely felt the ground as they both came to a stop. As Siddha let his hand go, Manu started feeling dizzy again and was about to fall. Siddha held him for a while to make sure that he got back his bearings.

"Feeling all right, my friend?" asked Siddha.

"Yes, I am all right. But tell me, how did you do that?" asked Manu, still awed by Siddha's power. He still could not believe the experience he had just gone through.

Siddha just smiled back. "That is not important now, Manu. Let us just focus on why we are here. We are here for you to experience the spiritual awakening," replied Siddha.

"All right then, you do not have to tell me about your secrets. Anyway, where are we now?" Manu was still a little frustrated that Siddha continued to be very mysterious.

Siddha was quiet and did not bother to answer Manu. As they were walking slowly, Manu noticed that he was in an unspoiled wooded area. He saw no signs of human imprint whatsoever as he walked between the bushes and trees. He was a little concerned that he would step on a thorny bush, a sharp rock, or a snake and would hurt himself.

"Nothing is going to harm you right now, Manu," Siddha assured. It was as if he was reading Manu's mind.

"Are you sure about that? This place certainly looks like an unexplored territory. There may be lions or tigers or even cobras."

"Stop worrying about all that, Manu. You are not physically here. Your presence is just in spirit. Let me assure you that no one can see you or touch you. No one is going to hurt you either," replied Siddha.

Manu noticed that Siddha was getting a little impatient. Manu himself realized that he was too worried about his well-being, which was somewhat uncharacteristic of his nature. He was like a distracted student or an unfocused warrior, which was not at all like Manu. He decided to stay focused.

Meanwhile, Siddha's reassurance made him feel relaxed, and he started admiring the unspoiled beauty of that forest. As he looked around, he sensed that it was early spring. Although it was a new place and he was a stranger to that forest, he felt like he had been there before. He knew he was in the past, but did not know where exactly in the past. He kept walking through the woods for what seemed like forever, when suddenly, Manu realized that he was approaching civilization. He saw some cows and fawns grazing the green meadows and noticed that there was a group of small houses not far from where he was standing. He could even hear some voices. As he tried hard to make some sense of what he was hearing, he felt that it was something very familiar to him. He struggled hard to understand the voices but the wind kept shifting in direction making it hard for him to decipher the words. As they approached the houses, he noticed that he was in an ashram complex. From his vantage point, he could see the flower and vegetable beds in the garden. He could also see the priests who all seemed busy, and men and women who were helping them. He could now hear their chanting more clearly, and he knew right then that they were chanting a hymn from Rig Veda.

Manu stopped and hesitated to proceed further.

"There is nothing to worry Manu. Believe me, none of these people can see you or hear you. They can neither harm you nor comfort you. Come, let us go and see what they are up to," coaxed the Yaksha.

Manu and Siddha slowly approached the ashram. There was a *yagna shala*[31] in the center of the garden with a large fire at the center. Priests had gathered around the fire and were performing a Vedic homa. He also saw a lamb tied to a nearby tree. He looked at its innocent eyes and wondered if it knew what was about to happen to it. He felt sick thinking about it. He looked away from the lamb to suppress his distress.

"Are they going to sacrifice the lamb?" he asked Siddha.

---

31 A place where yagna or homa (fire ritual) is performed.

275

"There will only be a symbolic sacrifice. No killing will happen. It will be back grazing in the meadows soon," replied Siddha.

Manu felt extremely relieved, and focused on the priests who sat on wooden platforms around the fire. All of them were chanting enthusiastically in unison, while the one, who appeared to be the head priest was busy pouring some liquid onto the fire. The fire kept burning vigorously. Manu recognized that they were chanting a hymn honoring Varuna, the sky god. It was the twenty-eighth verse in chapter two.

"What is he pouring onto the fire?" he asked. Manu was curious as he had not seen that liquid before. He had only seen clarified butter used in performing a homa.

"Oh, that is Soma, the divine drink. There is nothing better than Soma to please the gods," replied Siddha. Meanwhile, the chanting continued vigorously.

> ... *Having extolled thee, with thoughtful service. Oh! Varuna, may we have fortune in thy service...*
> *Let us be under your protection Oh! Varuna...*
> *Free us from sins Oh! Varuna, as from a bond that binds us....*
> *Keep us away from fear Varuna, the emperor of Rita (cosmic order)...*
> *Strike us not Varuna with those dreadful weapons which at thy bidding wound the sinner...*
> *Oh! Mighty Varuna, even as of old, we will speak forth our worship...*[32]

The chanting was going on in full vigor with many priests and people in the audience closing their eyes in prayer. Suddenly, a little boy who sat on his mother's lap raised an innocent question.

"Mother, is Varuna really God?"

The child's mother looked embarrassed by the question. She was afraid that the question might upset other women around her and tried to hush her child. "Do not talk, my child. There is an important yagna going on. You do not want to upset Varuna as bad things may fall upon all of us."

---

32 Rig-Veda 2.28.

Manu could see that the woman was trying her best to keep the child under control. Indeed, Manu himself had wondered about that same question. Who is Varuna? He knew that he is the keeper of Rita, the cosmic order. He was the sky god who punished the bad ones and protected the good ones. However, was he really God Almighty?

The child was getting restless and was angry that his mother was trying to suppress his natural inquisition. He felt angry and his first instinct was to cry. However, the child was determined to find the answer. He suddenly stood up and shouted, "Can someone tell me if Varuna is really God Almighty? If not, who is God Almighty? Where is He?"

There was a collective gasp, and the priests stopped their chanting. Their faces were red and were extremely upset that an important sacrifice to the great god, Varuna, had been disturbed. They were concerned that Varuna would strike back at them, and something harmful would happen. All the men and women who had gathered around looked extremely worried. It was as if time was standing still; everything was frozen. Some of the younger priests were upset that the child had derailed their rhythmic chanting. The parents and relatives of the boy felt embarrassed as everyone in the audience started staring at the boy. The boy grew scared and realized that what he had done was not right. He had disturbed an important yagna. Would his parents punish him for this? Just the thought of punishment made him cry; he had heard about punishments, but had never gone through one before. Realizing that crying may cause more problems, the boy did his best to control his emotions. He quietly sobbed, and the child eventually became silent. There was now absolute silence all around the yagna shala.

The silence was especially intolerable for the mother of the boy. She was hoping that the priests would ignore the boy and would continue with the yagna.

An old priest who was not part of the yagna, but was observing all of this from the audience, started walking towards the sacrificial fire. He had watched the whole incident from a distance, and he knew exactly what was going on in the boy's mind. After all, almost everyone had asked the same question at one time or another; but no one really knew the answer. The old priest was no longer performing the sacrifices. He was too old from the physical stress of doing the sacrifices day in and day out. As he walked towards the center of the sacrifice hall, many younger priests looked worried. This puzzled Manu. What Manu did not know was that the old priest had some unique ideas about the Vedas, and many thought that he was senile. He often got into spiritual arguments with conservative priests.

He stopped at the center of the sacrifice hall in front of the gathering and started addressing the child. He talked very slowly as he was approaching one hundred years of age.

"My child, you are asking a very valid question. The trouble is we do not know the answers to the second part of your question," began the frail priest.

There was a collective gasp one more time. The priests seldom admitted that they did not have the answers for anything. His candor surprised many in the gathering.

"Who is God Almighty? None of us knows the answer to that. While we do not know the answer to that question, we do know the answer to your first question. We know Varuna is not God. He is just a glory of God."

The boy was extremely pleased. For once, a priest took his question seriously. The mother was relieved too. The old priest suddenly started chanting a hymn from Rig Veda.

> *...He who gives life, who gives strength, whose commands all the gods obey...Who is the God to whom we shall worship with this oblation?...*
> *He by who the awesome earth and sky were made firm...*
> *Who is the God to whom we shall worship with this oblation?...*
> *He who fathered the earth and created the sky, whose laws are True...*
> *Who is the God to whom we shall worship with this oblation?...*[33]

As the old priest was reciting the hymn, Manu, overcome with a desire to know more about the old man, wanted to get closer to him. Manu recognized the hymn. This was one of Manu's favorite hymns from the Rig Veda. He had always debated in his own mind about the significance of the hymn. Was it saying that God is yet to become manifest, and if so,

---

[33] Rig-Veda 10.121.

when would that sacred event occur? How would He reveal Himself? Is the hymn saying that Indra and Varuna were nothing but glimpses of God's glory? As he pondered the meaning of the hymn, Manu felt like there was a spiritual bond between him and the old priest. Manu wanted to know him, talk to him, and debate with him just as he had done with the monks in the monastery. He felt frustrated that the old man could neither see him nor hear him.

"Manu, go and take a closer look at the old man," encouraged Siddha.

Manu walked to the man and stared at his face. He was very, very close to the old man; but he was not worried as he was aware that no one there could see him. He looked at his old sunken eyes, wrinkled skin, his cheekbones, his high forehead, and the long nose. As he stared into his eyes, he could not believe what was going on. He felt goose bumps all over. It was as if Manu was looking at his own image, perhaps an incarnation several thousands of years ago. He could feel a surge of electricity go through his body and felt extremely pleased. He was excited that he was witnessing his own incarnation from the ancient time. Was there a Divine reason behind all this? He looked at Siddha as if begging for an answer.

"Yes, Manu; it is you. You will find the answers to your questions as we progress in our journey. Now hold my hand. I need to take you somewhere else," replied Siddha as if he had read Manu's mind.

Chapter 24
The Revelation

anu did not know where Siddha was going to take him this time. Was he taking him further back in time, was he going to take him into the future, or were they going somewhere in between? He was nervous and was apprehensive about the gyrations, the swirling sensations, and the feeling of weightlessness he was going to experience. He found it too torturous. While he was excited about reaching the destination, whatever it was going to be, he was not looking forward to the physical excitation he was about to experience. He was physically too weak and emotionally too drained to experience that. The previous stop had made him feel much older, and he did not find either flying or time travel exciting. He, however, accepted the journey as a part of his karmic cycle.

"Are we going back in time again?" Manu asked Siddha.

"Not really; let us move the clock forward this time. You will be still in the past, however," replied Siddha.

"Where are you taking me this time? To the snow covered Himalayas?" Manu's expectation was that he was going to meet an ancient seer or maybe the Enlightened One himself and find all the right answers to his spiritual questions.

"Why do you think that we are headed towards the mountains, Manu?" asked Siddha, a bit puzzled by Manu's question.

"I thought you might take me to an ancient seer who would have answers to all my questions. I have read that the wisest ones are in the mountains," clarified Manu.

Siddha simply smiled. Manu did not even have the slightest idea where Siddha was going. He had no idea that he was going to witness the holiest and the most sacred event in human history.

Manu held on to Siddha as they both lifted into the sky. As he lifted upwards, Manu could see the holy ashram and all the people disappear beneath the clouds. To his surprise, he found the journey to be more relaxing this time around. There was neither the headache nor the dizziness he had experienced the first time. The journey was more soothing. Perhaps it was because they were traveling forward in time, Manu reasoned.

As they landed this time, it was pitch dark, and Manu could not tell where he was. He nevertheless sensed that he was closer to civilization. He could deduce this from the ground he was standing on. It seemed to be a paved pathway. As Manu looked around, his surroundings became a little clearer. The terrain was similar to Pataliputra, but for some unknown reason, Manu felt that he was nowhere near Pataliputra.

Both Siddha and Manu kept walking on the paved road. They had walked for tens of miles when they came across a river. The river was full, yet calm. However, it was too wide to cross at that point. The paved road had made a turn and was running along the river until it came to a spot where the river had narrowed into a ravine. Manu saw a bridge across the ravine and started to follow the road.

"Where are you going, Manu?" asked Siddha.

"Aren't we going to cross the bridge to get to the other side?"

Siddha smiled, "We do not need a bridge. Let us cross the river right here."

Manu had not expected this. The physical laws meant that it was simply not possible to "walk" over the river to the other side. Wouldn't they both sink down and drown? Manu was scared to walk over the river; nevertheless, Manu knew he should trust the Yaksha. After all, he could not have made this incredible journey without his help. He started walking over the flowing river, which felt wobbly and made him almost dizzy. He was again scared that he might sink into the deep river and drown himself. He quickly leaned towards Siddha and grabbed his shoulder with his left hand. The Yaksha smiled again.

"It will take just a few minutes before you get used to it," Siddha assured Manu.

As they walked towards the center of the river, Manu was getting more and more confident. He took his hand away from Siddha's shoulder and started walking on his own.

"By the way, Siddha, can you tell me the name of this river?" asked Manu.

"This is Saraswati River, Manu," Siddha replied in a matter-of-fact way.

"You mean the Saraswati River mentioned in the holy texts?" There was a sense of excitement in Manu's question.

Manu was in disbelief and could hardly breathe. He had read about the Saraswati River in the sacred texts, but everyone knew that the river was no longer visible to human eyes. Everyone believed that it had gone underground, perhaps several miles below the surface of the earth. Why would it just disappear? Manu had raised this question to many wise teachers but never had gotten a satisfactory answer. Perhaps, Siddha might know the answer.

"Of course, it is *the* Saraswati River. She disappeared because she could not bear to witness the world moving away from dharma into the clutches of Māya," replied Siddha.

He went on to explain, "Māya is a test, a barrier to overcome. Alas, most of the humans fail to pass the test, fail to overcome the barrier, and are caught in the cycle of Samsara."

"So Saraswati disappeared because we are drowning in the ocean of Māya?" asked Manu.

"Yes, you are right, Manu. It is something for you to think about and analyze. It will get you primed for what you are about to witness," added Siddha.

Manu was not happy with the answer he got from Siddha. The answer seemed very ordinary. He expected such an answer from ordinary scholars, but not from Siddha. His expectation was that Siddha would reveal answers that he had never heard or read anywhere. He was utterly disappointed and even started wondering if he should have embarked on this journey. Again, did he have a choice? Certainly, there was a bigger reason why the Saraswati had disappeared. The Yaksha must know the reason. Why was he not telling him? Was he supposed to realize it himself? He remembered the age-old wisdom, "one has to find the Truth in his own Self." If that was all he was going to learn from this journey, he was going to be disappointed. He did not want to be disappointed again. He wanted to turn back and go to the present.

"Siddha, please stop. I don't want to go back in time. I want to go to the present," Manu stopped and held Siddha by his hand.

Right then, the wind started blowing strongly. It was gaining strength by the minute, and waves, which were mere ripples a minute ago, started rising. Manu started losing his balance. He knew he was going to fall into the river and drown. He cried for help but no one could hear him. He tried to find Siddha, but the storm was so furious that he could not see anything beyond his own nose. Soon the waves were as tall as Manu, and he lost his balance as one high wave struck him on his head. The headache started coming back, and he had excruciating pain in his head. He tried to feel the water, but there was barely any feeling in his palms. Instead of water, he felt clothes and leaves. He did not know what was going on. He was lost, and he started to cry, almost like a baby in pain. Then, from a distance, he heard a voice, "You will be all right, Bikku. Just relax. We will take care of you."

"Siddha, is that you?"

It did not sound like Siddha. It was as if it were coming from some place far away. It even sounded somewhat boyish. Manu was confused. There was a long silence. He wondered where he was. Was he back in the present? He was now repenting that he had wanted to go back. He wanted to continue with his journey, and he felt his headache easing.

"Siddha, please come back. I am sorry. I want to apologize, and please do not punish me like this," he cried out as loud as he could.

There was no answer, and the silence was killing him. Finally, he heard Siddha. At that moment, Siddha's voice seemed like a voice sent from the heavens.

"Are you sure you want to continue, Manu? You are not afraid of the Truth?"

"No, it is not that. I am sorry, Siddha. I was out of my mind when I questioned your intentions. It was that I did not want to be disappointed again."

Manu was yet to recover from all the disappointment he had experienced as a bikku.

"You will not be. You have my promise," Siddha reassured him.

By the time Siddha finished speaking, Manu noticed that they had almost crossed the river. Siddha stepped on the banks first and helped Manu come to the shores. Then, they both started walking briskly along the paved road. He felt no pain and was relaxed. He looked up in the sky and noticed that it was a clear night with innumerable stars gazing at him. He noticed the thin slice of the moon and could see that it was the eleventh day of the lunar cycle, Ekadasi. He wondered if there was any significance to that.

As they walked further, he noticed bright lights coming from an area that was not far from where they were. Siddha had kept silent and was not saying anything. Manu did not want to question him anymore. As they approached the general area, Manu realized that there were thousands of people gathered with hundreds of oil lamps illuminating the area. A closer look revealed that they were two armies in battle formations, and there were literally tens of thousands of soldiers facing each other. There were thousands of chariots, elephants, and horses. He sensed that he was about to witness something monumental, something important. He wanted to find out more about it on his own.

Manu and Siddha reached a small hillock that was not too far from the battlefield. Siddha stopped, sat on a large rock, and asked Manu to rest on the other side of the same rock. From that vantage point, they could see the entire battlefield. Manu started purveying the battlefield. He noticed that the chariots on one side of the battlefield had flags with a monkey's image. Right then Manu felt a surge of electricity through his entire body. He had experienced some exciting moments in this mysterious journey, but nothing had come close to what he was experiencing.

Can it be happening to me? Am I witnessing the Epic Battle? Am I dreaming? He could not control himself and began to laugh. He could not believe that he had almost turned back, and was about to miss witnessing the most sacred event in human history. He felt ashamed that he had expressed his dissatisfaction at Siddha – the very one who had brought him on this amazing journey. The immense joy and excitement he was experiencing was almost too much for him that he couldn't contain it. He fell on the ground and kept murmuring, "Thank you God! Thank you God!"

Finally, he got up, and looked at Siddha. "Siddha, where are we? Is it possible that we are about to witness the Epic Battle?" Manu was humbled and he spoke as softly as he could.

Siddha did not answer his question. He was intently looking at the battlefield. Manu noticed that one of the main chariots started moving towards the center of the battlefield between the opposing forces. A prince stepped down and slowly laid his weapons on the ground. He saw another prince, who was the charioteer, step down and walk towards the first prince. At that time Siddha spoke, "Yes Manu, it is the beginning of the Epic Battle."

Manu was too far to hear anything said between the two princes. However, he knew exactly what was going on. The prince who had laid down his weapons was Arjuna, and the charioteer was none other than Lord Krishna, incarnation of God Almighty. He knew that Arjuna was refusing to fight the war, and the Lord was about to deliver the sacred Bhagavad-Gita. He wanted to hear each verse spoken by God. He pleaded to the Yaksha, "Siddha, with your magical power, can you help me hear the exchange between the Lord and Arjuna down in that battlefield?" Manu pleaded.

It was his only wish. It was his last wish.

"Unfortunately, Manu, I cannot do that. We have limited time, and I cannot keep you here forever," replied Siddha.

Manu got frustrated. He did not understand why the Yaksha was being so unreasonable. What was this time constraint? Manu had all the time in the world. He was not in a hurry to go anywhere.

"I do not understand, Siddha. You bring me to this sacred event, and before I can experience it, you are trying to take me back to my miserable material existence?" Manu did not try to hide his anger.

"It is like this, Manu. I do not have all the time in the world for you. The truth is there are millions of others who need my help, who need me to take them through the same journey, to see the Truth. However, I will try to help you as much as I can," Siddha replied calmly.

Manu had a ray of hope and waited for Siddha to tell him more.

"But, I do promise this. You will hear the most important verses, but not necessarily in the order that you have read in the holy text. Just hold my hand and close your eyes. You will see and hear through your spiritual senses. Now, give me your hand," commanded Siddha.

Manu obeyed his order, and held the Yaksha's hand. "Now, close your eyes," instructed Siddha.

Manu followed his instruction, and tightly closed his eyes. "Take a deep breath, and hold it until I tell you to breathe normally," Siddha said, giving his last instruction.

Manu had no problem with that instruction either. As he took a deep breath, he started feeling a tingling in his whole body. He was amazed that he could see everything clearly in spite of having his eyes closed. He looked at the battlefield and realized that it appeared closer now. He also noticed that everything was frozen in time except for Arjuna and the Lord Himself. Then something amazing happened. What he was witnessing became a picture frame and kept moving. Frames kept coming one after another. They were moving so fast that he could not make any sense out of the pictures, nor could he hear anything; and then the moving frames stopped and his vision came to a focus. He heard the Lord speak, *"I am the origin of everything, and everything emanates from Me. The wise who know this worship Me with total focus."*[34]

Then there was a silence, and the images blurred. What did the Lord mean by that? What does He mean by the things that emanate? Manu needed help and waited for Siddha. As if Siddha had read his mind, he began to elaborate, "What the Lord means is that He is not just the Creator of everything that is material in this universe, He is also the source of all forms of energy that sustain the material and spiritual worlds. The source of the spiritual energy that sustains all living beings is He. He defines the way the universe evolves; He also defines the way creatures evolve, physically, emotionally, or intellectually. He is the Creator of the entire universe, the one who sustains it, and in the end who destroys it. In other words, nothing exists or moves without His will. Once you know that, nothing else matters to you, Manu, and you will adore Him; you will worship Him with fervor and endless devotion."

---

34 Bhagavad-Gita 10.8.

Manu was just beginning to understand the glories of God. He wanted to know His nature and was eager to hear more. He wanted to know the Lord's relation to the material world. The images started moving again, and as they stopped and came to a focus, he heard the Lord speak again, *"My eight-fold nature in the material world is earth, water, fire, air, space, mind, intellect, and time limited ego. But, Oh Arjuna, this is My inferior nature. My superior nature is the one which upholds the entire universe and has taken the form of individual souls."*[35]

There was a silence as the images stopped, and Manu waited for Siddha's explanation. "Manu, the Lord's material creation is obvious. The eight-fold nature of the Lord in the physical world is something you can easily comprehend. However, what is more important is His higher nature. Every living creature in this universe has a soul that is an extension of the Lord's superior nature. Yes, your body consists of the eight elements that the Lord mentions including your false ego, which is time-limited. It is Māya that drives the false ego. However, the real you is the soul which upholds your material body. Your false ego dies when your material body perishes, but your soul lives forever. The soul spiritually upholds you today and will continue to uphold you in your future incarnations. What is important is that your soul is just an extension of the Lord's spiritual energy. Similarly, the whole universe and its sustenance are due to the Lord's spiritual energy which upholds it."

Manu wanted to hear more. He was tightly squeezing Siddha's hand. The very verses he had read a thousand times before sounded different this time. Images moved again. They were jumping backwards and forwards. He wanted to know more about the Lord's nature, and right at that moment the Lord spoke to Arjuna, *"Oh conquering prince, there is nothing whatsoever higher than Myself. I am the life in all beings. Oh Arjuna, I am the eternal seed of all beings. I am the intellect of the intelligent; I am the courage of the courageous."*[36]

This was getting very complicated for Manu. He really needed Siddha to distill the meaning of what he just heard from the Lord. The Yaksha was pleased to oblige his wish.

---

35 Bhagavad-Gita 7.4 and 7.5.

36 Bhagavad-Gita 7.7 and 7.10.

"Manu, there is no one higher than the Lord," he explained. "He has no enemies nor is there anyone who can challenge His supreme authority. Anyone who thinks otherwise is simply deluded. Respect life because life is God. Know that spiritual life is eternal because the Lord sustains it; your soul will be eternal even after your material body perishes. Use your intelligence correctly because it exists because of Him and be courageous to do the right things, for that courage is a gift of God."

It was now very clear to Manu. The Lord's nature was around us all the time. It was in life. It was in intelligence, in courage, and our own soul was nothing but an extension of His spiritual nature. Nevertheless, why did we find it so difficult to understand the true nature of God? Once again, reading Manu's mind, Siddha took him to the point where Lord Krishna was clarifying the same doubt that was bewildering Arjuna. The Lord said, *"The divine Māya of mine which consists of the three qualities of material nature is difficult to overcome. Only those who take refuge in Me alone can go beyond the veil of Māya."*[37]

There it was, the divine Māya, spoken by Krishna, the Lord Himself.

"Siddha, can you explain Māya to me? Can you tell me about the three qualities of material nature?" asked Manu.

"It is not easy to understand Māya, Manu. When the Lord created this material world, He permeated it with a lower form of energy to drive the world – to keep it going. That material energy is none other than Māya. Māya has several components. Nevertheless, the three important qualities of Māya are *Satvic, Rajasic, and Tamasic* nature. Satvic is all things that appear to be good and things that embrace harmony and purity like peace and compassion. Rajasic are things that represent passion, whether it is love or hate. Tamasic is inertia, inactivity, and ignorance. However, remember none of these are real, and they are there to distract you from the ultimate goal, which is to reach God's abode or *Moksha*. Until we can overcome the pull of Māya, our souls are not Saved. Māya keeps the soul in an endless cycle of birth and death, or transmigration. It is Māya that brings your soul back to the material world. There is only one way to overcome the pull of Māya, by taking refuge in God Almighty."

37 Bhagavad-Gita 7.14.

Manu cried aloud as he heard Siddha's explanation. He knew all along that he was drowning in the ocean of Māya. He had failed to overcome Māya while the answer was so simple, take refuge in God. If the path to God was so simple, why did so many fail? As he wondered about the answer, the moving frames stopped when the Lord Himself answered Manu's question.

"After many cycles of birth and death, one who has attained the knowledge - that God is everything - comes to Me. But such a great soul is rare indeed."[38]

Manu eagerly waited for Siddha's explanation.

"For many of us, it takes a long time to realize the supreme knowledge that God is everything; He is the beginning, the middle, and the end. Except for Him, everything else is temporary. As long as something is not permanent, it is really an illusion. Only the Lord is eternal. That is the ultimate knowledge. Nevertheless, enslaved by Māya, it takes many cycles of birth and death before one realizes that knowledge. A soul which gains that knowledge is bound to reach God's abode, and such a soul is indeed a great soul".

Manu wanted to know more. He was ecstatic that he was finally getting all his questions answered, answered by the Lord Himself. He was infinitely thankful that the Yaksha had brought him to witness the most sacred event in human history. He wanted to know more. Why did we resort to deities when we can go directly to God? At the very moment, the Lord gave the answer to Arjuna.

"People deprived of the knowledge that God is everything and driven by desires for material goals, resort to other deities guided by their own nature."[39]

Did that make the Lord angry? Manu was curious to find the answer. Siddha smiled and cleared Manu's doubt. "Why would the Lord get angry? After all anger is Māya, and the Lord, being the controller of Māya, is not subject to it. Instead, if you are devoted to a deity, which is only

---

38 Bhagavad-Gita 7.19.

39 Bhagavad-Gita 7.20.

an aspect of His glory, He will strengthen that faith, and He will reward those material goals. Whatever desired result one gets by worshipping deities of his choice is truly a gift from God Himself. However, Manu is that your wish? Are you after material goals? Listen to what the Lord says," explained Siddha.

Manu heard the Lord tell this to Arjuna, the Pandava prince.

"The fruits so gained are only temporary. The worshippers of gods go to gods, but My devotees come to Me."[40]

Manu understood what exactly the Lord meant by this. He did not need any help from Siddha this time. Temporary material gains were not what he was after. He wanted the ultimate fruit – to reach Him – to be with God. He was not going to put anyone between himself and God.

Manu still wanted to know more. He wanted to know how God had created the material world. He wanted to know the Lord's relation to him and all other creatures. He wanted to know all His glories. Siddha took him to the exact time when the Lord was revealing the same thing to Arjuna.

"Under My supervision, My nature (Māya) gives birth to all moving and non-moving things, and by this means the world revolves."[41]

"Manu, the material world owes its existence to the Lord in every aspect whatsoever. Both the material world and the energy that drives it (Māya) are God's own creation. However, the very energy that makes this world revolve also binds us to the material world. Māya holds us to the material world and causes endless transmigration of the souls. You will not reach God until you have overcome Māya. Fortunately, for all of us, all we need to do is focus on God's spiritual presence to overcome Māya." Siddha kept stressing the need to go beyond the veil of Māya.

---

40 Bhagavad-Gita 7.23.

41 Bhagavad-Gita 9.10.

Manu now understood the true nature of Māya; he understood that although Māya was a distraction that pulled one away from the ultimate goal – the goal to reach the Lord – it was essential for the material world to move forward. As Siddha explained, the Lord's spiritual presence in the material world balances the effect of Māya.

"Siddha, can you take me to the verse when the Lord explains His spiritual presence in the material world?"

Siddha took him to the verse where the Lord was answering the very same question for the brave prince.

"I am the basis of the Brahman, the Immortal, and the Immutable. I am the basis of the Eternal Dharma and of absolute bliss."[42]

Siddha explained, "The Lord at the time of Creation not only blankets the material world with His material energy (Māya), but He also permeates it with His spiritual energy or Brahman. We do not see it, but the spiritual energy is everywhere. It is in us as our Souls. Our Soul (Atman) is just an extension of the Lord's spiritual energy. In the tradition of Monism, the Atman and Brahman are considered the same. In the tradition of qualified Monism, the Atman is considered as an extension of the Brahman. In addition, Atman and Brahman are considered separate entities in the tradition of Dualism. "

"Which tradition is right then?" asked Manu.

"They are all right," replied Siddha.

"How could that be?" Manu was puzzled.

"They are all man made interpretations, and as long as those interpretations are helping the followers to reach God, they are all correct. Manu, remember what you heard before. God is everything, and what matters is Eternal Dharma as defined by the Lord. Synthetic traditions are just that – mere traditions. What is important is that one needs to lift himself from the realm of Māya to the realm of Brahman, which is God's spiritual presence," explained Siddha.

---

42 Bhagavad-Gita 14.27.

Manu still had more questions. He asked Siddha, "Why would the Lord create Māya if it only causes pain and distracts us from reaching Him? Besides, what was the purpose of all of this creation and when did it all happen?"

Siddha smiled and quoted a verse from the sacred Rig Veda:

> *"Who verily knows, and who can here declare it, whence it was born, and whence comes this Creation? The gods are later than the world's Creation, who knows then whence it first came into being?"*[43]

"No one knows when it all began, let alone why the Lord did it. Not even the gods in the Vedas know how it all began. Indeed, you will have the answer to that question the day you have overcome Māya."

"You mean, I will know the answer when I reach God's abode," Manu replied.

"Indeed you will. But at that point does it even matter?" Siddha commented. Manu nodded his head in agreement.

"At least, please take me to the verses where the Lord gives more details about his nature and presence in this world, Siddha," Manu pleaded again.

Siddha, who seemed ever ready to help Manu, took his hand and brought him to that point in the delivery of the sacred Scripture where the Lord clarified exactly that point.

> *"I am the father, the mother, the supporter, and the grandsire of this world. I am the ultimate object of knowledge, I am the sacred symbol Om, and I am the sacred Vedas."*[44]

Manu understood what the Lord meant by those words. He knew very well that the Lord was everywhere in a spiritual sense, and all one had to do was focus on His spiritual energy. Indeed, since He created the world, He had to be its father and mother. He always knew the Vedas were sacred, but for the first time he understood that the holy Vedas represented the Lord Himself. Indeed since the Vedas were the ultimate

---

43 Rig-Veda 10.129.

44 Bhagavad-Gita 9.17.

object of knowledge, he now understood that the ultimate object of True knowledge was the Lord Himself. Every time he had meditated on the sacred Om, he had felt at peace, and he had felt spiritually elevated and closer to God. He now understood the exact reason behind that feeling. It was now clear to him that the sacred sound Om represented the Lord Himself.

Manu still had one more question. "Siddha, do you know what the word Krishna means?" Manu asked.

"It means 'one who cuts'," replied Siddha.

"One who cuts? I don't understand."

"Well, now you know that Māya is like a bondage that prevents a soul from reaching the Lord, and the soul will go through transmigration until the realization that God is everything. This transmigration of the soul is a bondage that is impossible to break by anyone other than the Lord Himself. The cycle of birth and death is what the holy texts call Samsara. Only He can release you from that bondage. That is why He is known as Krishna – the one who cuts. He is the one who emancipates you from Samsara. *Remember, there is no Savior but the Lord Himself.*"

Manu had many more questions. He looked at the Yaksha for help as he had developed a special bond with him. He was now confident that Siddha would take him to where the Lord had revealed the answers he was looking for. "Siddha, do you know if the Lord projects Himself to the material world? If so, why would He do that?"

"Of course, the Lord appears all the time Manu. The Lord does that to uphold Dharma. Let me guide you to that point in time when you will hear that from the Lord Himself."

Manu could now hear the words as Krishna was answering the same question from Arjuna.

"Whenever Dharma (righteousness) declines and Adharma (un-righteousness) rises, I manifest Myself."[45]

Siddha explained, "Manu, there is *Dharma*, and there is dharma. *Dharma* is righteousness as defined by God, while dharma is adherence to traditions and rules as defined by man. *Dharma* is time invariant, and

---

45 Bhagavad-Gita 4.7.

it is space invariant, whereas dharma is evolving and is subject to rationalization and whimsical logic. When the material world goes astray with the decline of Dharma, the Lord descends into the material world in an incarnation. He descends on earth to destroy the evil, to protect the good, and to reestablish *Dharma*."

"Knowing that the Lord is always there to protect the good, how would I worship Him?" Manu asked. Siddha took Manu to the point where the Lord was answering the same question from Arjuna.

"Whoever offers Me with devotion a leaf, a flower, a fruit or water, I accept as long as it has been offered with pure devotion."[46]

Manu, surprised by what he just heard, looked at Siddha with astonishment.

"The Lord does not want bigger things? Would He not want us to offer things that are more valuable? Just a leaf or a flower or a fruit will do?" Manu enquired.

"The offerings you make are only symbolic, Manu. What matters is devotion, pure devotion," replied Siddha.

"What about a temple? Would he not want one to build a big temple for Him?"

Siddha smiled knowing that Manu, still deluded by the Lord's Māya, was asking such questions.

"Building a temple is good as long as you are doing it with a pure heart. It will help others develop devotion to God. However, the ultimate test is your Faith, your Faith in God. Good deeds will help you in developing devotion to the Lord, but the deeds themselves will not take you to Him. If it were just deeds that took one to God, His abode would be full of rich people only! The poor would have a lesser chance of reaching Him. Certainly, the Lord would not discriminate between the poor and the rich," explained Siddha.

Manu was still puzzled. It was hard for him to accept that the Lord would be happy with an offer of just a leaf or a flower or a fruit. He wanted more clarification. He thought about the Yagna he had witnessed earlier, and the sad sight of the white lamb tied to the tree came to his mind.

---

46 Bhagavad-Gita 9.26.

"Doesn't the Lord want some sort of sacrifice? Maybe a lamb, even if it is symbolic?" questioned Manu.

"You will get the answer to your question here," replied Siddha.

There were the moving frames again. They stopped as he heard the Lord explain his relationship to individual souls.

"I, the Supreme Lord, reside in the heart of all creatures.
But they all revolve like machines deluded by My Māya."[47]

There was the answer. Manu understood what the Lord meant by that verse. Deluded by Māya, humans would do the most heinous crimes. They would forget that the Lord is in the heart of all beings – after all, the soul is an extension of the Lord's spiritual energy. Some would kill an innocent lamb thinking it would please Him. Instead, we are only hurting our chances of reaching Him. Manu was now ashamed that he had even mentioned sacrifice. He should be thinking only about the way to serve God and nothing else. He knew being completely devoted to Him was the necessary criteria. But he was in anguish as he wondered how he would develop such a deep devotion. Realizing his anguish, Siddha guided him to the moment where the Lord had yet another answer.

"Oh Arjuna, whatever you do, whatever you eat, whatever
you offer as a sacrifice, whatever gift you give, whatever aus-
terities you perform, do that as an offering to Me."[48]

"Manu, remember that you are in this material world to do the Lord's work. Once you realize that, your work becomes a way of serving God; everything you do results in the dedication of all acts to God. You become unattached to fruits of your work. This dedication will help you develop devotion to the Lord. However, do not be tempted to think that just dedication of your work to God without attachment to its fruits will lead you to Salvation. It is only the first step."

"Then tell me about the other steps. Show me the way that guarantees Salvation."

---

47 Bhagavad-Gita 18.61.

48 Bhagavad-Gita 9.27.

"All right, Manu. I will take you to that verse. The verse you are going to hear now is central to the entire Eternal Dharma or God's Dharma. You will learn about the five steps for reaching God. Listen to it carefully."

Manu was excited and patiently waited for the moving frames to stop so that he could listen to the Lord.

> *"One who does My work, holds Me as the supreme Goal, is devoted to Me, is devoid of attachments to the material world, and is free from enmity towards all beings, attains Me."[49]*

The answer was straightforward. Those were the five simple steps to achieve Salvation. He had to do the Lord's work, without any attachments to the fruits. He had to be devoted to the Lord and hold Him as the supreme Goal. He had to be free of attachments to the material world, and he had to be free of enmity towards all beings. It seemed simple enough, but Manu knew that Māya would always be in the way and take him away from those five simple steps. He wanted an anchor that would not divert him from that *five-fold path*. He was looking for a guarantee. Siddha then took him to the verse where the Lord had made the very assurance Manu was looking for.

> *"Abandon all forms of dharma (traditions). Take refuge in Me alone. I shall free you from all sins and grant you Salvation. Do not grieve."[50]*

Manu was ecstatic. He had finally found the answers to all his questions; he now knew the path to God. He knew the guaranteed way to reach the Lord. He had accepted Krishna as his Lord and Savior. He was not going to put anyone between himself and God. God had descended as Krishna and had delivered the sacred Gita. He thanked Siddha continuously for the incredible journey he had just experienced. He sat there motionless, immensely joyous and in complete bliss. He kept saying repeatedly, "I accept Krishna as my Lord and Savior."

---

49 Bhagavad-Gita 11.55.

50 Bhagavad-Gita 18.66.

Now that he had reached the pinnacle of his spiritual quest, he did not see any reason to continue to be on Earth; he just wanted to leave the material world and reach Him. He was eager to leave the material world, which was the strangest feeling he ever had. Just then, Siddha woke him from his trance.

"I know what you are thinking, Manu. I want you to listen to one more verse before you make up your mind on your next step," guided Siddha as he took Manu to that important verse.

"He who, with supreme devotion to Me, will speak of this highest secret to My devotees, shall doubtless come to Me."[51]

When Manu heard the verse, God's call for spreading the true meaning of Dharma, Manu felt ashamed that even the thought of leaving the material world had crossed his mind. He felt ashamed of his selfishness. Manu realized that he still had unfinished business in the material world. He had the sacred duty to spread God's message to the rest of the world. As he thought more about that task, he was thrilled thinking about it and could not control his enthusiasm.

"How would I do that, Siddha? How would I spread the Lord's message?" asked Manu. Manu had his eyes still closed.

"You will come up with the answer on your own, Manu. Now you can open your eyes," prompted Siddha.

As Manu opened his eyes, all he saw was an empty field that was shining in the moonlight. Everything he had just witnessed had disappeared. Manu stared at the empty field. The journey he had just completed was the most thrilling journey anyone could ever make. At the same time, he was energized like he had never been in his life. He had finally found the Truth, and he was ready to spread the Truth to all corners of the world. Nothing else mattered to him. He then heard Siddha's words as he urged Manu to get ready for the next stop.

"Hold on to my hand, Manu. There is one more place where I need to take you."

"Where are you taking me this time, Siddha?"

"You will know when we get there," replied Siddha.

---

51 Bhagavad-Gita 18.68.

Manu was not afraid any more; he was ready to go anywhere, whether it was a place in the past or a place in the future. Siddha's magical prowess – the ability to transport him to any place and time in a matter of seconds – did not bother him. Nothing mattered to him anymore; after all, he had reached the ultimate blissful state in the material world. He felt devoid of emotions triggered by the effects of Māya.

As they landed in the new place, Manu realized that they were near an ashram. This time it was a full moon day. The ashram was a small building set on the top of a small hillock, surrounded by a well-kept garden. The garden looked so exquisite in the moonlight that Manu could not help admiring the beautiful flowers. A small stream that was flowing a few yards from the ashram added a special sense of serenity to the surroundings. Manu realized that it was early in the morning, several hours before the break of dawn. As they went inside the ashram, Manu saw a room with the door half open. He could see an old seer seated on a platform with an oil lamp to his side. He had a book of palm leafs and appeared to be deeply engrossed in his thoughts as he etched his writings on the palm leafs. The seer's deliberations were intense, and it appeared as if he were taking hours to compile his sentences.

"What is he writing?" whispered Manu.

"Go and see for yourself. You know he cannot see you or hear you," Siddha encouraged.

Manu walked closer to the seer and stood behind him. As he read the writings, he realized that the seer was compiling a set of rules – like a book of law. Perhaps laws for a king or an emperor?

As the seer wrote the rules, he flipped the old leaves for cross reference, giving Manu an opportunity to understand the context of the text. He realized the text was none other than the *Laws of Manu (*Manusmriti*)*, and the seer was the ancient Manu himself. Manusmriti had defined the traditions his ancestors had followed. The tradition as defined by Manusmriti was the tradition followed by all his teachers and relatives. Indeed, it had defined the tradition of the entire Aryavarta. He realized that he was witnessing the birth of Manusmriti. The old Manu would have been thrilled to be a witness to this important event. However, there was nothing thrilling about this to the new Manu. He had realized the Truth, and the laws compiled by a mortal seer did not mean anything to him.

The seer was writing about the rules of warfare prohibiting killing of innocents, women, children, and civilians. He was writing rules for the Brahmins, kings, and servants. He was writing rules for self-control and the practice of yoga. They all seemed logical and moral. However, as Manu read more about the rules, there were things that started making him feel uneasy. There were rules that were degrading to the working (*Shudra*) class and to the peoples outside the four Varnas, whom he called untouchables. There were rules that were degrading to women as well. On women, the seer had written,

> *"Her father protects in childhood, her husband protects in youth, and her sons protect in old age; a woman is never fit for independence.*

> *"Women must particularly be guarded against evil inclinations, however trifling they may appear; for, if they are not guarded, they will bring sorrow on two families.*

> *"For women, no sacramental rite is performed with sacred texts, thus the law is settled; ..."*

As he read those rules, Manu got very agitated. The words he had heard directly from the Lord came to his mind, *"I, the Supreme Lord, reside in the heart of all beings."*

How could the seer say such disparaging things about women? How could he discriminate against women when it came to the sacramental rites and the study of the Vedas? How could he go against God's own Dharma? He then read another line the seer had written which had glorified women,

> *"Wives who bear children are worthy of worship; between them and the goddess of fortune, there is no difference whatsoever."*

As he read the rules that neither conformed to God's Dharma, nor had any logic in them, Manu got more and more agitated. He was now convinced that the seer was deluded, just like the Lord had said, *"I, the Supreme Lord, reside in the heart of all creatures. But they all revolve like machines deluded by My Māya."*

Manu felt saddened by what he was seeing. He even felt sorry for the seer. He wanted to jump in front of the seer and argue with him about the fallacies in the rules. He felt frustrated since he knew that the seer could in no way see him or hear him. He felt sick as he thought about all the suffering it would cause to millions of people in future years. He looked at Siddha helplessly, and began to plead, "Let me talk to him, Siddha. Please make me visible to the seer."

"I cannot do that, Manu. I do not have that power. But, go in front of him and take a closer look at his face," replied Siddha.

Manu froze when he heard this. He remembered the last time Siddha had asked him to take a closer look at the old priest who was reciting a hymn from Rig Veda. Suddenly, he was afraid to do what the Yaksha had suggested.

"It is all right Manu. You need to know what is going on here. Do not be afraid. Take a closer look at the seer," Siddha encouraged.

Manu reluctantly went close to the seer and stared at his face. Despite the fact that the seer was very old, he could see that it was the same long nose, the same high forehead, the same eyes, the same cheekbones – it was his own image. As Manu realized that he was indeed the ancient Manu reincarnated, it felt like he had been hit in the face. He started trembling, fell on his knees, and started sobbing. He stretched his hands seeking God's forgiveness.

"What have I done? How could I be so deluded? Please forgive me, Krishna."

He grabbed Siddha's hand for solace. Instead, he felt a hand that was soft and tiny.

Chapter 25

Reaching the Ashram

G ovinda and Sugata were returning from Devapuri with the materials they had just garnered from the fair. Devapuri was a small town that was about ten miles northeast of their ashram. A fair took place twice a month in Devapuri where farmers and merchants from several surrounding villages came to buy and exchange goods. The two boys would often go to the fair to collect all the material that their guru needed for the ashram. They did not need any fancy goods; all they needed were little things like clothes for the students, brass cups or plates, and items for cooking like rice and spices. They often took fruits or vegetables grown in the ashram and bartered them for the items they needed. The merchants knew that the boys were from the ashram run by the seer Bharadwaja. Bharadwaja was a very well known spiritual master, and he was a household name all over the Maurya Empire. The merchants were all eager to supply anything the boys came for, and they considered it an honor to send the items that the great spiritual master needed. They accepted the fruits and vegetables from the boys as a blessing from the seer, as they were never equal to the items the merchants supplied in a monetary sense. A tax collector from the Empire also came to the fair to collect sales taxes from the merchants. He would enquire about the status of the ashram, and if any help were required, he would make sure that royal soldiers and servants went to the ashram to provide the necessary help. The great seer Bharadwaja wanted minimal interruptions from the secular world. After all, he had built the ashram to provide a pristine environment for studying the Vedic scriptures. He did not want outsiders to come and cause any distractions for his students. He only accepted help from the royal soldiers on major projects like expanding the ashram or a major clean up after a storm.

Govinda was fifteen years old, and Sugata was two years younger than he was. Govinda had joined the ashram when he was eight years old as it was the tradition to start the study of the Vedas at that age. Sugata had joined the ashram two years later. It was the tradition for students to spend eight years in the ashram before the seer declared them as young scholars in the knowledge of the Vedas. In addition to the scriptures, the students learned about medicine and the art of cooking, and they gained a basic knowledge of animal husbandry and farming. The students, once graduated, would go to cities and villages to help Arya families in the practice of the Vedic tradition.

This time around, the boys did not have many items to take back to the ashram. They had collected a few cotton clothes and a few herbal items like turmeric powder, cinnamon, and cardamom. Their bags were not that heavy, and they were quickly on their way back to the ashram.

The trail from Devapuri to the ashram of Bharadwaja went through the rice fields for a few miles and then entered a dense forest. The trail went up a small hillock and reached a resting spot. The resting spot was a stone structure with four tall pillars and a sculptured stone roof. Folklore said that hundreds of years ago a king built it as an observation tower for his hunting expeditions. The trail ran down the hillock and crossed a small stream. Once they were on the other side of the stream, it was a distance of around just three miles to reach the ashram.

"Let us walk briskly and reach the ashram before it gets dark," said Govinda. Sugata nodded in agreement. Sugata being the younger one often worried about surprise storms. He remembered the time when there was a vicious storm for hours, and they had to spend the whole night underneath the stone structure at the top of the hillock.

"I hope it does not rain before we reach the ashram," added Sugata.

"Do not worry; we will be all right, Sugata," assured Govinda.

"How can you be so sure?" Sugata protested, "I always worry about the floods in the stream. I am not a very good swimmer you know."

"Yes, I know that. We will be careful. Moreover, we have our guru's blessings. That will protect us all the time," replied Govinda.

Sugata agreed. He knew from ancient texts that the guru's blessings were very important. It is true that the Lord Himself has ordained this.

As they walked briskly, the rice fields on the two sides of the trail looked like giant green blankets. There were miles and miles of rice fields on both sides that reflected sunlight as they rippled in waves due to the mild breeze.

"The fields look very healthy this year. There should be a good harvest, and the farmers will be very happy," said Govinda.

"I wish we have good harvests every year. I do not like it when we have droughts," replied Sugata. He remembered the year when they had a severe drought and many animals had died. As one who loved animals, Sugata was very unhappy that year.

Govinda agreed. He wondered why they had droughts. Was it because people were not ethical some time and that made Varuna angry? Varuna was the keeper of Rita, the cosmic order, and unethical behavior made him unhappy. Did Varuna punish people by withholding rains?

As they were walking briskly, they had entered the forest ahead of their planned time, and soon they were at the bottom of the hillock. The forest was so dense that sunrays could hardly reach the bottom of the forest floor. The boys noticed that all of a sudden the forest seemed darker. As they looked up, they saw dark clouds gathering in the sky. They knew that there would be a severe storm soon and wanted to reach the top of the hillock before it started to rain heavily. They wanted to reach the stone structure for whatever protection they could get.

They started running towards the top as fast as they could. They could feel heavy raindrops falling on their heads as they raced towards the top. Their experience had taught them that it was going to be a major storm. The wind was gathering speed by the minute, and the rain continued to pour incessantly. There was deafening thunder following the lightning streaks. They knew the lightning streaks were reminders of Indra slaying the dragon. Soon there would be flash floods, and they wanted to be at a higher elevation to be safe from the floods.

"It is going to be a bad storm, Govinda," Sugata lamented.

"Of course it is going to be a bad one, Sugata. Come, let us run and make sure that we are underneath the stone structure. I am afraid that the wind is going to knock down some trees. We do not want to be struck by a major limb," replied Govinda.

They finally reached the top, sat on the stone bench that was underneath the stone structure, and tried to catch their breath. They sat there staring at the rain, which was coming so hard that they could hardly see anything beyond a few feet. They could hear trees falling even in the middle of the howling wind and the deafening thunder. The sound of large trees falling reverberated throughout the forest. As the water rushed from the top of the hillock towards the bottom, it had created several muddy streams. Rainwater was beginning to collect at the bottom of the hillock. As they looked down, it appeared like the forest trees were floating on a muddy lake. The boys were worried but were not very scared. They had seen many storms like this in spite of their young age. They knew the storm would eventually stop, and all they had to do was walk a few more miles to reach the ashram. The only thing that worried them was the stream they had to cross to get to the ashram. They knew that the stream would be flooded, and it would not be safe to cross for several more hours even after the rain stopped. They sat on the bench patiently waiting for the rain to stop.

Finally, the rain eased, and in a few more minutes, they began to see breaks in the clouds. They sat on the bench until all the rain stopped, and there was no more water streaming down the hillock. They looked at each other as if to sense a cue for their next move.

"Let us get going, Sugata. Be careful though. The forest floor is very slippery," Govinda said, breaking the silence.

"Yes. We have to be extremely careful. There could still be some loose limbs on the trees. Watch out for them," replied Sugata.

They started walking down very carefully, close to one another so that if one slipped, the other was close by to help. They reached the bottom of the hillock and stopped there to take a closer look at the havoc the storm had created. Several large trees had fallen down and were blocking the trail. The boys had to go around them as they progressed in their journey. As they were slowly making their way towards the stream, Govinda noticed something saffron in color beneath a fallen tree a few hundred yards ahead of them. He stopped and stared at the tree. He immediately realized that there was a man lying on the forest floor.

"Sugata, look over there! That man seems to be unconscious. Let us go and help him," Govinda alerted.

They both started to run towards the man ignoring the fact that the forest floor was still slippery. They knew every minute counted in a situation like this.

"He looks like a bikku," observed Sugata.

They saw that a medium sized limb had hit the bikku's head, and he was bleeding. They went close to him and tried to move the limb away. Luckily, the limb was not very heavy, and they managed to move it away from the bikku's head.

"Is he still bleeding?" asked Sugata.

Govinda kneeled down next to the bikku and took a closer look at bikku's head. The bleeding seemed to have stopped.

"Let us not take any risk. Let us put some turmeric powder and tie a piece of cloth around his head," replied Govinda.

He knew that the turmeric powder had the power to stop bleeding. He always carried pieces of cotton cloths in his bag for emergency cuts or bruises. He took a cloth piece from the bag and began to clean the bikku's head and face. He then sprinkled the turmeric powder on the cut, put another cotton cloth around the head, and tied it. He then sat on the floor, raised the bikku's head and placed it on his lap.

Govinda sat like that wondering how they were going to save the bikku's life. He was aware that the bikku was not going to recover from his unconsciousness soon, and the burden of saving his life was upon them.

"What do we do next, Govinda?" said a worried Sugata.

"We need to take him to the ashram. That is the only way we can save him," replied Govinda with a worried look.

"How are we going to do that? The ashram is still a few miles from here. Moreover, there is a swollen stream that we need to cross," Sugata replied.

"Let us not panic, Sugata. We will see what we can do. Do you think we can build some sort of a stretcher to carry the bikku?" asked Govinda.

Sugata thought about that suggestion. They both carried daggers for protection. They also carried ropes in their bag for emergencies. He looked around to see if he could locate some strong broken limbs from trees. There were also vines he could use for making a stretcher. He felt energized and was ready to get to work.

"Yes, we can build one. Let me start getting the pieces of tree limbs," Sugata replied.

As Govinda sat there holding the bikku on his lap, Sugata went around collecting broken tree limbs that were just the right size to make a stretcher. He also cut some strong vines and brought them for reinforcement; he wanted to make sure that the stretcher was strong enough to hold the injured bikku. He then started assembling the stretcher in a meticulous manner. Both Govinda and Sugata were at ease when it came to woodwork. They had built or repaired many rooms in the ashram over the years. After a while, they traded places, and Govinda worked on building the stretcher. Soon the stretcher was ready, and they carefully lifted the bikku and placed him on the stretcher. Then, using the ropes they had, they tied him to the wooden frame they had built so that he was securely on the stretcher.

They were exhausted from the work, but they were very proud of their accomplishment. Their guru had taught them that a chance to save another life is the best way to serve God. They prayed and asked for Almighty's blessings as they lifted the stretcher and started walking towards the ashram. They carefully took each step to make sure that they would not slip and fall. They were less concerned about their well-being; their main concern was not to cause any further injury to the bikku.

As they walked at a deliberate pace, they could hear the bikku muttering words. This encouraged the boys and gave them an extra push to reach the ashram as fast as they could. As they approached the stream, they could see that it was in a swollen state even from a distance. On a normal day, they could just wade across the stream to the other side, as the water was shallow at several points in the stream. That was impossible today as the stream was at least five to six feet deep. They realized that they had to take a detour to go over a wooden bridge that was upstream. That would add another mile to their journey.

Once they reached the bridge, they started walking slowly over it. The bridge was a wooden bridge with rope guards on each side. The wooden planks were very slippery from the storm and a major slip would put them at the bottom of the ravine. Despite their precaution, Sugata slipped. Nevertheless, he managed to hang on to the stretcher with one hand, grabbed the rope guard, and slowly regained his control. The stirring caused by the slip caused more pain to the bikku. They could here him muttering louder.

"You will be all right, Bikku. Just relax. We will take care of you," Govinda tried to assure him.

The bikku muttered in a faint voice. They heard it as, "Siddha, is that you?"

Govinda did not understand why the bikku was calling out for "Siddha." Perhaps he was referring to his friend or companion, reasoned the boys.

Once they reached the other side of the stream, they were confident that they would be able to save the bikku's life. All they had to do was walk for a couple of more miles, and they would be in the ashram. Seer Bharadwaja would be able to give him proper medical attention and heal his wound.

Meanwhile, at the ashram, Bharadwaja was worried about the boys. He was concerned about them having to stay too long in the forest. He kept looking out of the window for any sign of his students coming back. Suddenly, he saw the two boys carrying what appeared like a stretcher on their shoulders. He immediately called four of his students and asked them to run and relieve the boys. He knew that they would be extremely tired and was not sure how long they had been carrying the stretcher.

The students brought the stretcher inside and placed it on the floor. They immediately untied the ropes and looked at their guru for further instructions. Bharadwaja kneeled next to the bikku and checked his pulse. He then put his hand over the bikku's forehead to see if he had a fever. "He has a fever. Let us put him on the bed in the guest room. I will clean his wound and put some medicine on it. We need to cool his body so that he does not get into a coma."

The students carried the bikku to the guest room and carefully placed him on the bed. Bharadwaja cleaned his wound, added some medicine, and then put a new bandage. He then called his daughter Sharada.

307

"Sharada, I want you to stay next to the guest all night. We need to watch his condition during the night."

"I will be happy to do that father. Is there anything else I need to do?" replied Sharada.

"Yes, there is something important. Take a wet cloth and cool his forehead during the night. Let us hope he will be all right by the morning. Let us all pray for his recovery," instructed the seer.

The students went back to the kitchen as it was time for them to have dinner. Sharada brought an oil lamp and kept it at the corner of the room. She then stayed in the guest room.

"Are you not joining us for dinner?" asked Bharadwaja.

"No father. I would like to skip dinner if it is all right with you," replied Sharada.

That was acceptable to Bharadwaja. A fundamental tenet of eternal dharma is to make sure that a guest is properly treated. He was, indeed, happy to see his daughter so concerned about the bikku.

Sharada sat next to the bikku all throughout the night. She hardly had any sleep, as she was extremely concerned about his well-being. Periodically, she would dip a cloth in cold water and wipe his forehead. As she attended to the bikku, she stared at his face. She found his features to be clean like a chiseled sculpture. He had a long nose, high forehead, and high cheekbones. Hair was growing back on his shaved head. He was tall, as his body covered one end of the bed to the other. However, he was so frail and skinny that he looked almost like a skeletal figure. Of course, that had to do with his ascetic life style. What was he before he became a bikku? From his physical appearance, she surmised that he was probably a prince or a high-ranking warrior. Why did he leave the Vedic dharma and join a Buddhist monastery? How did he get hurt? Where was he going?

Sharada was curious to know more about the bikku. In a way, she felt like she had known him before. She felt a special bond towards him that she could not explain. Maybe it was because of the way she had become part of the ashram. She remembered how Bharadwaja had brought her to the ashram. He and his students had found her lying unconscious on the banks of river Ganges. They had brought her to the ashram and had provided her proper care until she was healthy. Bharadwaja wanted to send her back to her parents once she was feeling well. However, she could not remember anything about her past. She could not remember even her name or her hometown. Her name, her family, her town, her origins were all blank to her. The seer had concluded that she had experienced something traumatic, which had erased her memory. Out of love and compassion, he had adopted the girl as his own daughter and had named her Sharada, the goddess of knowledge. This was four years ago.

Bharadwaja had lost his wife long ago and had no children. He had considered Sharada as God's gift and had cared for her with tremendous love. He had taught her the Vedas and the Upanishads, which by itself was against the laws according to ancient Manu. Nevertheless, as an enlightened soul, Bharadwaja did not care about man-made rules. True to her name, Sharada had learnt the sacred scriptures with astonishing speed. She had even studied the Manusmriti on her own. Over the years, she had developed tremendous respect for the Vedic tradition and was a strict adherent to all aspects of the tradition, so much so that even her father was astonished by her devotion to the Vedic tradition. Unfortunately for Sharada, she could not discriminate between traditions born out of convenience from God inspired traditions.

Chapter 26
Getting Well

Sharada sat in the guest room next to Manu's bed checking his fever throughout the night. It was quiet in the ashram, as every one had fallen asleep. The room was dark except for the dim oil lamp that flickered in the corner of the room. She took a wet cloth and periodically wiped Manu's forehead to control his fever. Next to her was a bowl that contained some medicated soup. Bharadwaja had brought it from the kitchen before he had bid goodnight to his daughter. Sharada tried to feed it to the bikku in small amounts hoping it would help him cope with the pain

Throughout the course of the night, she could see the bikku tossing and turning in the bed. She could sense that he was in extreme pain, and he kept talking in his sleep. She tried to make sense of what he was saying, but found it extremely difficult to understand his words. She moved closer to him to listen to him more carefully. She could now sense that he was uttering what seemed like verses from the scriptures. She was not surprised, as she knew that many pious people chanted verses from holy texts to forget pain and suffering. However, his muttering was so soft that she could hardly decipher any of the words Manu was saying.

The flickering lamp made a large shadow of her that danced on the wall. The light from the lamp fell on Manu's face, which revealed his distinguishing features. She was tempted to run her fingers over his face almost involuntarily. She knew it was inappropriate to do so, but she felt like she was compelled to touch his nose. She slowly moved her index finger over his nose and then circled his lips with the same finger. She could not understand why she felt so close to him as if she had known him before. She then withdrew her finger somewhat ashamed that she was touching him in an inappropriate manner. She looked away from him, dipped the cloth in the cold water, and started wiping his forehead again. As she slowly wiped his forehead, she realized that his fever had subsided. She glanced over his body and realized that the bikku was not in pain anymore. The medication was working, and his face looked peaceful. However, she could still hear the bikku muttering words. She leaned closer again to hear his words. This time they were a little clearer.

As she listened very closely, she realized that they were verses from the Gita. He was talking in between as if he was debating with someone else. Why would a bikku recite verses from the Gita? Sharada was a little perplexed.

She heard him utter a sentence again. She heard it clearly this time. He was asking a question.

"What does Krishna mean?"

She tried to answer it, but came out empty. She knew that the answer Manu was seeking was a spiritual answer. She felt frustrated that she did not know the answer. What does the word Krishna really mean? she wondered, and then to her astonishment she heard Manu whispering the answer.

"It means the one who cuts. He is the one who emancipates you from the bondage of Samsara. He is the one who Saves. *Remember there is no Savior but the Lord Himself.*"

He kept uttering the last sentence repeatedly. Finally, he stopped talking in his sleep, and there was a deep silence. She put her palm against his forehead to check his fever and saw that he was sweating. She was somewhat pleased; after all, sweating was a sign of a fever subsiding. It was her sincere hope that by dawn he would come out of his unconscious state.

She sat next to him holding his hand, waiting for him to come out of his deep sleep. She was tired from the lack of sleep, and without realizing, she had fallen asleep.

Sharada felt a sudden tug and looked anxiously at Manu to see if he was doing all right. She put her palm on his forehead to assure herself that his fever had not relapsed. She then heard his soft murmur and bent towards him to understand what he was saying.

She heard the all-important verse in the Gita, when Krishna was as-suring Arjuna about Salvation.

"Abandon all forms of dharma, Take refuge in Me alone. I shall free you from all sins and grant Salvation. Do not grieve."

She then heard Manu chanting the same verse repeatedly. Suddenly, Manu started crying. Then he started chanting, "I have accepted Krishna as my Lord and Savior," almost as if it were a mantra.

Sharada was taken aback from all this. She was a little scared and did not know what to make of his outburst. She knew the bikku was experiencing some debate in his own mind and hoped that he would calm down and go back to sleep. She was worried that his excitement would complicate his injury. Slowly, Manu went back to his sleep and stopped talking. Everything in the ashram was silent again. Sharada realized that she was witnessing the bikku's conversion in real time. What she was witnessing was the bikku walking away from the spiritual path laid down by the Enlightened One and coming back to Eternal Dharma. Although the whole thing had scared her somewhat, she was now happy to see that the bikku had come back to Krishna, God incarnate. Soon she was asleep again.

Bharadwaja and his students were up before the dawn, and were get-ting ready to go towards the forest for the sacred rituals, and the morning yoga. They always went to the nearby stream for morning bathing and for practicing the yoga positions. The noise from the rooms woke up Sharada, and she got up to check on Manu's condition. Manu's fever was completely gone, and his body seemed to be at ease. She kept there waiting for him to wake up; she wanted to make sure that she was in the room when the bikku came out of his unconscious state. As she sat there looking at the bikku's body, which was meatless from years of the ascetic way of life, she noticed that he was beginning to move as if he was trying to come out of his sleep. She got alert and waited for him to open his eyes. Then, suddenly, the bikku got up, sat down on his knees, and started crying. He threw his hands up, and declared, "What have I done? How could I be so deluded? Please forgive me God."

He then grabbed Sharada's hand. Manu was puzzled that it was soft and tiny. He was expecting Siddha's hand, of course. He opened his eyes, looked at Sharada, and felt completely baffled. He had no idea how he had landed in a room next to a beautiful woman. His head was still hurting, and he could not properly focus on Sharada's face. He sat down covering his face with his palms, trying to regain a sense of bearing. It all seemed too confusing to him. "Was it all a dream? The long journey with the Yaksha seemed so real. The Yaksha himself seemed so real. How did I get here? Where am I?"

He then slowly opened his eyes again and looked at Sharada. This time she was more in focus. She looked very familiar, and as he focused on her features, he was astonished how closely she resembled Kusuma. It was the same face but a different hairstyle. The attire was different, and the woman in front of him looked like a Brahmin woman. Nevertheless, was it possible? Could it be that she was really Kusuma. Is she alive?

"Kusuma, is it you?" Manu murmured as he tried to adjust his position on the bed.

"Please be careful, Bikku. You have hurt your head and I do not want you to strain yourself. Please do not overexert," Sharada replied anxiously to make sure that he did not overexert himself.

She did not bother to find out why he was calling her *Kusuma*. Her only concern at that point was his wellbeing. She helped him lean on the wall next to the bed and offered him water. Cold water had never seemed so tasty, and Manu drank all of it without even stopping to breathe. He then opened his eyes and started staring at Sharada, which made her very uncomfortable.

"I am sorry," Manu replied softly. Manu apologized, realizing her discomfort. He then asked if he could get something to eat. Right at that time, Bharadwaja and his students entered the ashram.

"I think my father just came in. I will have him take care of you. I will go to the kitchen and prepare a hot meal for you."

She then walked out of the room and announced the good news to her father. Manu watched her intently as she walked out of the room, still puzzled how he ended up in that ashram. Even more puzzling was her remarkable resemblance to Kusuma. It all seemed surreal to him.

313

"He is awake now. He seems to be extremely tired and hungry. I will prepare him something healthy. Can you take care of him until then, father?" Sharada requested to her father.

"Of course, I will do just that, Sharada. You look very tired. Why don't you get some rest?" replied the seer.

She smiled as she walked into the kitchen. It was obvious from her smile that she was not going to rest until the bikku recovered. He knew her too well; she was dedicated to treating guests right regardless of age or creed.

Bharadwaja sat next to Manu and examined his head. He was pleased that the bleeding had completely stopped, and Manu's fever had subsided. He asked one of his students to bring his medical bag. As he waited for his bag, he took Manu's hand and started checking his pulse.

"You know you were lucky, Bikku. If my students had not found you in time, you would have been dead by now," Bharadwaja spoke softly.

Manu shook his head acknowledging that. He wanted to know more about the seer and his ashram. However, he was too tired to have a long conversation. Bharadwaja opened his bag the student had just brought and took out some herbal medicine.

"I am going to give you this medicine which will make sure that you have no infection. It will also reduce your headache. I want you to take this right after you eat your hot meal today," instructed the seer.

Manu was all right with that. He was now beginning to feel hungry with food mentioned repeatedly.

"I would like to find out more about you, Bikku. I do not even know your name or your family background. However, right now you need all the rest you can get. There is no need to cause any unnecessary strain, and I want you to rest some more," advised Bharadwaja.

The seer stood up and began to walk away from him. He stopped and turned back to Manu as if he had forgotten to tell him something. "Oh, I forgot to mention this to you, Bikku; the medicine may have a temporary side effect on your voice. Sometimes there is a temporary loss of voice. But it is not something to worry about; you should have your voice back within a few weeks," Bharadwaja tried to assure Manu.

314

Manu sat on the bed alone as the seer, and his student walked out of the room. He sat there alone with the medicine by his side waiting for Sharada to bring his hot meal. He was now a little apprehensive about taking the medicine. What would he do if his voice never came back? He then smiled realizing that he was about to fall into the Māya trap again. What was there to worry once he had accepted Krishna as his Savior? Moreover, he trusted the seer in his abilities and did not think about it anymore.

After a while, there was increased activity in the ashram. He could now hear the noise made by the morning activities in the ashram. The students were busy walking from room to room getting ready for the morning classes. He felt lonely sitting in the room; it seemed like almost an hour had passed when he finally saw Sharada bringing him a plate containing boiled rice, vegetables, and a cup of soup. He eagerly ate it, and food had never seemed so tasty to him. He ate it so fast that he looked like a tiger devouring a fresh kill. He then took his medicine and drank the fresh water Sharada had brought him in a brass cup. He wanted to talk to her but was tired, and he fell asleep with the effect of the medicine taking hold on him.

This was the routine for the next twenty-four hours. He would wake up, eat something fresh, consume the medicine that the seer had given him, and would quickly go to bed. However, every time he woke up, he felt a lot better and more relaxed.

The next morning, Manu was up before anyone else in the ashram. He felt fresh and energetic and was eager to go for a walk. He wanted to get back to his morning routine, his meditation, his yoga, and finally spending time in solitude communing with nature. He slowly got up from the bed and very carefully walked out of the ashram into the front garden. It was summertime, and the morning air felt very refreshing. The fragrance from the flowers in the garden felt so pleasing to his senses that he stood there closing his eyes to absorb the entire sweetness of the aroma. He had goose bumps all over his body, and he was inspired to chant. He wanted to chant his favorite verses from the Gita. As he tried to chant, it suddenly dawned on him that he had lost his voice.

Manu was not worried this time. He knew it was just a temporary setback. It was not just Bharadwaja's assurance. He was now convinced that his next phase of the spiritual journey was to spread the Truth – the one he had realized through that remarkable journey with the Yaksha. He had to fulfill that destiny, and his voice would come back. To his mind, it was God's will. He felt like he was a *Mauni*, one who has taken the vow of silence, like the Sadhu he had met in the temple on his way to the monastery. However, he did not mind being a Mauni, since it was only a temporary state. He was fascinated to see that his sense of hearing had magnified several times due to his loss of speech.

He kept strolling along the pathway that led from the ashram to the stream and noticed a large rock beneath a tree that looked like a perfect place for his meditation. As he sat on the rock during his meditation, he felt relaxed like he had never felt before. His rhythmic breathing along with mental chanting soon had lifted him into a spiritual plane where he felt completely at peace.

Almost an hour had passed when Manu finally came out of his meditative state. He opened his eyes and looked around to familiarize himself with the area. There was silence all around except for the whispering wind. He focused hard on that whisper, and he could hear God's message, the one he had heard during his journey with the Yaksha. God's message was simple. He was everywhere and in everything. Why were we so deaf to that message? How could he open everyone else up to hear that message? It was the noise from the day-to-day routine, which masked that message, he reasoned. How would he help others to suppress that noise to help hear the message without having to renounce their chosen professions? That was going to be his next challenge.

He got off from the rock and looked around to find an open space for his yoga practice. A flat area nearby which was devoid of any bushes and trees looked like a good spot for his exercise. He walked to the spot and slowly started his yoga positions, first with the simple ones, hoping to move to the slightly difficult ones later. He then remembered the seer's advice and decided to do only the simple ones. Soon he was completely engrossed in his yoga.

As he completed his yoga practice, he was soaking wet from the deep perspiration. Just when Manu was winding down his yoga practice, he heard some voices approaching him from a distance. It was almost dawn, and Manu noticed that some people were walking towards him from the ashram. He recognized them as they got closer. Bharadwaja was walking

316

with his students to the stream. As they came closer, the seer addressed Manu, "I see you are back in good spirit, Bikku. However, do not strain yourself. It is still early to be doing strenuous yoga positions," advised Bharadwaja.

Manu wanted to reply, and signaled to the seer that he had lost his voice.

"This happens every time I give that medicine. No need to worry; you should be talking again soon. I am confident that you will be able to speak in a month or so," the seer assured him.

A month of silence seemed too long for Manu. However, he had begun to appreciate the power of silence. He was getting addicted to that power. It had given him a deeper sense of appreciation for the nature around him. He had found himself to be a better person at listening to others. His mind was at peace and his senses were sharper than ever. He now realized why ancient seers sometimes took a vow of silence, sometimes for years. He felt bad that he had gotten upset at the Sadhu at the temple for having taken the vow of silence. Again, it was long before he had realized the Truth. It was all right to wait for a month, he reasoned. He looked up from his seated position, smiled, and nodded his head.

"Would you like to come with us and take a cold bath?" enquired the seer.

Manu was eager to do that. He was eagerly waiting for the moment when he could dip into a pond or a lake or a flowing river. Nothing rejuvenated him like a cold bath on a hot summer morning. Moreover, he wanted to get to know everyone in the ashrm. He had started to like Bharadwaja and his students. Their hospitality and friendliness had won him over, and he did not mind staying in the ashram for a while. He joined Bharadwaja and his students and started walking with them to the stream.

Chapter 27
Life in the Ashram

Manu was now an integral part of the ashram life. He had built a small hut for himself with the help of the young students. He had also made a bed made of ropes for his night's rest. He kept his possessions, the scriptures, and the few clothes he had with him in the hut. Manu's possessions were the barest minimum one needed for subsistence. He could now feel the power of detachment, something he did not truly experience when he was at the monastery. He had never been so content and at peace. He had finally overcome the pull of Māya.

He spent his time helping everyone else in the ashram. Sometimes, he would spend time in the kitchen helping Sharada. He would cut vegetables, do cleaning, or even cook without Sharada asking for his help. This pleased her immensely. Indeed, even his presence made her happy. She smiled a lot at him not being able to communicate much. Of course, every time she smiled, she had the two dimples that continuously reminded Manu about Kusuma.

She wanted to know him better, but Manu's inability to talk made it difficult for everyone to find out more about him. They did not know his name. They all wondered what his Varna was. Was he a Brahmin? On the other hand, was he a Kshatriya? Sharada was very curious to find out. Manu had changed a lot since the day he came to the ashram. He had regained his strength, and his hair had grown back. He now had a full head of hair with a short beard around his face. He was beginning to look like a young Sadhu.

Manu made sure that he took part in the spiritual studies as well. He sat along with the students during the morning Vedic chants and prayers. Although he could not chant aloud, he chanted with them in silence. He would watch and listen to Bharadwaja and his students during the evening discourses. He would watch them debate on the meaning of important verses in the Gita. He was often tempted to interject his interpretations but kept quiet for the silence of his vocal chords.

One day, Manu was up early in the morning, much before anyone else. He had finished all his morning rites and was cleaning the prayer hall, getting it ready for the morning classes. Just then the students returned from their morning Yoga and bath. As they entered, Sugata noticed Manu and said to his friends, "Look, he does not look like a bikku any more. He looks more like a Sadhu." The other students agreed.

"From now on, we are going to call him Sadhu. Is that all right with you, Bikku?"

They all looked at Manu, waiting for his reply. Manu turned towards them and nodded in agreement.

"That is excellent! We always wanted to have a Sadhu in our ashram," said Sugata.

All the other students laughed. From that day onwards, every one started addressing him as Sadhu and had no interest in knowing about his past, except for Sharada.

Time went by quickly, and Manu realized early one morning that he had regained his voice. He was going through his morning chants mentally along with the other students, when suddenly he started humming the verses. Everyone was startled a bit, but at the same time, they were extremely pleased to see him recover his voice. They all wanted to talk to him and find out everything about his past.

"What is your real name, Sadhu?" asked Sugata.

"Does it really matter? By the way, I like the name you gave me. It suits me fine," replied Manu. He felt odd hearing his own voice after a long period of silence. Sugata looked disappointed.

"You know Sugata, it is said that one should not dig into the origin of a Sadhu. Let us not waste time on where I came from. What matters is where we are going," added Manu.

"Where are you going, Sadhu? Can you at least tell us that?"

Manu smiled and looked at him and Govinda. He had developed a sense of affection for them. After all, they had saved his life, and he was truly grateful to them.

"I meant figuratively. I will tell you all about it, Sugata. Do you remember the day you and your friend Govinda brought me from the woods to the ashram? I had the most exciting dream that day. In that dream, I had come across the Lord Himself. I now know the true meaning of all the verses in the Gita. I want to spread that Truth to each and every town and village in the great Mauryan Empire."

"How are you going to do that, Sadhu?" asked Govinda, curious to know Manu's plan.

"I plan to traverse the plains on foot just like Gautama did hundreds of years ago. I want to spread the true meaning of Eternal Dharma all over the Empire," explained Manu.

"Can we help you in any way, Sadhu? We would certainly be thrilled to help you in any way we can. We want to join you in that journey," Govinda said eagerly. They really liked Manu's plan and wanted to be part of it.

"That is all right with me if it is acceptable to the seer. Next week, let us go to the fair, and I will start preaching the Lord's message there," Manu replied, as he was more than happy to bring them into God's Dharma.

Sugata and Govinda felt thrilled by that. They were confident that Bharadwaja would not object to them accompanying the Sadhu.

That evening, Bharadwaja and the students, along with Sharada, were having a discourse on *Purusha Sukta*, the tenth hymn in the second book of the Rig Veda. Manu thought it was appropriate for him to start talking about its meaning in light of what he had learnt during his encounter with the Yaksha. One of the young students led the chanting of the verse, and every one including Sharada joined him. The students were engrossed in it; the chanting, the spacing between the words, and the pace were perfect, just the way it was meant to be. The chanting went on.

> "...When they divided the great Purusha, how many parts did
> they make?

320

What did they call his mouth, his arms? What did they call his thighs and feet?

The Brahmin came from his mouth, of both his arms the warrior was born,

His thighs became Vaishya, and from his feet came the Shudra..."

At the end, the seer asked one of his students to explain the significance of that verse to other students. The student seemed extremely eager to give his interpretation of the verse.

"It is very straight forward," he started his explanation. "You know, the speech comes from the mouth, and the mouth is part of the Purusha's head. Since the head is the most important part of the body, the Brahmins are the first among all men and women. The Rig Veda is very clear about that," the young student gave the widely accepted interpretation.

None of the students seemed to object with his interpretation. The young man continued, "Next are the arms. Arms are the most important part of the body for defending or attacking your enemy. Therefore, the Kshatriya group is second among men and women. Vyshyas are next since the legs represent them, and Shudras are the last since they came from the feet of the Purusha, and of course, the feet are at the bottom of everything," the student completed his interpretation.

There was a moment of silence as everyone tried to reason in his or her own mind about the young student's explanation. The student was proud of his interpretation; he stood there beaming with confidence. However, some were confused. They thought the order was somewhat arbitrary, but were afraid to speak out. Manu finally broke the silence.

"If the seer gives me permission, I would like to comment on the interpretation we just heard," Manu requested.

Bharadwaja nodded his head and gave permission for Manu to speak.

"Let us take his interpretation further along. Let us take a Kshatriya or a Brahmin who feels superior to a Shudra. Let us put this person in a forest and make him face a hungry tiger. Fortunately, he is a quick

321

thinker and a good runner. He saves his life by running away and by climbing a tree. Would he feel that his feet were the least important part of his body at that time?" Manu began his explanation.

No one said anything.

"Of course, we all know that every part of our body is important. Likewise, all the four Varnas are equally important. No one is above or below the other. That is true even for those who are outside the Varnas. After all, the Lord has explicitly stated this in the Bhagavad-Gita," Manu continued to explain his interpretation of Purusha Sukta.

"Which verse in the Gita?" asked Govinda, who really liked Manu's interpretation.

"Well, you have the verse,[52] when the Lord explains that he is in the heart of all beings. Certainly, that means that we are all equal from the Lord's perspective. Do we want to have an interpretation that is against His teachings?" asked Manu.

The whole room was stunned. No one had interpreted Purusha Sukta the way Manu had just explained. Everyone liked his analysis, except for Sharada. For some reason, she liked the traditional interpretation.

"Do you agree with that analysis, Father?" she asked the seer.

"Yes, I do agree with his analysis. Indeed, that has always been the theological interpretation. The trouble is with the social interpretation," the seer sided with Manu.

This disappointed Sharada a little bit. Nevertheless, her faith in ancient Manu's analysis was still intact. She then looked at Manu as if to understand him even further.

"So, you do not believe in Varna-ashrama?"[53] asked Sharada.

Manu smiled at her question. He could sense that she was somewhat troubled by his interpretation.

"Of course not; I only believe in God's Dharma. I call that Dharma-ashrama. In Dharma-ashrama, there are no divisions,"[54] replied Manu.

---

52 Bhagavad-Gita 18.61.

53 Varna-ashrama refers to the Varna or caste system.

54 Dharma-ashrama refers to rejection of Varnas or castes.

Sharada did not want to continue with that discussion any more. As someone indoctrinated by the laws of ancient Manu, she was very troubled with the whole discussion. At the same time, Bharadwaja was very pleased with Manu's analysis. In Manu, he saw a thoughtful young man who really understood the true meaning of the Holy Scriptures. He wanted to find out more about him.

"I really like your knowledge of the Scriptures, Sadhu. If you do not mind, can you tell us about your past?" asked the seer.

This time around, Manu did not want to hide his past. He did not mind revealing his identity to them.

"Well, my name is Manu," he revealed. "I was a warrior under the Mauryan army. I left my warrior duty in search of eternal Truth and joined a Buddhist monastery. I was not satisfied with the answers I got there. Therefore, I am here now, and you all know how I came here."

When Sharada heard the name Manu, she had a strange tingling in her head. Soon the tingling was almost like a buzzing in her head and she felt dizzy and passed out. Everyone got very worried and quickly sprinkled some cold water on her face to wake her up. She slowly opened her eyes and looked at her father.

"I have a sudden headache father. Can you please take me to my room? I want to get some sleep," Sharada addressed the seer very softly.

The seer, with the help of his students, carefully led her to her room and ended the class for that day. The next day, Sharada was feeling better and was back in good spirits. However, the name Manu continued to puzzle her. It was as if she knew someone by that name from her past life. She tried hard to make any sense of it with no success whatsoever.

The next day, when he was alone with his daughter, Bharadwaja wanted to find out about Sharada's feelings towards Manu. The seer had thought about getting Sharada married to a deserving man but had not seriously explored it. Suddenly, he had the idea that Manu might be the perfect match for his daughter.

"Sharada, do you like Manu?" asked the seer.

Sharada was a little surprised by that question. However, she guessed why her father was asking that question. She even felt a sense of excitement. Of course, she liked his good looks and his pleasant personality. She blushed a little thinking about Manu.

"I like him father; may I know why you are asking me that?" replied Sharada.

"Well, you know Sharada; it is time that I found a husband for you. It is my duty as your father to do just that. If you like Manu, I would like to propose that," explained Bharadwaja.

Sharada had to take a deep breath before she could answer that question. It was all happening too fast. Of course, she liked Manu a lot. However, she was not sure about marrying him. She had to think a lot more about that before she could give an answer.

"I need some time before I can give you an answer, father," replied Sharada knowing it was not going to be easy to find the right answer. All that she could think about at that moment was the laws according to ancient Manu. Was it right for her to marry Manu?

Meanwhile, Manu wanted to know more about Sharada. Of course, the only thing he wanted to know was if she was really Kusuma. When he had a chance to be alone with Bharadwaja, Manu addressed that question.

"Bharadwaja, can you tell me how Sharada came to the ashram?" Manu asked the seer.

Bharadwaja was pleased that Manu was interested in Sharada's story. That only meant that Manu liked Sharada, which pleased him.

"It happened four years ago," the seer began his story, "My wife had reached God's abode, and I had cremated her body and performed the last rites. It was time for me to sprinkle her ashes in the Holy Ganges. Along with some of my students, I went to the place where the river Sita joins the Holy Ganges and was chanting the names of the Lord as I sprinkled the ashes. That was when I saw a wall of water coming from river Sita. I realized that there was heavy rain upstream, which had brought the water surge. Strangely enough, there was no rain whatsoever where Sita merged with Ganges.

"We moved to the shore just to be safe," the seer continued with his story, "Suddenly, I saw the body of a young woman wash ashore, and we quickly brought her to higher elevation and tried to revive her. We had almost lost all our hopes when, after several minutes of trying, we saw some movement in her body. We were so thrilled to see that and continued to revive her. She finally regained her consciousness, but, unfortunately she was in a trauma and could not remember anything including her own name."

"Do you remember the exact date? Do you remember how she was dressed?" Manu asked with a lot of anticipation.

"Yes, I do remember the exact date. It was the first ekadasi of that year. She looked like a girl from the hills like a hunter class. It really did not matter to me what her Varna was. I considered her as God's gift to me and adopted her. I named her Sharada and raised her in the Vedic tradition," explained Bharadwaja.

Manu knew exactly what had happened now. His worst fears about that tragic day had not come true. Although Kusuma drowned in the flash flood caused by the heavy rains, she had somehow survived the monstrous floods. Of course, she had lost all her memory. At least, she was fortunate enough to have ended up as Bharadwaja's daughter.

"I agree, Bharadwaja; Sharada is lucky to have you as her adopted father," replied Manu.

When Manu and Bharadwaja were discussing her past outside, Sharada was extremely agitated. She kept pacing up and down inside the ashram. All she could do was think about her father's desire. She knew very well that Bharadwaja really liked Manu, and was going to propose her marriage to him at an appropriate time. Of course, he would only do that if Sharada gave a positive answer to proceed with that proposal. She liked Manu a lot; there was no doubt about that. However, she was not sure about marrying him. She kept wondering what the reason for her hesitation was. Suddenly, it struck her that Manu was a warrior, and she was a Brahmin woman, a woman of the highest Varna. Of course, she remembered that the ancient Manu had forbidden a Brahmin woman from marrying a man from a lower Varna. She could not go against the laws specified by the first man. In her mind, the ancient Manu had to be right, as the Lord Himself had ordained Manu to write the rules. At the same time, she felt uncomfortable saying no to her father, knowing how much he liked Manu. She kept looking for a solution to get out of her predicament, when she finally thought of getting help from Manu himself. She decided to talk to him the next day, as Manu was always the first one to get up in the morning for his Yoga practice.

Sharada hardly slept that night, eagerly waiting for the morning hours that seemed like eternity for her. She heard the footsteps of Manu next to her room as Manu walked from the ashram to the tree beneath which he practiced his yoga every morning. Within a few minutes of Manu's departure from the ashram, Sharada got up, and quietly left the ashram walking briskly towards Manu's morning yoga spot.

He glanced up and noticed that the sky was clear with nothing but the shining stars and the half moon that brought enough light for him to do his meditation and yoga. As he sat there getting his senses together to focus on his meditation, he had a strange feeling in his heart that seemed so familiar. It was the same feeling he had at the monastery just before he walked out of the place. He knew right then that he was not going to stay in the ashram for a long time. At the same time, he heard some footsteps approaching him. He turned around and saw that it was Sharada walking towards him, which made him wonder if she was all right. His immediate thought was that she was sleepwalking.

As she got closer, he knew that she was completely awake and realized that she had come there for some important reason. He greeted her with a smile to make her feel comfortable.

"What brings you here so early in the morning, Sharada?" asked Manu.

"I need to talk to you about something important. However, I do not have a lot of time," replied Sharada with a worried look.

"Is something wrong? I am more than happy to help you any way I can." Manu tried to assure her.

"Manu, I will be quick. My father wants to propose my marriage to you. I am not happy with that." Sharada was almost abrupt in bringing up the main reason why she was there. The fact that she was so worked up about it amused Manu.

"That should not be a problem. Just tell him that you are not interested in marrying me," Manu replied.

"No, I do not want to do that," Sharada sounded worried, "I do not want to hurt his feelings." There was a brief silence as she struggled to express her thoughts.

"That is the reason I am here," she continued. "Please tell him when he comes to you with the marriage proposal that you are not interested in me."

Manu found the whole thing to be amusing. He was a bit confused as well. Seeing the puzzled look on his face, Sharada realized that she had to give him more details.

"It is like this, Manu. It is not that I do not like you. It is just that I am a Brahmin woman and you are a warrior. It is just not right, and I do not want to do anything against the laws of dharma as specified by ancient Manu," Sharada explained.

Manu now understood what was going on. At the same time, he was amazed at the power of indoctrination of the laws of ancient Manu. Moreover, since his journey with the Yaksha, nothing really bothered him as he had now overcome Māya. He felt like it was his third life within his present incarnation. He had been Manu who was in love with Kusuma, he had been Manu in love with Chitralekha, and now he was Manu the emancipated. He remembered the verse from the Holy Scripture, "*After many cycles of birth and death, one who has attained the knowledge - that God is everything - comes to Me.*"

He was thankful that he had attained that knowledge in the present life itself.

"I will just do that Sharada. There is absolutely nothing to worry about here. You can go back to the ashram and relax," Manu promised her.

Sharada was infinitely relieved and smiled broadly.

"I am grateful forever for your help in this regard, Manu." She thanked him and went back to the ashram.

Manu was now convinced even more about his mission. It was time for him to leave the ashram. He had to work hard to remove the ignorance that had swept the land. It was the laws of ancient Manu that had corrupted the minds and hearts of people of Aryavarta. He had to bring them the teachings of the Gita as instructed by the Lord Himself. He did not want to leave the ashram abruptly and waited for the right moment to inform the seer.

The right moment came when Bharadwaja approached Manu about bringing his daughter and Manu together in marriage. As expected, Bharadwaja had gotten approval from Sharada to approach Manu on that subject. When they were alone together in a secluded area, the seer brought up the topic.

"You know, Manu, I have been thinking about getting my daughter married soon. I wanted to talk to you about that," Bharadwaja began.

Manu knew exactly what was in the seer's mind. He had already decided how he was going to answer that question.

"I have observed you over the months in the ashram and have concluded that you are the ideal man to marry my daughter," the seer continued.

"It would be an honor if you accept her hand," concluded Bharadwaja.

"You know, Bharadwaja, I really like Sharada. She is beautiful and intelligent. Not only that, she is well versed in all Vedic scriptures," Manu started his preamble. "While I am honored that you think that I am a suitable husband for your daughter, I need to tell you about my immediate plans," Manu replied.

Bharadwaja, while he was pleased with the lavish praise that Manu bestowed on Sharada, was a little concerned when he heard the last words from Manu. What were his plans?

"Well, I have decided to become a Sadhu and go from village to village to spread the Lord's words as specified in the Gita. Given that plan, I am not sure that I can marry Sharada," Manu concluded.

When Bharadwaja heard this, he was a little shocked, but not really surprised. He knew deep inside someone as wise as Manu would not stay at the same place for a long time. Although disappointed, he accepted Manu's decision and gave his full blessings to his plans.

Chapter 28

The Wandering Sadhu

Everyone in the ashram now knew about Manu's decision to become a Sadhu. All of them, including Sharada, were sad to see him leave the ashram. However, they all knew that Manu's destiny was somewhere else, and no one could change his decision. Sugata was the one who was the saddest. When Govinda and Sugata heard about Manu's decision, they rushed to the seer seeking his permission to join Manu in his spiritual journey.

"I am all right with Govinda joining Manu; however, Sugata has to stay back," was Bharadwaja's reply.

"Why cannot I go with Govinda?" Sugata had protested.

"Because you are still in the middle of your studies whereas Govinda has completed his work," replied the seer.

Sugata had to accept his teacher's decision. He knew that he had an obligation to his family and to his guru to complete his studies. He only hoped that he would be able to join Manu and Govinda once he was done with his work.

Manu was getting ready to go on his next phase of his spiritual journey. He put his belongings into his old bag; there were so few items in his bag that it almost appeared empty. Soon Govinda joined him with his small bag, ready to accompany Manu.

"Are you sure you want to come with me, Govinda? It is not going to be easy, you know. We may face a very hostile world outside. They might not like what we are going to tell them," warned Manu with genuine concern for Govinda's welfare.

"I have thought about it for a long time, Manu. I know it is not going to be easy, and we may have a severe hardship. I am willing to face it; after all, like you told me once, there is nothing more beautiful and exciting than doing the Lord's work," Govinda replied calmly.

Manu was satisfied, and as they started walking out of the ashram, everyone, including Bharadwaja and Sharada, came to see them off. They slowly walked with them for a few hundred yards without saying anything. It was as if everyone was holding back his or her sadness on one hand and, at the same time, praying for Manu's success on the other hand. After a while, they all stopped, and every one of them knew they were at the end of the road. Govinda bowed to the seer and touched his feet. When he got up, the seer hugged him and Manu, drawn to both of them, joined them in a hug. They were like that for a few seconds when they finally separated and bid goodbye to everyone in the ashram. Manu and Govinda started walking away from the ashram slowly at first and briskly later as if to make it easy on their compatriots. Sharada could not hold back her sorrow any longer. She briskly went back to her room, closed the door, and cried the whole night.

Manu and Govinda kept walking in a direction that was not familiar to Govinda. They had traveled for hours without coming across any village or town. Finally, they reached a small village and decided to rest there as night was fast approaching. Govinda suggested that they should go and see if any one in the village was willing to provide shelter for the day.

"There is no need for that Govinda. It is still summer, and we can sleep beneath that banyan tree," replied Manu.

As they were getting ready to relax under the tree, Govinda was getting hungry. Of course, Manu was used to either fasting or eating just fruits during the night and was now conditioned to eat only one meal a day. Govinda, who was not used to that, was getting extremely hungry and looked at Manu, hoping he would notice his condition. Realizing that Manu was not going to help him, Govinda decided to prompt Manu.

"I am very hungry Manu. Can we go inside the village, and ask for alms?" Govinda made a polite request.

"I know you are hungry Govinda. We are going to be in this situation more often than you may imagine. It is a good idea to see if you can build will power to overcome the feeling of hunger. The sooner you develop that power, the better it is for you," replied Manu.

Govinda was disappointed. Nevertheless, he agreed to do just that. Right at that point, they saw a man walking towards them. The man seemed like a household servant who stopped in front of them and bowed to them as a sign of respect. He then addressed Manu.

"Sadhu, I am a servant in the house of Vamana Gupta. He is a wealthy merchant who lives in the large house you can see from here. His wife, Janaki, saw you from the house and sent me here to request that you take shelter for the night in my master's house," the servant reported in a polite fashion.

Govinda was very happy to hear that and eagerly waited for Manu's answer. However, Manu was hesitant and did not answer right away.

"Please, Sadhu, accept my master's invitation. He is a very religious man, and he will really be hurt if you refused," insisted the servant.

That really changed Manu's mind as his first commandment was not to hurt anyone (*"the Lord is in the heart of all beings"*). He agreed to take refuge in the wealthy merchant's house.

When they reached the merchant's house, Vamana Gupta and his wife Janaki greeted them. They took them inside and asked them to join them and their servants for dinner. Manu and Govinda accepted their invitation and sat in the dining room along with the rest of Vamana's family. Vamana had no children and treated his servants as his own family. They all ate together every night, and his love for his servants told Manu that Vamana was not an ordinary man. While Manu had only fruits as part of his dinner, Govinda had a full meal. As they were relaxing after the fine dinner, the merchant wanted to know about Manu's plans.

"What are your plans for the next few days, Sadhu?" the merchant asked.

"We do not have any definite plans, Vamana Gupta. All we want to do is go from village to village preaching about God's Dharma," replied Manu.

That really awakened Vamana's interest. He was one of those enlightened souls who had always questioned the laws of ancient Manu.

"Can you tell me more about that, Sadhu?" The merchant wanted to know everything about Manu's plan now. He was even interested in how he could help Manu in his endeavor.

Manu was about to give him more details about his intentions when suddenly it occurred to him that he had met Vamana before. As he focused hard to recall where he had met him, it all came back to him in a flash. Manu realized he was the merchant who had placed the Goddess's silver feet below the temple tower. He had visited that temple just before Manu had joined the Buddhist monastery. He had placed the silver feet so that those who were outside the four Varnas could pray to the Goddess. Suddenly, Manu's respect for Vamana increased tenfold.

"It is like this, Vamana. Blinded by Māyā, people of Aryavarta are adhering to senseless laws attributed to ancient Manu. Deluded by Māyā, they have placed those laws above the Lord Himself. They would rather break the teachings of the Lord than free themselves from the bondage of ancient Manu. I want people to reject Varna-ashrama and accept Dharma-ashrama. I want everyone to come to God according to the Bhagavad-Gita."

As Manu explained the basic goal, Vamana got very excited. It was as if the Lord had answered his prayers; he had wondered even from his childhood days what could emancipate the people of Magadha from the shackles of the laws of ancient Manu. The young Sadhu who was sitting in front of him was the answer to his prayer.

"Sadhu, it is like my dream has come true. I have always wondered if any learned man would speak out against the grotesque practices of Varna-ashrama. I am happy to offer any help you need in your mission," Vamana replied as if he were relieved of a major burden.

The servants and Vamana's wife listened to the conversation with great interest and nodded their heads. Govinda, who was observing the whole thing, noticed that Manu had now developed a persona that had begun to put a spell on people around him.

Govinda was amazed that their mission had such an auspicious beginning. Whatever happened to the hardship they were supposed to go through? What Govinda did not realize was that their mission was still a long journey with many invisible pitfalls.

"That is very thoughtful of you, Vamana. I will accept your offer," replied Manu.

Over the next few months, Vamana's house became the base for Manu and Govinda. From there they went to village after village spreading the teachings of the Bhagavad-Gita. Vamana had offered his horse-drawn carriage to help Manu in his travels, which made his travels much easier.

Manu's fame was now spreading like a wildfire all over the region. There were always large crowds that eagerly waited for Manu to give his sermons wherever he went. Indeed, the crowds were often getting out of control, as people were eager to touch him and talk to him. While most of the people liked Manu's teachings and realized the fallacy of the laws of ancient Manu, there were many who saw him as a danger to their vested powers. They first ignored him as a "crazy" Sadhu, but as his fame grew, they became very concerned. There were secret backroom meetings on how they could get rid of him. Some suggested they should slander him, while others even considered eliminating him.

Manu's teachings impressed many others who decided to become his disciples. Manu, along with Govinda and his disciples, kept traveling across the land whether it was the rainy season, winter, or summer. Some of these trips were very taxing on many of his disciples, who were not as well conditioned as Manu. Some even fell ill in the winter. Seeing this, Vamana Gupta suggested that he should build an ashram and preach from the ashram most of the time while occasionally traveling to other towns and villages. That was acceptable to Manu, and he agreed to start his ashram near Vamana Gupta's village on a large track of land donated by Vamana himself. In addition, Vamana and other wealthy merchants from the region donated money to Manu to build his ashram. Manu decided to call his ashram "Dharma-ashrama."

Volunteers from across the land came to help raise the ashram. Within months, Dharma-ashrama was a simple yet beautiful ashram. It was now easy for Manu to give his sermons day after day without having to travel long distances. People poured from villages and towns to listen to Manu.

Meanwhile, those who were unhappy with Manu's teachings continued to plan on how they could eliminate Manu and his disciples. In their mind, Manu was attacking the whole structure of dharma, as they knew it; for those deluded souls, ancient Manu was more important than God Himself.

One late, dark night, a small group of thugs slowly entered the ashram premises and hid behind the large bushes. There were five of them, and they waited for several hours for activities in the ashram to subside. It was now past midnight, and all the visitors had left. Manu, Govinda, and other disciples were sleeping in their rooms. It was so quiet now that the intruders could hear even the smallest animal move around the ashram grounds. They had no problem getting into the main hall of the ashram, as the door was always open. They started crawling into the main hall when one of them kicked a lamp, which made a loud noise and woke up the residents. One of the disciples quickly lit a lamp and was horrified to see that the intruders had drawn large swords. They looked like they were about to go on a killing spree. Before he knew what was going on, two other disciples had quickly grabbed the clubs that were near the corner of the room and had attacked the intruders. Those two disciples looked like experts in martial arts and were able to disarm the intruders. The intruders appeared to be in considerable pain, realized that they were no match for the two disciples, and quickly ran away from the ashram.

All the commotion and noise woke up Manu, and he came to join his disciples to see what was going on. All he could see was a group of strangers running out of the ashram and two of his disciples holding long clubs.

"What happened here?" enquired Manu.

"There were several intruders with knives and swords who came here to kill us. I think you were their main target. Fortunately for us, we were saved by these brave disciples," replied Govinda and pointed to the two who were still holding the clubs.

Manu looked at their strong physical appearances. It was not difficult to guess that they were probably elite warriors.

"Who sent you here? Can you tell me who sent you here?" Manu questioned the two.

"Please do not get upset at us, Manu. We were sent here to protect you by Kautilya," replied the two warriors.

334

Their answer really surprised Manu. Why would Kautilya do that? "Does any one know about this?" asked Manu.

"No one other than your father knows about this. Ever since you left Pataliputra, your father asked Kautilya to send some agents to protect you. We have been checking on your safety ever since. When Kautilya received intelligence reports that some were plotting to kill you, he asked us to join your ashram to guard you," replied one of the disciples.

Manu could not still believe that no one knew about this.

"Not even Vishnu Gupta?" he asked his disciples.

"No one else knows about this, not even Vishnu Gupta," assured the disciples.

Manu was thankful for his father's love and caring. It was not that he was afraid of death. He was thankful that his father's love for him had saved the Dharma mission. He was not yet sure that his disciples had the conviction to continue with the mission once he left the material world to Krishna's abode.

"What if the intruders come back?" asked Govinda who was a little shaken up.

"Do not worry Govinda; they will not attack us anymore. They were just hired people, and the people behind them will be afraid to try it again," assured the two disciples.

After that incident, things in the ashram settled down, and Manu's mission blossomed very well. His fame had now reached Mayapuri, which was the main town in that region. The head of Vishnu Gupta's secret service network for that region, Kumara Verma, lived in Mayapuri. When he heard about the *wandering Sadhu*, he decided to pay a visit to the ashram to get a first-hand understanding of what was going on.

Of course, Kumara Verma's intention in visiting the ashram was not to learn spiritual aspects of life. His purpose was to find out if there was any threat to the Mauryan Empire from this Sadhu or his cohorts. He wanted to know if the Sadhu had any hidden agenda, and if he had any subliminal messages that would inspire people to do anything that was damaging to the Empire. In the worst case, he could be an agent of enemies of the Empire.

To his surprise, his first visit to the ashram was a pleasant experience, and Manu's sermon completely mesmerized him. Everything he was hearing seemed like music to his soul. Like everyone who came to the ashram, he left that day feeling a little closer to the Lord. Moreover, it made him go back to the ashram as often as he could.

In spite of his spiritual attraction to Manu, Kumara Verma had his agents check everything about his background and found nothing sinister about the Sadhu. He was tempted to ignore Manu's Dharma mission and treat it as one of thousands of spiritual fads that sprouted across the Ganges valley every year. However, out of conditioning, he decided to report about the Sadhu to Vishnu Gupta in his next monthly meeting.

When Vishnu Gupta heard about the Sadhu and his movement, he was deeply concerned. He decided to use his top agent, Chitralekha, to eliminate any sliver of threat he posed to the Mauryan Empire.[55]

Chitralekha was getting ready for the last mission of her life. She had the strange premonition she was not going to be involved in any more missions. She packed everything she needed for the mission and had the two expert flute players meet her in a secret place. They were not ordinary flute players; they hid poisonous arrows inside their flutes and shot them while playing. They did it so well that it was difficult even for those standing next to them to notice the arrows. She had chosen two of the best flute players for her mission – Rama and Soma. They had been involved with her in several past missions, and Chitralekha had used them effectively to eliminate many potential enemies of the Mauryan Empire.

Chitralekha left Pataliputra along with Rama and Soma in the middle of the night in a carriage. When they reached Mayapuri, Chitralekha asked Rama to stay behind with the carriage. She and Soma left for Manu's ashram on foot. When they reached the ashram, it was already afternoon, and hundreds of people were pouring into the ashram for Manu's evening sermon. There was a large crowd near the patio in front of the ashram eagerly waiting for Manu. Chitralekha and Soma, who were dressed as visitors from the western province, joined them. They slowly moved closer to the front of the crowd so that they were in the right position to carry out their mission. There they waited eagerly for the Sadhu to come out of the ashram building.

---

55 See prologue.

The crowd waited eagerly for several minutes for Manu to come out. Suddenly, Chitralekha started feeling very warm and started perspiring profusely. Her hands started getting very sweaty as if she were extremely nervous. She felt like she was about to do something wrong; she had never felt like this on any of her previous assignments.

Finally, the Sadhu emerged. Chitralekha looked at the tall figure who was clad in saffron robes. He had long hair and full facial hair. His beard had grown long enough that it was touching his chest. She had a strange feeling that she knew the Sadhu; it was as if he were someone close to her. She just brushed aside that feeling as a last minute jitter before carrying out her mission. She quietly prompted Soma to get ready with his task by nudging him with her elbow.

Manu sat on a small platform and settled down to begin his sermon. His disciples sat in an arc next to him. Soma quietly got his flute with the poisonous dart ready and began to set his aim on Manu's neck. Normally at this point, Chitralekha would look away from the target. For some strange reason, she could not do it this time, and she stared at the Sadhu's eyes. She knew those eyes, and in a fraction of a second, she realized that the Sadhu was none other than her beloved Manu. She screamed and lunged forward to prevent Soma from shooting the dart. Unfortunately for Chitralekha, it was too late and Soma had already blown the dart. The dart came out of the flute and struck her palm as she was lunging forward. She let out another scream and to everyone in the crowd it sounded like she had screamed "Manu."

There was a sudden pandemonium, as the crowd did not know what was going on. Some thought that Manu was hurt, and they got extremely agitated and confused. However, they were somewhat relieved when he got up and started walking towards Chitralekha. As soon as he had heard the scream, Manu knew that it was Chitralekha. He was not surprised to see her there; however, he was concerned that something terrible may have happened to her.

He quickly walked to her and put her head on his lap. Manu noticed the poisonous arrow on her palm and quickly realized what had happened; Chitralekha had sacrificed her own life to save Manu. Manu looked around to see who the assassin was; however, Soma had vanished from the scene and was nowhere in the vicinity. As a trained assassin, he knew exactly how to vanish.

Chitralekha looked at Manu in a way she had never looked at him before. She remembered that when she was his lover, she had a recurring dream that she would die in his arms. She knew it was a strange dream and had always wondered about it. Now her dream had come true; she now knew that it was a premonition. Manu looked at her with tenderness and said, "I am sorry." She did not know why he had uttered those words, but it made her immensely happy.

As the poison in the dart rapidly entered her blood stream, she was slowly losing her consciousness. She knew that there was one last thing she had to do before she left the material world. She uttered the words "Om Krishna" ever so faintly and closed her eyes as her soul departed the material world. While Manu was sad that Chitralekha's life had ended tragically, he was happy that she had reached God's abode.[56]

The news of Chitralekha's death reached Vishnu Gupta the same day she died. Soma delivered the news personally to Vishnu Gupta; he had realized that it was better to tell the truth about how it had happened. His hope was that his honesty would prevent Vishnu Gupta from having him imprisoned or even worse, executed. When Vishnu Gupta heard the news about Chitralekha's death, he was devastated. He was so hurt that he froze on his chair and was immobile for several minutes. He was so motionless that Soma thought that something had happened to his heart, and he was about to collapse. However, after several minutes, Vishnu Gupta slowly got up and took one long look at Soma. As Soma stared at Vishnu Gupta's face, he could not find any emotion whatsoever. It was as if his body was still alive while someone had stolen his soul. Vishnu Gupta stood at his desk motionless for a long time not saying anything. The long silence along with Vishnu Gupta's emotionless face really worried Soma. Then ever so slowly, Vishnu Gupta's face dropped and drops of tears started flowing down his face as he closed his eyes.

---

56 The Lord states in Bhagavad-Gita (8.13) that one who thinks of Him along with Om at the time of death will reach Him.

Vishnu Gupta had never cried since the Nandas had ruthlessly murdered his parents. From that day on he was a different man who had completely buried his human feelings. Only his mentor Kautilya understood his mental constitution. Suddenly one day, Chitralekha had appeared in his life. Chitrasena, who wanted him to protect her, had brought her to him, and he had gladly accepted. However, he had never realized that he was going to be attached to her as a father would be attached to his daughter. The news of her death was immensely painful. He knew that he was partly responsible for the way her life had ended. After all, he had sent her on that mission, and he had done it all in the name of dharma.

"Take me to the Sadhu's place," he ordered Soma.

He then called out one of his trusted assistants and ordered him to inform Kautilya about his impending journey.

The next day, when Vishnu Gupta and Soma reached Manu's ashram, there was a large crowd that had come to view Chitralekha's body. Many a legend about her beauty flourished all over the Empire, and people were very curious to see her, even in her death. As Vishnu Gupta entered the hall and saw his adopted child dead, he broke down again in a way he had never done before. He walked to Manu, held his hand, and asked for his forgiveness. He then asked Manu to cremate her and do the last rites. Vishnu Gupta knew that Manu was the only man she had loved as a free woman. It was only fitting that he was the one to perform the last rites.

Chapter 29

Chandra Gupta's Spritual Journey

Vishnu Gupta was never the same man after Chitralekha's death. Even his own parents' deaths did not affect him the way her death haunted him. Perhaps it was because the brutal death of his parents happened right in front of his own eyes. The shock of his parents' killing was so deep and enduring that even Vishnu Gupta had not realized that he was a troubled soul since that day. Only Kautilya knew his mental status, and he protected Vishnu Gupta as any mentor would protect his or her protégé.

Vishnu Gupta was a confused man since coming back from Manu's ashram. He was confused about dharma; he was confused about what was right or wrong, and more troubling to him was that he had lost his spiritual bearings. What he had once thought as non-negotiable – the laws of ancient Manu – now seemed irrelevant to him. What is more, he was even questioning the existence of God Himself.

Vishnu Gupta stayed locked up in his room for endless hours completely immersed in his work trying to forget his grief. He could not eat or sleep, and he cried until he had no more energy to cry. He was lost and scared as a child lost in a dark forest. For the first time, he realized that he needed help. He knew that the only one who could help him was Kautilya.

Meanwhile, Kautilya had gotten independent reports about what had transpired at Manu's ashram. He now knew about the assassination attempts on Manu, including how Chitralekha had died. He called Vishnu Gupta into his office to understand exactly what was going on. When

Vishnu Gupta entered his office, he could not believe how distraught his protégé was. He looked weak, out of focus, and seemed like he had lost interest in life. Kautilya was alarmed at his mental status.

"Is everything all right, Vishnu Gupta? You seem to be taking Chitralekha's death too hard," asked a concerned Kautilya.

Vishnu Gupta gave a blank stare and did not bother to answer him. This was the first time Vishnu Gupta had ignored Kautilya.

"Can you tell me, Vishnu Gupta, what really happened in Manu's ashram?" asked Kautilya. He had a general idea about what had transpired. Nevertheless, he wanted to know all the details.

"He has started an ashram that he calls 'Dharma-ashrama'. He wants to spread God's Dharma across the Empire. He has been going around telling people that Varnas are all man made. He quotes the Bhagavad-Gita as the basis for his sermons. I did not like this, thinking his message would destabilize the Empire," replied Vishnu Gupta. He then paused as if he were struggling to find the right words. Kautilya waited patiently for him to continue. "I now know that I was wrong; I was deluded, Kautilya. I tried to have him eliminated, and sent Chitralekha on that mission. Now I have lost my own child. I am a very lowly person, and I feel lost and miserable, Kautilya," added Vishnu Gupta, and he started crying uncontrollably.

Kautilya felt terrible for his protégé. He knew very well that Vishnu Gupta treated Chitralekha as his own daughter. He also realized that Vishnu Gupta was emerging out of that impregnable cocoon he had built around him. He realized that Vishnu Gupta needed special attention at that point.

"Do not be so hard on yourself, Gupta. You were just doing what you thought was right, albeit misguided by the power of Māya. You need a teacher who can help you overcome the veil of Māya. You will be all right very soon," assured Kautilya.

"But who is that teacher that is going to help me? Can you be that teacher, Kautilya?" pleaded Vishnu Gupta.

"I cannot be that teacher, Gupta. I have strayed too far from that venerable role. The web of Māya has entrapped me as well. I can only think of one who can help you," Kautilya sounded a little bit sad as he admitted his own predicament.

341

"Who is that someone special who can help me?" Gupta asked Kautilya with a sense of hope.

"That is Manu, Gupta. From everything I have heard about him, he seems to be the one who can be your spiritual master," explained Kautilya.

Gupta was surprised to hear Kautilya's assessment. Of course, he had complete trust in Kautilya's judgment. Indeed, Gupta had always considered Kautilya as the true authority on dharma. However, how was that going to happen?

"Are you suggesting that I go and join Manu's ashram?" asked Gupta.

"Not really, Gupta. The current ashram location is too dangerous for Manu. There is ample intelligence that there is a constant threat to Manu's life. His ashram is located where the laws of ancient Manu are too entrenched in people's minds. He needs to start his movement from the fringes of the Empire," suggested Kautilya.

That sounded perfectly logical to Gupta. After all, that was how the great Mauryan Empire was born. "How can we help him, then?" enquired Gupta.

"Well, I have an idea. Let us send our agents to bring Manu to Pataliputra. Tell him that I personally want to see him. He will not refuse to come," instructed Kautilya.

Gupta's mood had a swift turn. His energy level went up as he was eager to accept Manu as his guru. He nodded his head in agreement and quickly went back to his office to carry out Kautilya's instructions.

As expected, Manu felt honored that Kautilya had sent for him. He gladly accepted the invitation to see Kautilya. Manu and some of his disciples including Govinda traveled to Pataliputra in a coach provided by Kautilya. When they reached the entrance to the city, Kautilya personally went to meet Manu and his disciples. He then took them to his office where Vishnu Gupta was waiting for them.

Manu was not surprised to see Gupta, as he always assumed that Gupta's agency was involved in all Mauryan affairs. However, he was not sure about the reason why Kautilya had requested the meeting.

"Manu, you are probably puzzled why we wanted you to come and meet us in Pataliputra," Kautilya stated, laying the foundations for the plan he had in mind. Manu and his students sat there waiting for Kautilya to continue with his explanation. "I will explain why Manu," continued

Kautilya. "We all admire that you are passionate about spreading God's Dharma. Indeed, many of us have had similar dreams, but none of us had the courage to do what you are doing."

Manu realized that there was going to be some sort of disapproval from Kautilya. He wondered what was bothering him about his mission.

"However, there are hundreds of people who are against your mission, and who are willing to kill you. The place where you have your ashram is too dangerous for you Manu," added a concerned Kautilya.

"I am happy that you are a man of wisdom who can distinguish between God's Dharma and the laws of ancient Manu, Kautilya. I know there are many who want to stop us, but that is not going to distract us," assured Manu.

"I am not questioning your commitment, Manu. For the sake of the mission, for the sake of spreading God's Dharma, it is important that you start the mission from the edges of the Empire," replied Kautilya.

Manu began to understand what was in Kautilya's mind. He wanted to hear it directly from him. "What are you suggesting, Kautilya?" asked Manu.

"My suggestion is that you relocate your ashram to Taxila in the west. Indeed, I want you to run your mission from my old school. I will arrange for that. The current location is too dangerous for you. Remember, the best way to conquer any land is to conquer it from the edges. The same applies for Dharma as well," explained Kautilya.

Govinda and others who were sitting on the side listening to the conversation were very saddened to hear Kautilya's suggestion. They loved Manu so much that they were not willing to lose him.

"What happens to the ashram?" asked Govinda.

"The ashram will stay. One of you can continue with Manu's work, albeit with a low profile," suggested Kautilya.

Manu thought about Kautilya's suggestion. Although he was not afraid of death, he did not want his mission to end abruptly. He paced around the room for a few seconds, stopped, and addressed Kautilya.

"All right, Kautilya. I accept your suggestion. I want Govinda to run the current ashram. I will go to Taxila with whoever wants to go with me," said Manu.

"I want to go with you, Manu," said Gupta. He was the first one to volunteer. Manu was surprised to hear that.

"What about your work, your secret service agency?" asked Manu.

"I have had enough of this material world. I am a seeker now. Please accept me as your student and show me the path to God. Teach me about God's Dharma," requested Gupta.

"You are welcome to go to Taxila with me, Gupta. We will spread God's Dharma together."

Within the next few days, Vishnu Gupta and Manu arranged to leave for Taxila while Govinda and other disciples went back to Manu's original ashram. Mukunda, one of Kautilya's students from Taxila, took over Vishnu Gupta's job. Vishnu Gupta himself had trained Mukunda in all aspects of his agency, and it was an easy transition for Mukunda.

With Vishnu Gupta gone to Taxila, Kautilya often felt lonesome. Chandra Gupta was the only other person who was close to him. However, with Chandra Gupta being the Emperor, Kautilya did not spend as much time with him as he did with Gupta. Furthermore, Chandra Gupta was now intensely involved in the matters of the Empire and had developed an independent style of governing. Although he always came to Kautilya for advice on all matters, he made his own decisions in the end. Thanks to the intelligence apparatus established by Vishnu Gupta, the Maurya Empire ran like a well-oiled machine. With the enemies kept at bay, people felt secure and were happy. It was now twenty-three years since Chandra Gupta and Kautilya founded the Mauryan Empire. Chandra Gupta's son Bindusara was now almost eighteen years old and was getting ready to succeed his father.

Meanwhile, Kautilya was feeling old. It was not a feeling of age in the time sense, but rather a feeling that he had not completed his spiritual journey. After twenty-three years of establishing the Mauryan Empire, he felt that while dharma had been re-established, the quality of dharma was suspect. He often thought about Manu's mission and was tempted to go back to Taxila. However, he was not ready to abandon Chandra Gupta before his son took over the kingdom.

Months passed by without anything exciting happening from Kautilya's perspective. Suddenly, all that changed when one day a special messenger broke that peace and tranquility. He was not any messenger. He was a messenger who brought messages only from the Emperor's parents. After Chandra Gupta had become the Emperor of Aryavarta, he wanted his parents to move from his childhood village to Pataliputra. However, his parents had refused to move to Pataliputra, and only visited the Emperor occasionally. Chandra Gupta had accepted the decision knowing that his parents were simple people who did not enjoy any sort of luxury. He, however, made sure that there were permanent guards to protect them, and he had placed a special messenger with them.

"Sir, I have an important message to take to the Emperor," said the messenger, who looked very tired and worried.

"What is it? Is something wrong?" replied Kautilya, although he knew very well that something was terribly wrong just by looking at his face.

"Yes, the Emperor's mother is very ill. She is on her deathbed. Her last wish is to see the Emperor before she leaves the material world," replied the messenger.

Kautilya did not want to waste even a single minute, and they both quickly went to see Chandra Gupta. When Chandra Gupta heard the news, he was extremely distraught. He wanted to go and see his mother immediately. Kautilya agreed, and sent the messenger back to tell Chandra Gupta's father that the Emperor was on his way to his mother. In addition, he instructed the messenger that no one other than Chandra Gupta's father was to know that the Emperor was on his way to see his mother. He immediately had two of his top agents shadow the messenger to ensure that no enemies of the Empire attempted any foul play on him.

Within hours of the messenger's departure, Kautilya and Chandra Gupta left Pataliputra through a secret passage, with all arrangements in place to handle state matters. Of course, whenever Chandra Gupta left Pataliputra on a secret mission, he always traveled incognito, which made it impossible for strangers to recognize him.

When Chandra Gupta reached his childhood village, he was overwhelmed and had to struggle to suppress his emotions. As he entered his mother's room and saw her barely alive, he knelt next to her and took her hand. Kautilya stood there as he watched Chandra Gupta's mother open her eyes, and struggling to say something.

"Are you doing all right Chandra Gupta? I am so happy to see you again," she whispered feebly.

She slowly lifted her hand and touched Chandra Gupta's face. It made Chandra Gupta feel both happy and sad at the same time. He was happy that he was there to see her before she left the material world, and at the same time sad that the moment was not too far away. He looked up at Kautilya, as he wanted to know if it was the right time for him to whisper the sacred words in her ears. Kautilya nodded his head in agreement, and Chandra Gupta whispered the words "Om Krishna" in her ears. She felt happy and content as she repeated the same words in her own mind and closed her eyes. Chandra Gupta put his head down and started silently crying. His father broke down as he knelt next to Chandra Gupta. Chandra Gupta put his arms around his father as he tried to comfort him.

Kautilya was sad to see Chandra Gupta's mother die, but at the same time, he was happy that Chandra Gupta had a chance to be part of the last few minutes of her life. Chandra Gupta, in spite of all the grief that engulfed him, was happy that he had a chance to plant the sacred words in her ears. However, Kautilya was thinking about the next steps. His immediate concern was to make proper arrangements for her cremation. He sent one of his men to go and fetch the head priest of the village to assist Chandra Gupta in the cremation rituals.

The news that came back from Kautilya's man was very disturbing. He slowly walked to Kautilya and whispered the bad news to him.

"The priest refuses to perform the cremation rituals, Sir," the man sounded sad as he broke the bad news.

Kautilya was shocked to hear that, although deep inside, he was not surprised. Throughout his life, he had encountered hundreds of priests who misinterpreted the scriptures and perpetuated several wrong notions of dharma. Kautilya took the man outside the room and asked him quietly.

"Why did the priest say he was not going to perform the rituals?"

"He says he does not want to because she is of a lower Varna, and a high priest like him will not get involved with a person of lower birth like her," replied the man very quietly.

"Does he know he is talking about the Emperor's mother?" asked an angry Kautilya.

"Yes, he does, Sir. Nevertheless, he really does not care. He says he is doing what the laws of ancient Manu dictate," replied the man.

Although the whole conversation took place just outside the room where Chandra Gupta was grieving, he could not help but hear the news that the man had brought. What he heard deeply saddened him. He, however, did not think about it too much as he knew that Kautilya was going to take care of the situation. Kautilya, who was terribly upset at the priest, decided to perform the last rites himself as he was an ordained priest.

Chandra Gupta stayed with his father the next few days trying to comfort him. He knew whatever he did was not going to help his grief. He even tried to convince his father that he should move to the palace in Pataliputra with him. He was not successful, however, as his father wanted to spend the last few years of his life in the same house where he had spent all his life with his wife. Once the last rites were completed, Chandra Gupta had to go back to Pataliputra. After all, he was the Emperor, and he had to take care of all his subjects. His responsibilities were beyond his immediate feelings and passions.

Chandra Gupta continued to grieve for his mother for several weeks. Witnessing her death had shaken his spiritual foundations. He wondered about life after death. He wondered about God and his own relation to Him. He was also questioning his own understanding of dharma. The priest's comments that he would not perform his mother's last rites because of her lower birth kept echoing in his mind. He questioned the Varna foundations of dharma and felt helpless that even he as the emperor of the mighty Mauryan Empire could not do anything about the Varna practice. He decided to ask those questions to the Jain scholar who had come to Pataliputra from the province of Karnataka. He had come to Pataliputra several years ago when the king of Karnataka decided to become a satrap of the Mauryan Empire. His name was Nagarjuna, and he had aged over the years. He always wore white garments and had long flowing gray hair that came up to his shoulders. He was part of Chandra Gupta's religious council, which consisted of representatives from several faiths including the Jain faith. Chandra Gupta had always liked his mild manners, his unassuming nature, and his depth of understanding of the Jain theology. He decided to send a messenger to bring the scholar to his court for a one-on-one session.

The Jain scholar was pleasantly surprised that the emperor had requested a meeting with him. He hurriedly groomed himself so that he was presentable and went to the palace with the messenger where a guard took him to one of Chandra Gupta's private chambers.

Chandra Gupta got up, welcomed the scholar, and took him to a chair that was next to the royal seat.

"Please sit down, Nagarjuna. You are probably wondering why I have asked you to be here," Chandra Gupta said.

"Your Majesty, I am not really certain. However, I would venture to guess that it has something to do about the Jain faith. After all, that is the only thing I know in this world," replied the scholar very politely.

"You are absolutely right, Nagarjuna. Since my mother's departure to Heaven, I have been thinking a lot about spiritual aspects of life. I know what the eternal dharma tradition says about it. I wanted to understand the Jain perspective on that," explained Chandra Gupta.

Nagarjuna felt honored that the Emperor had come to him for answers to such profound questions.

"Your Majesty, I am honored to answer those questions, however long it may take. Your Highness, please do go ahead with what you have in mind," replied the scholar.

"My first question to you, Nagarjuna, is about Varnas. Does the Jain faith believe in Varnas?" asked Chandra Gupta.

"Your Majesty, in our faith, we believe in the equality of souls because all of them can reach Moksha. We believe that the purest qualities of a soul are nothing but God. Thus, God exists in all our souls," replied the scholar.

Chandra Gupta thought about that. That all souls are equal is what people who follow eternal dharma believed as well. How was Jain dharma different from eternal dharma? "I find that similar to what is said in eternal dharma, Nagarjuna," replied Chandra Gupta.

"That may be true, Your Majesty. However, unlike the followers of eternal dharma, we practice what is in our scriptures," asserted Nagarjuna.

Chandra Gupta thought about that claim. He indeed had seen so many instances where followers of eternal dharma had flaunted the true teachings of God's Dharma. However, he had seen that the adherents of Jain dharma were faithful to their teachings.

"Tell me about Moksha, Nagarjuna. In your faith, how does one attain Moksha?" asked Chandra Gupta.

"Your Highness, just like in eternal dharma, when you have reached Moksha, you have ended the cycle of birth and death. Unlike in eternal dharma, Moksha is not what a Creator God grants you. Indeed, there is no Creator God in the Jain faith. Emancipation is purity of your own soul, controlled by your own karma. You have achieved Moksha when all your karmas cease to exist," elaborated the Jain scholar.

The more that Nagarjuna explained the Jain religion, the more Chandra Gupta liked it. The fact that there was no Creator God in the Jain faith did not bother him. He did not know if it was a weak moment in his life caused by the death of his mother, or if it was because of the fact that the head priest had hurt his feelings. He only knew that he was not happy with practitioners of eternal dharma. He could not accept the fact that the head priest had refused to perform his mother's last rites. To him she was the purest soul he had ever known, and the head priest's behavior had only repulsed him from eternal dharma.

"Nagarjuna, I am very intrigued by your faith, and I want to continue to learn about your faith. Can you come and teach me the tenets of your faith every week?" asked Chandra Gupta.

Nagarjuna was extremely pleased that his faith fascinated the Emperor of the mighty Mauryan Empire. He only hoped that it was not a passing interest and Chandra Gupta would embrace his faith some day.

"Your Majesty, I am always at your service. I will eagerly wait for your messenger every week," replied Nagarjuna.

Over the next several weeks, Chandra Gupta spent long hours studying the Jain faith. The more he studied that faith, the more he was attracted to it. He looked back at his life to see if it was the right time for him to transfer power to his son. Bindusara was an able son who was now well versed in all aspects of governing the Empire. He was a compassionate and caring young man who respected the tenets of dharma just like his father. There had been peace and stability all over the Mauryan Empire for more than twenty years. Chandra Gupta felt that his warrior journey had ended. He was satisfied that he had completed all his duties as a warrior. It was now time for him to begin his spiritual journey.

Meanwhile, Kautilya noticed that Chandra Gupta was spending many hours with Nagarjuna. He was suspicious that something major was brewing in Chandra Gupta's mind. Therefore, when Chandra Gupta arranged for an unscheduled private meeting with him, he was not surprised.

Kautilya went to the same private chamber where Chandra Gupta had been meeting Nagarjuna on a regular basis. He found Chandra Gupta engulfed in his deep thoughts. Kautilya had never seen Chandra Gupta in such a somber mood, and he knew that it was going to be a pivotal meeting in the history of the Mauryan Empire. They sat in their chairs for several minutes without saying anything. Kautilya realized at that time that Chandra Gupta was struggling to tell him something and was somewhat emotional about it. Finally, Chandra Gupta mustered enough strength to reveal his decision to Kautilya.

"Kautilya, I have made an important decision, and I want you to be the first one to know that," began Chandra Gupta.

Kautilya nodded his head waiting for Chandra Gupta to continue.

"I have decided to abdicate the throne and coronate my son Bindusara as the Emperor of the Mauryan Empire," continued Chandra Gupta.

Kautilya was actually happy to hear that. He was all for orderly transfer of power. In his mind, an unplanned transfer of power was dangerous as it always tempted enemies to launch an attack.

"That is a good decision, Your Majesty. I am happy to hear that decision, and I am confident that Bindusara will be an excellent ruler," replied Kautilya. However, he wondered about Chandra Gupta's plans.

As if Chandra Gupta read Kautilya's mind, he continued, "Kautilya, this may come as a shock to you. Once Bindusara takes over the Empire, I plan to become a Jain ascetic and join a monastery in *Sravana Belagola*[57] in Karnataka," added Chandra Gupta.

This, indeed, shocked Kautilya. It was hard for him to swallow the fact that his own protégé was walking away from eternal dharma and embracing the Jain tradition. However, he was not going to persuade

---

57 Sravana Belagola continues to be a sacred place and a spiritual center for the followers of Jainism.

him to change his decision. All his life he had preached that the greatness of eternal dharma would survive all tests and would be the only faith to last to eternity. Chandra Gupta knew that Kautilya was disappointed. He tried to give his reasoning behind the decision.

"It is important that I do this, Kautilya. I have done a lot of soul searching, and I have concluded that the spiritual path according to the Jain tradition is the right one for me. I have to do this for my own sanity. All I ask you is to stay with Bindusara for at least a few more months to facilitate smooth transition of power," Chandra Gupta pleaded.

Kautilya agreed to that. The security of the Mauryan Empire was, of course, his paramount concern. "I will be happy to help Bindusara, Your Highness. I will stay with him for at least six months after the coronation," promised Kautilya.

When he left the chamber, he felt old like he had never felt before. He knew that he had accomplished all he had to in Pataliputra, and it was time for him to get back to his beloved school in Taxila.

When Kautilya returned to his office, he felt extremely tired. He felt like his own son had walked out of eternal dharma. Chandra Gupta embracing the Jain tradition felt like he was going to lose a part of his own heritage. Although he had always preached tolerance towards other traditions, he never knew before how it felt to lose someone very close to him to a different faith. He did not like the feeling at all and felt miserable inside. He decided to close his eyes and relax. He started meditating to cleanse his thoughts.

When he opened his eyes, he was surprised to see the same old man standing in the corner of his office. He was the same one who always appeared whenever his thoughts were in disarray. He had not seen him in a long time, which told him that there had been no self-doubts for a long time.

"You seem to be terribly upset," the old man addressed Kautilya.

"Yes, I am very agitated. The great Chandra Gupta has decided to become a Jain ascetic," replied Kautilya.

"Are you upset because your protégé chose a tradition other than yours?" quizzed the old man.

"No, not that. I am upset that I failed to impart the true meaning of eternal dharma to him. If I had succeeded in it, he would not have done what he is doing now," replied Kautilya.

"So it is a sense that you failed your duty that is upsetting you?" asked the old man.

"I suppose so," replied Kautilya.

"Why are you so blind, Kautilya? Don't you know what the Lord says about those who stray?" asked the old man.

"What are you referring to?" Kautilya was too dejected to think straight at this point.

"It is the nineteenth verse in Chapter seven of the Bhagavad-Gita, that immortal Celestial Song. *After many cycles of birth and death, one who has attained the knowledge - that God is everything - comes to Me. But such a great soul is rare indeed,"* clarified the old man.

Kautilya's eyes brightened as he felt a fresh stream of energy through his veins. "You mean, eventually he will come back to God?"

"Of course, he will, Kautilya. Remember there is no Savior but God," replied the old man.

Kautilya now felt that he was being unnecessarily agitated about Chandra Gupta's decision. He was now thinking about his own spiritual journey.

"It is now your turn, Kautilya. Your work here is complete. It is time for you to go back to Taxila and be part of Manu's Dharma mission," suggested the old man.

He is right, thought Kautilya. I should have done that a long time ago, he mused. Did he waste his time by coming to Pataliputra?

"No, you did not waste your time, Kautilya. It was your karma - you had to do that, because it was God's work. Now that you are free of that karma, it is time for you to join Manu," answered the old man.

Kautilya nodded his head in agreement. He could not wait to go back to Taxila. He felt nostalgic and looked out though the window at the western sky. The sky was turning orange as it was getting close to sunset time. As he stared at the orange hues, he realized that he had never felt so peaceful deep inside. When he turned back towards the corner of his room, he noticed that the old man had disappeared.

Epilogue

A s promised, Kautilya stayed in Pataliputra for six months after Bindusara's coronation to help him establish firm control over the Empire. Once satisfied, he bid goodbye to Bindusara and traveled back to Taxila. After Kautilya reached Taxila, he spent the last years of his life dedicated to God's Dharma. He trained several young missionaries of Dharma who went to all corners of Aryavarta. Vishnu Gupta, on the other hand, dedicated his life to serving the poor. He used his relationships with rich merchants to raise money to build orphanages and schools. Once Kautilya reached Taxila, legend has it that Manu decided to travel further west to teach God's Dharma to desert tribes. Some people believe that these tribes incorporated the teachings of Gita into a new religion. Indeed, many of them still cling to the verse where God states that whenever dharma declines, He shall descend into this world. Some tribes have concluded that, indeed, He has already visited this world. Many, however, believe that those tribes misunderstood the teachings and only got the partial Truth. The debate still rages on about who is right and who is wrong.

It is interesting to note that for Manu and Kautilya, Dharma without a Creator God was not acceptable, whereas for Chit-Ananda and Chandra Gupta, the existence of a Creator God was immaterial. What mattered to them was the spiritual experience in the material world. The greatness of people of Aryavarta is that they respect and honor all these paths with or without a Creator God.

There are some, however, who believe that Manu never died and that he is traveling all over Aryavarta even to this day. Of course, no one knows what really happened to Manu. Nevertheless, the Dharma mission he started still lives in spirit, if not as an institution, all over the world. There is eternal hope that Manu will come back some day to reignite that mission. Until then, Dharma waits.

Glossary

Ancient Manu: Manu is the first man created by God in Dharma theology. He is the progenitor of humankind. He is also the author of Manu-Smriti in which he specifies the laws or codes for the followers of Dharma.

Artha Shastra: One of the oldest treatises on statecraft. It addresses economic and tax policies, political and military strategies, and internal security issues in governing a vast Empire.

Arya: Sanskrit-speaking people of ancient India that adhered to Vedic traditions.

Aryavarta: Ancient name for the Indian sub-continent.

Atman: The individual soul that is eternal.

Bhagavad-Gita: This is the book of Revelation in the Dharma tradition. Theologians consider it the summation of Dharma theology, and thus the most sacred Scripture for followers of Dharma. God Himself descended to earth as Lord Krishna to distill the Vedas to humankind.

Bikku: A Buddhist monk.

Brahman: God's spiritual presence in the material world.

Chanakya: Means the genius, which was a title given by Emperor Chandra Gupta to Kautilya.

Chandragupta Maurya: The first Emperor of the Mauryan dynasty (322 – 185 BCE) that ruled the entire Indian subcontinent and the present day Afghanistan and upper Iran (Bactria). Indian tradition believes that Kautilya helped him in overthrowing the Nanda dynasty.

Ekadasi: Eleventh day of the lunar fortnight; there are two ekadasi during a lunar month. Followers of Dharma traditions fast during the Ekadasi day.

Ganges River (Also called Ganga): Sacred River that washes away sins. When the ashes of one's body are washed by river Ganges, the departed soul will reach Moksha.

Karma: Means action. In Dharmic traditions, accumulation of fruits of bad karma perpetuates the cycle of birth and death known as *Samsara*.

Kautilya: Artha Shastra identifies the author by the names Kautilya and Vishnu Gupta. Although many consider that the two names refer to the same person, some historians consider them as separate individuals.

Māya: God's energy that permeates the entire world, and keeps the material world in motion.

Moksha: The state of liberation (or emancipation) from *Samsara* when an individual soul reaches God's abode.

Nanda Dynasty: Ruled Northern India 424 to 323 BCE. Chandragupta Maurya overthrew them.

Om: The sacred symbol in the Dharma tradition that denotes God. This is the highest symbol, and the sound Om symbolizes God.

Panas: Unit of currency in ancient India.

Pooja: Worship service.

Rita: Cosmic order in the Vedic tradition that punishes the evil and rewards the good.

Samsara: The endless cycle of birth and death (incarnation) until an individual soul reaches God's abode.

Saraswati River: Mentioned in Rig-Veda several times. Believed to have dried up centuries ago.

Senapati: Chief General.

Soma: Ancient drink offered to gods in Vedic fire rituals.

Upanayana: The "sacred thread" ceremony. Symbolizes the rite of passage when one begins the study of Vedas.

Upanishads: These are discourses on theology, meditation, and the nature of God. These are sacred texts that are considered part of the Vedas (in a larger context).

Varnas: The ancient Vedic society was divided into four classes (sometimes referred to as castes) based on the chosen profession: Brahmins were the priestly class, Kshatriyas were the warrior class, Vyshyas were the merchant class, and Shudras were the working class. Historians believe that originally people were free to move between castes. However, as time progressed, castes became hereditary.

Vedas: Vedas are the fundamental scriptures in the Dharma tradition. There are four Vedas, the oldest being Rig-Veda which is considered the oldest text in an Indo-European language. However, for followers of Eternal Dharma, Vedas are timeless and are Divine Revelation.

Yavana: Indian term used to describe foreigners in general and Greeks in particular. It is said to be the transliteration of the Greek word "Ionians."

Bibliography

Artha Shastra: There are several translations of *Artha Shastra* along with analysis and commentary. A detailed treatise is presented in: *"Kautilya, The Arthashastra"*, L. N. Rangarajan, Penguin Books India (P) Ltd., 1992.

Bhagavad-Gita: There are innumerable translations and commentaries on The Bhagavad-Gita. There are essentially two types of commentaries: (1) theological commentaries that are by ancient Dharma theologians that subscribe to their tradition, and (2) secular commentaries ranging from Mahatma Gandhi to western scholars of religious studies. For theological commentaries please refer to the following:

Commentary in the Advaita (monism) tradition: *"Bhagavad-Gita, with the commentary of Śankarācūrya, Translated by Swāmī Gambhīrānanda,"* Advaita Ashrama, India, Second Edition, 1991.

Commentary in the Vaishnava tradition: *"Bhagavad-Gita As It Is, by His divine grace A.C. Bhakti Vedanta Swami Prabhupāda,"* Published by Bhaktivedanta Book Trust, 1972.

For a secular commentary, please refer to:
"The Bhagavad-Gita according to Gandhi," Berkeley Hills Books, Berkeley, California, 2000.

Rig-Veda: There are ten books in Rig-Veda with 1,028 hymns (in Vedic Sanskrit). For an overview of Rig-Veda go to http://www.answers.com/topic/rigeda. One of the earliest translations of the hymns was by Ralph T. H. Griffith (1869). His translations can be found at: http://www.sacred-texts.com/hin/rigveda/index.htm.

About the Author

Satya Avatar grew up in the South Indian city of Mysore that is famous for its temples and palaces. He came to the United States in 1978 to pursue graduate studies at State University of New York at Buffalo where he received his Ph.D., in 1981. Since then he has worked in the high-tech industry where he has held several technical and management positions in Research and Development, Product Management, and Marketing.

Satya's other interests include World History, History of Religions, and Dharma Theology. His first novel "The Courtesan and the Sadhu (a novel about Māya, Dharma, and God)" brings aspects from all three areas to illustrate the moral struggles experienced by both individuals and societies as a whole.

Satya Avatar is married with two children and resides in Plano, Texas. His other interests include tennis, gardening, and music. He is currently working on his second novel about a Texas teenager who travels to the Himalayas to meet a yogi.

Satya Avatar can be reached at satya_avatar@dharmavision.com